the cursed beauty

A SLEEPING BEAUTY RETELLING

VALIA LIND

SKAZKA PRESS

Copyright © 2024 by Valia Lind

All rights reserved.

No part of this book may be reproduced in any form or by any electronic or mechanical means, including information storage and retrieval systems, without written permission from the author, except for the use of brief quotations in a book review.

This is a work of fiction. Names, places, characters and incidents are either the product of the author's imagination or are used fictitiously, and any resemblance to any actual persons, living or dead, organizations, events or locales is entirely coincidental.

Cover by Sanja Gombar

Map by Hanna Sandvig

My soul attained its waking moment:
    You re-appeared before my sight,
    As though a brief and fleeting omen,
    Pure phantom in enchanting light.

And now, my heart, with fascination,
    Beats rapidly and finds revived
    Devout faith and inspiration,
    And tender tears and love and life.

— "I still recall the wondrous moment….", Aleksandr Pushkin

note from the author

Dear Reader,

Welcome to the world of Skazka! If you're picking up my books for the first time, you might be wondering why I chose to write Russian fairytale retellings. The answer is simple; I was born and raised in St. Petersburg, Russia. These fairytales, these stories, are my childhood. They were the first to teach me about magic and what it means to see the world a little differently.

The Cursed Beauty is a retelling of the Russian Sleeping Beauty fairytale. The story is inspired by the folktales, as well as by the Russian ballet, as I have always enjoyed the fairies interpretation in that.

This retelling is filled with some of my favorite tropes and elements, infused with my heritage and language.

I have included a glossary of Russian words and phrases at the back of the book for your convenience.

The variations in the Russian words' spellings come from the way the words' endings are changed in the Russian language. There will be a letter off every now and then, as it would be in the native tongue. I believe keeping the language as close to the original as possible brings that sense of "realness" to the experience.

Alyonka and Nikolai have stolen my heart and I hope you love their story as much as I do. I hope you find a little magic between these pages that you can take into your day. Thank you for picking up this book and letting me share a part of myself with you. Thank you for reading.

Much love,
    Valia

My soul attained its waking moment:
	You re-appeared before my sight,
	As though a brief and fleeting omen,
	Pure phantom in enchanting light.

And now, my heart, with fascination,
	Beats rapidly and finds revived
	Devout faith and inspiration,
	And tender tears and love and life.

— "I still recall the wondrous moment....", Aleksandr Pushkin

prologue

NINETEEN YEARS AGO

In a land where snow falls year round, where the magic sneaks through the shadows of the forest, on a day when the sun stood still for fifteen hours, a baby was born.

The *Tsar* and *Tsarina* of *Holodnovo Tsarstva* have long ago gave up on an idea of a direct heir. But then, a miracle happened and Tsarina gave birth to a healthy baby girl.

Tsarevna Alyona, the pride and joy of *Holodnovo Tsarstva*.

The kingdom cheered. There were celebrations throughout the land. The *Tsar* couldn't be more proud.

Just like everyone in the land, he knew the stories of Skazka, a living land full of magic and all the creatures that resided therein. However, his fascination was not in on *znakhar*, a witch doctor who could cure any illness or the firebird who could bring him riches. He wanted the six fairies who are called Good, the blessing that would make his daughter the greatest ruler who had ever lived in this kingdom.

So an invitation went out to the utmost parts of the kingdom: asking for a blessing from Skazka herself. A christening to be held, nobles from across the land traveled to see this miracle babe and the *Tsar* and *Tsarina* hoped to see a magical gift for their child.

On the day of the christening, while everyone congregated in the main hall, the doors suddenly opened and six women stepped into the room. Only simply calling them women wasn't right. They were beings unlike anything anyone has ever seen.

Led by a gorgeous woman dressed in a lavender gown, her hair light purple in color and seemed to carry its own wind, they walked forward. The woman in lavender was adorned in golden jewelry, but it was an otherworldly glow around her that drew the attention. Her ears pointed, her eyes sparkling, and translucent wings pultruding out of her back, she almost glided across the floor.

The other five were just as striking, each carrying their own color. Green, blue, yellow, red, and pink. They glowed as they moved, leaving behind a trail of sparkles in the air.

"*Dobrii den, Tsar* and *Tsarina*. We have come to honor your daughter and her birth. I am the Lilac Fairy, the eldest of the Good Fairies."

"Oh!" *Tsarina* exclaimed, bowing deeply to the fairies. "*Spasibo* for coming on such an occasion. We welcome your presence in our midst."

Tsarina thanked the fairies, while the *Tsar* looked on. He has always been a proud men and now, the pride grew, watching the creatures of Skazka at the christening for his daughter.

The green fairy approached and gifted *Tsarevna* Alyona with the gift of tenderness - may *Tsarevna* always be gentle and kind.

The blue fairy approached and gifted *Tsarevna* Alyona with the gift of playfulness - may *Tsarevna* always be light-hearted and full of fun.

The yellow fairy approached and gifted *Tsarevna* Alyona with the gift of generosity - may *Tsarevna* always be generous and helpful.

The red fairy approached and gifted *Tsarevna* Alyona with the gift of serenity - may *Tsarevna* always be peaceful and poised.

The pink fairy approached and gifted *Tsarevna* Alyona with the gift of courage - may *Tsarevna* always be spirited and brave.

The Lilac Fairy took a step forward, a kind smile on her face, "The gift *Tsarevna* Alyona has received will make her into a wonderful person. Her beauty will flourish with her kindness, her talents will grow with her courage. She will—"

Suddenly, the double doors of the hall burst open and a wind as strong as a storm entered the space. People screamed, covering their heads as if it could protect them.

A shadow followed the wind and when it dissipated, there stood a woman. As strikingly beautiful as the other fairies, her hair as white as snow, her gown a gorgeous shimmering gold. Her wings matched her hair, sparkling in the light. She walked forward slowly, her eyes shifting quickly to the baby in the cradle, before she looks at the *Tsar*.

"What an event!" The woman said, even her voice breathtakingly beautiful. "My invitation must have been intercepted by *leshy*. We all know how mean that forest troll can be."

"You are not welcomed here," the Lilac Fairy said, taking a stance in front of the cradle.

"But *sistrichka*, if you are to give a blessing, I am to give a blessing as well."

"You are no longer our sister, not since you have taken the name of the Dark Fairy."

Tsarina took a step forward then, her eyes on the dark fairy.

"*Prosti nas pozhalusta*," *Tsarina* begged for forgiveness, her hands clasped in front of her. "We did not know. We thought there were only six fairies, we did not know you—we could not know of you to invite you."

The dark fairy's eyes narrowed, all pretense of niceness disappeared and she raised her arms high in the air, bringing them down in a sweeping motion, a screaming ripping out of her.

"Forgotten? You have forgotten ME?"

Everyone around the baby flew back, as if pushed by a great force, just as the dark fairy flew to stand beside the babe. The rest of the hall was frozen, unable to move, unable to speak, watching everything that happened in terror. The six fairies, suspended in the air, trying to break through the barrier put around them. But nothing worked.

Glancing down at *Tsarevna* Alyona, the dark fairy spoke, her voice laced in venom,

"You have insulted me in the worst way." She looked up, meeting the eye of the *Tsar* and *Tsarina* who were trying to get up from the floor, but the dark fairy's power was keeping them put. "You will answer for your ignorance. I will never be forgotten again."

She turned to the babe then, a smile back on her face, but so terrifying that *Tsarevna* Alyona began to cry.

"Heed my words, little babe," the dark fairy said, "receive this gift and cherish it always."

A sudden darkness fell over the hall, as if thunderclouds had appeared indoors. The dark fairy, with her eyes as black as the night, raised her palm in the air, looking directly at the *Tsarevna*.

"On the year of the nineteenth moon,
When the darkness cannot be held at bay,
A curse will befall on the babe,
And a sleep like death will descend.
For a thousand years she will slumber,
And the land and her people with her,
By a blade, or a thorn, or a prickle,
She'll be doomed to roam no more.
No magic can break it, no help can come.
The land will forget her, the place she calls home.
Say your goodbyes, sing the last song,
She will be alone, alone, alone.
By my words, her destiny is sealed,
She will bleed, she will die, she will sleep.
For her legacy always will be,
That she lived a life that was unfulfilled."

"*Pozhalusta,*" *Tsarina* pleaded, tears running down her face. "Don't do this. Don't—" But the dark fairy only looked on, with a grin on her face and a spark in her eyes.

"It is done, it is done." She proclaimed and a loud crack of thunder shook the foundation of the castle. Bringing her hand down, she blew a kiss at the babe and then with a twist of a wrist, another gust of wind and she was gone.

The other fairies now free from the barrier moved forward, but it was already too late. The dark fairy was gone and the curse was in place.

Everyone started yelling and crying at once. *Tsarina* on her knees, sobs shaking her body, the *Tsar*, now standing on his feet, looking like he doesn't believe any of it.

"You can fix it," he said, turning to the Lilac Fairy. "Fix it now!"

"It is not so simple, Your Imperial Majesty—"

"You will fix it or you will suffer a wrath much greater than you can imagine."

The *Tsar* would not stand by and see his rule destroyed by some magical being throwing a fit. He was the *Tsar* of *Holodnovo Tsarstva*, he would not be insulted in such a way. He looked at his daughter, the cause of it all in his eyes, and he turned away.

"I cannot undo another's curse," the Lilac Fairy said, stepping over to the child. "But I can finish my own gift."

She picked up the babe, cradling in her arm as she ran a finger over her eyebrows, smoothing them out.

"A time will come when the curse sets in,
But death will not take, it will only put you to sleep,
A bond between two, a partnership made,
Will undo the slumber, it will wake the beautiful maid."

The Lilac Fairy places a gentle kiss on the babe's cheek, sealing the gift.

"But she will still sleep?" *Tsarina* asked, taking a step

forward. *Tsar* pulled her back, putting distance between them and their daughter. "What are you doing?"

"Did you hear her words?" The *Tsar* said, his eyes hard. "She is in danger from anything. Us included."

"I don't understand—"

"Think of it, woman. A blade, a thorn, a prickle? She must be isolated."

"Even from us?"

"*Da*, as much as possible."

The Lilac Fairy watched the exchanged, sadness falling into her heart. Already, it seemed that the *Tsar* was putting between him and the babe, creating a wall as strong as his pride.

"She will sleep," the Lilac Fairy spoke up, "But she will not die. There is hope in a bond, she can—"

Suddenly, her words were stuck in her throat and she glanced at the other fairies. But all of them were experiencing it now, they were being pushed out, as the curse took place. They were the magical help that the dark fairy spoke about.

The Lilac Fairy hugged the *Tsarevna* close, whispering softly in her ear,

"I will see you in your dreams."

Then, she placed the babe back in her cradle and took a step back, just a shimmer started to descend over her.

"There is hope. Don't lose sight of it. This curse is not the end. It's only the beginning."

ONE

ALYONKA

I overslept and it might be the death of me. Well, I suppose not yet, since the ticking clock that's been hanging over my life since the moment I've been born still have ten months left on it. But regardless of that little respite, my time is still not my own. I must be more careful with it.

Pulling back the covers, I struggle out of the near cocoon of pillows and blankets that reside on my bed, and swing my legs over the side. The weather has been getting chillier by the day, and the protective measures have been rising with the temperature. I've learned that is the best way my parents can love me—in their own strange, keeping-their-distance-from-me way.

But, now is not the time to dwell on all the ways my

life is not what I would imagine it to be. Right now, I have an appointment to keep.

Being as careful as possible, so I don't disturb the guards outside my door, I tiptoe toward the bathroom and close the door behind me. Both my bedroom and bathroom are huge in comparison to other rooms in the palace. I honestly can't tell if the size of them is supposed to help keep me safe or it's simply a coincidence. This room, much like the other, has tall ceilings outlined with crown molding made out of gold, and heavy tapestries on every wall covering the wallpaper. The wallpaper itself is a dark blue velvet and it barely peaks through all the tapestries.

Holodnoye Tsarstvo is always cold, as the name suggests.

We're not called the Cold Kingdom for nothing. But I love everything about it. For generations, the snow stayed year around. But once Queen Calista defeated Baba Yaga over thirty years ago and my family was once again allowed to rule the kingdom, the land of Skazka became kinder to these parts. We still have snow most of the year, but we also see a lot of Autumn.

The location of the kingdom may play a part in my current lack of suitors, but my parents are working hard to remedy that situation.

Which is why I cannot have them finding out about my night escapades.

Moving past the large bathtub that's almost in the middle of the room, I head for the vanity table.

I study myself in the mirror quickly, to make sure I'm presentable. My light green eyes are framed by long dark eyelashes, my cheeks rosy even thought I just work up. The blonde of my hair carries a bit of a glow to it, always shining, even in the low light.

My hair is typically braided before sleep, so I run my hand over the braid now to make sure it's all in place. A few of the strands have escaped around my face, but I let them be. Moving closer to the mirror, I pat the space underneath my eyes to appear more awake, before I pinch my cheeks just a little. The movement actually makes me laugh, and I stare at myself in the mirror, amazed at how ingrained this behavior is in me. I cannot leave my rooms without looking completely put together, which definitely does not matter at the moment. It really doesn't matter if I look a little disheveled.

Reaching for the long coat I snuck in to the bathroom earlier, I shrug it on over my long night dress. A hood is attached to the coat, so I pull it over my head, before I head for the balcony doors.

My room has two balcony entrances. One in the main bedroom and one off of the bathroom. The main bedroom balcony doors make the most awful sound when opened, so they haven't been used in years. So finding out that the windows in my bathroom have a little step on the other side was the best discovery. Second only to the secret that part of the balcony carries.

I discovered it on my sixteenth birthday when I wanted to disappear, so I hid out on the balcony. I'm surprised no one else knows about it. But I suppose no one but a select number of people come to this side of the castle and they're not having out outside of my window for entertainment.

Pulling the glass doors open as quietly as I can, I step out into the chilly night air. It's some time in the middle of the night, if the millions of stars that are out is of any indication. I make sure the doors are closed behind me, before I turn to the right and walk all the way to the end of the balcony.

Here, much like in the rest of the castle, the vines have taken over the walls. It has always been such a fascinating sight to me. A castle in the midst of a snow kingdom with green vines growing on its walls. When winter comes fully, the leaves stay green, holding the snow on them like decoration and making everything look magical.

Very appropriate, all things considered.

Skazka is a land that lives and breathes anyway she chooses. Whether it's the ever green vines growing on the castle walls, magical creatures coming straight out of beloved stories, or snow in the middle of summer, she does what she wants. There are many stories about the wonders of Skazka and every time I hear one it gives me hope that my life is not a hopeless case. That even though magic has cursed me, there is a possibility of magic saving me as well.

Which is why my night adventure is so important to me. It gives me hope in the way nothing else has recently.

Glancing around, I make sure I don't make any unnecessary noise as I pull the vines away from the wall. The moon is just bright enough to illuminate the set of stairs leading up to the lower roof. The castle has many roofs, and a few of them are flat, so there's space to eat outside when the weather is nice.

The stairs themselves are carved into the side of the castle, with a tall wall on the outside, so even if the vines didn't grow down over them, it's impossible to see them unless someone is already aware of them being here. One of the many interesting things I have found out about this castle. After all, it's been my playground my whole life.

Looking from the outside, the castle seems like a standard blueprint of winding hallways and colorful domes and turrets. I will admit I love the artistic liberty the builders of the domes took by making sure the every color of the rainbow was involved in painting them.

But every now and then, the castle doesn't seem ordinary. Not when some of the hallways seemed to have been created specifically to send one walking in circles, or the gardens that protrude from various levels. This place holds as many secrets as there is magic in Skazka.

When I reach the top of the stairs, I push more vines out of the way and emerge from under them into the smaller roof. It's more like a larger balcony actually. I never would've even know it existed, because no one comes up here. Well, almost no one. There is one door that leads to the rest of the castle, but other than that, it's just open space. And the view? The view from here is beautiful.

I step to the edge and lean against the stone barrier. The stars and the moon are fully out tonight, not a cloud in sight. As I gaze beyond the castle grounds, I see the forest open up in front of me. It's almost like one of the paintings hanging inside the castle, as if someone used the best shades of blues and silver to create the night sky, blending almost seamlessly with the forest.

I've only been outside the castle grounds a few times in my life, with very specific protocols in place. But every time I look out into the forest, all I want to do is get lost between the trees. I think Skazka would be a wonderful companion to explore with, but alas, that is something I don't think I will every have a chance to find out for myself. After all, there aren't many aspects of my life that are actually my own.

A gust of wind comes then and I pull my coat tighter around my shoulders, making sure the hood stays on. I also check my pockets, to make sure I haven't forgotten anything.

I'm giddy with excitement, as I usually am before my nightly meetings. It doesn't matter how many times we meet, the anticipation still fills my stomach. This is my favorite part of my day and I can't believe I almost missed it because I overslept. When I hear a slight nose behind me, I turn slowly, a smile lighting up my face.

There he is.

I take a step forward immediately, not even bothering to wait until he approaches first.

"Hello, *krasavitz*," I say, stopping right in front of him, because handsome he is. "Who's a handsome boy? You are!"

He's nothing like I've ever seen before. He moves a little closer, inclining his head toward me and I reach for him before I can stop myself.

The moment my fingertips touch his forehead I feel a now familiar sense of warmth spread throughout my body. I've never had a pet before—they weren't allowed for a reason I will never understand—but I've read about them. About the kind of a companionship one can develop with a cat or a dog, the way their presence makes one feel a little less alone in the world. I believe that this sense of comfort is part of the gift Skazka has given me—my own personal dragon.

The first time he landed on the balcony, I thought I was hallucinating. I've read about the magical creatures that live in the sentient forest—I know the stories that have spread across the land over generations. But I've never seen any of the creatures myself.

My only experience with magic happened when I was only born and that experience was a curse. So not exactly a winning endorsement for all things magical. But as the deadline of the impending curse draws near, I see signs of it everywhere.

The days are shorter, the nights are longer. There are less flowers blooming in the warmer months. It's as if the kingdom itself is preparing for slumber.

Then, Chudo appeared.

I don't know why that was the name that came to me immediately when I met him, but he answers to it. I think it suits him. He is sort of a wonder in my life and definitely a gift from Skazka.

My knowledge of dragons comes only from history books. There are those who have dedicated their lives in collecting as much information about Baba Yaga—the notoriously evil children-eating creatures that loves to bestow curses on people. I was honestly shocked when I found out I wasn't cursed by her, like it seems everyone else in the kingdom previously was. Not that I trust the information I've been given about my own life. Everyone is always so secretive. I'm not sure if they expect me to break under the weight of too much knowledge, but when I was thirteen, I stopped asking. Now, I try to learn things on my own as much as possible.

There are only a few people in the whole world that I

actually do trust—one being my personal maid and best friend—Daria. The other, the man who probably raised me more than my own father has—Ivan Popyalof, my personal bodyguard. Named after the great hero of old, who went up against the three headed *Zmei* and conquered the snake dragon, he's been with me since I was ten and he's the one who told me every story I know about Skakza. He's always been very good about letting me read whatever I wanted during my library time and I devoured every history book I could find.

But I haven't even told Ivan Popyalof about him. I'm sure he's think it's too dangerous. He's more protective of me than anyone, which is partially his job, and partially the fact that he has been with me for such a long time.

I haven't seen my parents in close to six months. They left to visit *Vodnoye Tsarstvo* for some political reason they didn't disclose and then decided to stay. Before then, they've always kept their distance. So, Ivan Popyalof? He really is my family.

"*Zdrastvuite*," I say to the dragon now, my hand reaching for the treats I saved for him earlier. Thankfully, I ate in my room today, so it was easy to keep all of the *pirozoki* for him. The slightly sweet buns with stuffing seems to be his favorite. Doesn't matter the stuffing, strawberry jam or potatoes, he eats it up. I pull one out and he takes it eagerly, nearly licking my hand in the process.

I don't think I can say this out loud, but he's like a

giant cat. One time, he curled up like one and I leaned against him for an hour, gazing up at the stars.

Even though he came to me three months ago, I'm still amazed every time I look at him. He's about the size of a bear, with a long neck and tail. Almost like a snake, except for the four legs and the giant wings on his back. He has scales, purple or blue, depending on where the light shines across his body. But there's also some fur around his legs, as if he's wearing socks. He also has a little bit of fur on his wings, maybe to keep him warm.

"You seem hungry today," I say, just as he devours another *pirozok*, giving me a look that says I must be crazy to think otherwise. I can't help but chuckle. He butts his head against my hand impatiently and rub my free hand against his forehead. If I didn't know better, I'd think he was purring. Then, his bright green eyes meet mine and that sense of peace and comfort washes over me again.

"What adventures have you been up to the last few days, Chudo?"

He nudges me again for pets and I oblige, when a feeling of air rushing past me, as if I'm the one flying overcomes me. I freeze for a second, giving myself a moment to enjoy it, before the feeling is done.

I'm not sure what it is that allows him to share these feelings with me, but I will never complain. For someone who has lived her life on the strictest schedule, even the glimpses of his adventures gives me a freedom I will never experience.

"That looks feels," I say, as Chudo settles on the floor and I follow. He curls around me, the warms of his body keeping me incredibly comfortable in the cold weather. At least there are not storms when he's around, so with my fuzzy socks and fur coat, tucked beside him, I'm comfortable. His head is near my hand and I run my fingers over his forehead. This time, he definitely sighs in contentment —I can feel it against my back.

"Tomorrow, another suitor is arriving," I say, keeping my voice low. This time, Chudo makes a sound of protest and I agree with that feeling. "Tetia Tatiana says that he's very lovely. He comes from *Oceniye Tsarstvoe* and is directly related to the royal family. That puts the number at four. I think Tetia Tatiana is waiting on two more before the battle for my hand truly begins."

My voice is dramatic at the end and Chudo makes a huffing noise that I interpret as laughter. I run my hand over his forehead, petting him gently as I lean fully into his body. The comfort I feel in his presence is something magical. I think he was sent by Skazka to make sure my belief in magic isn't so one sided. At least, that what I've been telling myself. I think it's kind of wonderful to think that maybe the land cares about me enough to try and brighten my days.

"I can't say that I liked meeting the suitors one by one," I continue, as Chudo definitely makes a purring sound. "But since we're running out of time, Tetia Tatiana talked my parents in hosting a competition of sorts. I'm not sure how I feel about it, but I guess it doesn't matter. I'll do my part. I have to."

That's the bottom line in all of this. With my nineteenth birthday coming up in less than a year, I've spent the last few in nicely furnished rooms, with no less than fifteen guards surrounding me, as I sat across the table from suitor after suitor, trying to find someone who fills the mold of a man who will break the curse. When I was little, I always thought the love of my life will come into my life and sweep me away and all will be well. But the more time I spend on this so-called dates, the less I believe true love is something that exists. Instead, I'm just hoping for a good enough match.

I look up at the stars, leaning my head against Chudo. Tomorrow seems like it will be just another regular day. But for right now, I can at least pretend that I don't have a deadline rising on the horizon and a curse that will put me to sleep when I turn nineteen—something that will destroy this kingdom and everyone in it.

two

ALYONKA

When Daria pulls the curtains open in my room the next morning, I have absolutely no desire to get out of bed. I keep my eyes closed and my blankets pulled over my head for as long as I can. My night adventure gave me about five hours of sleep. Even though I would like to see Chudo every night, it's probably a good thing I don't or someone would notice me continuously tired.

"*Dobroye utro, Tsarevna.*" Daria uses my title as the daughter of the *Tsar*, which means Tetia Tatiana is in the room. Tetia Tatiana and Daria both came to the castle around the same time three years ago. Before then, I was under the care of a very stoic governess who retired. And even though I can dress myself most of the time—some of the dresses are a little difficult—my parents wanted me to have a lady's maid for all of the matchmaking adventures. Daria has become like a sister to me, but I don't think Tetia Tatiana likes me all that much. She's just here to do her job.

I pull the blankets down, one of which is a quilt Daria sown for me, and peak out to look at the room. Daria is near the window, hiding a smile, while Tetia Tatiana is near the doors, looking less than pleased with me. Then again, that is her typical resting face.

"*Dobroye utro,* Tetia Tatiana." I greet the perpetually unhappy woman, before giving Daria a quick nod. I much rather it be just the two of us, but since we're having another suitor arrive today, Tetia Tatiana must oversee my getting ready.

"It is nearly past the morning, *Tsarevna* Alyona. We have much to do and not much time for it." She looks down at her ever present notebook, scribbling something down. I have no idea what she writes in there, but it's always very aggressive. She glances up at me then, her eyebrows raised, and I realized I'm not moving fast enough. With a quick nod, I push myself of the bed, just as Daria comes over to hold a robe open for me. I step into it, and head toward the bathroom as Tetia Tatiana continues to speak.

"You will have breakfast downstairs in the main hall and then head directly to the sun room. *Knyaz* Georgiy

Leonidovich will arrive at approximately one in the afternoon, at which time you will meet him there."

I don't miss Daria's quick roll of the eyes in the mirror as I sit. There are too many nobles in these parts for my liking, but I especially don't like anyone with the given title of *knyaz*. I find them to take on the role of a prince in the most obnoxious of ways, since the title is often given as an appointment of a position.

"Are you listening to me, *Tsarvena*?" Tetia Tatiana's voice pierces my thoughts. I glance over my shoulder in the mirror to find her in the doorway to the bathroom, her eyebrows raised once more. Daria is behind me, untangling my braid and keeping her head down. I give Tetia Tatiana a small smile.

"Of course, Tetia," I say and she holds my gaze long enough to show her disapproval before she glances down at her notebook again.

"After the initial introduction in the sun room, you will to the library for your reading time. After which, you will head to the gardens for a stroll."

"Alone?" I perk up immediately. Tetia Tatiana doesn't hesitate to give me another disapproving look before glancing down at the papers.

"Of course not. The three nobleman whom you have met earlier, including *Knyaz* Georgiy Leonidovich will be present. Dinner will be held in the third dinning room tonight and you will dine with them. Ivan Popyalof will provide you with the rest of the information for today. Please do hurry, you are making us late."

With that, she turns on her heels and speed walks out of the room as if her skirt is on fire. Daria and I are still for half a minute before we both burst out laughing

"I think she's getting more intense with each arrival," I comment as Daria proceeds to tame my hair into presentable waves.

"She was scary before, but now—" Daria agrees. She makes a little face, then walks with me to the sink so I can wash my face and brush my teeth. Skazka is a land of magic and history, but we do carry some pretty cool human amenities now. While Father keeps the dealings with the human realm to a minimal, he at least gave us indoor plumbing. Compared to other kingdoms, so much of our current customs belong in history books, so I am thankful for this small gift.

Also, I'm thankful for the gift of Daria. She's only been with me for the last three years, but she's become my best friend. Growing up, my nanny was one of the captains in the royal army. My parents thought it was the best way to protect me. She was a lovely woman, but it's not like we were friends. She took care of me and then when I could take care of myself, only Ivan Popyalof stayed as my bodyguard. She went to have her own family after retiring.

But when my parents decided it was time to find me a suitor, they knew I needed help, so after much searching and vetting of maidens, Daria was selected. Even though her ultimate dream is to be a seamstress, we clicked instantly. And I finally felt like I had someone in my corner, besides my bodyguard.

"Quick, before she comes back," Daria says as I settle back in front of the vanity. "I have to tell you about the gorgeous *gorgeous* soldier everyone is talking about. I only got a glimpse of him this morning, but oh my goodness, Aloynka, he is what dreams are made of."

I can't help but chuckle at Daria's dramatics. She's a very big enthusiast of all these eligible gentlemen. She's also the only person beside Ivan Popyalof who calls me by my nickname, Alyonka. No one else dares, no matter how much I tell them to.

But *da*, Daria's outlook has been keeping things a bit light for me all things considered. She says "if I can't have, I can at least look"—which is basically everyone's outlook at the moment. I can't deny that the suitors are attractive. They're just not...for me.

A point that is driving my parents—and the rest of the kingdom—crazy I'm sure. Not that I know much of what my parents are thinking. Our interactions are so minuscule I no longer feel the sadness when it comes to their absence. Their only goal has been finding me the perfect match. Someone who will marry me in a binding ceremony before the land of Skazka and who will kiss me in front of the land and the kingdom to break the curse.

They think as long as I find someone who fits all the

boxes, love will come. But the more I spend time with these men, the more I think love is not for me and my future is simply doomed.

"I see what you're doing." Daria's voice breaks through my thoughts, just as she motions for me to step into the dress she positioned in front of me.

"I have no idea what you mean."

"Yes, you do. It's the morning gloominess. I can see it on your face." I sigh, as Daria steps behind me to weave the dress's corset together. She's not wrong, of course. I do have a bit of gloominess about me. But I can't help it. All of my days are the same and putting on a happy face in front of yet another new suitor is draining.

My eyes shift to the mirror and I study myself carefully. My complexion is fair, since I'm hardly ever allowed in the sun, my cheeks perpetually rosy. Light green eyes framed with dark eyelashes. Daria added some shimmer to the corners of my eyes and bright pink glossy substance to my lips. My hair is free from its braid, falling in soft waves around my shoulders and down my back. There are a few jewel clips in my hair, attached to the strands to make my hair sparkle in the light when I move.

The dress I'm wearing today is light green—a mint color according to Tetia Tatiana and her knowledge of all the latest fashion. It's tulle sequins and long, all the way to the floor. The sleeves are transparent and come all the way to my wrists, and the bodies is low-cut in the front, with three golden straps running around my middle. It comes together at the back with in a form of a corset.

Green and pink are the two of my signature colors and every time a new dress is made it brings me a little bit of joy. It brings immense joy to Daria since she takes part in creating these dresses for me whenever she can. She might not like Tetia Tatiana, but she does want to be her best friend if only they can talk fashion.

"What do you think?" Daria asks as she steps back.

"It's beautiful and I love the extra sparkle," I say, shaking my head back and forth gently to make the jewels in my hair dance. Daria beams at me and I can't help but smile in return.

Just then, I hear my bedroom door open and in the next moment, Ivan Popyalof steps into the doorframe. He gives me a quick bow and a smile.

"*Dobroye utro,* Alyonka," he says, then bows again.

"*Dobroye utro,* Ivan Popyalof," I reply with a smile.

Out of all the people in the world, he's been with me the longest. His hair is fully grey now, but still as thick as it was when he first became my bodyguard. Styled in the typical military cut, his uniform the deep blue of the royal guards—a heavy suit jacket with golden buttons and white pants. The only thing that has truly changed are the wrinkles around his face. He's coming up to his seventies now and the closest person I've had to a father. In even the smallest things. While the Tsar hasn't asked me how I'm feeling in the last ten years, Ivan Popyalof checks in regularly.

"Are you ready? Breakfast is served."

I give Daria a quick squeeze on the upper arm as a thanks and head toward the bedroom door. Slipping into my standard silver flats—that I only get to wear because they're completely covered by my dress—I head for the door. As usual for the days I eat breakfast outside my rooms, Ivan Popyalof will accompany me down, where I will eat alone, with guards at every corner of the room. Then, Tetia Tatiana will come and fetch me for the next set of activities and Daria will meet me in the library for some company.

Every day, the same thing. For my whole life, I've done nothing but eat my meals, study, and dance behind closed doors. That last one isn't a proper activity for a princess to do when the said princess is not supposed to put herself in the harm's way in at all. According to my father, dancing is dangerous.

Yet, I carry music inside of me and I can't help but let it out through guided movements. I've never had any proper training, only what has come to me naturally, but I love it just the same.

But at least now, there are suitors arriving to the castle, so a new item has been added to the repetition.

I lead the way past the guards outside my door, heading to the staircase that will take me down to two floors down to the main hall.

"Oh!" I suddenly remember Tetia Tatiana's words and turn to face my bodyguard as I walk backwards. I know these halls like the back of my hand. I have no problem doing this. "She who shall not be named has mentioned you have some information for me about today. What could it be?" I raise my eyebrows at him, as Ivan Popyalof tries to suppress a smile. He knows just how much I dislike Tetia Tatiana and I'm the only one who sees his face full of any kind of emotion. Amusement included.

But now, the amusement is gone as fast as it comes and there's something else that replaces it.

"I think it would be best we spoke after breakfast."

Well, I don't like that at all. Still walking backwards I narrow my eyes. That sounds much too mysterious.

"Ivan—"

"*Tsarevna,* watch out!"

Ivan Popyalof reaches for me the same moment something slams me from the back. His hand doesn't catch me, as I'm spun around and toward the stairs. I have a second to wonder if this is how the curse decided to take me out, before I'm flailing backwards on the stairs.

But before I can fall to my doom strong hands catch me and I'm swept straight off my feet. Automatically, my arms wind around his neck and I shut my eyes as I try to calm my racing heart.

"Well, I'm glad your reflexes are still on point," I say, eternally grateful for my bodyguard. But the moment I say it, I realize that the arms holding me feel nothing like Ivan

Popyalof. The scent of the man hits me next and I inhale automatically at the smell of woods and rain...comfort?

My eyes fly open and I lift my gaze up to meet dark brown ones, framed by the longest eyelashes I have ever seen. I know those eyes. I haven't seen them in nearly ten years.

The features of a young sad boy have now grown into the strong silent type. I can tell simply by the way his eyes seem to pierce right through me. Strong jaw, his hair longer than I remember and escaping the combed back look he tried for, his lips set in a firm line. He looks like someone who would make people swoon simply in his presence, right before he reprimands them to behave accordingly.

"*Zdrastvuite, Tsarevna,*" he says, his voice vibrating against my whole being. But I can't answer even if I wasn't out of breath at the near death experience.

Daria was right. The new soldier is gorgeous *gorgeous*.

NIKOLAI

Alyonushka.

She's more beautiful than I remember. Same wild hair now adorned with carefully placed clips and eyes full of mischief. It's been ten years since I've seen her and yet, she still somehow looks like my best friend. Only all grown up.

I give myself half a second to take her in, before I push it all away. Along with the childhood nickname I have no right to call her.

She fits so perfectly in my arms that I would like to keep her here forever. But then I realize I'm still standing on the stairs, with her cradled against me. Shifting forward, I place her gently on her feet and when I'm sure she isn't going to topple over, I stake a step back.

Regardless of my history with her—or how well she grew up into the gorgeous woman before me—she is off limits as anything but the Grand Duchess. It would do me well to remember that.

"*Tsarevna* Alyona," I say, bowing at ninety degrees for a long moment, before I stand up straight again. When my eyes meet hers, she's starting at me as if she's seen a ghost. Which I suppose is pretty close to who I am to her. If she was anyone else, she could hate me. But Alyonushka —*Tsarevna* Alyona has never been that person. Even though I disappeared without a trace back when I was shipped off to the military. On her birthday.

"Am I hallucinating?" She whispers, still not taking her eyes off me and I have to keep my face impassive, even though I want to smile. Even when I was a small sad child, she always had that effect on me. She radiates sunshine even when she's not wearing jewels in her hair.

"*Tsarevna* Alyona," Ivan Popyalof steps up, after calming down the palace worker that ran into Alyona. He glances between the two of us and I give him a respectful bow as well. "You remember *Podpolkovnik* Nikolai. He has returned from his latest assignment."

"A lieutenant colonel?" She asks, her eyes big and still trained on me. "*Pozdravlyayu tebya.*"

I'm used to hearing congratulations, but for some reason, it means more coming from her. It shouldn't, but maybe it makes sense. She will be my queen someday and receiving an honor from a queen is always pleasant.

"*Spasibo, Tsarevna* Alyona," I reply, bowing ninety degrees at the waist. When I straighten once again, I feel Ivan Popyalof's eyes on me. I suppose even that thank you was more familiar than it should be. He warned me keeping myself at a distance is of utmost importance. My presence will already be a distraction to her and there isn't exactly a lot of time to spare.

"We should head down," Ivan Popyalof addresses Alyona, but her eyes won't leave mine. I step out of the way, so they can use the stairs, but she's still standing there frozen. It's taking every ounce of my self control not to stare at her. The rumors about her beauty weren't exaggerated enough. No wonder every eligible and vetted suitor is at the doors of this palace.

"*Tsarevna* Alyona." Ivan Popyalof speaks again and this time, she seems to come to her senses.

"Of course, of course. Let's go."

She moves past me down the stairs and I stay as still as possible while they descend. Ivan Popyalof gives me another look and I incline my head as he follows her close behind. I stay like that until they're completely out of sight and have rounded the staircase to head down to the first floor. Only then do I allow myself a full breath.

"So that's her, huh?" My second in command—and the first friend I made when I was sent to the military camp—Timofey, steps back over to the staircase. He was only a few steps in front of me, but ended up too far away to do anything when one of the castle workers tripped and ran into the princess. The worker has moved on as well, along with anyone else that might've been in the hallway.

"*Tsarevna* of our kingdom, *da*." I reply, coming up the rest of the way and stopping near him. We're mostly the same height, and while my hair and eyes are dark brown, his are dark blonde and light brown. None of our other features are similar, yet, people often call us brothers and I suppose that's what we've become to each other anyway. Along with the teasing and the annoyances. I don't have to look at him to know he's making that face, like he's about to torture me on the spot with his teasing.

"Don't start, Timofey," I say, as I begin to walk down the hall to our original destination.

"Come on, you have to tell me. How are you feeling? It's been what—ten years? And you didn't just see her. You caught her in your arms. That's—epic. I mean—"

"Timofey, knock it off," I say, because I have to stay

focused on the task at hand and not take any trips down memory lanes or anything else that might divert my attention. Including the emotions I'm currently suppressing after seeing Alyona.

"I want to check every single room on this floor," I continue, before he can say anything else. "Doors, windows, and any secret passages that might be lurking in the shadows."

Timofey snaps to attention immediately at my tone of voice. He's been with me long enough to understand me, sometimes better than I understand myself. And right now, I need this.

We reach the farthest room down the hall and step inside. Most of these remain unused, but that is why I want to do a thorough sweep of each one. It eliminates the chance of anyone being where they're not supposed to be.

"Let's get to work."

three

ALYONKA

I eat my breakfast of barley porridge and blueberries while experiencing what I would call an out of body experience. I can't stop thinking about Nikolai's arms around me or his eyes peering straight into my soul.

I've clearly am loosing my mind if I think of Nikolai as anything but a solider—who grew up looking better than any prince I have ever seen. But *nyet*, I can't even allow that thought in my mind because he *is* only a soldier in my army and nothing else. He can never be anything else.

It's been ten years since I've seen him. Ten years since he promised to dance with me on my ninth birthday and then never showed up. I worked so hard to sneak out of my room that night and I waited until the cold seeped under my *shuba*. Not that I would admit it to myself, but I wore my best dress under that fur coat. I only ever danced alone and I've been begging Nikolai to be my partner just once. He finally relented, saying it was his birthday gift to me and we would meet in the garden that night so that I can get my wish of dancing under the moonlight.

But then he disappeared. I was so sad, I think I made myself sick. Or maybe it was the cold. Either way, it was a week later that I found out that he was shipped off to military camp. His mother, our palace cook, was finally able to tell me when I snuck down to the kitchens.

Even though I had my answer and my only friend didn't actually abandon me by choice, I still cried.

But now he's back. I have no idea how I'm supposed to feel about it. Am I even allowed to be excited that he's back? He seemed so removed from me when he greeted me, standing tall and proper. Am I the only one who missed him?

Probably. Which of course doesn't matter, because who cares if he missed me? I need to shut down immediately any residual nice feelings I might have and think about just how mad I was at him disappearing. That will keep a nice firm barrier between us.

"*Tsarevna* Alonya."

I blink my eyes at Tetia Tatiana's sharp tone and I realize she'd called my name more than once.

"*Da*, Tetia Tatiana?" I give her a small smile and she narrows her eyes. As usual.

"If you are finished, we should head over to greet your guest."

I glance down at my plate, and even thought I haven't finished, I'm done eating for now.

Pushing my chair back, I leave it all behind and follow Tetia Tatiana out of the dining hall, with Ivan Popyalof close behind. He didn't get a chance to tell me whatever Tatiana said he was going to go over with me, but I suppose it wasn't that important.

As usual, there are guards stationed everywhere. Sometimes it feels like half of the royal military lives at the palace just so they can watch over me.

Which has never made much sense to me. The curse isn't a physical danger to me in any way. It's not something anyone can actually protect me from. But my parents insist, so here we are.

I greet each one of the guards with a smile and a nod, but they're unmovable. I used to think it was useless to be nice to them, but Ivan Popyalof told me that they actually appreciate it. I glance back at my bodyguard now and he gives me a small smile. Even though everything seems like any other day, it also feels like something is going on. Maybe it's all the years I've spent with him, I know him better than anyone. I raise an eyebrow in question, but he shakes his head just a bit, glancing at Tetia Tatiana. The woman is powerwalking toward the sunroom, but we both know she's paying attention to everything. I'll have to ask Ivan Popyalof about it later and ask I will.

When we reach the double doors that lead to one of the many rooms in the castle, I pause. I really don't like this part.

The men who have come here have been nice enough, but it's always the same questions and typically, the same answers. It's not exactly how I would like to spend my time.

Tetia Tatiana doesn't bother to ask if I'm ready, but nods to the guards to push the doors open.

At least the room is one of my favorites. There are floor to ceiling glass doors right across from me and trees growing right on the other side. They're evergreens, so they stay fresh even in the coldest times during the year. There are also plants everywhere inside the room, making this as close to a green space as we can get right now. The two divans are right near the glass doors, with a table between them.

My gaze shifts to the man who stands up as we enter. He seems to be about 182 centimeters—six feet according to the newer measurements Skazka has been adapting. Brown hair, blue eyes, straight teeth that are so white, they're blinding. He's wearing a dark blue three piece suit and even from here, I can tell that the tie is silk and clipped with a golden clip. His cufflinks have diamonds in them. He looks expensive. They always look expensive and proud. I would rather he look kind.

Tetia Tatiana makes a small noise at me and I realize I haven't moved from the doorway.

"*Tsarevna* Alyona, may I present to you *Knyaz* Georgiy Leonidovich."

Tetia Tatiana does the honors of introducing us. The man bows before standing up and flashing me another blinding smile.

"*Priyatno poznakomitsiya*," I say, with the standard nice to meet you. The rule is that he can't speak to me until I speak to him first and sometimes I would like to put that to the test. But Tetia Tatiana is here and she has advised me that it would be best for me to keep my manners in place.

"Oh it is such an honor. You may not even know how much it took for me to be here. I have traveled quite the way and the kingdom isn't exactly kind this time of the year. The snow and the rain have been playing a game to see who can stay the longest, and it really was such a journey for me to arrive safely," Georgiy Leonidovich says and I inwardly cringe and celebrate at the same. He seems like a talker, which means I won't have to do much to lead the conversation. "Please, please, take a seat."

He motions to the divan opposite the one he's been sitting on and that gives him a point immediately. There have been a few who insist on sitting beside me and that is my least favorite.

Ivan Popyalof moves to stand behind the divan and

Georgiy Leonidovich glances up at him, studying him for a moment, before settling on his own divan.

"It really is true you go nowhere without your bodyguard. It must be exhausting always being watched." I open my mouth to reply, but then realize he's not actually asking me. "I, of course, have guards. Anyone in my position would, but at least they aren't present when I'm on a date."

He chuckles then and I cock my head to the side, genuinely wondering where Tetia Tatiana keeps finding these men.

"You must have so many questions for me," Georgiy Leonidovich continues, undeterred by my silence thus far. "I have a lot of knowledge to share, I have traveled and seen much of Skazka. I have even crossed into the human realm, which I'm sure you want me to talk about. It's truly fascinating. It's a shame you won't experience it, but hearing about it will be enough. I am the best storyteller. Everyone says so. Do you want to hear about the time I visited *Volkovskoye Korolevstvo*?"

"*Nyet.*"

Georgiy Leonidovich face instantly changes from the bright smile to confusion to annoyance. One word, and he shows his true colors. Tetia Tatiana is already moving forward, to diffuse the situation.

"What she means is she would much rather hear about you, before she hears about other people and places," Tetia Tatiana says, before throwing me a look only I can see and one I'm accustomed to. It's that "behave or else".

Georgiy Leonidovich is instantly placated though and he offers me another smile, this one more smug somehow.

"I can definitely tell you more about me. I have accomplished so much. You would be surprised at how impressive I truly am."

He continues to speak, but I'm only half listening. Enough that if he actually gives me a chance to speak, I can reply. But mostly I tune him out and wonder if my parents truly believe that marrying me off to someone like him is our only salvation.

Since my feet are covered by my skirt, I map out a few dance steps, moving around carefully enough that it's not noticeable. Not that the current suitor would even notice if I got up and started dancing. He's deep into whatever he's talking about.

My eyes roam over the plants behind Georgiy Leonidovich and I also wonder, what Nikolai is doing, right now, somewhere in the castle and why he's returned. After all this time, we're once again under the same roof. I never thought that would happen again.

Not that it matters. I don't care at all. It's simple curiosity.

When Tetia Tatiana steps over to where we're seating, I realize the allotted time with me has been reached and I will now have a chance to escape.

"I look forward to seeing you later this afternoon,"

Georgiy Leonidovich says with an exaggerated bow. I incline my head just barely, but I don't speak. Not that he notices. When he stands back up, there's smugness in his smile and I fight the urge to roll my eyes.

Tetia Tatiana leads the way out of the room, with Ivan Popyalof close behind. The moment the doors close, she spins on me.

"You couldn't have been a little bit nicer?"

"I could've been one of those plants for all he noticed and you know it." It's not often I allow myself to talk back to Tetia Tatiana but sometimes I can't help it. She narrows her eyes at me as if I'm not her Grand Duchess and she opens her mouth to argue when Ivan Popyalof steps in.

"It would be best to head to the study now, *Tsarevna* Alyona. You will be needed in the gardens in just a few hours." That last is directed at Tetia Tatiana and she relents.

"It's like all of my efforts are for nothing," she mumbles, before she pivots on her heels and walks off. Ivan Popyalof and I watch her go and I shake my head.

"She really forgets I'm to be her queen, doesn't she?"

One of the guards at the door makes a choked sound and I turn and grin at him. Ivan Popyalof ushers me away immediately, heading back up to my floor and the study I love so much.

"You really should not be making waves with her, Alyonka," my bodyguard keeps his voice low as he walks right behind my right shoulder. "She is doing what she is told."

"*Da*, but she is doing so with the worst attitude. Which I think reflects in her choice of men. My parents clearly thought they were hiring the perfect matchmaker in the land, but did you hear him? Could you see me spending the rest of my life with him by my side?"

This time, it's Ivan Popyalof that makes a choked sound and I know it well. He's always found my temperament entertaining.

"Let us get through the study hour and then we will face the rest of the—"

"Firing squad? Evil entities from the Skazka forest? Baba Yaga and her minions—"

"The rest of the gentlemen who are in competition for your hand." But even though he interrupted me with the stern tone to his voice, I can tell he thought that was funny. Between my bodyguard and Daria, they're the only two who do. I am thankful I have them.

NIKOLAI

"He's polished and proper in that way all nobles are, but he would not stop talking about himself."

The words reach us just as Timofey and I step inside the training courtyard. There are many courtyards on the castle grounds, and this one has been dedicated to the royal guard for practice. There are hallways on the other side of the wall to the left where the barracks for the soldiers are housed. The accommodations are the nicest I have ever been in since being set to the military. There are never more than two or three men per room and it has beds for each person, dressers, and even a desk and chairs. They're not decorated like the rooms in other areas of the castle, but they're well insulated against the cold, with one color tapestries and there are plenty of blankets to go around.

At least I don't have to worry about my shoulders freezing at night. Something I've had to worry about in the past.

"Did she seem interested at all?" Another voice says and I can't see the two soldiers speaking as they appear to be on the other side of the pillars leading to the open space for hand to hand practice. Timofey glances over at me as I stop in my tracks.

"She didn't. When she left with her bodyguard she definitely looked relieved. Which I can't even blame her for, but it is disappointing. Everyone wants this to be over already."

Of course they're talking about *Tsarevna* Alyona. I've been back for two days and that's all anyone talks about. Not that anyone can blame them. A lot is riding on her finding a good match—the whole kingdom is holding its breath at this point.

The two soldiers round the pillar to head toward the barracks, coming face to face with Timofey and I.

"*Podpolk—* oh, Nikolai," the taller of the two says as they both bow. I told the unit when I arrived that I wanted to be called by my first name and nothing else. While I'm sure *Marshal* Anatolyivich won't appreciate it, he's in another kingdom right now on some business, so I'm off the hook. He probably won't appreciate me asking to stay with the men, instead of taking the fancy room offered to me.

"Everything okay?" I look at the two men and they nod in unison. Oleg and Daniil: both good soldiers, came to the castle two years ago, and have been placed on *Tsarevna* guard duty.

"*Tsarevna* Alyona met the new suitor today and he's —" they exchange a quick look, "not great?"

"I'm happy to see that you are knowledgable on the latest gossip within these walls—it really escalates your standings within the unit," I say and Timofey covers up a chuckle with a cough. I glare at him before I turn back to Oleg and Daniil. "But why are you here and not upstairs with the *Tsarevna?*"

"Oh, Ivan Popyalof gives us a break during study time. They typically lock themselves in the study for a few hours, so we have time to eat." Oleg replies.

"Make sure you don't miss your time to be back on

duty," I say and then motion for them to carry on. I can feel Timofey's eyes on me even without looking.

"What?"

"For someone who says he doesn't care, you sure seem to care a lot," Timofey comments as we walk on the outskirts of the training field, my eyes scanning over the soldiers.

"It's my job to care about my unit."

"*Nyet*," Timofey says and this time I do glance at him. "It used to be your job to care about the unit. Your job is different now."

"Which is more the reason for me to be aware of everything that goes on within these walls."

"Mhhm, and it has nothing to do with *her*."

"I don't know what you mean."

"Right, as if you haven't mentioned her once or twice in the last ten years that I've known you."

I stop then and look over at Timofey. He's back to wearing that grin I dislike so much, the one full of mischief and of a particular annoyance to me.

"Come on, lighten up a little. This assignment is the best anyone could've asked for and I am eternally grateful you brought me with you. But can you live a little?"

"Timofey, I am the highest ranking officer here while *Marshal* is out of the kingdom. I don't have time to 'lighten up' or 'joke around'."

"You're such a *kislaya kapusta*."

This time I do stop in my tracks and look at him.

"I don't think anyone has called me a sour cabbage... ever. In my whole life."

"Maybe not to your face," Timofey grins and I roll my eyes. I've only been back for two days and everything feels different and same somehow.

Alyonushka—I have to stop thinking of her as my childhood best friend and put the sweet nickname to rest once and for all. She can't even be Alyonka to me, we're not familiar as friends.

She is *Tsarevna* Alyona and she needs my help. The curse deadline is getting closer and the Tsar and Tsarina are both clearly worried if they've hired a matchmaker to bring in suitors. The rest of the kingdom is worried too. But in the midst of all that, *Tsarevna* Alyona must be safe and must be taken care of. If I can play a part in that, then I will do it for my kingdom.

"Let's finish the rounds and head to eat. We have a long evening in front of us," I say, leading the way toward the barracks.

"Always changing the subject," Timofey tsks, but falls into step beside me.

"Watch yourself, or I'll have you scrubbing the showers."

"*Nyet*! Anything but the showers! Have you seen some of these guys?" Timofey shudders and this time I do crack a smile. This is a new environment for me and I'm glad to have my friend here. Now, if the rest of it will just fall into place as well, that would be great.

four

ALYONKA

I'm at my regular spot in the study—the windowsill cushioned area adorned with pillows—right against the large glass window. Ivan Popyalof is in his usual spot, near the door in the velvet chair. During my reading time is one of the few times he allows himself to relax just a smidge. But today, something is different.

My book is open on my lap, my legs stretched out in front of me, but I can't concentrate on the words. Something is definitely up with Ivan Po. Even his morning greeting today felt a little off. Then there were those intense glances between him and Nikolai—I can't quite figure it out, but it's there.

"Alyonka, you should be reading," Ivan Popyalof's

voice jerks me to attention. He raises only his eyes, smirking a little at me being caught.

"How do you always know when I'm looking?" I ask, closing the book and putting it aside as I pull my knees up so I can lean my head on them. Flexibility is often the pride and joy of a dance and I take it very seriously. I wrap my arms around my legs and tug them even closer, as I keep my head on my knees and my eyes trained on Ivan Popyalof.

He sighs, something that's a little unusual, and closes his own book, placing it on the table beside him. Then, he leans forward on his elbows, his eyes trained on me. Immediately, I feel it. That sense of foreboding. The intensity in his gaze, the way he's clearly trying to make me comfortable with his body language—he taught me to look out for all of these signs.

"What is it?" I ask, stretching out slowly so I can sit up. It seems like I need to be up to my full height for whatever comes next.

"I did not want to tell you until the end of today," he says and Tetia Tatiana's words suddenly spring to mind. She said Ivan Popyalof was going to give me more information about something.

"What it is? You know you can tell me. There's no secrets between us," I say these words with my whole heart because he's the only person I've known all my life to whom I can say them. Nikolai's face comes to mind immediately, but I push it away. That man is not my childhood friend anymore. We don't share secrets like we used to.

"You are correct, Alyonka," Ivan Popyalof says, his voice heavier somehow, as if he's trying to hold back emotion and none of this makes sense to me. I stand then, walking over to where he's sitting and drop down to my knees in front of him. Placing my hand over his laced fingers, I give them a little squeeze.

"*Pozalyusta*, Dyadya Ivan. Tell me."

There have only been a few times I've allowed myself such a familial way to address him. Last time it was over a year ago, when I was horribly sick and delirious from fever and he stayed by my side, like a father would. My own father never even came to see me.

But right now, it seems like whatever he's about to tell me is going to change things for us and I wanted to say it before it may be too late.

"This was not easy for me, I hope you know that. But I knew this time was coming and I know that making the decision that I made is what is best for you."

My heart drops in my chest as he moves his hands from under mine so that he can hold mine instead.

"I want you to know that being your bodyguard has been my greatest joy in life. To see you grow up, from helping you discover your favorite genres of books to which breakfast kasha is the one you hate the most—the dance recitals in your room—thank you for being the daughter I never had.

Alyonka, I—" he takes a deep breath then, his hands trembling around mine and I know what he's trying to say.

He's leaving. He's leaving me.

Ivan Popyalof bows his head a little and I feel like all the air is gone from my lungs. He's been the one person, my whole life, who has stood beside me. He could never leave me like this. Not if it was—

"My father," I say, and Ivan Popyalof jerks his head up to meet my eyes. The sadness there breaks my already broken heart all over again and I see all the answers I need in that one look.

"My father has ordered you to step down. I'm right, aren't I?"

"*Nyet*, your father—"

"Please don't lie to me, Dyadya Ivan. Don't protect him because he is your tsar. King or no king, he's supposed to be my father. And would he really do this if he cared?"

"I chose to step down now, Alyonka," Ivan Popyalof says, in that calming voice I've come to know so well. It's what finally brings the tears to my eyes, spilling down my cheeks in the next breath. "I was told that if I choose to step down now, I can appoint my own replacement."

"What?" That stuns me for a moment. Why didn't I think he would be getting replaced? But another person, to come guard me? It seems ludicrous to even think about. My parents go through so many avenues to vet the people who come into this castle. Where would they find someone—

I freeze as a thought enters my mind. It can't be true, can it? But after everything, I think it would make sense. Or as close as it can get. I meet Ivan Popyalof's eyes and he nods a little, a gentle smile on his face.

"You have always been the brightest mind," he says, which brings on more tears, even as his own eyes fill up. "You trusted him once, you can trust him again."

"Why him?" I ask, barely containing the sobs that threaten to overwhelm me. I take three deep breaths, trying to control myself even a little.

"Because I trust him with you."

"You do?"

"He is a good man, Alyonka. I followed his career closely after he left for military training. He has always been exemplary."

Coming from Ivan Popyalof, that is the greatest compliment. I study my bodyguard—the man who raised me—and I realize sometime when I wasn't looking, he got old. His hair is grey at more than just the temples now, there are wrinkles on his weathered face. Even his hands show signs of age. That's when I realize something else.

"You knew this was coming?"

"*Nyet*," he sighs, eyes full of compassion as he looks at me. "But I wanted to be prepared for any outcome."

So like Ivan Popyalof. I can't even be mad at him for keeping this a secret.

"What...what will you do now?" I ask, pushing the words past my lips as I grip his hands as hard as I can.

"My sister lives in a neighboring kingdom with her son and daughter in law. They have a little boy now. I cannot wait to meet him."

It hits me then, all over again, how unfair all of this is. How he's given his whole life to me.

"You don't regret it, Dyadya Ivan? Never having a family?"

He's on his knees in front of me immediately, his hands on my shoulders as he looks me right in the eyes.

"You are my family, Alyonka. Do not ever doubt my love for you. You may not have been my daughter by blood, but you are my daughter in every other way that matters. When I leave this castle, know that my care for you never changes. When you are queen—and you will be queen because you will beat this curse—we will see each other again."

He pulls me into his arms then, holding me like he did when I was six and fell out of the tree after I climbed it for the first time. Back then, he was the first to wipe my tears, the first to see me cry. I never doubted his love for me, not the way I doubt my father's.

"Do not worry, *Tsarevna* Alyonka," Ivan Popyalof whispers as I cling to him. "Nikolai will take good care of you."

WHEN IT'S time for us to head to the gardens to meet the suitors, it feels like I can't do it. What I wouldn't give to hide away in my rooms for just one day, where I would be free to process and feel everything the way I need to. But I know what my duty is and in that, there is no time for me.

"Come in," Ivan Popyalof says and I glance up at him as he stands to head to the door, just as it opens. Daria slips in through the space, before she shuts it again. I haven't moved from my position on the divan after Ivan Popyalof placed me here and now I look between the two people in the room.

"I sent for her so she can help you get ready," Ivan Popyalof says and the tears return immediately. His own eyes glitter before he looks away. "I will be right outside."

He doesn't wait for a response, but steps out of the room, shutting the door softly behind him. Daria looks at the door and then at me, confusion and worry on her face. She hurries over to me, dropping to her knees in front of the divan so she can pear at my face.

"Alyonka, what is it? You're crying, I haven't seen you cry in—"

"A long time, I know," I hiccup over the words, before I force myself to take a deep breath. It takes a few tries, but

I finally seem to calm myself down enough to offer Daria a small smile.

"Ivan Popyalof is being pushed out. Did you know?" I always assume the staff knows everything before I do, but Daria shakes her head.

"There hasn't been any talk. Are you sure?"

"My father's idea," I nod, flicking the stray tear off my face. "Ivan Popyalof won't tell me why, but I assume it's his age. You know how paranoid the tsar has always been about my safety. I mean, he's so afraid I'll get hurt he hasn't seen me in over a year." I laugh, but there's no humor there. "Ivan Popyalof is choosing to leave now so he can appoint a replacement."

"A replacement. You mean—" her eyes grow big as she gasps. She's a smart one. "The gorgeous gorgeous soldier?"

I chuckle, because I can't help it. I wonder what Nikolai would think if he knew that's how he's being talked about.

"This was before your time, but he and I used to be friends. Secretly."

He was my refuge when I had no one else. My parents have been paranoid about my safety my whole life. In their own way, I suppose, they wanted to protect me in case someone decided to kill me off before the curse's deadline and be the hero that saves *Holodnoye Tsarstvo*. It happened once when I was still a baby and it seemed to have solidified my parents plan to never be in my life. I've stopped being hurt by it a long time ago.

I remember hearing about the assassinating for the first time when I was seven years old, and hiding in a corner so no one would see me cry. But then, Nikolai showed up. He made me feel less alone.

"Oh my! That's incredible. That means you'll have someone by your side who will care about you, like Ivan Popyalof does."

"I don't know, Daria. Nikolai and I are no longer friends. We haven't seen each other in ten years. And then this morning—I don't know. He seemed standoffish somehow."

"I did hear about that," Daria smiles sheepishly, "him catching you like that on the stairs? It's making everyone swoon." I glance up at her fanning herself and shake my head. "But Alyonka, like you said, it's been ten years. And you're the Grand Duchess. It might've not felt like that when you were kids, but it's very evident now."

She's not wrong, of course. But I hate how my position divides us. I have no idea what to expect of him as my bodyguard, but I can tell that he takes his job very seriously. He won't let me fall.

"Come on, we need to get you ready for your group date," Daria says, standing up and then pulling me to a more comfortable sitting position. That's when I notice the pockets on her apron are filled with things and bulging. She begins taking out a brush, a handkerchief, lip tint and some other things.

"Does my face look puffy?" I ask, as she begins fixing

my hair. I had it all piled to the side and was leaning against it earlier. It's probably a bit frizzy now.

"You know that's impossible. You were gifted with magical beauty." Daria smiles and I return it, but the reminder of my baby presentation ceremony instantly adds a sour note to my already sour mood.

The six fairies and their six gifts. The fairy of tenderness, the fairy of playfulness, the fairy of generosity, the fairy of serenity, the fairy of courage, and the Lilac Fairy, the one to seal the gifts. But then the seventh fairy came, cursing me to die when I am nineteen, putting the rest of the kingdom into slumber as well. For a hundred years or more. The Lilac Fairy couldn't undo the curse, but she did change it a little by making me sleep instead. No one actually know how that will happen, so this has simply been my life. Loneliness for years, and now, suitors to win my hand in marriage. Now I'm getting ready to stroll through the gardens with some noblemen and princes. I just need to keep it together until I can get back to my room and have another good cry. Maybe dance myself until exhausted. That promise of the time that is my own is what makes me sit up a little straighter. Just a few more hours and I'm free.

five

ALYONKA

We leave the study behind, as I lead the way down to the gardens, with Ivan Popyalof and Daria at my back. The one aspect of these garden outings I do enjoy is the fact that Daria gets to come along. There have been multiple sets of suitors in the last two and a half years, but this part doesn't change. Tetia Tatiana typically meets us and does the greetings, before she leaves to take care of whatever it is she needs to take care of. Personally, I think she just finds the garden time incredibly boring. But it works in my favor.

There are multiple gardens on the castle grounds, but since it's the end of Autumn season, the trees and plants that do come alive for a few months during the year have gone to sleep. Except for the evergreens and the magically enhanced variations.

Being a magical, living and breathing land, Skazka often does whatever she wants. And I truly believe she wanted to give the castle grounds an extra gift in keeping two specific gardens—and my evergreen vines—well, green throughout the year.

The garden we're walking in today is the biggest and the oldest on the castle grounds. It looks a little bit like a miniature forest. The trees are planted close together and there's a weaving path that takes us from one entrance, to the outskirts of the grounds, before it weaves back to the courtyard area. I've read that many of the castles across the Skazka land have similar setups and I find that kind of beautiful. Even if I can never visit these areas, I can almost feel connected to them.

When we reach the hallways that will lead to the garden entrance, Tetia Tatiana is waiting. But so is Nikolai. For some reason, that causes me to trip on my own feet and Ivan Popyalof is there to steady me, with a hand on my elbow.

"Shoulders back, head high," he whispers, before taking a step back. It takes all of my self control not to burst into tears immediately. I'm going to miss his soft words of encouragement.

"I was told you know about the new arrangement. The transition can begin immediately then." Tetia Tatiana says by the way of greeting and my desire to cry turns into annoyance. I freeze in my tracks, my eyes on her, but she's not even looking to see how her words might affect me.

"The men are waiting in the courtyard already. Ivan, Nikolai, and Daria will accompany you. I expect you—"

"Ivan Popyalof," I say sharply, interrupting her. She glances up at me immediately, shock on her face. I think everyone else in the hallways is frozen as well. I can count on one hand the amount of times I've stood up to Tetia Tatiana, because I agreed to be obedient for the sake of the kingdom. But her blatant disrespect of the man who's been by my side my whole life will not be ignored.

I take a step toward her, my eyes trained on her, unblinking.

"I understand you have a job to do," I say, keeping my voice leveled, "and you appreciate efficiency. But Ivan Popyalof is a man who demands your respect so the least you can do is use his proper name." It truly is the most basic way to show respect for someone, by using their first name followed by the patronymic name. Especially someone of Ivan Popyalof's standing.

"I apologize, *Tsarevna* Alyona," Tetia Tatiana says, inclining her head.

"Don't apologize to me. I'm not the one you disrespected," I reply, raising an eyebrow. She makes a tiny noise, but turns to Ivan Popyalof immediately.

"I apologize," she inclines her head and he responds in the same matter. When they both straighten, she doesn't meet my eye as she carries on speaking. I glance over at Daria and Nikolai. One is trying to hold in her laughter, the other looks like an unmovable force. I tear my gaze immediately off Nikolai and focus on Tetia Tatiana.

"Please stay with the men for at least an hour. The dinner will be served in the third dinning room and those will be the only events for today."

Tetia Tatiana motions for Daria and the girl hurries over to grab my fur coat and help me into it. It's not fully winter outside, but the weather is colder than it usually is during this time of the year. Maybe the kingdom itself is feeling the impending doom of my curse.

Once I'm bundled in my coat, Tetia Tatiana leads the way to the double doors. The guards push it open and four men turn as once. I've met each one this past week, much in the same way that I met today's suitor. None of them have impressed me thus far, but I think I like them a little better than the last contenders.

I walk over to stand in front of them with a practiced smile on my lips. This part, where I play my role, I know the best. I think back to all the times that I've had to do this, with Ivan Popyalof right beside me and how going forward, he won't be there. Swallowing the emotion down, I turn my eyes to the first man, knowing I have to greet them first in order for them to speak to me.

"Baron Denis Alexandrovich," I say, addressing the blond man at the end of the line. He's the shortest of the four, only about a dozen centimeters taller than I, but he's also been the nicest.

"*Dobrii den, Tsarevna* Alyona," he replies, bowing deeply at the waist.

"*Knyaz* Boris Stepanich." I transfer my gaze to the next man. Boris is also blond, but he's about a head taller than Denis and very broad shouldered. He seems like someone who would make a better soldier than a prince. He, as well, greets me with a deep bow.

"Baron Lev Ignatovich." He's tall like Boris, and the only one with black hair and green eyes. He bows deeper than the rest and I try not to change my expression. Even in such a small thing, they're competing.

Then I turn my attention to the man I met a few hours ago. "*Knyaz* Georgiy Leonidovich."

He bows, but even as I meet his blue eyes I see the disapproval there. He thought I would greet him first, as he is the closest to me. I file that observation away with the others.

"Have a lovely time," Tetia Tatiana says, as she spins on her heels and walks back inside the castle. The men turn to me and I walk forward, leading the way into the miniature forest.

The men were briefed before I came out: they will walk behind me, and then one at a time, come to walk beside me. Tomorrow the last of this group will arrive and then the competition will really begin. I have been through this a few times now—I think this is the fifth group this year—and all it leaves me is completely hopeless that this curse will ever be broken. I want to keep my people from falling asleep for centuries, I want to make sure they prosper and not live the rest of their days in fear. I will do whatever it takes to keep my kingdom safe and this is just a small part of it.

NIKOLAI

I HAVE no idea how Ivan Popyalof has kept himself from punching these so-called suitors in the face all these years. I, along with everyone else in Skazka, had heard that the Tsar and Tsarina commanded a suitor to be found three years ago. If this is what Alyonushka —*Tsarevna* Alyona has had to deal with for the past three years, as her bodyguard, I would've thrown some punches by now.

"She can take care of herself."

I shift my eyes to Ivan Popyalof briefly, before I focus back on tsarevna and her companions. We've been walking for close to an hour now, moving slowly through this forest on castle grounds. There's really no other name for this supposed garden. The evergreen fill so much of the space you can hardly see the sky above. Between the trees and the snow that's clinging onto the branches, it looks like a winter wonderland.

My eyes shift to tsarevna again as an image of her as an eight year old in a pink flurry dress materializes in my mind. Even when it was snowing, she would shed her *shuba* and dance around in the falling snow like it was falling just for her. Sometimes I thought it was. Skazka loves Alyona—the older I get, the more I understand what I witnessed as a child.

But right now, the snow isn't falling for *Tsarevna* Alyona. Everything is completely still as we walk through on the path between the trees and the uninterrupted droning on of the men's voices is the only sound that breaks the silence.

This one in particular is grating on my nerves. Georgiy...even his name annoys me. He's been talking about some horse race he witnessed in one of the other kingdoms and I'm simply amazed that he's not tired of hearing his own voice. Daria, who is walking beside Alyona on her left, looks like she's completely tuned the man out. If I waved a hand in front of her face, I doubt she'd see it.

But *Tsarevna* Alyona is keeping her face perfectly pleasant for all of this nonsense. She clearly can handle herself. What she said to Tatiana back there was brave and much like a queen. But when Georgiy takes a step into her personal space uninvited I move automatically.

However, I don't make any progress forward before

Ivan Popyalof's hand is on my arm, holding me in place. I watch Alyona take her own step back and put up a hand when Georgiy moves with her.

"If you take one more step closer, you will forfeit your personal time with me," she says in a very clear and firm voice. The man shuts his mouth immediately, taking a step back. Alyona turns to glance at the other man, raising an eyebrow.

"Please, make sure to keep to the rules or we will have to rethink the way these meetings are led," she says and the men immediately bow, with agreements on their lips. I can't take my eyes off her. She's definitely not the same little girl I wanted to protect. She's grown into a very capable woman. For a second, I think she'll glance at me, but then she turns away and continues walking. I move to follow when I realize Ivan Popyalof's hand is still on my arm.

"Hold on a moment," he says.

"But I thought—"

"We will not lose sight of them." He reassures me and I glance ahead to see that this is a straighter portion of the path and we have some time before it weaves to the left.

"You cannot jump in at every little thing that happens," Ivan Popyalof says, bringing my attention to him. He's barely an inch shorter than I, so I can meet him eye to eye. I remember him from when I was a kid and he hasn't changed much. His presence still brings a calming kind of a comfort to me, much like it's always done with Alyona.

"How do you find the balance?" I ask, because this will be my job moving forward. "She knows, doesn't she?"

Ivan Popyalof nods and I glance at tsarevna again. I could tell there was a heaviness about her when she came up to the doors to meet us. She covers it well, but maybe it's the years I spent with her as a child that I can still tell when she's playing pretend.

"She was not supposed to find out until the end of day, but she is a smart girl and figured it out. I suppose we know each other too well now."

I look at Ivan Popyalof then and watch him watch Alyona for a moment. There's a heavy sadness in him and I can't even imagine what he's feeling right now. Regardless of what anyone else would say, I know the truth. This man raised her like her own daughter.

"She's smart and strong and resilient," the man says, turning his attention back to me. "She can handle these suitors well and she knows her own mind. What she needs from you, more than anything, is companionship."

"Ivan Popyalof?" I'm confused, because that's not what a bodyguard's job is supposed to be. Is it?

"I know I am asking a lot of you, Nikolai. But underneath all of that bravado is a girl who is mostly alone. You are smart, you can assess danger and I know you will protect her from harm. But I also know that you are one to keep to yourself. I had kept my eye on you all of these years, because of your friendship with Alyonka and I know how much your friendship meant to you both. You can keep it professional with her, but you can also be there for her when she needs someone."

This is such a contradiction to everything Ivan Popyalof told me originally. He told me to keep his distance, he told me that our friendship should never come into play here.

"I don't understand."

"Maybe it is because I am leaving," Ivan Popyalof sigh, looking tired for the first time since I've met him. "Maybe it is because I had made her cry—find a balance, Nikolai. For the both of you. Find a way to be her friend."

Ivan Popyalof begins walking again, but I stay frozen for just a moment longer. A way to be her friend? I don't know if we can ever be friends.

Six

ALYONKA

By the time we get back to the entrance of the garden, I'm exhausted. If I'm honest with myself, it might have nothing to do with the men themselves and everything to do with the fact that Ivan Popyalof is leaving. Although if I have to listen to Georgiy and Boris sing praises about themselves for a moment longer, I might start wearing the murderous look Nikolai sported back there.

I've been trying really hard not to look at him, but my mind still can't wrap itself around the fact that he's back. Or that he's going to be my bodyguard.

Tetia Tatiana meets us at the entrance and ushers the men away immediately. I take a deep breath as soon as my back is to them, before I glance up at the three people in front of me.

Ivan Popyalof and Daria look much like they always look, a bit concerned and like they'd like to hide me away in my rooms.

Nikolai looks—well, I'm not sure what I'm reading from him. Maybe curiosity? He's working at not meeting my eye, but every time he does, there's definitely something there.

"Let's get you upstairs and warmed up, before we get ready for dinner," Daria says and I transfer my attention to her. If it was just the two of us, she'd link her arm through mine and whisper some thoughts into my ear. I can tell she's barely containing herself.

I lead the way upstairs without a word, with Ivan Popyalof and Nikolai bringing up the rear. The one good thing about being in a situation where everyone is trying to make sure nothing happens to me before the curse can be lifted is that I get plenty of rest away from the suitors. If there was someone I actually wanted to spend time with, it would be different. But in the years since my parents began searching, I haven't met anyone who fit that mold. Of course, some of them have been plenty nice, but the nice ones don't last long in a competition. Sadly, while the men might be winners on paper, they have never been winners of my heart.

Now I'm being dramatic—or melodramatic I suppose.

"*Tsarevna* Alyona," Ivan Poplyalof interrupts my thoughts as we come up to the door to my bedroom. "Nikolai and I will meet you to escort you to dinner."

I glance between the two men, and nod my head, dismissing them. Nikolai is back at looking over my head, instead of meeting my eye and I watch as they turn and walk back down the hallway.

"Gorgeous, right?" Daria whispers and I tear my gaze away from his retreating back and roll my eyes at her. The men stationed in front of my room push the doors open without a word, as I walk inside.

"Annoying is more like it," I say, making sure the men heard me, in case they decide to gossip in the barracks. I know how these things go, within these walls, men are worse gossips than anyone else.

"What has he done to annoy you?" Daria hurries after me and I make sure to turn and meet the gaze of one of the guards.

"Come back all high and mighty," I say, just as the doors close. Daria stares at me for a moment, then glances at the door.

"What exactly am I missing here?"

"Nothing, I'm just being petty." I plop myself on the plush bench in front of my bed in a very dramatic fashion. Suddenly, I feel a thousand years old, like my whole body is incapable of movement. In retrospect, I know it's my heart that's heavy, but that doesn't make my body feel any better.

"Do you want to rest before getting ready?" Daria asks, watching me as I sink down slowly until I'm half laying on the bench, my legs hanging off the side.

"What gave you that idea? I am full of energy," I mumble and Daria laughs. I force a smile to my lips as well. She does help keep the sadness at bay.

I sit up suddenly, making her jump back a little.

"You're not also leaving, right? You're not allowed to be transferred to any outpost at the corner of the kingdom and if my parents decide to do that to you, I will keep you hostage," I say, staring right into her eyes. There's a small pause and then she bursts out laughing.

"I would never leave you, *Tsarevna* Alyona," she says, reaching for my hands as she crouches in front of me. "I am here every step of the way."

She squeezes my hands in reassurance and even though she's only a few years older than I, she suddenly feels decades apart. The calming look in her eyes, the soft way she speaks the words, they are all meant to reassure me. If I had a big sister, I assume she'd be a little her.

"You are good at this," I say, giving her hands a squeeze in return.

"It's because I care." She stands then, taking a seat beside me on the bench. I find more reassurance in those words than anything else, because she could've said it's her job. Which it is. She is tasked with taking care of me. But in my whole existence, there have always been two people who have chosen to care for me: Ivan Popyalof and Daria.

I do believe she would fight to stay by my side even if she was ordered to be sent away.

But then my mind goes back to those dark brown eyes that I once knew so well and I think maybe there was a third person who cared. He just doesn't seem to care now.

"Do you think people change?" I ask Daria and she replies immediately.

"*Da*, I think people change all the time." She glances at me, studying my profile for a moment, before sighing. "You mean the gorgeous soldier."

"Nikolai," I say, because the reminder of what he looks like is very unnecessary right now. "I could feel him watching me when we were in the garden."

"He hardly took his eyes off of you," Daria says and I glance over at her sharply. "What? Part of my job is to be observant."

"But he hardly looks *me* in the eye," I say.

"This is weird for both of you, you're different people now. Maybe he's not sure how to act? He's a soldier after all, and a good one if the gossip is to be believed."

"Which it usually is. The gossip mill within these walls is very reliable," I say, with a little smile. "I'm about to spend all my time with him, I guess I just want to know where we stand."

Daria nods and I look over at her as she meets my eyes.

"You'll figure it out. Right now, I can see the sadness on you and you're focusing on issues that don't exist—"

"Instead of focusing on my feelings, I know." I finish

standing up so I can stretch my limbs. It's been a few days since I've danced last and I can feel my body is restless for a multitude of reasons, that being one of them.

"You saw the men, right?" I ask Daria as I begin to go through a stretching routine. "They don't look like winners this time either."

"You never know, Alyonka. Someone might surprise you."

Which is what we say every time a new group of suitors arrives. But Daria is right, I am focusing on everything but the pain in my heart. Even within the walls of my own bedroom, I can't let go just yet. There's dinner to be had and then, maybe only then, when the night is dark and the moon is high I will let myself feel it all.

NIKOLAI

Ivan Popyalof leads me to the study down the hall from Alyona's room without a word. Once inside, he offers me a seat on the divan and sits across from me. I don't speak either, waiting to hear whatever it is he's mustering himself up to say.

"There is something you need to know," he finally begins and I go on full alert. I don't think this is another conversation on how I need to be Alyona's friend. This feels—heavier somehow.

"I am sure you are more than familiar with the story of Tsarevna Alyonka's curse." I don't miss the way he uses the sweeter version of her name when it's just the two of us. "Tsar and Tsarina were gifted a child when they thought they could never have one."

"And invited the six fairies to bless the princess," I say when Ivan Popyalof pauses. He nods, and the looks at me as if he's waiting for me to continue. So I do. "The fairies each represent the best attributes given by Skazka: tenderness, playfulness, generosity, serenity, and courage. Of course, the six fairy, the Lilac Fairy, is the one that seals the gifts."

"Except they were not the only ones who came to the dedication."

"The seventh fairy, the one who brought the curse."

"*Da*." Ivan Popyalof sighs and I notice just how tired he looks. When I was a kid within these walls, I remember how much I admired him and his strength. He always seemed so unmovable. But now he just looks tired.

"In recent years, Skazka has been going through many changes. Since High Queen Calista defeated Baba Yaga, the land has been healing slowly and answers that I have been looking for seem closer than before." I frown a little, but he's not looking at me. "Alyonka does not know about this, but I have been doing my own kind of research. The seventh fairy—she is hidden from us by magic. Whatever magic it is, it is old and powerful and I have not been able to find her."

"Isn't there a way to locate magic?" I try to think back to everything I've studied about the land and its power. There is so much we still don't know about and every day, we seem to learn more and more.

"If we knew her name, we could find her. But we have not been able to find that."

"You can't ask the other fairies?"

"The curse prevents us from finding them as well." He signs again. "Alyonka—" he glances at me then, as if he realized he's been calling her by her sweet nickname, but I show no reaction. Or maybe I do and whatever he sees on my face is enough.

"Alyonka is in a prison of magic. There are many aspects to the curse that we have discovered as the years gone by, and being cut off from anything that has to do with magic that might help break the curse is part of it. Just because I am leaving, does not mean I will stop looking. But there are many books within this room that might hold the answer. I have been smuggling books in, but I have not had a chance to read them all."

I let all of that information sink in, mulling it over. I always thought that the curse was unbreakable, unless it is broken by Alyonka's perfect match. Or whatever it is Tsar and Tsarina calls him. The whole point of these competitions to win Alyonka's affection has centered on the fact that that person carries the requirements needed to break the curse.

But then, it dawns on me.

"You don't believe she will find a match."

It's not a question, and Ivan Popyalof looks at me for a long tense moment before he finally nods. All air leaves my lungs as I think of the implications that carries. If Alyonka does not meet her match, then she will fall asleep for a hundred years and the kingdom with her. On the outskirts, there have been signs of the kingdom's impending slumber for over a year now. I traveled there myself when I was stationed out in the south. The plants there take longer to bloom, some animals are hibernating for longer periods of time. The officers have been taught to look out for these events as they travel across the kingdom, because everyone knows what that means.

But somehow, I never thought that Alyonka wouldn't be able to find a match. Her brightness and sassiness has always been a fascinating combination. She's beautiful, of course, but she's also smart and strong and someone who will lead this kingdom well. I can't wrap my mind around the fact that she won't find someone who'd want to spend the rest of his life with her.

"Have—have there been any prospects?" I push the question past my lips, as Ivan Popyalof watches me process all of this information quietly.

"There have," he replies, and something in me rejects those words immediately, but I push it away.

"What happened?"

"They were not strong enough to stay by her side."

I shake my head a little, because I don't understand how that plays into the situation. She needs someone to love her, isn't that it?

"You do not understand," Ivan Popyalof comments and I incline my head, seeing no reason to protest. He gives me a quick smile, leaning back against the divan as he considers his next words.

"Tsar and Tsarina believe that all they need to break the curse is a marriage of equal standing and an understanding between the two—a bond. Their idea of love is based on old traditions and rules. But love does not work that way. It is not about matching social statuses or noble blood. It is about two people coming together in a partnership, of understanding and acceptance, and making each other better just simply being in each other's company. Alyonka needs someone by her side who can handle the kind of a woman she is, but also someone who understands that she needs to be cherished and protected as well."

"But they only treat her as a trophy to be won," I say, because I saw it in the small amount of time I've spent with the group. I lean forward, placing my elbows on my knees as I try to find some potential in the men I've met. Maybe Baron Denis? Alyonka seemed the most comfortable with him.

"The competition is created to fuel their competitive

side," Ivan Popyalof says, "But it cannot be the only thing that drives them."

"That's why you told me to be her friend," I say. I can see it now, just how incredibly lonely Alyonka must be and I don't like it. The emotion is quick and fierce and I have to control the urge to go punch some people. Strange.

"She will need you, even when she pretends she does not. I will continue to do research on my part, but I need you to do the same. I can trust you with this, right?"

He meets and holds my eye and I know he's asking more than just about the books.

"You can trust me."

Seven

ALYONKA

Dinner is a particular exhausting experience. I can barely keep up with the conversation, as my whole attention is on the man who's standing just over my right shoulder. Who I was told is leaving as soon as dinner is over.

Tetia Tatiana announced it right before I walked into the dining hall, giving me absolutely no time to process or react. Daria's shocked gasp was the only indication that the words I heard were exactly what I thought I heard and then the smile was plastered to my face as the men greeted me.

This dining hall isn't my favorite, a rectangular shape that makes it bigger than it needs to be. It's also quite boring in that the decorations are minimal, with two humungous pictures of the Skazka forest hanging opposite each other across the table.

The walls on either side of me feel like they're closing in and I glance over Lev Ignatovich's head at Nikolai—who is to my right under one of the paintings—before I offer Lev a smile. Nikolai looks as stoic as ever, but maybe it's because I knew him as a child, I can read the anger on him. I'm almost positive that if it was up to him, he would've thrown Tetia Tatiana into the dungeons, just to teach her a lesson.

Dinner is typically the only dinner she eats with me, as she stays to monitor the progress between myself and the suitors. While I'm used to all of this, right now, I want them all gone and Ivan Popyalof sitting next to me so we could share our last meal together.

"I apologize," I say, when Georgiy Leonidovich is about to launch into another story about his escapades. Five pairs of eyes immediately turn to me and I offer them another one of my practiced smiles. "It appears that today has worn me out. I would like to retire to my rooms now and I will see you all tomorrow morning for breakfast."

"But you hardly ate," Denis Alexandrovich comments and this time my smile is a little more genuine.

"I am quite alright, thank you."

I don't wait for anyone to give me permission as I stand, Ivan Popyalof pulling my chair out for me, before I walk to the doors. Tetia Tatiana is on her feet, moving toward me just as I reach the doors. Because of the length of this room, we're far enough from the table that they can't hear us, but even so, Tetia Tatiana keeps her voice low. The doors open, but I don't move to leave just yet.

"You are being incredibly rude to your guests," she says, her face a mask of concern in case anyone is looking.

"And you were incredibly rude to deliver the news right before I stepped inside this room," I reply, raising my eyebrow at her.

"Is that what this is about?" She stands up a little straighter, her eyes flickering over my shoulders at the two men behind me. "You are a *Tsarevna*, you should act as such."

"Please do not tempt me to do just that." I hold her gaze, the warning clear in my eyes and she finally inclines her head, taking a step back.

"I will let you say your goodbyes," she says, her eyes still downcast. I don't reply immediately and when she finally glances up, I make sure there is steel in my gaze.

"If you try to manipulate me this way again, I will see that you are sent far far away," I say, before I turn on my heels and walk out of the room. Being around her for the last few years, I understand her game better than she thinks I do. I hear the doors close behind me and then only the sound of our footsteps.

The castle has always been a quiet place. But right now, it feels like it's already frozen in time. I don't look back, I don't pause, as I walk up the stairs toward my room. Tatiana has been pushing me more and more as the time goes by and sometimes I wonder if she wants to see just how far I'll go at the end of it all.

"Alyonka."

The soft sound of my name, said in that familiar way, makes me pause, but I don't turn.

"*Pozhalusta*, Ivan Popyalof," I say, the sound of my begging barely a whisper in the silent hallway, "Not here."

I start walking again and don't stop until we're at my personal study. This is the place that I spent the most time with him and this has to be the place I say goodbye. Once the doors shut behind us, I finally turn to face him.

Ivan Popyalof is right behind me, his eyes glittering with unshed tears in the low light. I'm not surprised at his emotion. What surprises me is Nikolai. He's by the door, seemingly trying to blend into the shadows.

"He needs to be here when I leave," Ivan Popyalof says and I nod, because it's the only thing I can do.

"We said most of our goodbyes already," I begin, my voice coming out stronger than I expect it to. "This is not a goodbye anyway. You have to take care of yourself and eat well. Sleep more during the night, as well. Enjoy the time with your nephew and your family. Find a hobby."

I can't hold back the tears anymore and they slowly trail down my cheeks as I speak.

"Make sure you go outside and breathe the fresh air, even when it's too hot. You should learn how to cook those cakes you're always sneaking from the kitchens. I think you—"

He steps forward, enveloping me in a tight embrace as the sobs overtake me. I cling to his uniform, to the comfort of his care as he pats my back gently.

"Dyadya Ivan," I hiccup over my words, "live a happy life."

"Alyonka," he says into my hair, "make sure you dance."

His quiet encouragement sends me completely over the edge and I let myself cry the way I've never cried before.

NIKOLAI

I DON'T THINK I'll ever be able to get the sound of her crying out of my head. It has been imbedded in my memory for the rest of my days. I wanted to wait outside, but Ivan Popyalof said it would be better for me to be in the room. I don't understand his reasoning, but I know that I want to be close beside her as much as possible.

This place—this castle—seems to be full of people who don't actually take her feelings into consideration. I can't wrap my mind around the games Tatiana keeps playing when it comes to Alyona but I know that whatever they are, she has me to contend with now.

I'm going to protect Alyona from all of it.

When her cries have subsided, I glance over at her and I see that she's asleep. Ivan Popyalof carefully places her on the divan, before pulling a blanket over her. He stands there for a long moment, gazing down at tsarevna and I can't imagine how he must be feeling right now. Well, maybe I can a little bit. I had to leave her once upon a time as well.

Ivan Popyalof sighs, before pushing some of the hair out of Alyona's face and then turns and walks toward me. With a quick nod, he leads me out of the room. The guards who were at the doors before had left, so it's just the two of us.

"I will leave before she wakes. I should have been gone an hour ago," Ivan Popyalof says and we both glance at the closed door.

"I will take care of her, I promise," I say, because I think he needs the reassurance.

"I know you will," he says in response, giving me a small smile. "I would not be able to leave if I did not believe that."

For some reason, he truly does trust me with her. I want to ask why that is, but in the end, it doesn't matter. I am taking on this responsibility with my whole being and I will not let this kingdom down. I will not let Tsarevna Alyona down.

"If you need to get in touch with me for any reason, tell your mother. She will be able to find me."

Those words take me by surprise, but I quickly store that information. My mother has been one of the main cooks in this castle since before I was born. I was not allowed to see her when I first returned, but not since then. She had written me letters while I was away, but I think not all of them arrived. Some pieces of information were always missing. One of these days, I hope to sit and talk to her like we used to when I was a child. But we both have responsibilities within these castle walls that keep us apart.

Now, I'm finding out she has more secrets than I first thought.

Ivan Popyalof raises his arm and I grasp it in a first shake. His gaze is steady on mine and I see everything he won't say out loud reflected there. This breaks his heart as much as it's breaking Alyona's.

Then, without another word, he turns and walks down the hall. He told me all of his things were packed this morning, so he will be gone in the next few minutes no doubt. I watch him until he disappears down the stairs before I step back inside the study.

Alyona hasn't moved.

She looks more like herself like this—with not a care in the world weighing down those beautiful features of hers. I noticed she still smells like flowers, which is such a contrast to a kingdom full of ice. I never could get over that scent, reaching out to me. When we were kids, she was my sunshine. Now, it seems that time and the curse has dimmed some of her light. Ivan Popyalof's departure has only added to that assessment.

I watch her for a long moment, before I decide it be better for her to sleep in her own bed. Walking over, I lean down, scooping her up into my arm carefully. She moves in her sleep, snuggling into my neck, her left hand automatically fisting the shirt over my chest.

I inhale sharply at the unconscious move. Her breath tickles my neck and I stand frozen, as she snuggles even farther into me. A fierce protectiveness rises up in me and I pull her closer without thinking.

She has changed during the years I've been gone, but I have too. Yet, I still feel the same kind of connection to her that I felt as a child. She fascinates me in a way no one else ever has. She's always been a force to be reckoned with, but holding her in my arms now, I can't help but think just how fragile she is under all that bravado. It makes me want to protect her even more.

When I reach her bedroom, Oleg and Daniil are on duty. They're surprised at the sight of me carrying their *tsarevna*, but they don't comment as they pull the doors open. Daria is inside, pulling back the covers and she turns when I enter. She stares me for a long moment, before she moves away from the bed and toward the door. I expected her to stay, but she's gone in the next moment, shutting the doors behind her.

I look at the girl sleeping in my arms and for a wild second I contemplate holding her for a while longer.

Then, as if realizing how stupid that thought is, I almost laugh out loud as I move toward the bed. Maybe it's all the events of today that made me temporarily insane. So instead of entertaining any thoughts at all, I place her gently on the bed.

When I go to move away, her hands tightens on my shirt, keeping me in place. A little protest escapes her lips and her brow furrows down. I stay suspended over her, watching her face for any sign of waking up, but all the distress seems to be in her dream. Before I know what I'm doing, I run my fingers gently over her brow, smoothing it out. She relaxes immediately under my touch, sighing in her sleep and the grip on my shift loosens enough that I can move away.

There's a blanket at the foot of her bed, so I pull it over her and take a step back. Leaving her right now seems like the wrong choice. After another moment of consideration, I walk over to the window that's directly opposite the door and take a seat on one of the chairs beside it. I can see the whole room from this vantage point. Most importantly, I can watch over *Tsarevna* Alyona as she sleeps.

eight

ALYONKA

I'm not sure what wakes me. When I open my eyes, the room is dark, with only the moon shining through the window. For a second, I'm confused on how I got here. I don't remember getting ready for bed and then I realize I never did. I push myself to a sitting position, glancing down to find that I'm still wearing my dress.

It comes back to me then. The study, the goodbye, feeling so exhausted that I couldn't keep my eyes open. A fuzzy memory of strong arms cradling me to a solid chest...

"Nikolai?" I ask the darkness and then I feel, rather than see him move. My eyes turn toward the window as he stands, coming up to the foot of my bed. "Ivan Popyalof is gone, isn't he?" For some reason, I need to hear him say it.

"He's gone."

I don't want to cry again. I think I cried more today than I've cried in my whole life. The only day that I can think that might rival it was the day Nikolai disappeared. I raise my eyes to his, but he's in the shadows and I can't read his expression.

"Can you light a candle?" I ask and he moves away immediately. In the next moment, there's a strike of a match and a soft glow chases away some of the shadows. Pushing myself off the bed, I reach for the candle next to my bed and walk toward Nikolai. Without a word, I light my own candle and head for the bathroom.

While my father allowed indoor plumbing to become a thing in this kingdom, the lighting situation is still handled mostly by candles. Although I have read that some kingdoms have embraced the human concept of electricity a lot better than we have.

"Would you like me to stay?" Nikolai's voice comes to me before I step inside the bathroom. I turn and look at him for a moment and then find myself saying,

"*Da.*"

Before I close the door behind me. I'm not sure why I want him to stay. I could send for Daria if I simply don't want to be alone. But for some reason, it's important to me that Nikolai is the one who stays.

"We have to build a bond somehow," I say out loud,

before I light a few more candles and wash my face. We don't exactly have time to get reacquainted. My father made sure of that when he basically kicked Ivan Popyalof out of the castle. That's the only way I can see his departure.

I clean up and brush my hair, before I change into my nightgown. When I finally step out into the main room, I see that Nikolai has lit the fireplace near the bed. Only then it dawns on me that it has gotten much colder in the evenings.

I hope Chudo lives somewhere very warm. Although I imagine a magical dragon that belongs to the cold kingdom forest can withstand the temperature drops. I have no idea how I'm going to sneak away to visit him. But that's something I'll have to figure out later.

Right now, I head for the bed, pulling back the covers the same moment Nikolai reaches for them.

"It's okay, you don't have to do that. I can handle getting into bed by myself."

He nods, dropping the side of the blanket he was holding and steps back. I climbed under the covers, but stay sitting as I watch him move back toward the fireplace. His eyes are on the flames, so it gives me a moment to study him.

Dark brown hair that's longer than normally allowed, but styled in a way that lets him pass. His profile is strong and reminds me of a painting. Everything in perfect proportion. Nikolai really grew into his boyish looks. I noticed a tiny mark on the left of his lips, a scar from a battle I know nothing about. There are laugh lines around his eyes that carry a history that I'm not privy too. He turns his head just slightly, catching me staring, but I don't look away. But neither does he.

At least his stubbornness hasn't changed. That makes me smile.

"After all this time, you really have no questions for me? I feel like the whole kingdom would love to be in your shoes and ask me about a hundred questions," I say, cocking my head to the side as he continues to stand near the fire. He truly does look like an unmovable force.

"Ivan Popyalof did mention that you are allowed to talk to me right?" I ask, because I can't help myself. I'm determined to get some kind of a reaction out of him. His eyes shift to me, meeting my own, and I feel like cheering.

"Ivan Popyalof said that you prefer to be called by your name, instead of *Tsarvena* or Grand Duchess. Why is that?"

Not the question I expected, but I'll take it. He's talking and that feels like a win. I sigh a little as I lean against the pillows at my back.

"My father—the Tsar—" I make sure to exaggerate, like I'm making the greatest of announcements. I raise an eyebrow and I don't miss the way his jaw twitches just a bit. Suppressing my grin, I continue, "He has always been big on tradition. He believes that the 'old ways' can keep us safe somehow. Which, as I'm sure you know, is why our kingdom still uses the historically accurate imperial terms. Even High Queen Calista doesn't use the outdated Tsarevna, but here we are."

Nikolai doesn't show any outward emotion, but he is listening. I can see it in his eyes, which are currently trained on me.

"It's not that I hate using the old titles or following the elder's ways, it's just—" I'm not sure why I say what I say next. I don't think I've ever uttered these words to anyone else, but they escape before I can stop them.

"It's just I don't feel much like a tsarevna."

I freeze in place, realizing just how dangerous that confession could be. My parents are already under scrutiny after having a cursed child that puts the kingdom at risk. What would happen if people realized that I don't even feel like I belong?

Not that I don't want to be a tsarevna. I love this kingdom and the people and I want to take care of them as a ruler. But the closer I get to the impending doom of my ninetieth birthday, the more I don't feel like I fit the role.

"Who do you feel like?" Nikolai asks, breaking the silence and stunning me into silence. I hold his gaze, trying to see past the handsome, but tough exterior and find the boy who would sneak pastries into my playroom after bedtime. But he's not giving anything away, not an ounce of emotion in those eyes.

Yet, I still feel seen somehow, as if he truly wants me to answer. Which is why I can't. Because the truth is, I don't know the answer to that question outside of being a cursed baby and a daughter of a tsar. Everything else, I never had a chance to figure out.

"If you could stay until I fall asleep, I would appreciate it," I say instead and I know he doesn't miss the way I change the subject. But he doesn't call me out on it either and for a moment I thought he would. Instead, he nods and then takes his place near the window as I snuggle back into my bed.

I usually sleep alone. The guards outside the door were always handpicked by Ivan Popyalof and he would take the time to go down the hall to the study. He didn't think I knew of his nightly research sessions when he was supposed to be resting, but I'm not oblivious. He had always tried to protect me.

But right now, the last thing I want to be is alone. For some unexplainable reason, I want Nikolai near. He has always been a strong memory, someone I trusted in a way I don't trust many people. And now he's here. His steady breathing is like a lullaby reaching out to me through the darkness.

The emotional rollercoaster of today is just the beginning. I think that I won't be able to sleep, but then, for some reason, I do.

THE NEXT MORNING, Nikolai is gone when I wake up. But I find a daisy the pillow beside my head and for some reason, I immediately think of him. I take the flower to the bathroom with me, finding it a home in some water on my vanity.

My body feels heavy and I simply go through the motions as I get ready for the day. Tetia Tatiana leaves me in Daria's care to get me ready for the day without going over the itinerary in full. I'm not really surprised, she seems to be pouting.

"Did you sleep at all?" Daria asks, after I pull on the dress and she begins lacing it at the back. It's very similar to yesterday's dress, except today, it's light pink.

"*Da*," I reply, shrugging a little. "I think the books call it emotional exhaustion."

Or maybe a part of it was Nikolai's calming presence. Not that I'm ready to admit that out loud. I can't believe what a long and exhausting the last twenty four hours have been. I'm almost nervous to see what the next few days will bring.

The last of the suitors is supposed to be arriving today. Then, the real competition can begin. Although, I'm not feeling very optimistic about these men either. If I were to be honest with myself, I'm not feeling very optimistic about any of this.

A knock on the door distracts me before I can fall into my melancholy. Looking at myself in the mirror, I wonder if I've always looked this sad. I've never given into this feeling before, but losing Ivan Popyalof might just push me into it. But then, Nikolai appears in the mirror and that feeling doesn't seem as true anymore.

His gaze holds mine in the mirror and my heart beats a little faster. I must be tired. Tearing my gaze away from his, I stand, turning to face him.

He looks just as immovable as he did yesterday. His hair is combed at the sides, his face clean shaven. His uniform looks like it's been pressed and then steamed for extra smoothness. He keeps his arms behind his back and I realize he's giving me the same once over I'm giving him.

"*Dobroye utro, Tsarevna* Alyona," Nikolai says, with a bow. I don't miss the way Daria wiggles her eyebrows at me from behind him. I bite the side of my cheek to keep from laughing. He stands back up, his eyes on me and I play innocent. He doesn't miss it though, narrowing his eyes just a little as he looks at me and then at Daria, who hurries to my side.

"*Dobroye utro*, Nikolai," I say and he shakes his head a little. "What?"

"Daria, you should bring a shawl for Tsarevna Alyona. We'll be going to the training courtyard after breakfast."

"Training courtyard?" I ask, then glance down at my very light material pink dress. "I don't think I'm dressed to be tumbling around in the snow." Nikolai's lip twitches and I take that as encouragement. "Although me wearing this dress might give you an advantage. Wouldn't want to embarrass you too much in front of your soldiers."

I grin, raising an eyebrow as Daria tries to stifle her laugh while she fetches a shawl. She's unsuccessful, but I don't even look at her as I watch Nikolai's eyes sparkle. It might be the early morning light, but I like to think I put that there. Slightly amused by me, he looks more like the boy I knew. He doesn't say anything, but takes the shawl from Daria and walks slowly up to me. He looks me over for a moment, and then reaches around me, wrapping the shawl around my shoulders. His proximity does strange things to my brain and then I'm back to last night, the darkness, and Nikolai's scent surrounding me.

Confused, I glance up at him only to find him still dangerously close.

"Be careful, Tsarevna, or I might take you up on that challenge." His words are low enough that I know they're meant just for me. So is the ghost of a smile on his lips. When he takes a step back, he's back to his stoic self and I wonder if I just hallucinated the whole exchange.

But the weight of the shawl on my shoulders tells me it was real. And so is the flower near my mirror. There is more to him that meets the eye. I pull the material closer, looping it over the crook of my elbows as I continue to watch Nikolai. He's back to not looking at me. Instead, he turns and walks to the door, waiting.

Daria's face if full of shock as she stares between the two of us and I wish I had an answer to the questions she's not uttering out loud. But I'm just as confused as she is.

Now is really not the time anyway because I have to

put my "please-marry-me" face on and entertain the suitors. Technically, they should be entertaining me, but it's been a long since I've been entertained.

We leave the room without another word. Daria walks beside me, casting a little look at me. Nikolai is behind me, in a place where Ivan Popyalof used to be. My heart feels heavy for a second, before I once again push it all away.

It's time to play my part.

nine

NIKOLAI

I must've had those momentary lapses of judgment. I've heard of medical emergency phenomenons where a person loses their sanity in a blink of an eye. That is the only explanation to what happened back there. But how can I even be mad at myself when I was rewarded with such a smile for my efforts?

When I left Alyona sleeping last night, she seemed at peace. Leaving a flower for her seemed risky, but when I saw a pot of them downstairs, I couldn't help but think of her—innocent and a tiny representation of the sun.

But when I stepped inside her room this morning, all of the peace and sunshine was gone. I could almost see her talking herself into all the right things she'll need to say and do when she goes downstairs. I just couldn't stand seeing her like this, I wanted that light back in her eyes. Even though she was teasing me, she seemed to do it with no feeling behind it. But when I stepped closer—that sparkle was back. Even if just for a moment.

After all, that is my responsibility as the bodyguard—to make sure *Tsarevna* Alyona is well taken care of.

Tatiana went over today's schedule with me and I can't say that I approve any of it. But of course, none of it is actually up to me, so I don't know why I bother having an opinion. Well, I will always have an opinion, but I won't be sharing it with Tatiana. Her role—while it is important to the kingdom's future—just makes me want to punch things. I haven't felt so wild about my emotions in a long time and I don't like it.

Now, as I walk behind Alyona and Daria, I wonder how well I can keep my emotions in check if I'm randomly losing my mind.

I can't be engaging with Alyona like that. It's not my place. It will never be.

"Why the training courtyard?" Alyona asks, glancing behind her for just a moment. She doesn't pause her walk as we head down the stairs.

"Tatiana has scheduled the first competition."

"I thought we were waiting for the last candidate."

"He arrived early this morning."

And looked like another one of the polished nobles

who only cared about himself. I may be slightly harsh, but none of the men are giving me good impressions.

"You will meet him at breakfast and have time to speak to him alone after the first competition."

She glances at me again and I see the confusion on her face. I would have to agree. From everything I've been briefed on when it comes to the way these meetings are set up, she was supposed to meet him before the competition.

When we're almost at the dining room, I see Tatiana and the new man standing in front of the doors. I haven't met anyone with hair like his, it's more reddish than brown and eyes light blue. For some reason, he makes me think of autumn.

Because some of my attention is always on Alyona I don't miss the way she straightens her shoulders just a bit, pulling the shawl tighter around her shoulders. The memory of her proximity from last night has been haunting me all morning. But now that's coupled with the way she smells and the tiny inhale of her breath when I move in close.

I really need to remember our places.

"*Dobroye utro, Tsarvena* Alyona," Tatiana greets her with a bow. The man beside her bows as well, an easy smile on his lips. I've noticed that about the men, they all smile with such an ease. I suppose for someone who felt like he had to work for his smile, it seems strange to me. But then again, Alyona offers him a smile as well and maybe it's just those of the noble blood. They know how to use their smiles as tools.

The man is average in hight, just like the rest of them which puts him a little shorter than me, dressed in similar expensive looking jacket and trousers. The buttons on his jacket look extra shiny and I think those are real diamonds within the gold setting. There's nothing remarkable about him, except that he's the only one with reddish hair and blue eyes. I suppose that will give him at least some of the advantage in standing out.

"May I present Graf Sergey Vladimirovich," Tatiana continues as Daria and I stand to the side. The man bows again and when he straightens I don't miss the way his eyes follow Alyona's dress, from the bottom up. Now I'm extra grateful for the shawl as it covers some of her exposed shoulders.

Alyona doesn't speak immediately, which makes me cheer internally. She's testing him, waiting him out, since he can't greet her until she does. It's a smart tactic. Not that it's my place to praise her for anything, but I am glad to see that her personality is still her own, despite all the rules and regulations placed on her by her always absent parents.

I will never understand their desire to be away from her for any reason. I would think they would feel the opposite—wanting to spend every possible minute with her in fear that they might lose her. But even when I was still at the castle, they would never venture to this part of it or having any dinners with her. They would only see her for official kingdom occasions and I was told that hasn't changed.

"*Doborye utro*, Sergey Vladimirovich," Alyona finally says and the man flashes her a grin.

"You look radiant this morning," he says and Alyona cocks her head to the side. I can almost hear the retort on her lips, but she's the future queen. She holds herself back and offers another practiced smile at the compliment.

"Shall we go in?" She asks, directing the question at Tatiana and the other woman's mask isn't as practiced as Alyona's. I see glimpses of annoyance, before the woman nods.

"Of course."

She turns to the double doors and notions for the guards to open them. Alyona glances back at me and Daria and I watch as her lady's maid bows deeply at Alyona's nod. I look between the two, as Alyona turns to walk into the dining hall.

"I will come over to the training grounds after," Daria whispers as she moves past me. "I don't eat with them."

My confusion must've been evident. I nod at the girl and then follow Alyona inside the dining room. This is a smaller room than the one the dinner was served in last night. It's a square shaped with only high windows on one side and another set of doors on the opposite end of the room. There is a gallery wall opposite the windows, with a variety of nature paintings. The men are seated around a rectangular table and instantly stand when Alyona enters. She doesn't speak immediately, offering them a simple nod as she heads for the head of the table.

Once she's seated, Tatiana takes the seat directly opposite her at the other end of the table and the other men all sit as well, with the last guest sitting closest to Alyona on the right.

"Shall we eat?" Alyona address the group, as I move to stand below the gallery wall paintings directly on Alyona's right. I'm close enough to her that it'll take me no time to reach her if need be, but also at the best place to see the servants entering and moving around the table.

Even as she picks up her fork, she seems to be moving automatically. Every single action, from taking a bite of her *oladi* to the smile she offers to the men is rehearsed. I don't see any of the Alyona I knew in her. She looks perfectly pleasant and also, completely removed from everything that's happening.

Timofey has always commended my ability for attention to details and right now, the more I watch Alyona the more I realize why Ivan Popyalof was so worried about her. She's miserable.

ALYONKA

Breakfast is too long and too exhausting. I eat my *oladi* with raspberry jam and listen as each man is given a few minutes to greet me and ask me a few questions. I can't help feeling that they simply read these out of some manual Tetia Tatiana secretly created and has been distributing for a good price.

I might also be extra irritable because I'm sad and I haven't danced in close to a week now and I think maybe my dragon friend misses me. Okay, *I* miss Chudo. I read in books that pets are good for comfort and while I think that he might be offended to be called a pet that's the closest term I have for him. I'm not magical like High Queen Calista or I would call my dragon a familiar. But I think the bond aspect of that term is appropriate.

Feeling too restless to sit any longer, I put my fork down and look up at Tetia Tatiana.

"Shall we move on to the next part of the morning?" I ask the table, but keep my attention on the woman. She chews the food she was eating, before she gives me a tense smile.

"We'll head down first," she says, addressing the men. "Please take your time and come down within the hour. We will let your food settle first."

I stand then, Nikolai next to me immediately pulling out my chair before the palace staff can get to me. The men also stand and bow as I walk past them and out the doors I came in. But instead of heading to my room or the study, I pivot to the right.

"Quick, before Tetia Tatiana comes out," I say to Nikolai and take off down the hallways. He springs into action immediately running up beside me. I glance at him and the easy way he keeps pace, his hair flapping up and down with each step and I can't help but smile. I'm making a decorated soldier run through the halls of the castle as I try to get away from my overbearing matchmaker. Nikolai catches my gaze, a question in his eyes, but I'm not stopping yet.

"This way," I say, pivoting to the left this time.

This castle is a maze of interconnected hallways that seem to go on forever. Each floor's layout is slightly different from the one below and I have no idea what my ancestors thought when they were adding on to the original structure. It seems that everyone had a different idea of what a castle should look like and all of the ideas were used. No matter how much I pride myself in knowing every in and out of this castle, there are still places unexplored, secret passages that's been locked away from even me. Or places I haven't explored in years that have been forgotten.

The hallways are wide and tall, with branching off hallways left and right. The first and second floor have gardens and some are hard to find, if one doesn't know where to look. The far north side of the castle has a hill and the first floor is slightly built into it, so there is a direct garden access from the second floor that leads down the hill and into the courtyard. Since our kingdom is usually covered in snow, the hill is a great place to go sledding. If I was allowed such things. I saw some kids do so the last time people were actually allowed at the castle. Although, I watched from the landing above.

When my parents are home they live on the far south side of the castle and I've never actually been to their rooms.

But that doesn't matter right now. I turn to the right one more time and then we're at the set of doors. I push them open before Nikolai can and then we're inside.

This one is one of the smaller sitting rooms that lead out into a garden. The room is similar to the one I usually receive the guests in, except that it's half the size. There's a fire place to the left, two plush chairs with blankets and a table in front of them and bookcase on the opposite side. But directly across from the doors is a gazebo type extension, as if someone took a gazebo from the garden and built it in place of the doors to the garden. There are doors within the gazebo, but if you stand right in the middle, it feels like you're surrounded by a snowy blanket.

"I have an hour of freedom," I say as Nikolai lets the doors shut behind us. "Tetia Tatiana won't find us here."

"How do you know?" Nikolai asks and I turn to find him right in front of the doors, as if he's afraid to take a step farther into the room.

"I try to rotate the rooms I hide in," I reply, giving

Nikolai a genuine smile. "She's been here for three years and still doesn't know all of my hiding places."

He still doesn't move from his position. I watch him for a moment, but he seems to be frozen in place, his eyes over my head and on the gazebo. At least that's what I think he's looking at.

"No further questions?" I ask and he only shakes his head once. This impenetrable persona of his is not something I'm used to. He was closed off when we met, but it was as if meeting me changed all that immediately. He was the one to ask all the questions, to push me beyond the proper *Tsarevna* that I always tried to be. But it's been ten years. Should I really pretend to know him at all?

But then, I can't help it. We're going to have to spend a lot of time together. I need him to be more comfortable with him, if even a little bit.

I walk up to him, so that we're face to face. He grew up to be so tall. We used to be the same size. I think if I squint hard enough, I might catch a glimpse of my old friend in there somewhere. He doesn't move an inch or meet my eyes as mine roam all of his face.

Cocking my head to the side, I stick out my tongue in a very un-princess like manner. His eyes flicker down to mine, before they look over my head again.

"Interesting. The military seemed to have turned off your smiling function," I say, taking a tiny step forward and peering up into his face. Because I'm so close and watching carefully, I see his jaw flex just a little. Trying to keep my own smile at bay is hard, but I've practiced enough.

Leaning back, I fold my arms across my chest and raise one hand to my chin as I look him over.

"There must be a special device somewhere, a cord I can pull? A lever?" I walk from one side of him to the other as if he was a statue. When I stop in front of him again, I reach out to poke him in the chest. His own hand snatches mine before I can move away.

I gasp at the contact as my eyes fly up to his and find that he's already looking at me. His hand, that is so much larger than mine, holds me captive. We stare at each other and I'm suddenly finding it hard to breathe.

"Why did you leave me a flower?" I find myself asking, because it seemed both a Nikolai thing to do and not. He watches me for a moment longer, before he replies.

"Because flowers carry meanings." He says it in a way that makes me catch my breath. He's still holding me captive, and suddenly, I want to know every little thought in his mind.

"What kind of meanings?" I whisper. He watches me, as if his eyes are looking straight into me and then he asks me something I don't expect.

"Why do you have to hide?"

Nikolai's words are barely audible over the sound of my heartbeat in my ears. But still, I want to answer him honestly. But how do I say out loud all the insecurities I feel when it comes to this curse and my part in it? How do

I explain the fear of failure that if I don't find someone willing to marry me that the whole kingdom with suffer? Sure, the whole kingdom knows the rules of the curse. But no one ever asks how I feel about it.

But Nikolai? I have to remember that he is a near stranger who is nothing more than my bodyguard.

I keep trying to find the boy I knew in him, but I have to be honest with myself and stop that. He can't replace Ivan Popyalof, and he's not the friend I had when I was eight years old. Just because he's the first friend I've ever had doesn't matter. He is here to do a job and I need to let him.

I take a step back and he drops the hand he's been holding.

"Being the belle of the ball can be exhausting. You've seen how intense Tetia Tatiana can be. Sometimes I need a break."

"You're the *Tsarevna*," Nikolai replies—as a statement and not a question—his gaze still steady on me even as I move closer to the fireplace. I contemplate calling someone to light it, but then my secret place would be discovered and I don't want that right now. I also don't want Nikolai calling me out on my status within these walls. Or the lack thereof.

"Nothing is as simple as that," I find myself saying, before I turn away from the fireplace and head toward the gazebo and the doors to the garden. The snow has begun to fall and I stand in the center of the gazebo, looking up at the glass ceiling, as the snowflakes cover it slowly. Nikolai doesn't move from his position by the door and I'm grateful.

It feels like I've already lived through a full day today and it only just started. It's going to be a long one.

ten

NIKOLAI

While Alyona watches the snow fall, I light the fireplace for her. She's clearly surprised, but she thanks me before she takes a seat in one of the chairs near it, pulling a blanket over her lap and snuggling into it. I move back to stand by the door, because I think we both can use the distance.

The shared history between us makes it difficult to draw lines. Seeing her sad does something to my insides. Ivan Popyaof asked me to be her friend, but it's not truly possible. Not the way he wants. Alyona has a destiny to fulfill. My only job is to see that she does so while staying as safe as possible. Which means I shouldn't be asking her any personal questions or trying to push her to reveal any kind of truths. Even if it's just for herself.

"Let's head over to the courtyard," she finally breaks the silence and we leave the room behind, with her leading the way to the training grounds. She really does know this castle well. Even as a kid, I remember marveling at how she could always find her way, no matter how turned around we got.

When we reach the training grounds, everyone is already there. The men stand in a row, staring at the space in front of them. All of the soldiers have cleared off the field and only Timofey is in the middle. He immediately steps up to us as we come up to the edge of the field.

"This is my second in command," I speak up, since Tatiana seems to have no intention of introducing him. "He transferred from the south with me. He will be conducting today's competition."

"*Spasibo* for your hard work, Timofey," Alyona greets him and the man is quick to smile at her.

"*Tsarevna* Alyona, it is my pleasure," Timofey bows deeply to greet her.

Alyona stops at the edge of the field, keeping left of the men so she can see all of them lined up. Daria steps up to her left, a warmer coat in her arms.

Tatiana steps out on the other side of the men, a bright smile on her face. Her eyes flicker over to Alyona and I don't have to be excellent at reading facial expressions to see the disproving glance she casts at the princess.

I'm directly to Alyona's right and I have the urge to move closer. Which I don't.

"Today's trial is very simple," Tatiana says, projecting her voice across the yard, even though we can hear her just fine. "It is a competition of skill. Timofey here will be your opponent and you will be graded on form, strikes, and control. Any questions?"

"I don't understand why we need to prove we're a good swordsman. I'm excellent with a sword." *Knyaz* Georgiy speaks out almost immediately and I'm not surprised. He would be the one who opposes. Out of all the men here, I like him the least.

"It is important to the Tsar and Tsaritsa that you are able to protect the Tsarevna." Tatiana replies, her tone that of a kindergarten teacher.

"Why would we protect her? Isn't that the bodyguard's job?"

I don't anticipate myself moving, but when Alyona's hand tugs on my sleeve I realize I had. I glance down at her slender fingers gripping the material of my coat and when I meet her eyes my heart does that somersault thing I've heard people talk about. Suddenly, she doesn't look like royalty who can handle anything, but a beautiful girl in need of protection.

But then she shakes her head once and drops her grip on my wrist and the image is gone. She's back to being her capable strong self and I feel like I hallucinated everything.

There must be something in the water or food at the castle. It seems I am actively losing my mind.

"If you're terrible with the sword," one of the men is saying—Baron Lev I believe—"then just say so."

"I am an excellent swordsman!" *Knyaz* Georgiy replies immediately, puffing up his chest. "I can take any of you on."

"Then prove it."

I don't realize that I've said the words out loud until Daria gasps from beside Alyona. All sets of eyes turn to stare at me, but my attention is on Alyona.

"If you allow it," I say. Her lips flex a little and I know she's trying to fight a smile. She gives me a nod and I leave her side, motioning for Timofey. My friend doesn't even bother hiding a smile as he passes me the sword.

"Stand beside her," I tell him and he takes my place next to Alyona as I turn to face the men. Tatiana looks outraged, but it's not like she can say anything when Alyona allows it.

"I can't fight you, you're a trained soldier," *Knyaz* Georgiy nearly whines, as if Timofey wasn't a trained soldier as well. I swing the sword in an arch, stepping closer to the men.

"The point of this competition is to see what you can handle," I say, looking each man in the eye. "If you cannot handle a simple sparring with a soldier, then you are not worthy to be here."

"Nikolai!" Tatiana finally speaks up, her voice high

pitched, but I don't care. One of these men could be a king beside Alyona one day. He should be able to handle a simple challenge.

"I will go."

I turn to the glance at the end of the line where Baron Denis is standing. He's the shorter of the bunch, but he has determination written all over his face. I motion to the wall that's been set up next to the men with a variety of swords and he walks over to pick one.

Out of all of the men who are here, I like him the best. From the interactions I noticed at the garden walk and then the breakfast this morning, he hasn't made Alyona uncomfortable. So he gets a point for that.

Baron Denis and I move to the center of the training yard, facing each other. He seems confident, but not in an obnoxious sort of a way. We acknowledge each other with a bow and then I attack.

I keep my movements fluid, striking on each side, before overhead and underhand. Baron Denis deflects each one, as he moves backward against the attack. There's no other sound but the clanks of the metal smashing together. I allow Baron Denis to attack a few times, deflecting easily. He's strong and sure on his feet and in his movements, which means he really does know what he's doing.

Tatiana calls it then and we separate immediately. I glance to the side and watch as Alyona, Daria, and Timofey start clapping. She meets my gaze for a moment, before she transfers her gaze to the men. She looks like she wants to say something, but she holds back. Interesting.

That's when I notice something else. Alyona is doing that thing again where she moves her hands in a rhythm only she can hear. I've noticed it a few times since I've been with her and I don't think she realizes she's doing it.

When I met her she was seven and I was nine and she was exactly the same. It was almost like she carried with her a melody, her very own song constantly playing in her mind, that forced her limbs to move with the flow.

She's doing it now as she watches Tatiana praise Baron Denis on his efforts. Her hand is down beside her, lost in the folds of her skirt, but every now and then, I see her fingers and wrist move to the right and then the left, and then in a wave motion.

It's not surprising. What is surprising is that I haven't seen her dance once since I've been back and even Ivan Popyalof didn't mention it before he left. I can tell it's still very much a part of her, so why is it nowhere in her daily routine?

But then again, I have a lot of questions when it comes to her.

Tatiana calls the next contestant up and I turn to focus on the task at hand. When I see that it's *Knyaz* Georgiy I can't help but smile a little. This will be fun.

ALYONKA

This day feels never-ending. This whole week feels like the longest of my life. I want to visit Chudo, I want to dance on the rooftop, I want to be everywhere but weighed down with this responsibility that feels like it's going to crush me.

I watch the men perform with the sword and I feel nothing. It would've been better to have them compete against each other, than Nikolai, but I didn't feel like saying anything. I know how it would go on the other side and I didn't feel like getting another lecture today. I'm sure she's already waiting to give me a talk about disappearing earlier.

I clap when I'm supposed to and smile when it calls for it. My body is tense for many reasons, but it also feels stiff because I haven't danced in a while.

"What a wonderful display of excellent fighting skills." Tetia Tatiana's voice penetrates my thoughts and I focus on the task at hand. I need to pick the winner.

I can tell which one Tetia Tatiana would like me to pick without her having to say anything. She's standing right next to Boris Stepanich with so much excitement I'm surprised she hasn't burst. Nikolai is walking back to take his place beside me and our eyes meet for a brief moment, but even with that one look, I know who he would choose. And the person is my choice as well.

"Thank you for your participation," I say, pulling the shawl a little tighter around my shoulders. The snow fall from earlier only lasted a short while, but the extra chill is still in the air. But I don't reach for the warmer coat, if only to keep myself slightly more alert right now.

"You have done an outstanding job and I am truly impressed by your skills." I make sure to meet each man's eyes as I speak, giving them a moment of my undivided attention. It really doesn't take much. I can almost see them puffing up their chests at such simple praise.

"But for today's competition, the winner—" Tetia Tatiana is not going to like this. "Is Denis Alexandrovich."

I clap and Nikolai, Daria, and Timofey clap with me. Lev Ignatovich and Sergey Vladimirovich also join in and they get points for that in my mind.

"*Pozdravlyayu*, Denis Alexandrovich," I address the man and he bows deeply.

"Thank you for your kindness, *Tsarevna* Alyona."

"Now, Tetia Tatiana, if you could go over the rules of the next competition?" I turn my attention to the woman and I think she really has stopped all pretense when it comes to her disapproval of me. My parents must pay her handsomely for her to continue her employment here. She would've quit a long time otherwise.

Her face is a perfect mask when the men turn to look

at her and she steps out onto the field, so we can all see her better. Nikolai stops beside me, as Timofey moves over to make room for him. He's closer than before, the heat of his body reaching out to me and now I don't feel as cold anymore.

"The next competition will happen in three days' time," Tetia Tatiana says, projecting her voice across the courtyard.

"Three days?" Georgiy Leonidovich mock whispers and I fight my impulse to roll my eyes.

"*Da*, Knyaz Georgiy, three days time." Tetia Tatiana says, leveling him with a look. "This competition is a bit different and requires some time in preparation on your part."

I can't help it, I chuckle a little. Thankfully, only loud enough for those immediately next to me to hear, but I don't miss the way both Nikolai and Timofey glance at me. Daria is fighting hard not to grin like a crazy person. She knows how long it took me to talk Tetia Tatiana into this one.

But I figured since all previous competitions didn't work out the way she wanted them to, I had a chance to put some requests in. This is by far my favorite.

"The next competition," Tetia Tatiana gives me one more look, "Is a poem writing contest."

eleven

NIKOLAI

"I truly believe that all of the men collectively had a small panic attack," Daria laughs as she transfers the food from the tray to the table in front of Alyona.

After the sword competition, the men retired to their rooms and Alyona went to the study. She has barely said five words to me since we left the courtyard and I can't seem to get a read on her. She told Tatiana that she will not be dining with the men, and while that wasn't received well by the woman, Alyona stood her ground.

Now, we're back in her rooms, with Daria serving dinner. I should leave her while she eats and have my own dinner, but I can't seem to make myself move. I'm sitting in the chair near the doors, my eyes on Alyona.

She's near the fireplace, that's been lit, on a chair of her own and a small table in front of her. She walked here from the study without saying a word to me and I have no idea why. Did she feel like I overstepped my boundaries by volunteering to lead the competition? That is the only reason I can think of and I can't understand it. From my observations since coming to the castle and meeting the men, plus the information Ivan Popyalof provided before he left, the suitors don't seem to care much about the curse aspect of it. It's like they've forgotten the gravity of the situation, as if marrying her will only bring them a seat at the tsar table and not any kind of responsibility. I'm getting mad all over again just thinking about it.

Alyona looks over at me for a moment and I because I'm already looking at her, our gazes clash. A strong current of awareness passes between us, before she pulls her gaze away and addresses Daria.

"Sit down, it's only us in here," she says. I can't help but feel a thread of annoyance at the familiarity with which she addresses Daria, which is followed by confusion. I have no place to be feeling any kind of emotions when it comes to *Tsarevna* Alyona.

Daria glances at me once, before she settles herself opposite Alyona. This would be the perfect time for me to go eat my own dinner, but I don't move. I'm interested to hear where this conversation will go. Purely to help me protect her better, of course.

"Did you see the one that likes to talk back?" Daria

continues, reaching for one of the bread rolls on the plate. Today's dinner is made up of potatoes and meat stew, with bread and butter on the side. The smell of it reaches toward me, reminding me I haven't eaten since early hours of the morning. The food looks like what my mother used to make for me and I need to see if I can visit her in the kitchens soon.

"Georgiy Leonidovich." Alyona's voice pulls me back to the conversation. The way she says his name tells me all I need to know on how she feels about him. My lips curl automatically, because I also don't like that man.

"Don't be smiling over there."

My head jerks up as I find Alyona's eyes on me. She's shaking her head and that makes me want to smile more.

"You know what you did," she continues, before she transfers her attention to Daria. "Because of his macho display, Tetia Tatiana is going to be on my case now."

"Technically," Daria says before I can defend myself, "She would be on your case anyway. But at least we got to see the men having to work for it."

"You don't think Timofey would've made them work for it?" Alyona asks Daria and I'm officially no longer part of the conversation.

"Maybe, but he didn't have the same motivation." Daria's eyes flicker to me as my own narrow. I have no idea where she's going with this and I'm not sure I like the insinuation.

"You have to admit," Daria continues, as she plays

with the piece of bread in her hands, "It was lovely to see them humbled a bit. They really didn't know what hit them."

"Sure they did. It was my supposed bodyguard, who went to play instead of staying by my side as is his job." Alyona takes a bite of her food and I think it's time I take myself out of this conversation. Before I say something I'm not meant to be saying out loud.

"I think my job involves protecting you from anything that can cause you harm," I announce, standing. They turn to me at once and I give Alyona a deep bow, before straightening. "If it is okay with you, I will be going to dinner now."

Alyona's eyes grow big for a moment and she puts her spoon down quickly.

"Of course," she replies, "You may go. Please." She motions for the door and I realize she must've forgotten that I haven't eaten yet. I give her one last nod, sweep the room with my eyes quickly and then turn and leave.

Oleg and Daniil are on duty again and that makes me feel better about leaving her. The greet me after they close the doors and I motion for them to be at ease.

"If she decides to leave or anyone comes to visit, please come get me immediately," I say and the men promise to do so. Not that it would do me much good, not with how massive the castle is.

It takes me some time to reach the training courtyard and even longer to reach the dining room setup for the soldiers. Timofey must've been busy since I saw him last, because he's only now getting in line for food. I join him.

"There he is," my friend greets me as one of the men scoops potatoes and meat into my bowl. I thank him and continue on, making sure to grab plenty of bread. The room isn't big, just big enough to house four wooden tables with benches, that seat six comfortably. But it's enough for us, as we are always rotating through here for meals.

"Well, that was a beautiful display, I have to tell you," Timofey says, as we take a seat at one of the tables. I stare at him as he takes a spoonful of potatoes and chews it thoroughly. "What?" He asks, as he takes another bite.

"Is there a reason why you're talking with your mouth full?" I ask, crossing my arms across my chest. Timofey rolls his eyes and swallows, before he puts his spoon down and mirrors my body language.

"Is there a reason why you're being so prickly?" He asks. I drop my arms immediately and pick up my spoon.

"I have no idea what you mean."

"Right, because you're going all possessive over the princess isn't something everyone saw."

I nearly choke on my food, swallowing before I look up at Timofey's smug face. He gives me a fake shocked face and then proceeds to eat. He's the only person in the whole military who isn't afraid to act like this with me. I'm not sure if I like that or not.

"Nikolai, stop staring at me like I haven't spoken the truth and eat your dinner."

"You really have no self preservation skills, do you?" I ask, before picking up my spoon again.

"I'm your favorite child, you won't do anything to me," Timofey replies and this time I do chuckle a little. We're basically the same age, but because of our ranking, he has always called everyone around me children, himself included.

But right now, I feel like I could use some parenting because if what Timofey is saying is true—*nyet*, it's not. I have nothing to worry about. All I did was my job. I'm good at that.

ALYONKA

"Are you really mad at him?" Daria asks as she gets me ready for bed. I'm surprised Tetia Tatiana hasn't shown up at all this evening to scold me. But I am grateful. It's so much better for my health when I'm not being yelled at every single day. However, it does feel like there's a storm brewing in that woman and I'm not sure when it'll burst free.

Nikolai hasn't come back either, but I know he will.

He'll have to make sure I am all snuggled in my bed. He might be a tad overprotective, but I can't blame him. He's new to this and we're still figuring out where we stand.

Which is why Daria's question is difficult.

"*Nyet*, I'm not actually mad," I finally say, as Daria runs a brush through my hair. I've taken a bath and changed into my long nightgown, but I still feel tense all over. I can't admit, even to myself, that Nikolai's possessiveness was a bit—exciting. Regardless of our history, he genuinely seems to care about my well being.

Or maybe, he's just extra good at his job.

"I'm mostly just annoyed," I admit, as Daria continues to work on my hair. It's already drying in its signature waves—one of those actually useful gifts from my baby presentation ceremony.

"At who exactly?"

My eyes meet Daria's in the mirror and this is the perfect example of our friendship. She's saying out loud all the things I'm trying not to face.

"I'm not sure, Daria," I reply and I turn so I can face her. She takes a step back and perches on the tub, waiting for me to put my thoughts into words. "I'm having so many mixed emotions about him being back. I mourned him as if I would never see him again. Those feelings don't just go away, do they?"

I can't even be sure about any of this because my experience with other people has been so limited. My whole life, I've been in this protective cage, only meeting people who are approved for me. The only decisions I've truly made for myself is becoming friends with Nikolai when I was seven years old and for keeping Chudo a secret.

And dance.

That's something my parents were particularly against, considering it could lead to injury. But regardless of their thoughts, I couldn't give it up. And when they stopped paying attention to me, I was happy in that sense, because I could continue on my own.

But Nikolai—they took that decision away from me.

And now he's back and I honestly don't know what to do with that.

"They don't go away, Alyonka," Daria says, folding her hands on her lap, a note of sadness in her voice. She carries heavy memories, just like I do, but she doesn't speak of her past often. I know she had to leave everything behind to be able to accept the position of my lady's maid and I will forever be grateful to her for that choice. Often, I wonder how I can repay her for her kindness. But she never asks for anything, just my friendship. Something I'm more than willing to give.

"Then what do I do with it all?" My own voice is tinged with sadness and exhaustion. No matter how much I want to see the good in everything, at times, it simply gets too overwhelming.

"I'm not sure, Alyonka," Daria replies, before moving to her knees in front of me and grasping my hands in both of hers. "But you have told me more than once that everything happens for a reason. Do you still believe that?"

"I have to," I reply immediately, because it's true. If I lose faith in that, I'm not sure how anything in my life makes sense.

"Then the truth is that Nikolai returning is part of that plan. These men—" Daria chuckles a little, rolling her eyes, "they're here for a reason."

"For entertainment purposes?" I ask and this time Daria fully laughs.

"At least that. I mean didn't you see that Georgiy guy puffing up his cheeks like that. He looked like one of those roosters walking around the hen house. The blond one with the blue eyes seems just as bad."

"Boris—Boris Stepanich," I roll my eyes at the name, "He seems to be Tetia Tatiana's favorite."

"Oh, I noticed that too. Maybe she knows him somehow."

"Honestly, I wouldn't be surprised. I'm not sure what she's getting out of this job, but if she can get a distant relative on the throne, I could see it being worth dealing with me."

"Oh hush," Daria stands and reaches for the hairbrush again. "She is privileged to deal with you and she knows it. It's why it drives her insane. But I will say, I could see her having a secret plan."

So can I. Daria gets back to brushing my hair and I mull over my own thoughts. With the way Tetia Tatiana has been acting, I've been wondering more and more why she's still here. Maybe it'll be worth looking into, just to give me a peace of mind. I wonder if this is something I can ask Nikolai to do for me. He seems to be resourceful enough.

I close my eyes as Daria continues to brush my hair out, trying to make myself relax. Which is counterproductive, but it's better than focusing on all the things that are currently driving my mind crazy. I desperately need to dance to get some of this nervous energy out. But it's not like I can sneak over to any of the ballrooms right now, so a little twirl around the room before bed will just have to do.

twelve

ALYONKA

I shouldn't go. I know I shouldn't. There are two many variables at play, too many changes. But I need this. So I wait at least two hours after Daria leaves me before I move from my bed.

Nikolai came by right before Daria left to check the room and to wish me good night. I have no idea what kind of danger he thinks is lurking behind the curtains, but I just watch him do his thing, before he bows and leaves. He seemed a little distracted, but I didn't.

Now, a few hours later, I'm still thinking about it. So since I'm clearly not going to sleep, I want to go see my dragon friend.

It's been colder the last few days, but I don't reach for a heavier dress, just my fur coat. There is not storm on the horizon as far as I can tell, so now is the perfect time. Pulling on my laced up half boots, I tiptoe to the door first and put my ear to the wood. While I know there are guards outside, I hear nothing. That's good enough for me.

Tiptoeing to the bathroom, I head to the balcony, pulling the glass doors open. A blast of cold air hits me in the face, but I'm undeterred. If there's even a chance Chudo will come, I want to try.

It doesn't take me long until I'm slowly climbing the step up my secret rooftop. I love being outside, but it doesn't feel the same when I'm surrounded by suitors and guards. This—this is my special time and I feel refreshed already.

When I emerge from behind the evergreen vines, the rooftop is only slightly covered in snow. It's a light dusting, as if it stopped snowing as soon as it left a little behind. It's perfect dancing weather.

I walk over to the edge, leaning my hands on the stone wall and look out over the forest. The moon is only half out today and everything is in the shadows. Even if I knew where Chudo came from, I wouldn't be able to see him.

The night is full of stillness. It feels like there isn't even a breeze in the air and every creature is asleep. Maybe Chudo is also asleep. Maybe he—

I feel a movement behind me and I turn with a wide smile.

"You're he—"

I freeze, my smile dying as I stare at Nikolai. He's on the other side of the roof, near the door I've never been able to open, just as frozen in place as I am.

Even though I've seen him just a few hours ago, this feels different somehow. Maybe because it seems like we're the only two in the whole land of Skazka. He seems like a stranger and like a friend all at once. But I have no idea which side of him is actually here on this rooftop with me.

"*Tsarevna* Alyona, how did you get here?"

I guess it's the stranger side. Which is better for both of us, but it still makes me annoyed. I almost sigh out loud. But I don't, because if I'm going to be the princess in this situation, I need to act as such.

"Am I obligated to answer?"

He cocks his head to the side just a little and it's too dark for me to read his expression from over here.

"Of course not. We will just wait and see."

And then he folds his arms across his chest, leaning against the wall behind him. I raise my eyebrows, but he's unmovable. I can't help the warmth that spreads across my chest, because we've been here before. We've played this game more than once.

But I think that this time, Nikolai might have the upper hand. He seems more unmovable than I've ever seen him. None of that shy sad boy he was when I first met him. But I'm also not the same girl.

"I thought you were my bodyguard." I sigh, very dramatic like. "Are you really going to put me in danger by letting me get sick while keeping me on this roof all night?"

I can't be sure from this distance but I think he might be fighting a smile. Yet, he doesn't move, but neither do I. Well, I move a little, by folding my own arms across my front and leaning against the wall behind me. This time, I swear he does smile.

"Can still talk yourself out of any situation," he says it so quietly that I almost don't hear him. Suddenly, my mind is back to one of those nights when we were kids and I had masterfully talked him into sneaking down to the kitchens during baking hours to steal *vatrushki*. As a kid, I had an absolute obsession with the cheese filled pastries and wasn't allowed to have any unless it was a special occasion.

Now that I think about it, it's been a while since the kitchen baked some. I wonder why.

"Are you really going to keep me prisoner on this roof?" I ask, because it's much safer for me to keep myself away from the memories. "How did you get up here?"

Nikolai pushes away from the wall and gestures to the door behind him. I stare at it for a moment in confusion, before looking at him.

"That door doesn't open."

"It doesn't?" He replies and then takes two steps and he's pulling it open. I'm not sure why I thought he was joking, as I stare at the darkness beyond the open doorway.

"Where does it lead?" Because this has actually been a mystery for me since I found this little roof area. Nikolai looks at me for a long moment, before replying.

"Down to the first floor directly," he says, "it's a turret with stairs winding in the middle of it. It connects to a study on the first floor."

"Interesting."

But not really surprising. Since this castle has been added on throughout the generations, it makes sense someone built more of the castle past the turret, encompassing it in more building, instead of having it at the edge of the castle like usual. But maybe since it doesn't have the typical design or location of a turret, it never occurred to me.

"You didn't know?"

"*Nyet*. I have never been able to open the door."

Nikolai reaches into his pocket and takes something out. He moves towards me, holding his palm out and I see that he has two keys.

"One is for you," he says.

"What?"

"In case you ever need it."

He holds it out for me to take and I stare at it for a long moment before I finally reach for it. Our fingers brush, just barely, but that small contract sends my heart racing. I take a step back and turn to stare out at the night stretching out in front of me. These are not reactions I should be having toward my bodyguard. Maybe instead of coming out here, I should've slept. My tired brain is confusing things for me.

NIKOLAI

I wasn't prepared on seeing her tonight. After dinner, I visited my mother in the kitchens. As usual, I couldn't speak to her for long, because she was so busy. But just seeing her was nice.

Then, I bypassed Timofey, lest he come up with some outrageous ideas again and went to say good night to Alyona. Thankfully, Daria was still in the room, so it kept our awkwardness to a minimum.

Once I left her room, I had fully intended on getting some rest. Since driving to the castle, I haven't really rested. But instead, I head toward the study down the hall from Alyona's bedroom. I also haven't had a chance to go over any of the materials Ivan Popyalof left or do any of the research he asked for.

The room is dark when I step inside. The one window's curtains are drawn, blocking out any of the moonlight. I reach for the candle near the door, and with it still open, I light the candle before I step fully inside.

I've been in here twice with Alyona but haven't given

myself a chance to look around. Now, I take the time to stop in front of each bookcase, looking over the variety of books. There is a plethora of volumes on Skazka history, a whole set of books about High Queen Calista's adventures, and even a section on various nature and wildlife of this land.

When I move closer to the bookshelves near the windows I notice an arrangement of bright colored hardcovers—different shades of green in a gradient and then turquoise, maroon, purple—all with pretty fonts. I pull one out and studying the pretty typography and the drawings arranged in a frame around them. Romance books from the human realm, I realize, after reading the inside cover. The bright green one appears to be about gates you can travel through and the bright turquoise one is about two rival authors. I smile to myself as I put them back on the shelf. It makes me glad to see Alyona reads for pleasure as much as for academics. It is important to have a balance of both.

Not that it's up to me at all. I keep forgetting that part, which is becoming increasingly irritating.

I walk over to the desk next, placing the candle on the side and taking a seat. There are stacks of books and papers left over from Ivan Popyalof and I take the next hour or so to read over it all.

As I read, I realize just how much information Ivan Popyalof has been able to compile. The notebook he left for me with notes written inside is at the bottom of one of the book stacks and it contains a lot of his observations. He has also recorded the competitions, making his own judgment on the suitors who have come through. An ugly emotion starts to rise from somewhere deep inside of me and I push it aside, reading over the names and the statuses of the suitors.

A year ago, he thought he might've found the Fairy of Serenity and the Fairy of Playfulness, but it ended up being wrong information. Alyona has only been allowed to leave the castle on three occasions, when her presence was required to represent the kingdom, and each time, Ivan Popyalof took that as an opportunity for more research and for making more connections. He is very well connected after all this time.

Placing the notebook where I found it, I blow out the candle and leave the study behind. My mind is full of bits of information I've never thought to think about before.

No wonder he's so concerned about the curse and its deadline. There has been seven competitions so far and none of them have yielded any kind of good results. There have been a few good candidates, someone who could've stood by Alyona as she ruled, but something always sends them packing. That was another mystery Ivan Popyalof was trying to solve.

Living in Skazka, of course I believe in magic. But it has never played a part in my life, so it's always been something that's been a little bit far from me. Now, I'm fully wrapped up in it.

The curse has always been something that everyone in the kingdom knew about, but it's one of those pieces of knowledge everyone simply lives with their whole lives. But not anymore. There's less than a year left until Alyona turns nineteen and the curse becomes reality.

I was so lost in thought I didn't realize I wandered into a part of the castle I haven't explored yet. Granted, there are many areas that I still have to visit, as this castle is probably the most confusing piece of architecture I have ever seen.

Looking around, I see that I'm on the first floor, but nowhere near what I've deemed the front of the castle. It's where the dining halls and sitting room used for the competition. It is also near the barracks. Now, I'm on the opposite end and if I'm correct in my assessment, I think I'm somewhere near the area where Alyona resides two floors up. Or maybe past that?

The hallways here are the same as anywhere else in the castle. The ceilings are high and painted with scenes from Skazka's history. The walls are heavily wallpapered with velvet dark blue wallpaper and various sized paintings in gold frames line them on each side. The crown molding is also gold, as well as the wall candle sconces. Everything looks very traditional.

I continue down the hall until I reach a few doors. One by one, I open the doors and find myself in various sitting rooms. When I reach the third door, it is opposite the other two, situated on it's own, with no other door on this side until way farther down the hall. When I push it open, my mouth nearly falls open.

Inside is a large ballroom, withs ceilings so high it at least takes up the second floor space. There are large chandeliers hanging from the said ceiling. I can't see it entirely, but it's painted with another picture. What really stuns me though are the giant windows that line the whole wall in front of me. They're tall, reaching the ceiling, but only coming down about three fourths of the way down. The glass panels are outlined with gold and they look like they would open from the middle and out.

The truly beautiful sight is the moon shining through, making everything looks almost magical inside the room. It's almost like the room was created to show off the moonlight and the star filled sky. Even with all the glass, it doesn't seem cold.

Alyonushka would love to dance here.

The moment the thought enters my mind I shake my head and walk back toward the door. I have no right to be thinking such things. I step out of the room without another look back. I stand in front of the door for a full minute, chastising myself for thinking of her in such a way. That nickname should never enter my mind again, and yet, it has happened twice.

Frustrated, I continue down the hall, past the ballroom and end up at another door, on the opposite side. Pushing it open, I find myself in a small study, with just four bookshelves and a divan near the fireplace. There are no windows, but right between two bookshelves is a door. Curious, I walk towards it and see a key already in the lock, with another one hanging off it.

Since apparently it's a night of discoveries, I unlock the door and find a set of finding stairs. When I reach the top, I unlock the door, only to find a medium sized roof landing and Alyona standing on the other side of it.

Now, as I hand the key to Alyona, I wonder if all of what happened tonight led me here.

"It goes all the way down to the bottom floor?" Alyona asks and I nod. She stares at the key in her hand, moving side to side to that melody only she hears. The more I watch her, the more I think she doesn't realize she's doing it.

My skin still tingles from where our fingers brushed and maybe that's what pushes me to say what I do next.

"When was the last time you danced?"

thirteen

ALYONKA

"When was the last time you danced?"

I jerk my attention to Nikolai, taken completely by surprise. The question seems to echo all around us, as if he shouted instead of speaking softly. I can't stop my body filling up with warmth, all over, at the simple way he remembered. My eyes fly up to meet his and I shake my head once. He can't be asking me this, he can't be making me feel anything.

"I don't think this is any of your business," I say, because one of us has to keep the lines drawn. He's getting under my skin in a way I couldn't even anticipate and this cannot be so.

"I think the wellbeing of the Grand Duchess is precisely my business."

He hasn't moved—there is still most of the roof between us—but I feel his words traveling across my skin like a caress. The only way I can explain it are residual feelings left from our childhood.

He was my first friend, he was my only friend, he was my everything at the age of seven and eight. I thought I found someone who could understand me even when I didn't have the words to explain myself.

But then he disappeared and even when I found out it wasn't his choice, I couldn't let go of the hurt. That hurt flares up its ugly head now and I shut my eyes against the memory.

"Then make sure no one assassinates me because they think killing me would keep the kingdom from experiencing the curse. That's all you have to do," I say, my voice hard, my walls desperate to be rebuilt.

"Ivan Popyalof said you need more than simple guarding—"

"Ivan Popyalof isn't here and he isn't your monarch. I am. So I suggest you remember who you're talking to."

I sound harsh even to my own ears, but I can't help it. The memories of him as a boy, the pain of him leaving, the man who stands in front of me now—all of these are mixing up in my mind and I can't let any of it affect me. I have no idea what I expect from him next, but isn't a soft smile and his next words,

"There she is."

My eyes are on him and I wish the moon would go back to not being so bright so I can ignore the way he's looking at me.

"What is that supposed to mean?" I ask.

At first, I don't think he's going to reply. He takes a step toward me, eating up some of the distance I'd deemed safe.

"It means that you went through most of the day forgetting to speak up. You didn't like the competition, you didn't like meeting your last suitor the way you did. I suppose you liked the potatoes and meat stew Tatiana had the kitchens prepare, but is that what you wanted to eat tonight?"

He smirks then at whatever he sees on my face and takes another step toward me.

"You have always been a fighter, Alyonka. Why were you hiding in some random room in the castle when you should be speaking your mind?"

It's the fact that he uses my name that gets me. He used to call me Alyonushka. The only person who ever did. I haven't heard that sweet endearment of my name since I was a child and suddenly, I'm desperate to hear it again. But the simple representation of distance also reminds me that we're not those kids anymore.

"You weren't here," I say and he jerks back as if I slapped him. I meet his eyes again and he's frozen in place, almost halfway across the roof toward me. I can't tell him that I gave up my own ideas on how my life should go in order to please my parents. Sure, I wanted to earn favor with them when I was younger, but that simply morphed into a life ruled by their rules. It's too late to change that now, especially since everyone seems to confident in the way this curse needs to be broken. It's not my place to be selfish.

"You weren't here," I repeat. "So don't pretend to know anything about me. Do your job. That's where you were trained to do, that is why you're here."

It's a good reminder for both of us. It's not like he came back of his own volition to be by my side. He was assigned here and chosen by Ivan Popyalof to protect me. I am a job to him and I have to make sure we both remember that. Regardless of how close we were as children, we cannot be that close now. The distance between us is a must.

"You didn't miss me at all?"

All air leaves my lungs at his quietly spoken words and suddenly the night air is the coldest it's ever been. I shudder in my fur coat, hands curling inside the pockets.

Did I miss him?

Desperately.

Will I ever tell him?

I can't.

So instead, I give him the exact thing he praised me for just moments before. I raise my chin, as I study him with my detached royal gaze. I have perfected it over the years and I know how it affects people. He stands frozen as I give him an assessment and then I finally...finally meet his eyes. One word, and I turn to go.

"*Nyet.*"

NIKOLAI

THE NEXT TWO days go by in a blur of activity. Alyona has her meeting with Graf Sergey and then her individual date with Baron Denis. They opt out to play chess in the sitting room, laughing together like old friends.

I can't let it get to me, but I'd be lying if I say it's not. I've been carrying that "no" with me for days. Even as I watched her disappear behind the evergreen vines and checked to make sure she made it back safely, I couldn't swallow the hurt that one word produced.

Because I missed her.

It feels like I'm missing her even now.

"Okay, Mr. Broody-like-Skazka's-winter-storm," Timofey set his plate of food in front of him, before he takes his seat. "Spill it. Whatever is brewing in there."

"Did you just compare me to the weather?" I ask, the fork full of food halfway to my mouth.

"You didn't like me comparing you to food, so I'm trying

something different." He winks at me, before he digs into his dinner. Tonight's menu consists of one of my favorite dishes: *pelmeni*. The pastry dumplings are filled with meat and then boiled and fried to maximum perfection. A dollop of sour cream and the food feels like a warm hug. I might've missed these a lot when we were stationed at the south border.

"How about you don't compare me to anything and I let you keep your mattress," I say, before taking another bite. Timofey chuckles as he chews, shaking his head.

"Your threats are useless when it comes to me. I would just steal your mattress." Now it's my turn to roll my eyes. "Now are you going to tell me what's been bothering you?"

He would be the only one to call me out on it. I'm grateful he lowers his voice when he asks, because I really don't need to become part of the gossip mill within these walls. Even though I've already been a start twice, according to my two gossip hens: Oleg and Daniil. They really are good kids and I'm happy to have them guarding Alyona when I can't be there.

"Ah, it's about her," Timofey says before I have a chance to reply. I nearly drop my fork.

"What are you talking about?"

"Oh, please." My friend points his fork at me, "I know that look. You've worn it often in the last ten years I've known you and it always comes down to *her*."

I glance around us to make sure no one is paying

attention and thankfully most of the soldiers have cleared out by now. I've been having dinner later than everyone else. Timofey won't admit it, but I think he's been waiting to eat so I don't eat alone. But at the moment, I kind of wish she didn't.

"Eat your dinner, Timofey," I say and he takes an exaggerated bite, before he chews it and points his fork at me one more time.

"You've been avoiding this conversation since we got to the castle."

"And you've been pushing it every chance you get. Don't you have some actual things to report to me?"

"Fine..." he makes sure to drag the word out, before he puts his fork down and leans on his arms toward me. "As per your instructions, I've been overseeing the training rotation. Every day, each person trains with at least three different opponents. Also, I've been monitoring the assigned patrol units and leaving the paperwork on your desk."

"*Da*, I have been reviewing it."

"Other than that, everyone is following the chores schedule you put together."

"What about their emotional well being? Are there any complaints? Fights?"

Timofey cocks his head to the side and gives me a quick smile. It's true, I might be going slightly overboard, but when I agreed to take over this post, I wanted to make sure the soldiers under my care had better experience than I ever did.

"Everyone is happy," he reports. "You don't have to worry about it. Maybe focus on your own happin—" he stops abruptly when he sees my look. "Or you can continue to be a *ploskiy blin* and scare everyone off with that face."

"A flat pancake is the best insult you can come up with?" I ask, swallowing the rest of my bite.

"Just look in the mirror. The resemblance is uncanny."

I reach for him then, but he's already jumping up and grabbing his dishes.

"See you in training," he calls over his shoulder as he drops off his plate and leaves the dinner hall. Maybe I'm not as good at hiding my emotions as I think I am. Or maybe my friend of ten years can simply read me better than most.

Either way, he's not wrong. I'm bothered when it comes to Alyona and there's nothing I can truly do about that. Which is frustrating.

The next competition is tomorrow and while I don't like the way Tatiana is parading Alyona around like a trophy, I do hope the poem writing contest goes well. We are running out of time.

fourteen

ALYONKA

I woke up feeling all kinds of anxious. I'm not sure what's causing it, except for everything. I haven't had a chance to dance in over a week now, I haven't seen Chudo in days, and the tension between Nikolai and I has been rising to unbearable heights.

The lie I told him that night on the roof has been eating at me. Even Tetia Tatiana noticed.

"Can you look a little less like you're heading to your execution?" She asks, as Daria finishes lacing up my dress. Today's is another shade of pink. This one is a little less fluffy, with a body hugging silk silhouette and a simple tulle layer over the skirt and shoulders. It's definitely more summer style, but it makes me feel extra pretty, especially with my hair cascading around my shoulders, hallway up in a braid. I'll be wearing a heavy cape over it anyway, and the whole ensemble makes me feel like I'm a heroine in one of those romance novels I like to read.

I fake grin at Tetia Tatiana and she simply sighs, before taking her frustration out on her notebook. Daria steps in front of me, placing the cape over my shoulders and buttoning it under my neck. It's heavier than I would like it to be, but it'll keep me warm.

It's similar to the coronation cape, except on a much smaller scale. It sits over my shoulders, with a top layer covering down to my elbows, and the bottom layer going all the way to the floor. It's dark blue, a nice contrast against the light pink of my dress and the only thing I wish it had are pockets.

Tetia Tatiana continues to scribble furiously, as Daria rolls her eyes at me while she can't see her. I stifle a smile and then sober up completely when Tetia Tatiana looks up at me.

"Since you insisted on eating breakfast in your room this morning, we'll be heading straight to the garden room for the second competition. The men are all eager to show off their poetry writing skills."

The way she says that leaves no room for guessing on how she truly feels about this test. Even if she didn't protest on how stupid it was when I pushed for it originally. But honestly, I'm so tired of all the competitions being about strength and historical knowledge. Anyone can train or memorize facts from a book. Something creative, like poetry writing, shows off a completely different set of skills. I would like to gauge their responses—especially if the poems turn out to be less than stellar. One can learn a lot from someone who has just been embarrassed and how they handle themselves in the aftermath.

But instead of saying any of that, I simply smile, "I can't wait."

Tetia Tatiana huffs another gust of air just as there is a knock on the door. My heart leaps in my chest immediately at the anticipation and then Nikolai steps through the doors. His eyes find me immediately and he does that quick sweep of his gaze over me, as if he's making sure everything is where it needs to be.

I've come to anticipate his quick study and I make sure I don't move until he's done. That's when I realize his uniform and my cape are the same shade of midnight blue and I almost let that matter.

"*Dobroye utro*," I say, and he gives me a deep bow. All of this is routine, but for some reason, my anxiety isn't as pulsing anymore.

"I hope you slept well, Tsarevna Alyona," Nikolai's deep voice travels over my skin even at this distance. "It is going to be a stormy day."

I haven't even looked outside, but now, I want to. Walking out of the bathroom, I head toward the window and peek outside. He's right. The clouds are gathering overhead. Which means there probably won't be outside garden time today. Or any escapades for me tonight. I sigh a little and turn toward the rest of the room.

"Let's get going," I say and Tetia Tatiana nods once and leaves the room. I already told Daria that she's coming to this competition with me. It feels like something she should experience first hand, which is why I insisted on eating my breakfast in my rooms. So we could eat together.

Nikolai takes a step out of the doorway to let me pass and I can't help but inhale his comforting scent as I walk out the door. He smells like fresh and sure, like the air right before first snowfall of the season. It's my favorite time to be outside.

He doesn't speak again as he falls into step behind me. But I can almost see him mulling something over and I make a mental note to ask about it when we're alone later.

My heart should not be jumping in excitement at that idea. Stupid, stupid heart. Calm down.

We reach the garden sitting room, which is the first room past the grand ballroom the balls are typically held. Well, where they would be held if my parents had any events at the castle since they've decided about seven years ago that even the annual winter ball is too dangerous. The ballroom is the closest to the front entrance and perfect for guests. It's where the whole curse thing went down.

While I hardly frequent that room, I do love the garden sitting room. It's large, not as big as the ballroom, but big enough that there are multiple divans throughout, and four separate fireplaces. The windows are floor to ceiling, so the room needs extra heating. But it's bright, and there are plants used for decoration throughout the large room.

The men are already inside when we arrive, which I'm not surprised about. Nikolai leads me to one of the individual chairs near the fireplace to the right of the door and I sit down in it gratefully. The men all bow, and when I motion for them to take a seat, they take up the divan and chairs around me.

"Welcome to the second completion," I greet them with a smile. This one, I'm actually excited about. There is a chair near the window, so Daria takes that. It's behind the men, which is kind of perfect because then I can see her reaction. Nikolai walks over to the fireplace, standing on the other side of it, so he can watch me and the whole room from his position. But it also means I can see his face as well.

Tetia Tatiana takes center stage, addressing the men from the other side of the room.

"As previously stated, this is a poetry writing competition. If you would like to go first—" three hands raise in the air, taking her by surprise. But I can't even say that, because the three who raise their hands are Georgiy Leonidovich, Sergey Vladimirovich, and Boris Stepanich. Exactly who would I expect to volunteer. Especially since the last time the one who volunteered won.

"Oh, we seem to have some excited participants," Tetia

Tatiana says, her eyes sparkling and I definitely need to talk to Nikolai about looking into her relationship with Boris Stepanich. I glance over at my bodyguard and he meets my gaze, almost like he's thinking the same thing.

"Let's start with Boris Stepanich," I say, giving the man a smile. Tetia Tatiana looks like I've given her the sun. The man stands, straightening his jacket, before he walks over to stand in front of the fireplace, between Nikolai and me. Clearly, he likes the theatrics.

He clears his throat and then he begins to read.

"The beauty of the frozen forest,
Compares not to the beauty of you.
There is no snow as pure as your skin,
No *brusnika* as red as your lips.
Your eyes sparkle like the stars,
Your hair moves like the river waves.
You alone, *Tsarevna, moya*
Beautiful like Skazka."

He finished with a flourish, bowing deeply, as Tetia Tatiana claps with unabashed enthusiasm. The rest of us clap a little more politely, as Boris Stepanich grins and returns to his seat.

I kind of wish Daria was sitting directly next to me, because did he just call my lips are red as the thorny looking wild cranberries? I glance at her and watch her purse her lips. That's all the answer I need.

"That was lovely imagery," I say, because I'm supposed to be giving them positive reinforcement. I should've brought prizes to give out.

"Sergey Vladimirovich, why don't you go next?" I motion for him and he stands up enthusiastically. That is something I noticed about him, he's rather enthusiastic about everything. When he begins reading his poem, he ends each line with an exclamation.

> "I was riding alone when I came upon you!
> A snowdrop rising from snow!
> There are days when live seems—!
> Like it will always be this way!
> But then a hope springs up!
> In the dull winter day!
> Yet, you pushed through the dirt!
> You clawed through winter's snow!
> Now you stand drooping!
> But don't fear!
> I am here!"

He raises his hand in the air at the last word and then bows deeply. I clap automatically, trying to keep the laughter off my face. That definitely started a lot better than it ended. Now I'm a drooping flower in the snow.

I really love snowdrops, but I'm not sure either of these men can be said to be good with words.

"I really like snowdrops," I say the only part of my

thoughts that can be said out loud, but Sergey Vladimirovich looks very proud of himself as he takes his seat.

"Georgiy Leonidovich, please." I motion for the last man who volunteered and he stands slowly, making sure to look around at each person in the room, before he finally looks at me. He walks toward me, not breaking the eye contact and I feel, more than see Nikolai moving closer to me.

Georgiy Leonidovich's gaze shifts to my bodyguard briefly and then he stops walking, and move to stand beside my chair, on the opposite side away from the fireplace. He's close enough that I have to move back to be able to look up at him. I fold my hands in a way that allows me to lean on the arm rest away from him and feel Nikolai's body heart reaching out to me as he stands directly by the chair now.

Knyaz seems completely oblivious to the fact that he's making me uncomfortable, or maybe he simply doesn't care. He glances at his paper once, and then begins to speak.

"Oh what wondrous thing it is, love.
Oh how I'm desperate to feel your touch.
Mountains move when I see you before me,
Skies open up, pouring rain upon me.
Nothing in Skazka compares to your beauty,
Even foxes are jealous of your wit and shiny hair.

If Baba Yaga would come through those doors,
I would fight and triumph over her for you.
I have traveled the world, and into other realms,
I have seen much, you can never imagine.
But I am willing to stand by your side in this kingdom,
And be your knight in shining armor forever!"

He starts clapping for himself before my brain finishes processing his poem. I nearly jump in my seat at the sound of the clapping and I join in with the rest of them. I'm not sure any of these were written for me. I think that even if I wasn't here, they could read these poems and enjoy themselves.

There's a slight pressure on my right shoulder and I freeze immediately. It's just a little tap, tap, tap, and then it's gone and I don't dare to look up at Nikolai. But I know it's him, offering silent encouragement.

I glance over at Daria, who is having the worst time trying to keep the laughter at bay. Her shoulders shake in silence, and I'm thankful no one is looking at her. At least she's enjoying herself.

While the men cheer each other on, I give myself a moment to breathe. Nikolai's soft taps on my shoulder replay themselves in my mind and I find enough encouragement in that to keep going.

Only two more to go.

NIKOLAI

I'M PRETTY sure dragging these men out of here by their hair and dumping them over the side of the castle's walls is not in my job description, but I wish it was. They've been given such an opportunity to be in the presence of Tsarevna Alyona and they're patting each other on the back for that terrible garbage of words they're calling poetry.

I can see her trying not to shrink into herself. Even her sentences are becoming shorter and shorter. Her hands are on her lap, but I can see her moving each finger to touch her thumb, before she restarts again. It's like she's performing a dance but only with her fingertips. The movement, just like everything else about her, is mesmerizing and I keep my eyes on her hands until her voice breaks through my thoughts.

"Denis Alexandrovich?" She says when the man stands. He doesn't do any of the boastful walking and smiling like the others have done. He simply bows to Alyona and then stands in front of the fireplace where they all should've stood.

"I apologize for my lack of poetic talent, Tsarevna

Alyona," Baron Denis says, before he clears his throat and begins to read.

> "There are many stories told about Skazka,
> Of the land where magic thrives.
> There is magic that can bring amazement,
> There is magic that can curse a child.
> But the greatest strength that Skazka has,
> Is the wonder of a loving heart.
> For every story that I hear,
> The good overcomes the dark."

There's a moment of silence when he's done speaking and then Alyona claps enthusiastically for the first time. I have to agree with her assessment. While this poem is in no way romantic, or very well written by normal poetic standards, there is a lot of beauty in it.

"That was wonderful, Denis Alexandrovich. Thank you."

The man grins at her and then takes his seat, just as the last contestant stands. I honestly have no idea what to expect from Baron Lev. Out of all of them, he's the one I have the most trouble figuring out.

He walks over to stand in front of the fireplace without a word, bows, and then begins to read.

> "A heart is an empty place,
> When love does not exist.

A smile is only a mask,
When joy is hidden away.
I met you, and everything changed,
The way winter turns into spring.
I met you, and the mask fell apart,
Since love is a spark that became..."

I think he has stunned everyone into silence, and I can't even blame them. That was a little bit beautiful and much more of what Alyona deserves. I glance down at her, trying to gauge her reaction and even though her mask is in place, Baron Lev is the clear winner.

But if I'm being honest, it didn't sound like this is something that he wrote in the last three days. It seems more like something he's carried with him for a while.

Just then, a thunder shakes the castle's walls, as if signaling the end of the competition. It's Alyona's study time after this and I'm looking forward to her having alone—

"Well, since the weather decided to show up suddenly," Tatiana speaks up, addressing the room, "Why don't we mingle here for a bit, before we announce the winner."

I stare at Tatiana, wondering how someone who is supposed to be an expert in human relations simply cannot read the room. Or more importantly, cannot see that Alyona was clearly ready to leave.

"What is the next competition?" *Knyaz* Boris asks and

Tatiana beams at him. I need to check with Timofey to see if he was able to find out anything about these two. They are giving me the wrong impression any time they're together.

"Oh, you're going to love it. The next competition is—"

"Ice skating!"

Everyone turns to look at Alyona and her outburst. Because the next competition was going to be a show and tell type of a competition. The men were going to show off some of the items and experiences they can bring to this kingdom. Clearly, *Knyaz* Boris knew of this, as he glanced over at Tatiana in disapproval.

The men were told to be prepared for anything, but they weren't given specific explanations. From what I've learned talking to people around the castle, and from what Ivan Popyalof recorded in the notebook, every set of suitors that come through here have had different competitions. There hasn't been any repeats, so no one could share any kind of information regarding what goes on here.

But ice skating was not on the table.

"Well, actually—" Tatiana starts, but Alyona silences her with a wave of a hand, as she stands.

"I think that's a wonderful competition," Alyona says, walking over to the set of windows, near where Daria is sitting. "We've only spent a little bit of time outside and as you know, my kingdom is of a colder variety. I would like to see how my future husband carries himself in these conditions."

The words future husband might as well have been shouted straight into my brain, because they seem to be echoing in there. Not a phenomenon I should be experiencing, but here we are. Alyona turns back to the room, the ready smile on her face.

"Shall we play some chess?"

fifteen

ALYONKA

I stay with the men for another two hours, giving each of them a chance to play chess with me. I'm not a genius when it comes to the game, but I've been playing long enough that I can hold my own. But honestly, half of them are a little overconfident and it is their downfall.

Tetia Tatiana has been glaring daggers at me since I announced the ice skating competition. I know I'm supposed to care what she thinks, since I promised my parents I would trust her judgment, but I'm caring less and less. I had to really fight her to get the poetry competition as one of the options, and she would never approve of ice skating. Mostly because she has to supervise and she hates that cold. I honestly have no idea why she lives in this kingdom.

But while I watched the men try and fail at poetry, I realized that it's the first time I had fun in the last year of these suitors coming and going. The competition might've not yielded a lot of results, but it did give me more information on what kind of men these are.

"Tetia Tatiana, shall we announce the winner for today?" I ask, after beating Sergey Vladimirovich in the match. He takes it much better than the last two did.

"Of course." The woman perks up immediately. The thunder sounds again, this time much closer than it's been in the last hour. There's a moment of stillness and then the rain begins. The sounds instantly soothes me and I desperately want to be away from this room and back in my own.

"Tsarevna Alyona, if you will." Tetia Tatiana motions for me. I stand, facing the men who are now seated on the divan and chairs, much like they were during the competition.

"First, I want to thank each and every one of you for your hard work. Poetry is not easy, but you brought your own flair to it and for that I am very grateful. But, there can only be one winner and for this one, that winner is—" I glance briefly at Nikolai, who has moved to stand by the doors and then transfer my attention back to the men, "Lev Ignatovich."

The man stands and bows, while the rest clap without

much enthusiasm. Another boom shakes the castle and Tetia Tatiana jumps into action.

"Congratulations, Baron Lev," she says, her smile tense, "For now, let's go ahead and retire to our rooms. Dinner will be served individually today."

I don't even wait until she's completely done speaking before I'm walking toward the doors. Daria and Nikolai at my back. I would like to be back in my room, so I can watch the rain without interruptions. We're halfway up the staircase when I turn to Daria.

"Oh, you can go ahead and go to the kitchens. You wanted to talk to your friend about a dress?"

"It's okay, Alyonka," Daria leans toward me, keeping her voice low. "I don't need to go right now."

"No, please go. You know I'll be sitting near the window for the next few hours anyway."

"And dinner?"

"Bring it up to my rooms."

Daria nods, giving me a quick bow, and then with a way at Nikolai heads back down the stairs. I glance at him, to find him already watching me. I simply shrug, before I turn and continue up the stairs. I greet Oleg and Daniil when I reach my room and then we're finally inside and I can breathe easier.

I'm not sure what it was, but I was nearly suffocating in that room. I unbutton the cape first, before pulling on the strings as well. The cooler air outside has seeped into the castle, but my room feels cozier than the downstairs.

As I put my cape on the bed, Nikolai walks past me and toward the fireplace. Without a word, he lights it back up, working quickly and meticulously. I watch him for a long moment and when he looks up at me, I still don't look away.

It feels like we've been walking around each other, both too aware of the other, since the night Ivan Popyalof left. Except that ever present tension between us is getting harder to ignore.

"That was at least entertaining, right?" I ask, as I make myself walk past him and toward the chair near the window. I pull the curtains to the side, so I have a clear view of the rain before I settle in. The sudden urge to fold in on myself is hard to resist, but I do.

Instead, I keep myself only slightly relaxed as I get comfortable in the chair. It's big enough that I can pull my legs up under me, but I don't. I'm not sure why I feel like I have to keep my princess persona in front of Nikolai, but here we are.

I almost jump out of my seat when a blanket lands on my lap. I look up to find Nikolai rearranging it over my lap, before pulling it up toward my neck. He holds it out enough that I can either take it from him or lean back and let him put it on me.

We stay like that for a long moment, staring at each other with only the blanket a barrier between us. I have the sudden urge to ignore the blanket and pull *him* closer, so instead, I lean back and allow him to cover me up to my neck. The moment it's over my shoulders, he moves back.

I snuggle in, instantly feeling better, even as my insides are in turmoil. He makes my whole body light up like I have been struck by lightning. My pulse quickens every time he steps into the room or I feel his eyes on me as we're walking to meet the others. It's maddening in the most exhilarating way and it's wrong. I shouldn't be feeling any kind of feelings when it comes to Nikolai. It must be that I'm tired, that's all.

"Oh," I sit up a little, remembering what I was going to ask him, "Can you check on Boris Stephanich for me? I'm not really sure what it is, but he seems to be Tetia Tatiana's favorite and—"

"I'm already checking on it," Nikolai replies when I trail off. The smile I give him is probably my most genuine one in the last few hours.

"I'm happy to see that it's not just my paranoia."

"I think you have every right to be paranoid," he says and this blanket must be extra warm because I'm feeling very toasty.

"Did you like how I was compared to foxes and berries? I never thought making them write poetry could be so interesting." I sigh, forcing my attention to the storm outside my window. If I keep looking at Nikolai, bathed in the firelight, looking at me like I mean something, I might do something crazy. Like ask him to hug me.

"*Da*, there are definitely better comparisons to be made," he says, his voice only a bit above a whisper, and I think that maybe I'm not supposed to hear it. But it perks me up immediately and I do turn to face him.

"Is that right? What would you have compared me to if you were writing a poem?"

"I don't write poems." His voice is so emotionless, he sounds more like a soldier than I've ever heard him before.

"Never?"

"Never."

"Have you ever tried?" For some reason I can't let it go and maybe it's because I'm enjoying the way he's gone completely still. He tends to do this when I'm teasing and I like the effect I have on him.

"I've never had any reason to try."

"But if you did, what would you compare me to?" I lean forward a little, holding my blanket close as I try to peer into his face. He has taken a seat near the fireplace, so he can see both me and the door. It's fascinating how alert he is at all times and also slightly annoying when I'm trying to get a visual reaction out of him.

"The ice skating is a good idea. It's different and will challenge them." Nikolai says, completely chaining the subject and I roll my eyes, before I lean my head against the back of the chair keeping my eyes on Nikolai.

"It might not happen. I forced Tetia Tatiana's hand by announcing it. But my parents might prevent it if they get wind of it. Which they might not, since they're so far away at the moment."

"Why? The pond is on the castle premises."

"Still. It's too dangerous to be out there, so exposed. Something could happen to me on the pond. Or if someone got high enough into one of those trees, they could see over the walls."

"So even on the outskirts of the castle grounds?"

"*Da*, even there I'm in danger." I close my eyes for a moment, exhaustion weighing heavily on my limbs. "Did you know I've only been off the castle grounds three times?" I ask, not opening my eyes. I don't have to see the shocked look on Nikolai's face to know it's there.

"I know, I know. Wild. But the Tsar and Tsarina are very strict about that rule. Only when Skazka demands my presence can I go."

Nikolai doesn't say anything for a long time, so I open my eyes to find him watching me. For some reason, it doesn't make me feel self conscious, so I just watch him back.

"You always refer to them as Tsar and Tsarina," he finally says and I shrug.

"That's who they are."

Because being parents is something they don't really know how to do. I'm not sure which one of them made that decision, but keeping their distance from me has been their whole plan my entire life. I've made peace with their absence, but it doesn't mean that a part of me still doesn't try to be the good daughter, who follows every rule they set out to me. I want to say that it's not so that I could earn favor in their eyes, but that wouldn't be true. I'm not sure things would even be different if I didn't have the curse hanging over me. But that's a whole other conversation to be had at a different time.

I turn to look out the window as the storm continues to rage. Already, the rain has turned into snow, the winds howling as they throw the snowflakes around in a dance of their own. Nikolai's presence is soothing, so I don't even think about it when I close my eyes again and let myself rest.

NIKOLAI

I STAYED with her while she slept and only left when Daria brought her dinner. The storm has let up a little bit by the time it was time to go to bed. It would be wise to let her rest. But while I know I shouldn't, I can't get Alyonka's sad eyes out of my head, so after everyone has gone to bed, I head back to her room.

There's so much protocol that I'm breaking here. But the pull toward her is undeniable and I think we both need this. She needs to dance and I need to see her dance. Maybe then my heart can settle enough to rest.

Halfway to her rooms though, I freeze. If I show up right now, the gossip mill in this castle is going to explode. But I also feel like I can't just let it be.

Pivoting, I head back to the first floor and toward the side of the castle that isn't usually frequented by people. Especially at this time of the night. The rest of the castle feels like it's frozen in time, as if there is not a living soul here except for me and Alyona.

I reach the study at the end of the long hallway and step inside, walking directly toward the doorway I discovered last time I was here. I expect the storm to be deafening inside the turret but I don't hear anything as I walk all the way up to the third floor.

When I step out to the landing I realize I couldn't hear the storm because it stopped snowing. Alyonka never did explain to me how she found the way to this roof, but I watched her disappear behind the vines and saw the stairs when I went to check.

Now, I walk over to the same spot, pull the vines aside and take the stairs down. As expected, I end up on her balcony, but the doors by her bedroom are sealed completely shut, so I look over the bathroom windows and realize there's a step on this side of them. For a second, I wonder how to go about this, when the glass panels suddenly swing open and Alyonka is on the other side.

"Are you trying to puff up your credentials by adding

breaking and entering to it?" She asks, folding her arms across her chest. There are only a few candles lit in the room behind her, but I can tell she's not wearing a coat and it's cold outside.

Immediately, I push inside, and shut the window behind me. She takes a few steps to allow it, but doesn't go far.

"Maybe don't stand in front of an open window in nothing but your nightgown," I say glancing around to see if I can find anything to put around her shoulders immediately.

"Nikolai," her voice brings my attention back to her. "Why are you sneaking around my balcony in the middle of the night?"

"How did you know I was there?" I counter and she rolls her eyes.

"I was looking out the window in the bedroom and saw you standing there like a lost puppy."

"I didn't expect the stairs to lead to your bathroom balcony—" I trails off as Alyonka chuckles a little and stands up a little straighter. "I was being considerate."

"You were sneaking onto my balcony in the middle of the night during a storm. I don't know if considerate is the right word here."

I stare at her for one moment, before I walk past her and into the bedroom. When she reaches the doorway that connects her two rooms, I'm already pulling her *shuba* off the hanger. Without a word, I walk over to her

and holds it out so she can step into it. She stares at me like she has things to say, but I can tell she's curious. She's always been intrigued by my adventures. Right now, that wins out.

She turns, placing her arms inside the sleeves as I pull the coat over her shoulders. I turns her around and begins to button the *shuba* quickly. I can almost feel her staring at the the top of my head before I straighten.

"Follow me," I say and then head back to the bathroom.

"Is this safe?" she asks, when I push the windows open. I look her over, before I reach over and take her hand in mine, tugging her toward the windows.

"Don't worry, I'm a trained professional," I say, but I can't function past those words because I'm too distracted by the feel of her hand wrapped around mine. This is probably a bad idea, but it's too late now.

sixteen

ALYONKA

Nikolai leads me up the stairs and then to the door without a word. It stopped snowing for now, the moon peeking through the heavy clouds. But once we step inside the small turret, the wind picks up again. It's pitch dark in here and I grip Nikolai's hand that much harder.

"Be careful. Let your eyes adjust."

We stand frozen in the small space and I can feel his breath on my cheek. It's very distracting. But after a few moments, the darkness doesn't seem as scary.

"Ready?"

I nod and then realize he probably can't see me.

"*Da*."

We begin our descent slowly, testing each step. I hold onto Nikolai tightly and he doesn't seem to mind. When it feels like the stairs will never end, we reach the bottom. Nikolai pushes the door open and pulls me inside the room. It smells like books in here, but that's all I can tell. Not that it matters because we're already moving and then we're out in the hallway.

There are candles lit here, so I let my eyes adjust once again.

"I'm sorry, I didn't think to bring light," Nikolai says.

"It's okay, we survived."

I glance around the hallway, trying to pinpoint where in the castle we are. This looks familiar, but also like I haven't been here in years. There are plenty of areas like that within these walls. Some are boarded up for reconstruction, some are simply forgotten by me because I don't visit often enough.

"Why are we here, Nikolai?" I ask when he doesn't say anything else. I glance at him and find him studying me in that way that I can only attribute to him. He seems to be looking inside of me, past all the masks and defenses I put up. It's disorienting and I'm not sure what to do.

"Because I think you need this."

I don't realize he's still holding my hand until he's tugging me behind him. It feels so natural, to be connected to him by simple touch. He comes up to a door on our right, pushing it open, before he motions me inside. I glance at him, then at the doorway, before I step inside.

My breath catches as I try to take in the gorgeous room. Suddenly, lightning flashes, a rare occurrence when it's only snowing outside. But it makes everything inside look that much more magical. The snow continues to come down, as the clouds part just enough to let the moon have a spot. It makes the ballroom sparkle as the light heats the gold and crystal accents.

"What is this?"

I turn to Nikolai and find him lighting one of the candles on the wall. It's a small glow, but it allows me to see his face. What I find there is not something I expect. He doesn't look much like a soldier, capable of anything. He looks more like my friend.

"I know you told me to stay out of it, in not so many words. But if I remember anything about you is that you hold a lot of your emotions in and let them out through dance. So I thought what better place to let yourself get lost then in the most beautiful ballroom. The moonlight makes it much more aesthetically pleasing, don't you think? It's fitting, of royalty, somehow."

"I'm not sure what you mean—" I try but he's shaking his head.

"Do you know that you create a pattern with your fingers any time you need to keep yourself in check?" I open my mouth, but no words come. "You do this thing where you touch each individual finger to your thumb, in different sequences. You've been doing it often."

I stare at him as if he's spoken a foreign language. Maybe he has and it's one only me and him understand. Because everything he says is true. He really did see past all of my carefully erected costumes and pretense and right to the real me.

The urge to hug him is almost overwhelming, so instead, I take a step away. Unbuttoning my *shuba* I drop it off my shoulders, leaving it on the floor. Then, I walk toward the center of the room, my mind already on the melody and the steps. The room falls into darkness as a cloud passes over the moon, but then, as the song of my heart begins to play in my head, the clouds part.

My dance is simple, just a nonstop set of fluid motions. I'm making up the steps and movements automatically. I don't have to think about the direction I might go, my body carries me toward it. My hands raised high above my head, I spin as I bring them down and then I spin again. My nightgown billows around me as I lean forward post turn, pointing my toes and arching my back.

I swing my arms overhead, left and right, and then I'm standing tall again, before I spin. My vision blurs with the next burst of the lightning and I realize there are tears in my eyes. It's been such a long time since I could let myself move so freely. Even thought I know Nikolai is in the room, I'm not shy or timid.

It feels like his presence does the opposite—it pushes me to be bold.

I dance until I'm exhausted, until I feel my muscles protesting. But even so, I feel more like myself than I have in weeks. When I finally stop spinning my eyes clash with Nikolai's and we stand frozen, as the lightning continues to dance around us.

NIKOLAI

I've been sneaking her down to the ballroom every night for a week. What started as a little bit of weather has turned into a continuous storm. The snow hasn't stopped falling in the last three days, creating a barrier between the castle and the rest of the world. The suitors are definitely getting agitated, since no progress toward the next competition has been made. But Alyona has been unmovable in her stance on it being a skating trial and I won't say this out loud, but it makes me quite glad that's the case. Watching the men squirm has its benefits.

For Alyona's sake, of course.

But because it's been storming so much, I think today I'll have to figure out a different way to get Alyona to the ballroom. Taking her up on the roof seems extra dangerous with the howling winds. The last few nights, I waited for it to die down, but it doesn't seem like that will be the case today. Since the early hours of the morning, the storm has been making itself known outside these walls.

"Has it ever stormed like this before?" Timofey asks and I shake my head. I'm buttoning up my uniform, while Timofey pulls a sweater over his head. He's overseeing some indoor exercises for the soldier today. I need to head up to meet Alyona before today's schedule begins.

"*Nyet*, this is new."

"Why do you think it's happening?"

I look over at him, wondering how much of my thoughts to share. It would do us no good if word spreads, but Timofey is the one I trust the most.

"I think it's the curse," I say, lowering my voice even though we're the only ones in the room. He stops what he's doing immediately, staring at me as if I've lost my mind.

"What do you mean?"

"I mean, remember when we were stationed at the south border? How the land there seemed to take longer to recover from the winter months? The flowers didn't bloom, the leaves wouldn't bud, it was almost like the forest was frozen in whatever state it was in last. The curse talks about slumber—" I trail off, but Timofey gets it.

"You think the kingdom itself is being affected by the curse as the times grows near."

It's a statement but I nod anyway. The more research I've been doing in the study at night the more I'm sure of it. I've been going there before meeting Alyona for her dance time and it seems like with each book I read, the answer feels farther away. Maybe that's the biggest reason Ivan Popyalof has been so intent on finding another way to break the curse. The kingdom itself is running out of time.

"Keep that to yourself," I say, tugging the sleeves of my jackets over my wrists. I'm wearing a dark blue suit today, with a button up shirt to match. Even though it's standard, for some reason I've been taking extra care every morning to make sure nothing is out of place. I stand in front of the mirror now, checking for any creases.

"Don't worry, boss man. Not a word will be uttered." Timofey comes up next to me, looking at me in the mirror. "Except maybe 'wow, you're looking mighty fine'." He makes sure to whistle as he wiggles his eyebrows at me in the mirror. I don't hesitate to push him away, rolling my eyes.

"Stop learning all the unnecessary phrases from the human world."

"But why?" Timofey knows how much I hate his whiny tone.

"But because," I reply, copying it exactly. He bursts out laughing, while my face remains completely stoic.

"You are a barrel of laughs, my friend," he says, shaking his head as he heads for the door.

"At least we've moved on from food comparisons," I mumble, as I walk out behind him.

With a quick wave on his part, we go our separate ways. I reviewed today's schedule with Tatiana last night and now as I head to Alyona's room, I wonder how Alyona is feeling about it.

It seems like to me, Tatiana is doing everything in her power to drive Alyona crazy. I've been watching her fuss and I swear she's underhandedly blaming Alyona for the weather. When I arrive at the doors, I'm let in immediately and like always, Alyona turns to face me with a bright smile on her face.

That hasn't changed.

The light she has always carried within her might've dimmed a little, but it hasn't gone out. I want to make sure it never does.

As her bodyguard, of course.

I do my typical visual assessment of her, noticing the signs of exhaustion. It seems like she hasn't been sleeping all that well. I think she might be even less excited to go down to the first floor than I am.

"We don't have to go down there," I say as Daria puts finishing touches on today's outfit. Alyona is wearing a heavier dress than usual. It's a deep green, with sleeves going down to her wrists and a layered skirt. The cold from outside has been seeping through the walls, so I'm glad to see her more bundled up. And protected from Tatiana.

"You know I do," Alyona replies, meeting my eyes. Something has definitely shifted between us since that first moonlight bathed dance. But I'm not ready to admit it, even to myself, so this is just a fleeting thought that doesn't mean anything.

"Tetia Tatiana is bringing everyone to the sitting room for tea and games. The whole point they're here is to spend time with me. Would it really make sense for me not to show up?" Alyona asks, raising an eyebrow, but I'm undeterred.

"It would make perfect sense because you are the Grand Duchess and you can make your own choices."

Alyona stares at me as I've spoken an unknown language, unblinking. Daria is right over her shoulder, trying not to smile.

"Should you be speaking to your Grand Duchess in such a way?" Alyona asks, cocking her head to the side.

"Absolutely." I reply without missing a beat. This time Daria does crack a smile, but so does Alyona.

"I appreciate the concern, but it's only for an hour or two. I will be okay."

She leaves no room for argument, so I don't push any farther.

When we reach the downstairs sitting room, the thunder is so loud it sounds like it's right outside the walls. The men all jump as Alyona enters, looking toward the windows and missing her completely. Even Tatiana isn't paying attention. I step forward to announce Alyona but she puts out her hand, stopping me in my tracks. When I look at her, she shakes her head once, her attention on the rest of the room.

I study her profile and I realize what she's doing. She's studying the men's reaction to the storm. The more I'm around her the more fascinated I become with how she handles herself. This is similar to what I do when I am present for any sort of negotiations. Watching people's response to what's going on around them when they don't know they're being watched can tell a person a lot about someone.

Currently, even an untrained eye can see Graf Sergey and *Knyaz* Georgiy squaring off against each other. But while *Knyaz* Georgiy appears fine, Graf Sergey is definitely nervous about the weather outside. Which is not something I would've expected.

Baron Denis and *Knyaz* Boris seem mildly concerned, but Baron Lev looks annoyed. He may have won the last competition, but he seems more and more like he doesn't want to be here.

"Oh, *Tsarevna* Alyona!" Tatiana exclaims and the men turn as one toward us. They bow immediately, and Alyona walks over to take a seat on one of the chairs near the fireplace.

"I hope you are *weathering* the storm well," Alyona says and the men immediately reply with affirmations. None of them comment on her use of the word and she seems a little disappointed. I step behind the chair almost automatically, my hand on the back of it, close enough to wind one finger around a hair lock and gently tug. She glances up at me and I give her the tiniest of winks.

It's all it takes for her to sit up a little straighter and I fight the urge to smile.

"Shall we play a game?" She asks, turning back to the room.

SEVENTEEN

ALYONKA

The whole game and tea time is an incredible bore. Well, except for the part where the men jump anytime there's a gust of wind. It's like they've never lived anywhere with a little snow before.

Granted, "little rain" has turned into a continuous downpour, but still. If they're afraid of a storm, how are they supposed to stand by my side when I'm the queen?

Inadvertently, my eyes are drawn to Nikolai, who is standing near the tall window, still as a statue. Except for his eyes, that keep shifting from person to person and then door to door, making sure everything is where it needs to be. I haven't seen him flinch even once.

As if he feels me looking, his eyes shift to meet mine and hold. There's intensity in his gaze that matches the rhythm of my heart. My hand curls over the material of my skirt, forcing it to stay in place. Because almost on its own, it shakes, as if it wants to be placed over my heart. Nikolai's gaze flickers down to my hand, before it comes to rest on me once more and it's like he knows exactly what I'm thinking.

He always seems to call me out on all the things I'm keeping to myself.

"*Tsarevna* Alyona, it's your turn." I jerk my gaze away, shifting to Denis Alexandrovich who's right beside me.

"Oh, *spasibo*." I pick up the dice and roll it, having no interest in the battle currently happening on the board.

"You must be tired," Denis Alexandrovich continues, giving me a kind smile. I glance at him again, after I move the soldiers to their appropriate places after the roll. "It must be tiring entertaining us."

"Not at all," I smile at him, because he's being kind. Of course, I'm tired. But I'm also worried about Chudo, who I haven't seen in over a week. The combination of the competition and grief of losing Ivan Popyalof, on top of worrying about my dragon friend is definitely taking its toll. Not that I can show it. So I appreciate the remark. "This is just an opportunity to spend more time together."

"Even so, I thank you for your time."

We exchange another smile, just as someone else huffs, rolling the dice. I look over at Boris Stepanich and he's staring at the two of us.

"This is the whole point of us being here," he says, directing that to Denis Alexandrovich, before he moves his own soldiers around.

"Still, it is a good thing to express gratitude," Denis Alexandrovich replies, surprising me. Out of the five men, he's been keeping the most quiet. But maybe he takes a little time to muster up the courage to stand up to them.

"What else are we going doing to do, being stuck here?" Georgiy Leonidovich huffs from behind his cup of tea and I can tell he doesn't think I'll hear him. He's next to Boris Stepanich, but farthest away from me.

"Georgiy Leonidovich," I call out, shifting to the left as I lean my elbow on the armchair. The man startles as he's taking a sip, looking up at me. "If you're going to complain, you should at least do it audibly enough for everyone else to hear you. What if they too want to join in?"

Tetia Tatiana looks terrify from her position near the divan the two men are sitting. I keep Georgiy Leonidovich captive with my gaze, waiting for him to come up with some sort of a retort.

"I think what Tsarevna is trying to say—" Tetia Tatiana jumps in, but I raise my hand to stop her.

"I said exactly what I meant. I would appreciate any kind of negative talk to be spoken out loud and with intention, instead of being hidden behind whispers and cups of tea." I hold Tetia Tatiana's gaze, before I meet the eyes of each of the men individually.

"I understand that this isn't exactly what you had in mind when you came here, but I do appreciate your patience and adaptability," I say making sure to keep my tone as pleasant as possible. I got irritated and I pride myself in not letting people see that side often. But maybe I'm more on edge than I thought, because I simply couldn't help myself.

"Since we have already planned to take our meals in our rooms, I will see you at a later time. Please let the staff know if there is anything you need."

I stand then, and Nikolai is immediately by my side. The men also rise to bow, but none of them say anything as I turn to leave. I'm only a few steps past the doors when I hear Tetia Tatiana's unmistakable heels against the floor. I sigh, stopping so she can catch up.

She steps around me, facing me, frustration written all over her body language.

"This behavior is unacceptable," she says without any preamble, taking tiny steps toward me until she's in my face. "They are your guest and you're treating them without any respect. You have been acting up since Ivan Popyalof left and I cannot stand by anymore."

I feel Nikolai move forward and I reach out blindly, grabbing for his sleeve. The little tug keeps him in place right beside me and instead of letting go, I curl my fingers into the material, gaining a little bit of strength from the proximity.

"They are guests of my parents," I say, keeping my

voice as calm as possible as I stare down at Tetia Tatiana, "they are here to compete for my hand and yet, it seems that I'm the only one behaving accordingly. They should be trying to gain my favor. I'm not here to entertain them or you. Now, if you excuse me, I'm tired."

I step around her, pulling Nikolai behind me, just in case he decides to go back and teach Tetia Tatiana a lesson or two. Even without looking up into his face, I can feel the frustration radiating off his body. So I keep my fingers pinched over his sleeve, so he has no choice but to move with me.

When we reach the stairs, out of the view of Tetia Tatiana I stop, dropping my hand from his sleeve as I take a deep breath.

"*Tsarevna* Alyona," Nikolai's voice ruffles the hair near my temple, but I still don't look up at him. "Are you alright?"

"It seems you're getting your wish," I chuckle without any humor. This time I do look up at him and he furrows his brow a little, as his eyes travel over my features. "You wanted me to be more myself, more outspoken. Now I can't seem to stop."

His eyes narrow as I chuckle again, my body suddenly feeling like it's two hundred years old.

"Is it better to suffer in silence?" Nikolai asks and his voice is but a whispers. There are guards stationed at the doors nearby, but it still feels like we're the only ones here. I have no idea what I'm reading on his face, only that we're standing very close, my fingers still pinching the material near his wrist.

"It's better if I do what I'm told. The kingdom depends on it," I reply and he nods once.

"And your wellbeing doesn't matter?"

"I don't think my wellbeing is much of a concern here."

And isn't that the truth that I try to keep as far away from my mind as I can. Because at the end of the day, it seems that everyone is concerned about the kingdom, but no one is actually thinking about me. I'm only a conduit for the curse and I must play my part in it. I sigh again, finally moving away, but then Nikolai's words stop me.

"I care about you."

My body jerks as if it touched a live wire as I meet his imploring gaze. He's unmovable as usual, but that just makes the impact of his words that much harder. Because as I watch him watch me, I believe him.

NIKOLAI

SAYING what I didn't probably wasn't the best idea. When it comes to Alyona, I simply cannot make good decisions. The moments when I catch her being herself sends my whole being into a spiral I cannot seem to get out of.

Even now, as I sit in the chair near the door in the study and she's behind the desk, my words continue to echo around us while my heart beats out of control.

As a soldier, I've learned many different techniques to help with tough situations. But this seems to be a situation no one has prepared me for. Alyona glances up then, catching me looking and I hold her gaze as usual, if only to keep some semblance of control.

"What is it that you like to do in your free time, Nikolai?" She asks and I nearly fall out of my chair at the casual way she says my name. There's something extra intimate about us being in the study, with the wind and the snow blanketing the world outside. Maybe it's the low light, maybe it's the small room—I clear my throat and sit up a little straighter.

"There isn't much free time in my schedule," I reply.

"Hmm, true. You must be busy, but still. There has to be something you enjoy, no?"

I'm not sure if I want to tell her, but the way she's looking at me, I'm not sure I can keep it to myself. Alyona leans forward, placing her elbows on the table and her face into her hands. She keeps her eyes on me, a small smile on her face and I swear I will tell her anything if she just keeps looking at me like that.

Shaking my head, I tear my gaze away and stare at the shelves to her right.

"You will find it odd," I begin.

"I absolutely will not," she replies immediately and it's my turn to sigh.

"Okay, there is something I like to do. I like—" I pause, clearing my throat again, thankful the room is bathed in shadows because I'm pretty sure my face is aflame. "I like studying about flowers. And collecting them whenever I can."

My eyes stay glued to the bookshelf, even though I want to know her reaction. But maybe I don't actually want to know her reaction—

"How do you collect them?" She asks and I detect no laughter in her tone, just genuine curiosity.

"I...I press them into my journal or a book."

The silence that follows makes me want to leave the room. But instead, I shift my gaze to her and what I see makes me grateful I'm sitting down because I might be on my knees.

The look on her face is one of pure wonder. She's staring at me as if she's never heard such a thing before, when in actuality she was the first person I ever saw pressing flowers in books.

"I used to do that," she whispers, and clearly, she remembers. We stare at each other and I think our minds are in the same place—ten years ago, in the garden forest down below us.

It was about half a year after Alyona and I became friends. We would sneak out into the garden a lot, keeping out of sight as much as possible. Even at that time, her every move was controlled. But Ivan Popyalof knew of our friendship and he never discouraged it, giving us time to adventure together. We would act out various stories we read in books—well, stories Alyona read in books. She would always carry one with her.

On days when we would come across a pretty flower or bush, I would watch Alyona pick one up, usually one that has already fallen or a flower that has begun to wilt, and put it between the pages of whatever book she had. I think it's her love of knowledge and discovery that first gave me the interest of nature outside of just appreciating it.

"You did," I say, and give her the tiniest of smiles. Her whole first bursts into a grin and I feel my heart skip a beat.

"That's amazing! Do you have many you've found?"

"*Da*. Being stationed in various parts of Skazka helps with that."

"Incredible." She pauses, her gaze far away on something.

"I want to see." Alyonka stands and heads for the door before I realize what she's doing. My body reacts automatically and I grab her wrist, intent on pulling her back. Except that she side steps me and instead of going backwards, ends up pulling me forward. She nearly runs into the chair and I nearly collide with the small table. There's a moment where we're in kind of a frozen motion—as much sense as that makes—and then I'm spinning both of us, as I yank her toward me.

Her back lands against the door, with my arm wrapped around her waist, and I'm right up against her, my other hand near her head, to keep myself from crushing her. Our chests rise and fall in sync as we both try to catch our breath. Her face is centimeters away from mine, and I can see every fleck of gold in her otherwise green eyes. She's so beautiful it makes my head spin.

A pressure in my chest makes me move forward just a fraction and I realize Alyonka's hand is fisted over my shirt. My gaze flickers down to her mouth and when it meets her eyes again, they seem to be glowing.

"Is everything okay in there?" A voice sounds from the other side of the door and we jump apart as if we've been caught doing something we shouldn't be doing. There's a quick knock and then the door opens, with Daniil poking his head in.

"We're okay. Just had a near mishap with the table," I say, nodding toward the offensive piece of furniture. Daniil looks between the table and then at us and I'm pretty sure my reasoning isn't what's going to make it down to the barracks. He looks up at me and the glare I direct his way might actually keep him from talking—if the way he retreats is of any indication.

"Thank you for checking," Alyona says from beside me, her voice completely normal, as if what just happened didn't scramble her brain the way it did mine. "You should go get lunch now, as I am heading to my rooms."

Daniil bows and then moves back, closing the door behind him.

"Your room?" I ask and when I glance at Alyona I think my heart is about to leap out of my chest. She's grinning at me, like a cat that's found a mouse.

"*Nyet*, Nikolai," she says, "your room."

eighteen

ALYONKA

My whole body feels like it's on fire and my head is spinning, but I can't let Nikolai see any of that. I thought it's bad enough when he looks at me with that intensity that's very much his own and tells me he cares. But to feel him nearly pressed against me, our breaths mingling—there's a possibility I'm losing my mind.

I'm not allowed to have any sort of thoughts regarding my bodyguard. I cannot entertain even an idea of a maybe, because Nikolai and I could never be. My parents are convinced a marriage to a noble blood is what the curse demands and I cannot fail my kingdom. No matter how much Nikolai's proximity is sending my heart soaring.

"*Tsarevna* Alyona," Nikolai calls as I leave the study

behind and head for the staircase. "Alyonka!" The last is a little more urgent and then I feel him beside me, before he steps in my way.

"I don't think this is a good idea."

"Perfect, then don't think." I smile up at him brightly and he blinks a few times, before he refocuses his never wavering gaze on me.

"Tatiana is already unhappy about the events of today, do you really want to anger her further? You know how quickly people talk within these walls."

I cock my head to the side, incredulous.

"I like how you went from telling to stand up for myself to now trying to tell me what to do." I raise an eyebrow at him. "You can't have it both ways."

Nikolai sighs, which is very unusual of him, and I take that as a little victory.

"I've created a monster," he says and I lean forward to make sure he sees my face when I grin. His eyes fly down to meet mine and then I realize how close we are once again. Straightening, I clear my throat, but I don't stop smiling.

"Come on, Nikolai. I want to see the flowers you've collected. Everyone will be at lunch, it'll be the perfect time to go."

"And how do you suppose we get past the guards on the first floor?"

"We go to the garden and then head down to the first floor from the outside and circle around."

"Why does it seem like you've done this before?"

"Me? Sneak around the castle unnoticed? I would never." I place a hand over my heart and I swear Nikolai's mouth twitches just a bit. This feels even more like a win. So I step around him and head for the stairs once more.

"Don't you need to grab a coat?" Nikolai asks falling into step beside me, but I'm already shaking my head.

"You're not talking me into going back to my room, Nikolai," I say, not breaking my stride. "I am filled with determination."

"You really haven't changed all that much," he mumbles, but I hear him. I nearly trip over my own skirts, but his quick grip on my elbow keeps me upright. I give him a quick smile, before I move away again, because touching him is definitely terrible for my mental health.

So is the reminder that he was the first to know me as just me and not a cursed princess.

I can't get away from the feelings he evokes in me and I can't tell if it's the past or the present him that's doing it. Obviously, I feel attachment to him I wouldn't feel for anyone else taking his position. But it's not the same feeling as that of when we were kids. Something has shifted between us and I can't seem to figure out what. These are not feelings I've had before.

When we reach the second floor, I turn toward the gardens. Nikolai keeps pace with me, but then we both freeze. Voices are coming down the hallways. I reach automatically.

Grabbing his arm, I pull him toward the first door on the right. Yanking the door open just enough, I nearly push him in and then step in behind him. But I don't close the door all the way, staying near it so I can hear who's out there.

There are a few rooms on this floor which are sort of like art galleries and this is one of them. There are a few windows at my back, but I know the rest of the room is filled with paintings. Back when people actually visited the castle, my ancestors apparently enjoyed showing off the collections. It's been a while since the doors were open for anyone to see this art besides me.

Nikolai is pressed up right beside me and I'm having a difficult time concentrating but I try. Because the voices become clear and I can distinguish one of the men from the competition.

"It's not the best scenario, but we should be spending more time with the princess. Even if it's not on one on one dates." The men come into view and I see the unmistakable reddish hair. Sergey Vladimirovich is speaking.

"You're right. But I cannot blame her for not wanting to spend all this time with us. If the pressure is getting to us, I can only imagine how she must be feeling." The voice belongs to Denis Alexandrovich and I have to smile. He really is the nicest one of the bunch.

"Do you think it's strange that the storm came once everyone arrived for the competition?" Sergey

Vladimirovich asks and I pause at that. I didn't even think about it, but he's correct.

"Nothing about this kingdom surprises me," Denis Alexandrovich replies and then they're past the doors and down the stairs. I look over at Nikolai, who's been facing the dark room behind me but now glances down at me.

"Those are my two top candidates," he whispers and I slap a hand over my mouth trying not to laugh. I'm so surprised I almost don't make it.

But I do agree with him. Those two are my top choices as well. Not that they're great choices, they're just better than anything I've had before.

I've been through this competition for my hand seven times now and there have been plenty of nice men. But in the end of it all, they aren't here to marry me so they can spend their life being my husband. They're looking to marry me so they can become the hero of *Holodnova Tsarstva*.

"Come on, we need to get moving before they come back," I say and then grab Nikolai's sleeve again, tugging him after me.

At the back of my mind I know that if he truly wanted to, he could stop me. The fact that he hasn't is making this all the more exciting for me.

We leave the gallery room behind and head down the hallway toward the courtyard. This garden has always been the one I visit the least because Tetia Tatiana thinks it's dangerous. Heading down a hill isn't exactly her idea of fun. But I like the feel of adventure it brings. It feels like I'm actually out beyond the castle walls, traveling through some part of the Skazka forest.

"You should've stopped to grab a coat," Nikolai says the moment we're past the doors and in the actual part of the courtyard that's outside. This area consists of pillars right as you get on the other side of the doors, and then two benches on opposite sides of the small stone square in the middle. Then, the forest. But since it's been raining and snowing so much, everything is wet and I feel the cold immediately.

"I'm wearing a heavier dress than usual. I can manage."

I take a step toward the path that will lead us downhill, but Nikolai stops me. I glance down at his hand wrapped around my wrist, an electric shock radiating from that one point of contact, heating me up instantly. Meeting his eye I wonder if he's feeling it, but he just looks a little...annoyed? He drops my wrist, shrugging out of his uniform jacket.

"What if you catch a cold?" he asks, stepping right into my personal space so he can place the coat over my shoulders. He holds it over me and motions with his head. I slide my arms into the sleeves, before he pulls it closed over me.

"I'll just get better," I reply, my brain malfunctioning at his proximity.

He sighs, then leans down so our faces are on the same level, as he holds the jacket closed over me.

"What if you get a cold and I get fired?" he asks, our breaths once again sharing the same space. Even though the light is dimmer here, it still looks like his eyes are sparkling. But it's the thought of him gone that slams into my heart, making me almost gasp out loud. I almost drag him back inside the castle right then and there, just so I can make sure nothing happens to him. But of course, that would be a little crazy of me. So I opt for the next best version.

Because there's no way I can form any coherent words, I instead just pull the jacket tighter against me, giving him my best smile. He blinks a few times, as if refocusing and then straightens.

"Let's go, troublemaker," he syas and I grin again.

"You haven't called me that in a while."

"I see that it still fits."

We walk toward the pathway and then he completely shocks me by reaching for my hand again. He pulls the sleeve up just enough to wrap his fingers round my own.

"Make sure you don't slip," he says and then pulls me into the garden forest.

It's so much darker here because of the tall trees. I will never understand the way the gardens at the castle grow, but I think it's one of those mysteries I don't actually need an answer to. My biggest mystery right now is if I can keep my heart inside of my chest while Nikolai's hand is holding my own. It seems like the answer to that is a very strong maybe.

When we reach the first floor from the outside, Nikolai doesn't even pause, turning us in the direction he needs to go.

"Wait, I thought you're second in command. Don't you stay in the commander's quarters?" I whisper, because we're heading toward the regular baracks.

"*Nyet*, I wanted to be closer to my men."

I don't know why, but that makes me happy. It's just so...Nikolai.

Since it's lunch time, many of the guys are eating and those who are not are in the indoor area for training. I overheard Nikolai telling Timofey about it a few days ago. They've been keeping the soldiers busy during the storm as much as possible, but also have been giving them extra rest. It's all about the balance.

We reach a door that looks like any other and Nikolai pulls it open, tugging us inside. Once the door closes, we just stand in front of it, my eyes taking in the room.

It's simple, with two beds on opposite sides of the room, a desk near the one on the left and a large wardrobe opposite that to the right. There are shelves mounted over the desk, full of books and that's where I turn to. After one step, we both seem to realize we're still holding hands and we separate with that nervous energy that's becoming very much our own.

"Which ones have the flowers?" I ask, thankful my voice comes out normal. Nikolai moves up behind me, reaching over my head and pulling down a book. I stay as still as possible, as his body brushes up against mine. I would think I couldn't feel him this intensely, not when I'm wearing a heavy dress and his uniform jacket over it, but I'm aware of his every move anyway.

"Herem" Nikolai steps back, opening up the book and I glance down to find multiple pages with dried flowers on them.

"This one is a pansy. It's strong association with remembrance and pondering."

I glance down at the beautifully preserved flower, the purple and yellow of it still vivid even in its dry form. Nikolai leafs a few pages over, landing on another one. This one is also purple and yellow but the petals look like a crown, with little antlers hanging down which are yellow in color. The flower is small and less vivid than the other, yet just as beautiful.

"A fawn lily," Nikolai says, his voice soft, traveling like little drops of rain over my skin. "It's often associated with warmth."

"In a physical sense?" I am so fascinated. When I was little and collected flowers this way, I didn't know anything about them. But Nikolai collects the flowers and the knowledge that they are. I find that...endearing.

"More so of the heart. Think of your heart being embraced in the warmest care."

I look up at Nikolai, this strong capable men, cradling a book full of dried flowers in his arms and I can absolutely picture that kind of care.

We stand frozen like that, much like the flowers in his book, stopped in time, until voices reach out to us.

"Oh no," Nikolai says, slamming the book shut and placing it on the bed, before he grabs my hand and is pulling me toward the door. But the voices are closer now and there's no way we can leave.

"There's only a few left," someone says and Nikolai grunts. I look up at him but he's not looking at me. He tugs me with him, pulling the wardrobe door open and pushing me inside.

"Are you crazy?" I manage to whisper, before his hand is over my mouth and he's in the wardrobe with me, shutting the door with his other hand.

We're immediately plunged into darkness and maybe that's why I'm even more aware of his hand on my mouth. I reach up, wrapping my fingers around his wrist—or try to—as I pull it down slowly.

"Nikolai?"

"It's Timofey. We share the room."

That shocks me.

"What do you mean? You don't have your own room?"

"I told you, I wanted to be closer to my men."

"How's that working our for you?" Because now I understand his panic. If we're seen, the whole barracks will gossip and if it gets back to my parents or Tetia Tatiana, they'll take Nikolai away.

The door to the room opens and the voices are now inside.

"I'll just grab the towel and we can go."

A towel? That would be in here with us, wouldn't it? The wardrobe is big enough that if Timofey only opened one side, he probably wouldn't see us. It seems that there are shelves on the other end, with the space for long coats where we are. We're in between coat hangers, so maybe he doesn't need this side at all.

I curl my fingers into Nikolai's shirt at his waist, tugging him against me. He moves forward but it still feels like he's too far, so I pull him closer. He inhales sharply when my forehead comes in contact with his chest, but I don't move away. Instead, I lean fully into him, placing my cheek against his chest and carefully sliding my arms from beside his hips to his back. I'm plastered against him, and the only thing on my mind is trying to find a way that I can protect him. But then his own arms move and he wraps them around me, one hand around my shoulders, the other around my lower back and I sink completely into him like I have always meant to be just here, in the circle of his arms.

I think the other side of the door opens, I think the men leave the room, but neither Nikolai or I move, locked in this moment in time and in each others arms.

NIKOLAI

"You haven't touched your food. *Sinok*, are you alright?"

It's after bedtime in the palace and I've finally managed to come see my mama in the kitchens. Most of the staff that works at the castle either lives at the castle or the small cluster of houses built right on the other side of the walls. But because of the storm, everyone has been staying inside these walls. Mama stayed up so we can finally spend time together and I'm spacing out.

"Yes, Mama," I reply, giving her what I hope is a reassuring smile.

She takes a seat in front of me, folding her hands on her lap, as she watches me and I know what's coming next. She's about to read me like a book. Even after years apart, she still has this power over me.

"Why don't you tell me about it?" she asks. The warmth from the fireplace to our right reaches out to us, while the shadows from the flames dance across my mama's face. She looks so much like the woman I remember, but also a stranger.

When I was sent away to the military, she fought for me to stay. But I knew that if I did she would lose her position at the palace and she loves cooking for *Tsarevna* specifically. I couldn't take that away from her. So I went willingly, even though it was the last thing I wanted for myself.

There was no choice for me. Not when the Tsar ordered it. I was one of three children age ten and up in the palace and all three of us were sent away. I never knew the other kids and they didn't end up in the same training camp as me. I have no idea what happened to them. But it was an order and an order is meant to be followed.

I missed my mama a lot growing up in that camp, she was my only parent and she loved me completely. Now, being back, and having a chance to sneak over to see her feels like a gift. But it seems foolish to talk about my feelings regarding Alyonka with her because I shouldn't be having them in the first place.

"I don't think there's anything to say." I reply, taking a bite of *pirozok*. This one is stuffed with potatoes and as usual, melts in my mouth.

"Is it the Grand Duchess?"

I try to swallow around the piece I'm chewing without choking on it. My mind is fully back in that closet, with Alyonka pressed tightly against my body, her arms holding me close. She fits so perfectly into the circle of my arms, it's like she was made to be there. If I close my eyes, I can still feel her there, her scent surrounding me, wanting to breath her in. In a land of perpetual winter, Alyonka has always carried the scent of flowers with her. Leave it to my mother to get right down to it.

"Mama—"

"I know, I know. But you have always had a soft spot for that girl, even as a young boy. I'm not surprised those feelings are still there, especially when you're in such close proximity again."

I stare at her completely stunned. How would she know any of this? Had word started circulating on the palace gossip mill?

"Don't look so surprised," she reaches over and pats my knee. "I could always tell what you were thinking."

"Could you tell *me* what I'm thinking? Because most of the time I don't know." I sigh. There's something about being back around Alyonka that makes my whole brain loose all coherence. I'm not a solider around her, not someone who has led armies across the land of Skazka. I'm just a man who wants to be near her at all times. I dont' know what to do with that.

"I wish there was something I could say that would help here," Mama says, reaching over to hand me a cup of tea she just poured. "But I'm only an old woman who wants the best for her son. I think I'm a little biased."

"Where's the old woman you're talking about?" I accept the cup. "I don't see her."

"Still as charming as ever. I'm glad to see the military didn't take that away."

She reaches over and I place my cup on the small table just so I can hold her hand.

My father died when I was only three years old. I never had any memories with him. But my mama—she has been my whole world since I can remember. I didn't fight the military taking me away for her sake, I took every assignment given to me, just so that she could be taken care of. Even when I couldn't see her for years, I was doing it all for her.

But for the first time in my life, I want to be selfish. I want to make the decisions that will be all my own.

Yet, I can't.

"Nikolai—" my mama's voice breaks through my thoughts. "Just don't overthink it. Follow your heart."

"You know that's not possible for me. I'm not my own person."

"You think it's that simple, but I think there's more to it than that. Nothing is as simple as we think it is."

nineteen

ALYONKA

It's been a good hour or more since I said good night to Nikolai and Daria. Instead of sneaking out to dance, I told Nikolai I needed to rest. I'm sure after what transpired between us today, he's suspicious. Or if he's not yet, he will be.

I've been laying in my bed, listening to the storm continue its dance outside, but I'm not sure how much longer I can wait. I doubt Chudo will come in this weather, but I want to at least check. The snow has let up a bit and has turned into rain for most of the day, but this seems like my only chance.

I've only ever read about familiars when it comes to magic, but that's who Chudo feels like to me. Maybe he's out there in the trees, sheltering from the storm, but close enough to the castle to see me. That's possible, isn't it?

I'm not exactly sure why this desire to see him is overwhelming me so much. I have plenty of other things to think about—like what in the world is going on in my brain regarding Nikolai. When we were hiding in the closet earlier, I—

Nyet. That's a train of thought I cannot entertain. I need to focus on seeing Chudo.

Pulling back the covers, I swing my legs over the side of the bed, before I reach for my boots that I stashed under it. This argument has been playing in my head for most of the day and I know if I don't try tonight, Nikolai will get suspicious of me saying no to dancing. He seemed curious on why I insisted on staying in my room, and I truly thought for a moment he'll ask me a question I can't answer yet. But thankfully, Daria was with me.

Who also has questions for me that I'm sure she's going to ask tomorrow.

Basically all of this just convinces me that trying to go out in this weather to see my magical dragon friend is a good idea.

I lace up my boots and then tiptoe toward the bathroom. The pathway is familiar enough that I don't have to light a candle or hope for moonlight. I grab my long coat, the heavier one I would wear for the rain, without the fur. It'll get wet as evidence anyway, but I'll deal with that tomorrow.

Pulling the windows open, I'm immediately assaulted with the wind. I gasp for a moment, before I climb over the ledge and out into the balcony. The rain isn't as much of a downpour as its been and I'm thankful for small favors. I stay close to the wall as I shuffle over to the vines and the hidden steps.

When I push the vines aside and step through I realize that the steps are all slippery. I guess I hoped for some protection, but the vines or the wall don't actually allow for any of it, when the rain is falling straight in.

Whatever snow fell, has been melted by the rain and everything is shiny in the moonlight. My hair is plastered to my forehead and I push it to the side, as I move up the stairs. They're stone and slippery, so I lower myself enough that I can kind of crawl up the staircase.

I stop for a moment, catching my breath and trying to figure out why it feels incredibly important to me to reach the roof landing. It's such a wild emotion, I can't even imagine it's coming from me. I've gotten strong feelings from Chudo before, so maybe it's him.

He could be calling out to me from the forest, desperate to see me like I am to see him. I would never say this out loud, but he reminds me of a cat. He wants attention on his own terms, but the attention is a must.

Maybe it's my own loneliness that's seeping through, or maybe I'm actually picking up the complicated emotions of a magical creature, but it still drives me forward. Even as I slip and nearly face plant on the stairs.

"Alyonushka!"

At first, I think I'm hallucinating, but then the same feeling of comfort I always associate with Nikolai overshadows me and I look up, finding him at the top of the stairs. He's looking at me with a combination of someone who has lost her mind and someone he would very much like to protect. The rain dissipates suddenly and when I blink my eyes, he hasn't disappeared.

I'm in so much trouble.

NIKOLAI

AFTER MY CONVERSATION with my mama, I told myself that I just wanted to check on Alyonka, but something more was driving me toward her. She's had this pull on me since we were little kids. But this is different and new and not surprising in the least—if I was going to be honest with myself, which I'm not. I have no idea how to feel about that.

Instead of going up the regular stairs, I decided to take the secret turret passage up to the roof landing. It was raining, but maybe just being close by would calm my restless mind. This afternoon has riled me up in ways that I can't put into words and now, I can't explain this pull.

There isn't much rational thought left in me when I stepped out onto the roof landing and headed down the stairs.

But that's when I saw her. She slips on the stairs, catching herself against the wall, her hair plastered to her face.

"Alyonushka!" I call over the rain and she jerks her face up to stare at me in shock. As soon as our eyes meet, the rain stops and I blink against the random change.

"Are you insane?" I ask, moving down the stairs, until I reach her. She's about halfway up, mostly on her hands and knees, crawling. "Did something happen in your room? Are you okay?"

Because now every terrible scenario rushes through my mind. Someone getting into her room past the guards, her hurt in any way—

"*Nyet, nyet.*"

She grabs my face as if she can see the terrible train of thought my mind has taken and moves it so I'm looking directly into her eyes. "I'm perfectly okay and nothing happened."

"Then why are you trying to hurt yourself on these incredibly dangerous steps in a middle of a storm?" I ask, my voice a little muffled because she moves her hands together over my face, squishing it.

"Alyonka, now is not the time for this," I mumble, sounding funny with my lips squished. But she laughs with so much glee I can't even be upset about it.

"There's something I need to do," she replies, dropping her hands from my face.

"What could be so important?"

"I can't tell you."

"Why is that?"

"Because."

"Because why?"

"Because you wouldn't like it." My heart drops in my chest.

"Are you meeting someone?" I barely push the words past my lips.

"*Da*," she replies and then clasps a hand over her mouth as if she didn't mean to say that. I feel it like a slap on the face or a punch in the stomach. I knew this was coming, this is the whole point of this competition. But the knowledge that she would've found someone, that her heart is being turned toward someone, it takes everything out of me.

"Oh!" she moves forward suddenly, grabbing my face once more. "Not like that. Not a suitor!"

I furrow my brow in confusion. One, because who else could it be? And two, why she feels the need to make sure I understand? It shouldn't bring hope back into my being, but it does.

"Come with me," she says and there's no argument to be hand. She motions for me to turn around so I can go back up the stairs and I do so almost automatically.

We come up to the roof landing and I step to the side

to watch her. She walks over to the farthest edge of the landing, overlooking the forest and stands there.

"If you can hear me, can you please come?" she says and I'm so confused I don't even know what to do. I walk over to stand beside her, because even in all the confusion, I need to make sure she's safe.

"I actually have no idea if your hearing is this good, but I miss you. It's been so long and I—" she pauses, her eyes focused on something far away, almost like she's listening to something I can't hear.

"Oh! This is...wow this is new. I—can I really? Oh! Oh!" she exclaims and I lean over so I can see her face.

"Alyonushka, are you okay?"

Her eyes refocus on me and she grins.

"It's been a long time since you called me that," she whispers, her eyes shining. My body shifts forward, as if it needs to be closer, but then something moves above us. I jerk my attention to the sky, trying to see past the clouds, but I can't pinpoint what pulled my attention. Then I see it. A large shadow moving below the clouds. And it's getting closer.

"Alyonka, we need to move," I say, grabbing her hand and tugging her toward the door, but she doesn't move.

"*Nyet*, wait," she calls and then the large shape descends and I throw my body over Alyonka's as best as I can.

The shape is on the roof landing with us and I turn my head just a little to see what it is. My whole body turns rigid as I try to wrap my mind around what I'm seeing.

It's a dragon. What I would imagine one to be, if I believed they existed. About a size of a bear, it's covered in scales that change color between dark purple and blue. There's fur around its legs and on the wings and the large green eyes are currently narrowed at me.

"Nikolai." Alyona's voice against my cheek pulls my attention and I realize I'm still cradling her close to my body. "You're very sweet to try to protect me, but could you let go now? You're slightly suffocating me."

I loosen my hold immediately, but I don't move away. Alyonka punches my stomach lightly, making me shift a little, before she wraps her hands around my forearm and pulls it down.

"Nikolai, I would like you to meet Chudo. Chudo, this is my bodyguard, Nikolai. Please be nice to each other."

The dragon seems to puff at me, lifting his head like he's assessing me, those eyes giving me a thorough study. For a moment, he looks like he might open up his mouth and swallow me whole. But then he gives me a nod.

"Did he just nod at me?" I whisper, unable to tear my eyes away.

"*Da*, now you do it." Alyonka whispers in return. I do so automatically and Alyonka claps her hands.

"Perfect, now we can all be friends."

twenty

ALYONKA

Apparently, Chudo and I can communicate telepathically. I've always been slightly aware of his feelings, but this is a new development. He doesn't speak in full sentences, more like a combination of words and emotions, but oh my goodness, we can communicate! I am in shock, I am elated, I may need to sit down...

"*I miss too,*" he says now, followed by a strong emotion of missing me. "*Want pets!*"

That emotion nearly rocks me where I stand and I'm glad I'm still holding onto Nikolai.

"I will give pets," I reply out loud and Nikolai jerks. "What?"

I pat his forearm a little and Chudo's eyes narrow.

"*No him pets. Me pets!*" He sends another wave of want toward me and I chuckle.

"*Da, da,* you, Chudo!" I push past Nikolai only to be stopped by him again. Chudo growls a little in protest which makes Nikolai tense up even more.

"Okay, I need both of you to calm down," I say addressing them, "Nikolai, Chudo is harmless. And he's demanding to be petted. I suggest you allow it."

"Is he your...pet?" Nikolai asks as he loosens his hold on me. He doesn't let go completely, however, moving with me as I reach for Chudo.

"*No pet! Greatest! Fierce! Not puny, pfft human!*" Chudo says and I try not to chuckle, lest I offend him in any way.

"Not a pet," I reach over, placing my hand between Chudo's eyes, scratching lightly. He closes his eyes for a moment, before opening one up so he can watch Nikolai.

"Have you read those stories about magical familiars? Or sidekicks?" I ask Nikolai as Chudo begins to purr a little. "I think he's mine."

"*Pirozki? Want! Want! Want!*"

I chuckle at the intensity with which Chudo is asking for the treat, and I make sure to give him an extra scratch as I say,

"Next time. I will try." He really does love *pirozki*. I should've tried sneaking down to the kitchens to find some. Not that it would've been that easy.

"How is that possible?" Nikolai can't stop staring and

I can't blame him. Chudo is magnificent. "I didn't even know dragons were real."

Chudo huffs a burst of hot air at Nikolai, making my bodyguard come to stand on the other side of me. The reversal of roles doesn't escape me, but I try not to smile too much.

"I'm not sure. But he's very much real."

"But you can't do magic like High Queen Calista," Nikolai continues. "How?"

"I've never been able to figure it out for sure, but I've always thought that maybe I carry some magic on me because of the curse. Or he's a gift from Skazka."

"*A gift!*"

"Oh!" I exclaim, turning my attention back to the dragon. I've never been able to ask him directly before, but now I can.

"Why do I hear you now? Are you a gift from Skazka?"

"*No tell, but gift!*" he purrs even louder, vibrating the roof landing.

"So he can't tell me how I can communicate with him, but he is a gift." I tell Nikolai.

"So you can communicate?"

"As of tonight. I have no idea why. Before I only got strong feelings from him. But now, we can talk."

"That's why you come to the landing?"

"*Da*, I haven't seen him in weeks now," I say, moving my petting near his ears. He curls in on himself like he usually does and I smile. I've always thought he was young and when he's like this, it seems even more so. I study this incredibly magical creature, who is currently curled up and purring like a cat.

"If he is a gift, maybe he was sent by Skazka so I'm not so alone," I muse out loud, forgetting that Nikolai is right there. He moves towards me just a little bit, his body heat reaching for me against my back.

"Are you often alone, Alyonushka?" he asks, his voice barely audible it's so low. I turn my face to find him watching me and I give him a sad smile.

"I'm always alone."

There's a moment of stillness, almost like the air around us is holding itself suspended, as I realize just how vulnerable I sounded. I never want anyone to know how heavily this curse weighs on me, because there's nothing anyone can do. I have to endure and I don't want others to have to endure it with me. But Nikolai has always had the kind of effect on me that leaves me feeling unbalanced. And more talkative than I should be.

"Alyonushka." The word is but a whisper on his lips but it travels through every part of me. I shut my eyes as tears pile up. I meant it when I said no one has called me that but him. It's the nickname that's given to someone with my name, said with the sweetest connotation. But now, it just hurts my heart.

"Don't call me that," I whisper, keeping my face turned toward Chudo. The dragon is watching me now, concern radiating off him, but he doesn't move.

No matter how much I want Nikolai to keep using that nickname I can't allow myself to get attached to it again. It's a nickname for someone who still has an option to dream. I've had to put away every notion about my future when I turned seven and my parents explained to me why I was so guarded, why there were so many things I couldn't do and couldn't have.

Nikolai came into my life shortly after I learned what was in store for me and he became my escape. We would sneak down to the kitchens to steal pastries, we would hide in the gardens, creating our own adventures. He became a hope for me, a possibility of having a life lived to the fullest.

And then he was gone. I was alone again and I've been alone ever since.

"I should call you that more often."

Nikolai's words break through my thoughts and I twist around to find him right behind me, almost no space left between us. I gasp, tilting on my heels, but his hand reaches out, wrapping around my waist and pulling me to him.

Our bodies come together and we stay frozen, as we try to catch our breaths.

"You should never feel alone again, Alyonushka," Nikolai says, staring intensely into my eyes. "I'm always by your side."

I can't keep the tears slipping down my cheeks. My heart feels like it's going to explode, my whole body tense with the emotions raging inside of me. Nikolai watches the path my tear makes and then he growls, pulling me fully to him. I gasp as he cradles me against him and my arms come up to wrap around his waist.

We hugged inside the closet just a few hours ago, but this feels like a conscious decision that will ruin both of us if we let it. The sound of rain arrives suddenly, but I don't even feel it against my skin as I cling to Nikolai like my whole life depends on it.

NIKOLAI

I CAN HOLD her like this for the rest of my life. The rain comes suddenly once more, but before it can reach us, it stops. I glance up and find a large wing placed over us. The dragon—Chudo—has stretched out, keeping his wing over us. I look at the dragon and even though I can't communicate with him like Alyonushka can, I know we share an understanding.

She must be more than simply protected, she must be cared for.

Alyonka hiccups a little and then pulls back, ducking her head as if she's embarrassed. She tries to move backwards but I'm not letting her go far. I reach for her and sweep her right off her feet. She gasps, her arms wrapping around my neck automatically.

"What are you doing?"

"Making sure you don't catch a cold," I reply, because that's all I can come up with. She looks over at the dragon and chuckles.

"*Spasibo*, Chudo," she says, glancing up at the wing that's serving as a shelter from the rain. "You can put me down, I'll stay under the wing."

"I don't know if that's a good idea. I think body heat is helping to stay off the cold."

I put on my most innocent expression and when she laughs, I feel like I've won a thousand medals.

"So you're going to keep me close for survival?" She asks.

"It seems like a very important reason to do so," I reply, my face a stoic mask of seriousness. But then her fingers tug on the hairs at the back of my neck and my whole body feels aflame. I meet her gaze and while the tears are still clinging on to the lashes, there's a light in her that got dimmed for a moment.

"Very important. But maybe set me down so I can say goodbye to Chudo?"

"Only because I must," I mumble, gently placing her back on her feet. She stays in the circle of my arms for a moment, before she turns to the dragon.

"It's bedtime, Chudo," she says and the dragon stares at her for a moment, before glancing at me and back at her. "He is. And he will make sure I am safe. Please be safe as well and I will come see you as soon as I can."

She steps forward so she can pet the dragon again and Chudo moves the wing so it stays over her. Which means I am soaked in a moment. The dragon meets my eye and I swear he's laughing at me. Alyonka scratched the dragon between the eyes a few times and then says something else I can't hear over the rain.

"We should head inside," I call out, stepping close to her. She nods and then waves at the dragon, who meets and holds her gaze for a moment. Then, the rain suddenly turns into a snow fall, as if someone the coin. I glance up, completely confused and then look back at the dragon, who glances at me and then immediately takes flight. I reach for Alyonka's hand, wrapping it tightly in mine as I pull her toward the slippery stairs.

"You'll get sick," I say, as I tug her behind me. She stares at the sky where the dragon went for a moment and then moves. I keep a strong hold on her as I lead her down the stairs and then to her balcony. The wind picks up when we reach the windows and I pull them open, ushering in, before I step in after her. It takes me two tries to shut the windows behind us, locking them in place.

I turn to glance at Alyona and see that she's lit a candle. She's dripping water all over and so am I. The rain was brief, but it was powerful.

"You need to dry off," I say, when she doesn't move. I step up to her, reaching for her coat and it's like my moving has sprung her into action. She unbuttons it and I pull it off, placing it on the bathtub. Before she can move, I'm already on my knees, unlacing her boots.

"You don't need to—"

"The faster we do this, the better." I don't stop, until I've unlaced both. She placed a hand on my shoulder as I pull one boot off and then the other. The bottom of her dress is also wet.

I stand up, walking around her and reach for her lace up corset.

"Nikolai."

My name is but a whisper, but my fingers freeze against the skin of her back. I glance down, to find myself unlacing the strings and I drop my arms immediately, taking a step back.

"I'm sorry, I went into problem solving mode," I say, and she turns to look at me over her shoulder, her hands at her chest to keep her dress in place. I avert my gaze immediately, focusing on the one candle that's burning right beside us.

"It's okay." Her voice seems far away and too loud at the same time, and I'm sure my face is as red as a tomato. I'm glad it's dark in here. "Can you check the fireplace while I change?"

"*Da*, of course." I turn away immediately, feeling my way up to the doorway and pushing it open. The moment I'm through, I shut the door behind me and take a deep breath. The whirlpool of emotions that today has been has suddenly left me exhausted.

I take another deep breath and head over to the fireplace. The room is aglow with the light from the fire, so I have no problem seeing. I shrug out of my jacket, hanging it on the back of the chair near the fireplace, before I add another log to the flames. My button up shirt is wet, since the jacket isn't made to withstand rain and the fire feels nice against my skin.

Another few minutes later, I hear the door open and I glance behind me to find Alyonka has changed into a long nightgown, her long hair wet and hanging down around here. She's holding a brush in one hand and a lock of hair in another, as she absentmindedly tries to untangle it while looking at me. She looks like a vision, straight out of every dream I've ever had. The gifts the fairies gave her before the curse have always made her stand out among others. But it's her expression that nearly brings me to my knees. There's something purely Alyonushka in that look and I want to do everything in my power to keep her safe and taken care of.

"Come here," I say, my voice coming out rough even to my own ears. She raises her eyebrows, but moves toward me. I pull an ottoman over in front of the fire and motion for her to sit. She cocks her head to the side in confusion, but sits anyway. I take the brush out of her hand and then move behind her.

I crouch down and pick up a strand of hair, before I

begin brushing it out. The room is silent, besides the crackle of the fire and our breaths. My heart is beating so loudly in my chest I'm sure she can hear it.

"You don't have to do this," Alyonka says, breaking the silence. But she doesn't move away or turn toward me. So I don't stop. I work on the ends of her hair first, moving slowly to the top, making sure I don't pull too hard.

"But I want to," I reply.

The room grows silent again, and I think the temperature goes up a handful of degrees because suddenly, I feel hot all over. Yet, I don't stop.

Once the hair is all brushed out, I put the brush down and reach for it all. Separating it into three sections, I begin to braid. I've only ever practiced on thread or vines hanging off a tree, so this feels entirely new to me.

"Are you—braiding my hair?" Alyonka asks softly, as if she's afraid to spook me. I chuckle a little, but don't stop.

"I am."

"How do you know how to do that? The military teach you?"

I chuckle again. "Nyet, this is not one of the requirement for becoming an officer."

"Then, how?"

"I taught myself." I say, and she turns to look at me over her shoulder. I'm almost at the end now, the feel of her hair against my fingers calming in a way I didn't expect.

"Why?" Alyonka asks, just as I reach the end. I don't have anything to tie it with, but it doesn't seem like it will come out easily. Still, I hold on to it for a moment longer, wondering if I should be honest with her. I glance up and find her eyes on me, surprised and filled with a little bit of wonder, so I reply before I can stop myself.

"So I could braid your hair."

She audibly gasps and I smile, knowing how wild that sounds, but also loving her reaction. I stay crouching, even as she turns to face me, the flames reflecting their dance on her face.

"Mine? Why?"

I try to keep my face free of emotion, but maybe there's another darkness in the room to keep her from seeing me fully. I take the risk.

"Do you remember the day we decided to climb the trees near the back of the northern wall? You really wanted to see what was on the other side and we had no way of finding out, unless we climbed.

You weren't allowed to climb and I'm pretty sure you've never done so before, but you insisted."

"Like I do."

"*Da*, in that special way of yours until I relented." I smile at the memory of an eight year old Alyonka, standing with her hands on her hips in front of that large tree, determination all over her face. "Your hair was pinned back, but then the ribbon got caught on the branch and your hair spilled all over, making it difficult for you to climb."

"I remember. I was very frustrated because I couldn't get it to stay and you couldn't help."

"So I decided that if it happened again, I would be able to help."

We both smile at each other, before her smile drops away.

"But then you left."

She's right. I was sent away shortly after. Without having a chance to say goodbye. But it didn't stop me from learning and practicing over the years on the off chance I could do this for her. Of course I can't let her see how over the years, I kept on practicing, because I never stopped having hope that I might see her again. I can't tell her that part. Not when we've already crossed too many lines between us.

"Oh, you must be cold," Alyona suddenly exclaims, looking over my shirt. "Take it off."

She reaches for the buttons on my shirt, unbuttoning the top two, before I catch her wrists, stilling her progress.

"Duchess, are you trying to undress me?" I whisper and her eyes flash. That electrifying sensation courses through me and I wonder if she feels it too.

"Only for your survival," she replies, her lips curling up in a teasing smile that I officially want to see every day for the rest of my life.

"Well, if it's for such an important reason." I drop my hands and spread them wide, motioning for her to continue. She rolls her eyes, pushing me slightly away, before she grins.

"What a lazy bum. Take off your own shirt."

She turns away, standing up and walking over to her bed. She grabs a blanket off the edge and turns back to me. I haven't moved.

"I'm serious. If you're so shy and embarrassed, I'll look away." She raises an eyebrow and I don't break eye contact as I unbutton another button. Her eyes immediately jerks down and back up and then she raises the blanket in front of her face, holding it open. I stand, trying to keep my laughter at bay, as I walk over to her.

Peaking over the edge of the blanket, I glance down at her hiding her face on the other side.

"I'm not undressing. I need to head back."

"*Nyet!*" She immediately pulls the blanket down. "You'll get sick. Stay here."

"Alyonka."

"It's an order. I'll give you blankets and you'll sleep in front of the fireplace and you can head back in the morning. I don't want you out there right now."

Just to make sure I can't make any arguments the wind decides to howl at that exact moment. We stare at each other and I finally relent. Even though we both know this is a terrible idea.

twenty-one

ALYONKA

Surprisingly, I sleep. When I open my eyes the next morning, Nikolai is gone. The blankets and pillow I had him use are stacked at the edge of the bed on the bench. It's almost like he wasn't here at all.

Last night, I wanted to stay awake and see if I can make him confess any other memories he carries with him. But the moment I climbed into bed, I passed out. It's the most soundly I've slept in ages. I can't even be mad at myself for falling asleep. Clearly, my body felt like it could finally relax in his presence.

My body seems to be knowing a lot of things that I am not familiar with, but that's for another time.

The next four days go by much the same way. I spend time with the suitors, I eat my three meals a day, I have my study time, and then I retire to my rooms. The storm has been picking up speed it seems and the rain has completely turned into snow, cutting us off from the rest of the world even more so than we usually are.

Even though everyone is cranky and tired, they're trying to keep up with appearances a little better since my little outburst. Tetia Tatiana is continuously unhappy with me, and I can tell even though she's trying not to show it. I asked Nikolai to look into it for me, but of course, with the storm, any information he might've been able to find out hasn't reached us yet.

Five days after Nikolai meet Chudo and slept in my room, I'm sitting on in one of the downstairs rooms, with the rest of the suitors and Daria. My lady's maid is on the divan beside me, a lap loom on her lap. There's a ball of yarn between us, as she expertly weaves the material horizontally across the warp—the foundation of the weaving design. Since sharp needles aren't allowed in the castle, she works only with a long wooden tapestry needle, which allows her to weave across the rows.

I have a book in my lap, but I can't stop watching her progress. No one knows this, but she taught me how to weave a few years ago. Some of the tapestries in my room are actually made by me. I know that technically, I'm not supposed to be doing such things, but just like with dancing, I wanted to do something for me.

I'm not the only one watching her. Lev Ignatovich and Sergey Vladimirovich both seem to be fascinated.

Their eyes follow her fingers as she threads the yarn as if they've never actually seen anyone do so before. Which, honestly, I would not be surprised if they haven't.

My eyes seem to shift to Nikolai on their own and I see that he has also noticed. He glances at me, holding me hostage with his look and I'm suddenly finding it really difficult to breathe.

The door behind him opens, breaking the eye contact and I feel like I am myself again. I try to focus on the book in my hands, just to hide my face from the rest of the room. No one can notice I'm having these—whatever they are.

The staff comes in, bringing an afternoon snack, distributing tea and some pastries in front of everyone. I glance at the plate in front of me and notice three different versions of *pirozkov*. I promised Chudo some, so now I need to figure out a way to smuggle some in.

I almost laugh out loud at the absurdity of my thoughts. I could just ask for the extra's to be brought to me before bedtime. I try not do to that, simply so I can keep the lectures about my eating habits to a minimum. Also, sneaking around is an adventure.

Except now, I don't have to entertain myself in such a way. I'm no longer alone.

Once again, my eyes find Nikolai's and he's already looking at me. There's an intensity in his gaze that I'm not used to seeing when others are present. It suddenly makes me dizzy and I shiver a little, tearing my eyes away and focusing on the food.

"Are you cold?" Denis Alexandrovich asks, before he stands and reaches for the throw blanket on the side of his chair and places it over my lap. I'm so surprised by how fast he moves, I simply lift my book so it's not in the way. He smiles at me, and takes his seat again, reaching for his tea.

The whole room seems to be frozen. Everyone is staring at the baron in shock. I look over his shoulder to find Nikolai with a blanket in his hands, stopped halfway to me. There's that moment of tension between us and then he takes a step back, folding the blanket back up. For some reason, that small move and the look in his eyes almost feel like a huge canyon has opened up between us.

"That was so kind of you, Baron Denis," Tetia Tatiana speaks up, her mask back in place. However, I can tell she disapproves of what he's done. No one is supposed to approach me without permission. Definitely not that close. But with all the time we've been spending in the same space, I'm not surprised some of that has grown lax.

"*Da, spasibo*, Denis Alexandrovich," I say, throwing a quick glance at Tetia Tatiana. The other woman raises her chin at me in disapproval, for what reason, I have no idea. At this point, she seems to like me less and less as the days go by, but I don't cower away. I'm working on that whole taking my power back. She holds my gaze for a moment longer, before putting on a smile and standing up.

"I think it's about time for *Tsarevna* Alyona to head to her studies."

She meets my eye again and I narrow my eyes at her. I really cannot figure out what her game is, but at least she's giving me an out. I'm definitely finished hanging out with the suitors. So I incline my head.

"*Da*, I think it's time."

The men stand immediately to bow, so Daria reaches for the blanket, pulling it away so I can stand. Denis Alexandrovich looks a little confused and I offer him a kind smile. Nikolai leads the way out, and I don't miss the hard look he throws at Tetia Tatiana.

Daria is right beside me, with Nikolai leading the way as we head toward the study. He's not looking at me and I can't help but feel like something is different. I glance at Daria and make a decision.

"Keep me company?" I whisper and she looks at me in surprise. This is the time that's usually just Nikolai and I in the study. I don't miss the way my bodyguard's shoulders jerk a little, so I know he heard me, even though he doesn't turn around.

Daria glances at him and then at me, giving me a firm nod. We reach the study and Nikolai opens the door, motioning for us to go in first. I nod to Daria and she steps inside, as I turn to my bodyguard.

"I need a little girl time," I say, keeping my voice low and Nikolai simply nods in affirmation. He's not really meeting my eye, looking over my shoulder or over my head. Which is more what he acted like when he first returned. It's been a month now and I thought we've reached a new level, but something is definitely different.

"I'll return in a few hours. Oleg and Daniil will be right outside," Nikolai says and I turn to see the other two soldiers coming up the hallway.

"*Spasibo*," I turn back to Nikolai with a thanks. He meets my eyes then and there's an emotion there I can't quite identify.

"You don't have to thank me, *Tsarevna* Alyona. I'm just doing my job."

With that, he steps around me and leaves.

NIKOLAI

I'M sure I'm being childish. If I told Timofey or my mama about it, they would probably agree. Technically, I can't be telling Timofey anything at this point. He already spent most of the morning teasing me about being "a good bodyguard" by staying "oh so close" to his mark. One of these days I will make him clean the bathrooms.

Timofey would probably call me foolish anyway but I can't get the sight of Baron Denis placing the blanket on Alyonka's lap with ease out of my mind. There was something about the way she looked that made it so evident how different we truly are. I could never get away from breaking the rule like that. I wouldn't just receive disapproving looks. I'd probably be demoted on the spot.

But because of his status, because of what his role is in all of this, there is no punishment. He got close to her, he approached her first, and after the initial shock, everything went back to normal.

Such a small event, but it feels like so much more right now. Because if I was going to be honest with myself, I'd admit that I've been entertaining notions I have no place entertaining. When it comes to Alyonka, she will always be off limits. I shouldn't think otherwise just because we share a history and a few secrets.

"Are you actually going to spar or only stand there looking handsome?"

Timofey's question breaks through my thoughts and I glance around at the men gathered. Since Alyonka requested alone time with Daria it gives me a chance to participate in some of the training. Timofey has been teaching more close combat, something that would be useful to the soldiers when they attend royal gatherings and do protection duty.

Eventually. After the curse is lifted.

"Do you think sweet talking is going to keep you from being squashed like a bug?" I ask, smirking. The soldiers gathered around "ooh" and "aah", while some of them clap a few times. There's no discrimination in the my unit, anyone can join and I train them all equally. They do enjoy the training, but they especially enjoy watching Timofey and I spar.

"Sweet talking has always helped in the past," Timofey grins, throwing a few winks at the surrounding people.

"Well, now I just think you're stalling," I comment, cocking my head to the side. He laughs and then he launches himself at me.

We've always been pretty equally matched, which makes him for a great opponent. Now, as the frustration runs through my blood, I focus all of my attention on the moves and the fight. The endorphins rush though my body as sweat starts to collect on my temples.

Timofey swings left and I dodge him, ducking, before I'm up again and swinging right. He jumps back, staying on his feet as I attack. Right, right, left uppercut, right again. It's a quick pattern, but effective one. He blocks and we switch, our moves practiced and flowing.

I give him a quick signal, letting him know we're switching it up. Instead of only using our arms, we add a few movements with the legs. We spar until I am covered in sweat, my limps nice and exhausted. That's when we finally call a draw.

"Hope you caught all that," I say, turning to the spectators, my voice authoritative. "There will be a test later."

The look of panic on their faces is worth it. I turn away to grab a towel, hiding the smile behind the material. Timofey glances at me and shakes his head.

"Forgive the commander, he often thinks he's funny," Timofey addresses the group and I can almost hear the collective exhale. "But do practice, because you never know who will be called next into the ring." He makes dramatic noises and the soldier scramble to get moving.

"Are you sure you're a soldier and not an entertainer?" I ask Timofey as we head toward our room.

"No one said I couldn't be both," my friend replies, shrugging. We reach the room and I head in to wash up first. My body feels exhilarated after the good workout, but my heart I still just as heavy. Once I step out of the bathroom, I glance at the clock and find that I still have at least an hour before I need to head back up to the study.

I can't fault Alyonka for wanting alone time with her lady's maid. I've learned that the two share a friendship, which is so necessary for the Grand Duchess. But even with the soldiers stationed outside, I want to be in the room to make sure she's safe. The desire to be near her at all times is becoming almost unbearable.

Which is not something I can allow. Picking up one of the books I took from the study, I sit down on my bed and begin to read. Ivan Popyalof wants me to keep doing research, but no matter how many of these books I've read, I haven't found anything useful.

That makes all of this feel more hopeless than ever before.

"Are you going to tell me what's on your mind?" Timofey asks when he finishes washing up. I don't look up at him, keeping my attention on the book in front of me.

"Nothing is on my mind," I say.

"Come on, man," Timofey sits on the bed opposite of mine, leaning forward. Even without looking directly at him, I know he's watching me like a hawk. "I could tell you were distracted even before we started sparring."

Sometimes, I don't like just how well he knows me. But while I've learned to confide in him at times—I was once told by a little girl of barely seven that it's not good to bottle up my feelings—I don't think I can share this with him. Not the burning sensation I feel in my chest any time Alyonka is with any of the other men, not the desire to grab her hand and whisk her out of this castle and this kingdom and never look back.

"It's nothing," I say, but of course he's no buying it. I sigh, putting my book down and turning to face him. He's sitting on the bed, elbows on his knees as he continues to watch me. "I know I'm handsome, but please, control yourself."

I swing my legs of the bed and head toward the desk. There are four other books on the table that I've read through, with absolutely no helpful information. I've even started looking for dragon lore, but that's just as sparse as the curse.

"If you won't talk to me," Timofey says from behind me, "you should talk to her."

I freeze, the book in my hand half suspended on top

of the stack. Timofey moves, opening the wardrobe and then coming up to stand behind me. He doesn't say anything else, just slaps me on the back and then walks out of the room.

The thing is, I really shouldn't be surprised. Of course he knows. He probably knew before I did.

I put on my jacket, before I pick up the stack of books and head out of the room. Even though I know it's not time to head to the study yet, I simply can't help myself. Being away from Alyonka for any length of time makes me uncomfortable. I'm her bodyguard after all. I should be there to make sure she's safe.

When I round the corner to the main foyer I pause. Tatiana is near one of the room, with *Knyaz* Georgiy beside her. They can't really see me, unless they turn and look, but I step closer to the wall anyway, keeping my eyes on them. They seem to be looking at something in her hands, whispering to each other. I watch as she levels him with a serious look and then tucks the paper—maybe an envelope—inside of her suit jacket. *Knyaz* Georgiy nods and smile at her and then pivots and walks away. She looks around briefly and then heads toward the stairs.

If I was expecting her to scheme with someone, it definitely wouldn't be *Knyaz* Georgiy. I wait a few minutes and then head upstairs toward the study. When I come up to the doors, Oleg and Daniil greet me.

"Tatiana just went inside," Daniil says and I thank him before I dismiss them both. I knock on the door once and then enter. Daria is right inside the doors to the right, and I nod at her as I come in. Tatiana is in front of the desk where Alyonka's is sitting.

"It would be best for you to choose a different competition," Tatiana is saying. I'm surprised it's taken her this long. She's been unhappy with Alyonka's choice since the beginning. And since the weather appeared, she's been even more dissatisfied with the Grand Duchess.

Alyonka's eyes meet mine as soon as I'm in the room and my heart thuds in my chest so loudly I'm afraid the whole room heard it. I bow automatically and when I stand, Tatiana is rolling her eyes before she turns back to Alyonka.

"I'm not going to change my mind," Tsarevna says. I can't see Tatiana's face, but the set of her shoulders tells me she's very unhappy.

"Think of your kingdom—"

"I am." Alyonka interrupts, "Now, I would like to get back to what I was doing." She bows her head, looking down at the book open in front of her and Tatiana doesn't even bother to bow. She turns on her heels and heads for the door. Except, I can't let her leave like this. She seems to be unraveling and now, she's hiding something I can definitely call her out on. So when she reaches the door, I step in front of her.

"Is there a problem?" She asks looking up at me. I study her face for a moment, honestly surprised this is the woman Tsar and Tsarina entrusted their daughter to. She seems to be more and more annoyed by her position. I can't find a better word to describe it.

"Show me what you have in your pocket," I say and she jerks a little. It's subtle, but because I'm watching her so closely I don't miss it.

"I don't know what you mean," she says, trying to move toward the door, but I'm an immovable force. Alyonka stands, looking at the two of us in confusion.

"Now, Tatiana. Unless you want me to take it by force."

She gives me a very angry look, before she rips the paper from inside her coat and hands it to me. It is an envelope and it has Alyonka's name on it. I pull the paper out and I can't say this is something I expected.

twenty-two

ALYONKA

"What is it?" I ask, walking over to where Nikolai is standing, holding the piece of paper he confiscated from Tetia Tatiana. Whatever is going on there, he looks very unhappy with the woman in front of him. I glance over at Daria, who's stayed near the doors but she just shrugs. But then Nikolai speaks and I'm in shock.

"An invitation to the coronation of Ivanna Sergeivna, the queen of *Korolevstvo Tsvetov*." Nikolai replies and the two of us turn our attention to Tetia Tatiana. Daria gasps, but doesn't offer much more than that, keeping to the shadows.

"Where did you even get it?" I ask, incredulous.

"Knyaz Georgiy had it on him," Nikolai replies for her, shocking me all over again. "I suppose his job was to deliver it when he came and he forgot."

He does seem like the forgetful type, I agree. But I can't do much beside that as I stare at Tetia Tatiana.

"You were keeping this from me? Why?" I ask, my frustration with this woman reaching new heights.

"It is no use for you to know. You cannot attend, so a polite congratulatory gift will be sent in your place."

"Why can't she attend?" Nikolai's question beats my own near outburst of frustration.

"She's not allowed to leave the castle." Tetia Tatiana replies, speaking extra slowly as if Nikolai can't understand her words. Which irritates me more. I'm about to give her a piece of my mind, but it's like Nikolai anticipates it. He steps forward, shielding me just a little with his body, before he speaks again.

"Is that your decision or did it come from the tsar?" He asks, and I force my expression into neutral indifference immediately. My parents have always been so unreachable, sometimes I forget most of the rules they set out for me. But staying in the castle has been a big one. However, I've never wanted to fight the matter as much as I do now.

I don't say anything yet though, I can't let Tetia Tatiana read my thoughts on this matter. I'm curious to see how this plays out. Nikolai is a formidable opponent.

"It was decided with a discussion, for the safety of *Tsarevna* Alyona."

"So, you pushed for it." It's not even a question and Tetia Tatiana's eyes narrow at Nikolai's voice.

"What is it that you're suggesting?" She asks.

"What I'm suggesting is that *Tsarevna* Alyona—if she so desires—attends the coronation. Everyone has heard of what's transpired in *Korolevstvo Tsvetov* and royal families from across Skazka, including the High Queen Calista will be present. This would be the perfect time to make connections with the other rules in nearby kingdoms. And safe, with the High Queen there." He glances at me for a moment, as if he's contemplating what he'll say next and I can't tell what he's thinking.

"And a good opportunity for meeting more eligible suitors without the pressure of the competition."

The last line was delivered so logically that it actually makes me hold my breath. There's no emotion behind those words, as if everything that's happened since he returned wasn't real. The last few weeks rush through my mind, but maybe that's all it was—things I made up in my head. It's harder to keep my face impassive now, but I was raised for this.

"Is that what *Tsarevna* Alyona wants?" Tetia Tatiana's voice carries a note of a challenge, as if she's sure I will keep quiet and follow her rules like I have so many times before. But really, after the last month we've had she should know better.

I step around Nikolai and level her with a look.

"*Da*, it's what *Tsarevna* Alyona wants," I say and she immediately loses some of the smugness. "It's a perfectly logical reason for accepting the future queen's invitation. You said it yourself just a few days ago that the current competition is coming to an end. This way, we can expand the pool of options. I can get her there and back safely, with minimal issues."

I'm close enough to Nikolai that I can almost feel the frigid air coming off him at my announcement, but wasn't he saying the same exact thing not a minute ago? But Tetia Tatiana is already talking, so I try to concentrate on her words.

"With the curse right around the corner, can she really be traveling to some kingdom and for what? A party?"

"To make alliances." Now it's Nikolai's turn to speak slowly, so Tetia Tatiana can follow. "She is the future queen. She can't ignore these kinds of responsibilities. Since the Tsar and Tsarina aren't here the responsibility falls to Tsarevna Alyona. She can make connections, make friends—"

"Friends? She can't have friends. She is a queen, which means her job is to be alone. Her position doesn't allow for such frivolous relationships as friends."

"Alone?" I finally speaks up, staring at the woman as if she's lost her mind. Because if that's what she's thinking, then what are we doing with the competition? Nikolai has moved even closer, our arms brushing and I keep myself from reacting to that small contact. Instead, I focus on the frustration.

"Since my parents aren't here to make that decision and you kept the invitation from me until now, there is no time to send for a reply, I will make the executive decision."

I stare at Tetia Tatiana as if daring her to argue. Which of course she does.

"Your parents gave me the full range of veto power when it comes to your activities."

"Unless you decide to keep me here hostage, I suggest you don't exercise that power," I say, lowering my voice a little. Which has the desired effect. She expected me to raise it, to argue loudly like I've heard other people argue in the few kingdom meetings I've been allowed at.

"Nikolai has a plan," I say confidently, even though he hasn't outright presented it. But I trust him. He wouldn't suggest this if he didn't have a solid way to protect me. "If he believes he can get me there and back with minimum issues, I believe it too."

I can't see his expression because he's standing beside me but I feel his body heat reach out to me like a reminder that I'm not alone.

"Can you get her there and back?" Tetia Tatiana addresses the man and I turn my head just enough to watch him nod.

"Fine, do what you will. But before you go, the storm must let up. If it does so, we will hold your ice skating competition and only then can you leave. It is only fair for the suitors who have traveled far to be here."

With that she walks around me and heads for the door. Once she's out of the room, I collapse onto the divan, staring at the invitation I've been gripping in my hand.

Am I actually going? Can I actually go? Am I leaving the premises of this castle after all these years? It seems unbelievable.

She's not wrong about the competition however. It wouldn't be fair for me to simply disappear and leave the men behind. But I can't help the excitement that rushes through my body at the thought of going to the coronation.

I have only been outside these walls four times in my entire life. And the last two were in the last four years, when my presence was required at council meetings. But even at the most recent one, I feared my father would think that I'm not actually needed and I will stop having these small outings. I mean, it's been two years at this point, so the fear is realized.

Daria waves her hand briefly to catch my attention and then she opens the door and slips out. Nikolai doesn't comment on her departure, so I turn my attention back to him.

"Do you really have a plan?" I glance up at Nikolai, who hasn't moved. Just continues to watch me.

"*Da*. The moment I read the invitation, I started

thinking over the options. If we can reach the village near the trading passage, High Queen Calista has set up a few portals for traveling. The military has used a few for meetings and important events. We can use one to cross the river and arrive at the coronation with time to spare."

I sit up immediately.

"Have you seen these portals?"

"*Da*."

"Wow, so you've seen magic. I envy you."

"Why? Magic is already part of your life."

"Ah, of course. How could I forget this stupid curse?" I slump back against the back of the divan, in a very un-princess like manner, but Nikolai is unfazed.

"I meant Chudo. He's magic and he comes to you."

He says it so matter of fact that I have a sudden urge to leap into his arms and hug him. But I'm sure he'll have a problem with that. I'm not sure what's going on, but it feels like something is off between us. Whatever is going on with him, I want to fix it. But I'm not exactly sure how.

I sit up, leaning forward so I can fold my hands under my chin and stare up at Nikolai. I blink at him a few times as he watches me, his own eyes narrowing a little. He knows what I'm doing, but I don't mind. I like seeing how I effect him.

"Nikolai—" I begin in my sweetest voice and watch as he swallows harder than usual.

"Duchess," he says and I grin.

"Tonight, I want to dance."

NIKOLAI

The next two nights, Alyonka dances. The storm hasn't let up even a little bit and I fear that we will miss the coronation all together. The way Alyonka's eyes sparkled when Tatiana agreed to not stand in her way is imbedded in my mind. I want to see that excitement have the proper payout. Somehow, someway I need to get Alyonka to that coronation.

Which is maybe why on the third night I'm on this landing balcony in the middle of the night, testing a theory. I've read in one of the books Ivan Popyalof left for research that have been times the land has answered requests. Specially, when it comes to the request High Queen Calista had made. True, I'm not a queen with magical powers, but I'm hoping since the land seems to like Alyonka—she sent her Chudo after all—my request might be answered.

"So I have no idea how good your hearing is," I say, facing the forest. The storm has mellowed a little, keeping the wind to less frequent gusts, which allows for me to be out here without freezing. "I never actually tried talking to any magical beings before. Never thought I would. But if you can hear me, is there a way to make the storm disappear for a few days?"

I take a deep breath feeling like a complete idiot, but I keep my eyes on the forest, which means I'm mostly staring into darkness.

"You see, Alyonka has an invitation to visit the queen of *Korolevstvo Tsvetov* for the coronation. Alyonka isn't allowed to leave the castle's premises, as you may know, being a magical land and all that. What am I doing?"

I run a hand over my face, before dusting some of the snow off my arms, before I tug the scarf farther up over my chin. I have clearly lost my mind if I think the land of Skazka can hear me. Being around Alyonka has jumbled my brain, for sure. Shaking my head, I turn to head back down the stairs when suddenly Chudo lands in front of me.

I've never been around him without Alyonka present and I have no idea how to respond. So I stand completely still, holding his gaze as he seems to assess me. We stay like that for a few moment and after he doesn't immediately eat me, I incline my head in a greeting. He narrows his eyes, crouching low and I step back, bumping into the edge of the balcony. He might eat me. I don't think I can handle him in a one on one the way I can handle Timofey.

Chudo stretches his head toward me, until we're only an arm lengths away, as he continues to stare at me. Then he puffs once, sending a gust of hot air into my face, before he leans back, with a smug look on his face. His body shakes and that's when I realize he's laughing at me.

"You think this is funny," I mumble and he nods his head once, surprising me. I thought only Alyonka could communicate with him, but apparently he understand me as well. "That wasn't very nice," I say, raising an eyebrow at him. He laugh again and wags his tail three times like a dog would. He clearly think this is entertaining.

I notice then that the snow has stopped falling. Glancing up at the sky, the clouds are still there, but for the first time in days, no snow fall. I glance at the dragon and it's my turn to narrow my eyes.

"Did Skazka hear my request about the weather?" I ask. I'm not sure what I'm expecting, but it's definitely not a nod from Chudo and another tail wag. "Really? How? I mean, it doesn't matter. I should say thank you!"

I turn around to face the forest when Chudo sends another gust of air at me. Looking at him, I watch as he puffs out his chest, holding my gaze for a moment, and then when he sees I'm watching, he sits up even straighter, showing off his purple and green scales with pride.

"You did it?" I ask, and Chudo nods ones, "But how? Wait, *nyet*. Once again, it doesn't matter. *Spasibo*! Can you keep it like this for a few days? So Alyonka can have the competition and can travel?"

Chudo nods at everything I say, looking like one of those cats who brought home a wild prey. I'm pretty sure the dragon is grinning at me. I think I find that more shocking than the weather change, actually. But I'm not about to dwell on any of it.

"Alyonka will be very happy," I say sincerely, and Chudo slaps his tail on the floor a few times. Then he leans forward again, this time toward my hands, which are deep in my pockets to chase the cold away. He sniffs at both pockets and I realize he's looking for a treat.

"I'm sorry, Chudo. I don't have any *piroshki* with me. I didn't know you'd be here."

I jerk as a bunch of snow comes out of nowhere, dumped straight on my head. I dust off the pile on my head and roll my eyes at the dragon.

Chudo is looking all innocent as he sits back on his butt and then his face morphs into the biggest pout. I have never seen an animal be so expressive before, but I guess I haven't been around a lot of them in the first place. I look around, trying to see if there's anything I can do, when it comes to me.

"Here," I say, unwrapping the scarf from around my neck. "This is my favorite scarf. It will look very nice on you."

The dragon watches me for a moment, as if he's going to deny my offer. But then he glances at the scarf and his eyes light up as he sits up straight and leans toward me. I step forward and reach over, wrapping the scarf around his neck once, and tying it. The scarf is dark grey made of wool, and somehow looks exactly right against the dragon's purple and green scales. It matches the grey fur around his neck, making it seem like he's wearing a fur coat with an extra fuzzy collar.

Chudo sits back for a second, before he stands and walks to the right and then to the left, as if showing off his new accessory. I can't help but grin.

"It looks great," I say. Chudo meets my eye and I think he might've said thank you, right before he pushes off and takes off into the night sky.

Я вас любил: любовь ещё, быть может,
　В душе моей угасла не совсем;
　Но пусть она вас больше не тревожит;
　Я не хочу печалить вас ничем.
　Я вас любил безмолвно, безнадежно,
　То робостью, то ревностью томим;
　Я вас любил так искренно, так нежно,
　Как дай вам Бог любимой быть другим.

　　　　　　——Я вас любил, Aleksandr Pushkin

(Translated by Reginald Hewitt)
　I loved you; even now I may confess,
　Some embers of my love their fire retain;
　But do not let it cause you more distress,
　I do not want to sadden you again.
　Hopeless and tongue-tied, yet I loved you dearly
　With pangs the jealous and the timid know;
　So tenderly I loved you, so sincerely,
　I pray God grant another love you so.

twenty-three

ALYONKA

The sun wakes me right before Daria comes into the room, nearly skipping. I sit up in bed, staring at the sight I haven't seen in a while—clear skies. I didn't realize I didn't pull the curtains all the way closed last night after I sat there, staring at the falling slow.

"Alyonka, did you see? The weather is so lovely this morning! You get to have your ice skating competition!" Daria leans on the bed, looking up at me with a big smile.

"You seem very excited by this prospect," I reply, shaking my head a little.

"Of course! My favorite competitions are ones I can actually watch and Alyonka," she leans in closer, almost like she's about to share a secret. "Some of your suitors have seen this much snow for the first time this trip."

I laugh then, because I can't help it, slapping a hand over my mouth.

"Daria, that is very...not nice."

"What? Expecting a disaster?"

I point a finger at her, keeping my face stern, but we both know I'm not serious. It's not like I want the suitors to fail. But I would like to see how they do in such an uncomfortable situation—how they handle themselves. I've seen them be dignified, I've seen them boasting when they win at board games, but the competitions are created to push them outside of their comfort zone and see how they do.

"Daria," I say, once I've washed up and she's working on brushing out my hair, "I think I would like to wear the blue dress today."

Her hands freeze on my hair and I watch her eyes grow big in the mirror as she gapes at me.

"Really? You mean it?"

"Of course," I reply, holding her gaze. "I'm only sorry I haven't had a chance to wear it until now."

Daria claps her hands, a grin splitting her face, before she gets back to my hair. Ever since I discovered Daria's love for sewing clothes, I've tried to nurture that by giving her chances to create some of my wardrobe. Tsar appointed a seamstress to create all of my dresses, and Tetia Tatiana is in charge of making sure I get all my clothes updated every few months. But at the beginning of the year, I asked Daria to sew me a specific dress without telling anyone. She worked on it in her rooms and when she finished, I knew she was the perfect person to bring this vision to life. However, up until now I haven't had a chance to wear it, since my wardrobe is planned out by Tetia Tatiana like everything else in my life.

But today, I'm feeling extra rebellious.

I'm thankful Daria came early and we could have breakfast together, before the rest of the day could begin. It feels like it will be a long one.

"What is that?" Tetia Tatiana asks as she steps inside the room a little while later. She's dressed in a heavier dress and boots, ready to head to outside. I won't say I was hoping she wouldn't come to the ice skating, but that would be a lie.

"This is a dress," I reply, turning so I can look at myself in the mirror. Typically, I stick to my signature colors of pink or green, but this dress is a light blue, made from a heavier material than my summer-like gowns. The sleeves go all the way down to my wrists, and they're a bit loose, to allow for movement. The sweetheart neckline is offset with the tops of the sleeves coming all the way to my neck. The skirt is full and goes all the way to the floor. My favorite part, however, are the white embroidered snowflakes that cover the whole dress in various places. Some of the snowflakes have blue gemstones in the middle, others have pearls. Daria added silver snowflake pins to my braid for embellishment and is holding the white fur headband she'll place over my hears.

"Where did you get it? It is not on a list of the dresses I had the seamstress make." Tetia Tatiana sounds disapproving, but I can tell she likes the dress. She keeps staring at it like she's never seen anything like it before.

"I had my own seamstress create it just for me," I reply, raising my chin a little. Tetia Tatiana opens her mouth to say something else, when there's a knock and Nikolai steps in.

His eyes find me immediately and he freezes right inside the doorframe, unblinking. There's a moment where time seems to stop as we stare at each other. Then his eyes travel quickly over my dress, before coming to rest on me once more. I inhale and the tiny movement jerks him into action. He bows and when he straightens, not an ounce of emotion is on his face.

"I've checked over the pond and it is perfectly safe and ready for Tsarevna," he says, addressing Tetia Tatiana.

I think the woman is fighting her urge to sigh dramatically as she once again scribbles something in her notebook.

"Very well, the men should be finished with breakfast by now. We can head down." She pivots in her signature way and then heads out of the room. Daria brings the hooded cloak over, so she can place it over my shoulders.

"Will that be warm enough?" Nikolai asks and I nod.

"It's more comfortable for me to move in than *shuba*."

After Daria secure the cloak over me, she places the fur headband and hands me the white fur hand muff to match. "See, nice and warm."

I smile at Nikolai and he blinks a few times as he stares at me, before he finally nods. He's dressed in his typical dark blue uniform, but today he's wearing a long coat over it as well.

We leave my rooms behind and head down to the lower floor garden and the path that will take us to the pond. This part of the castle gardens is the most unexplored by me. I've only been to the pond a few times with Ivan Popyalof and back when I was younger. Technically, I wasn't allowed to skate, as it would be considered a dangerous activity, but Ivan Popyalof taught me anyway. Not that I would be skating anyway. I think Tetia Tatiana might pass out if she saw me wearing ice skates with their oh-so-sharp blades. I can't blame her, but I do wish Ivan Popyalof was here.

My heart squeezes at the thought of him and I truly hope he's well. Missing him has become second nature, but I won't allow myself to dwell on it for more than a second, before I tuck that all away.

I feel someone's eyes on me and when I glance over my shoulder I find Nikolai watching me. I think he might know what I'm thinking, even though we haven't discussed it. He's become very good at reading me, even when I'm trying to hide.

"I will stop by the kitchens for refreshments," Daria

tells me when we reach the first floor. Tetia Tatiana tasked her and a few others to bring hot tea to the pond.

This leaves Nikolai and me to walk over to the pond alone. As usual, Tetia Tatiana has power walked ahead, but I'm okay with that. The air feels amazing against my skin and I turn my face to the sun the moment we're outside.

I stay like that for a minute, enjoying the crisp morning in the way I haven't been able to in a while. With Nikolai just an arm length away I feel at peace. But I know we can't just stay out here like that. I open my eyes and turn to face him.

"You look like a Snegurochka," he says the moment our eyes meet.

"The maiden made of snow?" I ask, "Wasn't she the one who danced with the girls in the village and ended up jumping over a fire and disappearing?"

"That's one story," he replies, his eyes still on me. "But she is also a beautiful maiden who is said to be the granddaughter of Grandfather Frost and helps him bring gifts to children."

"Ah, of course." I try not to show how much the word beautiful coming from his lips has affected me. I flex my hands inside the hand muff, trying to appear unaffected. Somehow, that one comment and his gentle gaze have made me feel better.

"We should go before they send out a search party," I comment and then walk past Nikolai and toward the pond. It really isn't fair that he is the only one who can make me feel all of these feelings, when he isn't even in the running for my hand.

NIKOLAI

I CAN'T STOP STARING at Alyonka and it's completely unacceptable. It also doesn't help that I'm about to watch her being courted by five very undeserving men. This attitude is also unacceptable. They might not be winning any endorsements from me, but they are still here for a good cause. I have to put my feelings inside and do my job.

"*Dobroe utro*," Alyonka greets the men as soon as we step into the learning. The pond isn't all the big, surrounded by tall trees on every side. I'm not really surprised the weather is holding out and I know I should tell Alyonka about Chudo's roll in all of this, but it's not something we can discuss at the moment. So I stay beside her as the men come up to greet her.

Two wooden benches have been set up on the side so the men have a place to change into their skates. On the opposite end is another bench where Alyonka can rest if she chooses to do so. But knowing her, she'll stay right near the pond the whole time.

"Thank you for coming out here. Isn't it a lovely day?" She asks and Baron Denis is the only one that replies with an affirmative. The others all look...a little concerned.

"Aren't you skating as well?" Knyaz Boris asks and I narrow my eyes at him. He was unhappy when she first announced ice skating and clearly, he's still unhappy.

"Unfortunately, it's not something I can participate in," Alyonka replies and the other men huffs—actually huffs in response.

"You will make us put ourselves in danger on this ice, but won't do the same yourself?" He asks, glancing at the other men. "That seems unfair."

I move forward before I can help myself, but I don't make it far before Alyonka steps right into my path, making me freeze.

"What is unfair is being cursed as a baby," Alyonka says it with a smile, but Knyaz Boris does realize his mistake at her words. Not that it stops him from speaking up again, because he clearly does not know how to shut up.

"Then why hold a competition you cannot participate in?" He asks and I can't tell if he's actually being serious or not. What kind of a question is that?

"Because, Boris Stepanich, I'm not the one competing, you are. A fact that you have seemed to have forgotten." Alyonka cocks her head to the side, looking very much like a queen. "I hope you skate better than you hold your tongue, because it has put you in the last place for now."

He bristles immediately as the other men try not to laugh out loud. But one look from Alyonka silences them. I'm surprised Knyaz Georgiy hasn't spoken up, he's usually the one who complains the most. But when I look at him now, I see that he looks the most at ease since the beginning of the competition.

Tatiana steps up and motions for the men to head over to the benches and put the skates on. Alyona walks over to stand near the edge of the pond, looking at it wistfully. It takes much of my self control not to reach for her. Instead, I focus on the men.

They're clearly cold, being out here for more than a few minutes, which tells me a lot. I'm sure Alyonka sees it as well. Baron Denis and Graf Sergey are both uncomfortable with cold, but they're the only ones not complaining out loud. The other three keep grumbling under their breath.

"Lev Ignatovich, why don't you go first," Alyonka calls out and the man stands up from the bench with a nod. He walks over to the pond a bit shaky, but not unusual for someone on skates. But when he steps on the ice, the shakiness becomes more evident. He wobbles a lot, but still continues to try, keeping himself upright by stubbornness at this point. He makes his way over to us, nearly running into Alyonka when he tries to stop. I have to catch him with one arm.

"*Tsarevna* Alyona, this is definitely the hardest thing I've ever done," he says and chuckles. Maybe not the response I expected from him, but not bad. "As your husband, will I be required to skate often?"

"Only on days the snow is on the ground," Alyonka replies with the utmost seriousness, making the other man laugh. I can't help it, that nasty green monster rises up in me and I fight the urge to push him down. It's official, I have lost my mind and reverted to being ten years old apparently.

Graf Sergey comes out next and he is a little more sure on his feet, but still not great. It's clear they haven't had much practice, which is to be expected. Baron Lev tries to move to the side as Graf Sergey skates over, but neither one of them do a good job of it, running into each other and ending up on their butts.

"Are you alright?" Alyonka asks and I can tell she's trying not to smile at their mishap. They look very frustrated with themselves, but not angry, so that's a good sign. I can see why Alyonka would've wanted this competition, beside simply having an excuse to go outside. Because that is definitely part of the reason. She looks so happy to be out here. I wonder if Chudo is somewhere in the trees around us and he can see how he made her happy by fixing the weather.

Knyaz Georgiy steps out on the ice next and immediately, I can tell why he was looking so smug. He's very good. He does a few laps around the pond, before he come to a step in front of Alyonka.

"Georgiy Leonidovich, where did you learn how to skate so well? You're from a kingdom the hardly sees winter." Alyonka asks and the man puffs up his chest much in a way Chudo did last night. He's looking to be praised.

"I am very good at a lot of things, *Tsarevna* Alyona," *Knyaz* Georgiy says, and does a little circle around Baron Lev and Graf Sergey, as the other two roll their eyes at him. "It really is a shame you can't come out here and skate. We could do circles around everyone else. I might even be better at skating than you. Would you be okay with that?"

He doesn't even wait for a response, before he skates off to show off some more. I glance at Alyonka just as she shifts in place, rearranging her cloak a little, before quickly putting her hand back in the hand muff. I narrow my eyes a little, but before I can comment, Knyaz Boris is on the ice and he is an absolute mess. He fall immediately and a very unacceptable word leaves his mouth.

"*Knyaz* Boris!" Tatiana exclaims, rushing over to him and trying to tug him to a standing position. *Knyaz* Georgiy zooms past them with a laugh and wow, I cannot stand that man. Daria arrives then, with another one of the staff from the kitchens, carrying thermos and cups.

Tatiana is still trying to help *Knyaz* Boris back to his feet, while the others simply look on. Well, *Knyaz* Georgiy keeps skating around them, forward and backward, but not offering to help.

"I think we all know who the winner of this competition is," *Knyaz* Georgiy calls out and this time Alyonka does roll her eyes when no one is watching her. Well, no one but me.

"I was going to have them play a game, but I think this tells me all I need to know," she comments. Baron Denis makes his way over to Alyonka through the snow and bows deeply when he reaches her.

"I apologize, *Tsarevna* Alyona, but I have never skated and therefore, it would be pointless for me to try." Admitting defeat is difficult, so I have to respect the man.

"It's quite alright, Denis Alexandrovich. I knew at least a few of you might have an issues, but I appreciate you being honest with me."

She doesn't have to say it, but she clearly wants to call *Knyaz* Boris on his lack of being up front of her.

"That's enough," she calls out and the men look more than relieved. Daria pours a cup of hot tea to Alyonka and hands it to her. Tsarevna looks at her hands and pull a set of mittens out of my pocket and hand them to her. She stares at them in surprise and I simply raise an eyebrow. She hands me the hand muff and pulls on the mittens, before she takes the cup Daria offers to her. She takes a sip of the drink, stealing a glance at me, while the others gather around.

"Like I thought, a waste of time," *Knyaz* Boris

comments low enough that he's not talking to us, but I know Alyonka hears him anyway. So do the others.

"It was not a waste of time for me. Did you see how amazing I am on skates?" *Knyaz* Georgiy comments. The men are shivering from the cold, very not used to it, and they nearly down the whole cup in one go.

"If it's okay with you, Tsarevna Alyona, I would like to head back to the room," Baron Denis asks and she agrees immediately. The others bows and head for the bench immediately, looking to take the skates off. Only *Knyaz* Georgiy lingers and I can tell he wants to hear he's the winner.

"Thank you for this morning, you were very impressive," Alyonka tell him, offering him a kind smile and that seems to satisfy him for the moment. He moves off as well and then one by one, they leave.

"I hope you're satisfied with this waste of time. The next competition will be a previously chosen one by me." Tatiana stops in front of Alyonka, her annoyance clear as day.

"Thank you for your time," Alyonka says simply, surprising Tatiana, who was definitely expecting an argument. The woman shakes her head ones and then looks at me, her dislike evident.

"When you return," Tatiana says, turning her attention back to Alyonka, "be prepared. We don't have a lot of time."

Which that, she pivots and heads off into the woods,

leaving Alyonka and me alone with Daria and the other staff member, who quickly pack up the thermos and cups, taking Alyonka's, and head off as well. But not before I notices Daria give Alyonka a look I don't quite understand.

Alyonka glances at the pond, sighs a little and turns to head back as well, when I reach out and catch her by her cloak.

"Stay."

twenty-four

ALYONKA

I don't want to agree with Tetia Tatiana about ice skating being a waste of time, but I kind do have to agree. What did I actually learn? That Georgiy Leonidovich is incredibly boastful and Boris Stepanich is simply irritating? I already knew both of those things. All this did is make me long to skate. I thought being near the pond, even if I couldn't participate will be enough, but it's not.

"What is it?" I ask Nikolai when he keeps me in place with a hand on my cloak. I curl my fingers into a fist and spread them out again, amazed at the fact that Nikolai brought me mittens. But should I be? He plans for every outcome.

"What's so special about skating? Why did you want

to do it so badly?" He asks and I almost forget how to breathe. I don't even realize it until this moment that this is what I wanted. I wanted the men to ask me why I pushed for it, why we were out here in the first place. But not one of them did that.

I meet Nikolai's gaze and find him watching me patiently. His hand is still on my cloak and I take a step toward him, closing some of the distance between us. With him looking at me like that and us being out here where it feels like we're completely removed from the world, I decide to be honest.

"There's freedom out here," I say, "It's like I'm a different person. The curse doesn't exist and I'm allowed to do what I want." Nikolai doesn't speak, simply continues to watch me. So I continue.

"For obvious reasons, I wasn't allowed to skate. Too dangerous, just like everything else that one would qualify as fun," I chuckle and Nikolai smiles. "But Ivan Popyalof taught me anyway and the few times that we were out here, I felt like I do when I'm dancing. Like I'm fully myself, even if it's just for a few moments. When I suggested this competition, I wanted to see if anyone else could find the magic in this simple pastime. But maybe it's just a me thing."

Nikolai doesn't say anything for a moment, before he turns and starts walking toward the lone bench, away from the others. His hand on my cloak pulls me alone with him and I'm too curious not to follow anyway.

He leads me to the bench and sits me down, before he walks into the forest. I turn, watching him disappear for a moment and then come back with two sets of ice skates.

"Nikolai?" I can't even put together words for the questions that are rushing through my mind. I watch him walk over to me, before getting down on his knees in front of me.

"I think that if you want to experience the magic, you should experience the magic."

He reaches over for my foot and unlaces my boots, before he carefully replaces it with the ice skate. I can't seem to move as I watch him tug the shoe in place and then proceed to tighten in. He does the same thing for the other foot, before he takes a seat beside me. In silence, he pulls his one ice skates on and then he stands.

"Come one, Duchess. Show me what you've got."

He offers me his hand and I don't hesitate to take it, as he pulls me to a standing position. Carefully, he guides me onto the ice, keeping himself facing me. When we're both on the pond, he continues to skate backwards as I try to find my balance. My body jerks forward and Nikolai is there to catch me against him, one hand on my elbow, the other around my waist. I stare up at him, my heart beating so intensity I'm sure he can feel it against his chest, even though all the layers of our warm outwear.

A light breeze ruffles his hair and I fight the urge to push it away from his forehead. I can feel us moving and I realize we're skating, with him going backwards to keep me in his arms.

"When did you plan this?" I ask.

"When I came to check on the integrity of the pond," he replies. He pulls back a little, keeping his hands holding onto mine as I feel more sure on my feet.

"Why?"

"Because I could tell how much you wanted to do this, so I wanted to give you a chance if the opportunity presented itself."

I don't even have words for that, so I act instead. I tug on his arms, pulling him closer to me, until we're chest to chest once more. I want to ask him how he can always tell exactly what I need, how he can read me so well. I want to pull him closer and stay like this for the rest of the day. I tug him to me when suddenly, he is hit with a snowball on his shoulder. I twist in the direction that it came and I find Chudo at the edge of the pond.

"*Play!*" He says and I grin at him. "*See gift? Handsome!*"

Chudo lifts his chin, showing off his neck and I see a familiar scarf.

"Why is my dragon wearing your scarf?" I ask, turning to Nikolai who's brushing the snow off his shoulder.

"Because I didn't have any piroshki for him," Nikolai replies. I furrow my brow in confusion and glance back at the dragon.

"*Helped. Made snow go away. Me!*" Chudo is very proud and I'm very confused.

"When were you with Chudo?" I ask Nikolai, "How did you make the snow go away?" I ask Chudo, as I skate over to him. He offers me his forehead for scratches and I oblige.

"He can apparently effect the weather," Nikolai replies, skating up beside me.

"Is that why we had good weather every time you came to visit?" I gasp, looking at the dragon in new light.

"*Good Chudo. Made happy! More pets!*" He purrs as I continue to scratch him, shutting his eyes in pure bliss.

"*Da*, you made me happy," I say, but I'm not looking at Chudo. I'm looking at Nikolai.

NIKOLAI

I COULD'VE STAYED out on that pond with Alyonka for the rest of the day, but Tatiana sent Daniil to come get us just a few minutes after Chudo arrived. I can't tell if she knew we were out there skating, or she simply wanted to make sure Alyonka didn't have any fun since she's been defying her. She called us back, sending Alyonka straight to the library to read.

After being outside, Alyonka was more than happy to put on her fuzzy socks, grab a giant fuzzy blanket and curl up on the divan with a book. While I went to discuss a few technical plans with Timofey regarding out trip. Hopefully, Chudo can keep the weather nice for a few more days, because the coronation day is approaching and we need to be leaving soon.

The rest of the day was spent much like our previous days. Alyonka had lunch with the suitors, begrudgingly announcing Knyaz Georgiy as the winner of the competition and then spending the diner time with him alone. He had not let her speak much, which she later said was fine, because she didn't feel like talking anyway. I watch her make patterns with her fingers again, which is why instead of making sure she is snuggled in her bed and resting, I'm sneaking her down to the moonlit ballroom after everyone else has gone to bed.

The fact of the matter is that I am absolutely weak when it comes to her. She turns those beautiful green eyes on me and I will do anything she asks. Which is why I fought with Tatiana on her behalf in the first place. The moment I mentioned the coronation and all the people she could meet, I saw the light come into her eyes. She has shared with me just how lonely she feels. I want to do everything in my power to make sure she doesn't feel like that often.

We've truly perfected this sneaking down to the ballroom routine. Even though everything is mostly dark, we have no issues finding our way. Alyonka keeps her fingers clasped on my jacket as I lead the way. All I want to do is reach down and take her hand in mine, like I had the chance to do on the pond today, but that's never going to be my place.

Once inside the ballroom, Alyonka walks over to the middle of the room immediately. Her eyes are on the large windows and the moonlight shining through.

"I want to try something," Alyonka announces turning toward me. I have moved away from the door, but I stay near the end of the room, giving Alyonka all the space she needs to move around.

"What is it?" I ask and she motions for me to come up to her. I walk toward her slowly, until I'm only about a meter away. She holds up her hand and I stop. Without a word, she turns back toward the windows and we stand like that for a moment, as if we're the only two people in the world, surrounded by glass and snow.

"Nikolai?"

"Duchess."

She glances at me with a smile.

"Catch me."

Alyonka moves before the words even register, taking two steps and then leaping at me. I react automatically, catching her around the waist. The movement spins us, as her arms come around my neck and one of her legs wraps around my waist. I turn with her, spinning to the left, as I hold her close. She laughs and I can't help it as I keep spinning us.

We move around the room and then she throws her arms out, arching her back and I shift my hands to support her. Her hair is wild, fanning out all around us, and she feels so perfect in my arms I have to blink against the sudden onslaught of images.

Alyonka and I dancing in the moonlight.

Alyonka and I on a picnic.

Alyonka and I laughing freely with other people in the room.

Small moments in time that we could never have.

As if she knows what I'm thinking, she leans forward, placing her hands on my shoulders and lifting herself slightly. I wrap my arms right over her thighs, keeping her in place as we stare at each other. Our faces are only a few breaths apart and she looks so beautiful it actually makes my head spin.

The way she's looking at me makes me feel like I'm the most important person in Skazka. A lock of hair falls forward over her shoulder, tickling my cheek and she slowly moves her fingers over my skin, to keep it away from my eyes. Her touch is slow and gentle and it sends a plethora of goosebumps over my body. My arms flex where I'm holding her and I swear she lets out a tiny gasp.

Every look across the room, every shared moment behind closed doors—each a memory I will carry with me for the rest of my life. But it's all it can ever be. The reminder of that, the weight of that truth, is what breaks me out of my stupor.

I squat, gently placing Alyonka back on the floor. Once I know she's standing, I move back, trying to put some distance between us. Her arms are still locked round my neck and she tugs them closer once, before she lets go. I take a step back and then another, giving both of us some room.

We're breathing hard, as if we've run a marathon while I can't take my eyes off her.

She's wearing one of her pink dresses, long sleeves, open neckline, and a lot of tulle. Her hair has fallen out of her signature braid, her cheeks are pink and her eyes are shining. There isn't enough air left in this room and I wish there was a way to open a window. Just so I would have something to do, instead of completely losing my mind over this gorgeous woman.

A sudden gust of wind outside is so strong it rattles the glass windows, making both of us jump. Alyonka chuckles nervously and I can't help but smile.

"Do you remember when we snuck down to the kitchen during a rain storm?" Alyonka asks, her voice unnaturally loud after so much silence. I glance at her, but she's watching the snow falling again. "I really wanted that milky chocolate drink that I was not supposed to know about. But we were playing in the smaller garden when my father had a stroll with the visiting ambassador."

"I remember," I say, unable to keep the smile from my

face. "When you heard the human realm had chocolate milk you were ready to petition anyone and everyone to smuggle you there."

"I was so determined. Even though my father was so against breaking tradition, I wanted to go. I wanted to find out for myself."

"And then we discovered that the ambassador brought some of the sweet powder with him and we could try it."

I remember how nervous Alyonka was, how tightly she held onto my hand while we tried to dodge soldiers stationed around the castle. We were in a sitting room, waiting out the shift change, when Tsar and the ambassador came in. Alyonka and I had to climb inside of a large trunk and wait them out.

"It was the first time you hugged me."

I twist to look at her, surprised. She's not looking at me, she keeps watching the snow, but there's a small smile on her face.

"Until then, I don't think anyone has ever held me. Maybe when I was a baby," she says, her voice low, sending pleasant shivers up my spine. "But that day, you opened up your arms and you wrapped them around me and held me close. It was such a small thing, but it made me feel like I was worth something."

I want to reach for her now, it's taking all of my self control not to reach for her now. She sounds so sad and I can't bare it. But I don't reach for her, because it's not my place and it never will be. Instead, I offer her a little bit of myself.

"You made me feel important that day," I say, and it's my turn to watch the snow fall because I can't look at her and stay in place. "There were kids at the village who would pick on me constantly. I wasn't going to school because I had to help my mama and with my father gone, I was the man of the house. But the kids who weren't in my situation didn't understand why I wore dirty clothes or why my stomach was growling when I should've had plenty to eat."

I take a deep breath, because a part of me can't believe I'm saying these words out loud. But it's Alyonka. If I was ever going to say this out loud, it would've been to her.

"That day, I was afraid that you would say something. My shirt was dirty and my shoes were falling apart. But you never seemed to notice. You didn't care. You were just happy to see me and when we climbed into that trunk and I pulled you close, you didn't hesitate. You clung to me like I was someone important, like I could protect you from anything. That moment…and you…you had always stayed with me."

I feel a tiny tug on my sleeve and I glance down to find Alyonka's fingers pinching the material. When I look at her, I find her eyes glittering in the moonlight, her face open and earnest.

"You had always stayed with me too."

twenty-five

ALYONKA

The moment between Nikolai and I haunts my every waking hour. Neither one of us expected to be so honest with each other, but it's as if we simply can't help it. I could always be myself with him and apparently all the time apart hasn't changed that.

It's been two days. We haven't really been alone since that night and maybe that's for the best, because I'm about to travel to another kingdom in a very secretive matter and I need to be focusing on that. It's been a long time since anyone tried to harm me in any way, but it would still be better for us to travel without anyone knowing it's me.

I still can't believe Chudo can affect the weather, but in a way it also makes sense. It makes me feel like Skazka is giving me this chance to prove myself. Because that is kind of how I'm feeling.

It's not about anyone else. It's me proving to myself that I can do this. It's about me being the kind of a leader this kingdom needs.

I know that I've always been determined to do whatever it takes and marry whoever my parents decided on. I've participated in the competitions, listened and done everything that is required of me, but at the end of the day, I still don't know what kind of Tsarina I would be.

Meeting other queens, seeing how another kingdom runs on my own, without the screen of my father being present and telling me how I should feel or think is going to be a new experience for me.

Daria and I talked about it last night. She is the only other one who is coming with us. The plan is to travel light, without telling anyone I am going. This will keep the rumors to the minimum and keep the danger at bay the best it can. I haven't left my rooms today at all, preparing the suitors to not see me for the next week.

The carriage will take us over to the village and the trading passage and then we'll take a portal. Nikolai's status has a lot of pull and we will have no issues securing passage even without telling people who I am. Apparently this is how a lot of people travel, especially the ambassadors when they have to jump around the kingdoms. Skazka is so vast, this allows for it to be a lot more accessible. High Queen Calista—the only queen with magic in the land of Skazka—has made a lot of amazing discoveries and opened up a lot of opportunities for the land to grow. The fact that I get to meet her at the coronation is enough of a reason for me to go.

By the third day, the weather has held up and it's time to get ready to leave. I wake up earlier than usual and instead of staying in bed, I put on my fur *shuba* and head for the rooftop landing. I need to see Chudo before I go. He flew away quickly when he heard Daniil approaching the pond. I can't just leave without saying something to him, but actually since I can communication with him now, I'm a lot less anxious. Almost like he let's me know he's okay without me even realize it.

At least, that was my thought last night when I wanted to go see him but instead stayed in bed, because I felt at peace.

"I'll be leaving," I say the moment I'm on the landing. I shuffle through the snow, walking up to the edge of the space, projecting my words in my mind and out loud. "It is for a coronation. I am excited and nervous," I admit, hoping he can hear me.

"But I will be back, so please watch over my home for me."

I stay like that for a few moments, but nothing comes back. Sighing, I turn to go back when suddenly Chudo appears, landing in front of me.

"*Long away, why?*" He asks and I walk over to scratch that space between his eyes.

"It is a long way, but it's necessary," I reply, as he purrs. "I'll be back soon."

"*I come. Keep no snow.*"

"Not this time. But I thank you for keeping the snow away." The disappointment I feel is so heavy I almost gasp.

"*I want.*"

"I know," I lean over putting my forehead against his and he sighs in relief. "I want it too, but not this time. I need you to make sure everything is okay here."

He doesn't seem happy by that, but he agrees.

"*Soon. Come. You.*" He says, as I give him an extra scratch and step back.

"I will come back soon," I reply and he gives me one last look and then jumps straight into the sky. Seeing him before I leave definitely makes me feel better, so I head back downstairs with a slightly more enthusiasm.

Nikolai arrives about a minute after I'm back inside of my room, surprising me.

"What is it?" I ask, studying his face. Before he replies, the door opens and Tetia Tatiana steps inside, with one of the staff from the kitchens.

"Daria is sick. Elena will help you get dressed." Tetia Tatiana motions to the girl and she steps forward. I glance between Nikolai and Tetia Tatiana, wondering how this is going effect our plans, because I am not backing down. I lean forward looking Tetia Tatiana in the eye before I whisper,

"It's still happening."

I turn to Elena where she waits in the bathroom, and shut the door so I can get ready. Let Nikolai talk it out with Tetia Tatiana. I get ready automatically, my mind on Daria and our journey. I would've definitely felt better having her with me. But I can't back down just because she's not coming along.

Elena doesn't speak much, but she is efficient. She helps me into one of my heavier dresses, with the neckline that goes up to my collarbone and sleeve that end halfway down my hand. The dress is a combination of a royal attired and a traditional *sarafan*. It's just instead of the jumper dress being worn over a blouse, I'm wearing a warm dress underneath. Once my hair is braided and my dress is in place, we step back out into the bedroom area.

Nikolai gives me a quick once over and I don't think I'll ever get used to the way his eyes travel over me. Or the tiny sparks they leave behind. I keep my face free of emotion when I turn to Tetia Tatiana, who looks less than thrilled.

"You may go," she addresses Elena and I barely have a chance to thank her before she's gone.

"Traveling without Daria is not a good idea," Tetia Tatiana says, turning her attention to me.

"Are you concerned with *Tsarevna's* reputation?" Nikolai asks and I demand for my face to keep itself from blushing. "Because I can assure you—"

"Oh please, don't be absurd," Tetia Tatiana waves him

away, "As if anyone would ever assume the two of you are together."

Her words feel like a slap, but not to me. To Nikolai. I glance at him and at his unreadable expression and have the sudden urge to go to him. But I don't.

"Tsarevna Alyona has never taken care of herself. She has never traveled alone. She has—"

"She is standing right here," I snap, my voice harder than I've ever allowed it to sound in front of Tetia Tatiana. The other woman stammers as I step closer to her. "Stop making excuses in order to get your way. I will be more than fine and perfectly protected. Now please, step aside. We have a schedule to keep."

I don't wait for her to say anything else, but walk over to take the *shuba* off the hanger and pull it over my shoulders before either of them can move. Then, I leave my room behind and head downstairs.

NIKOLAI

I WATCH as Alyonka says goodbye to Daria, my heart full of pride and concern at the same time. Seeing Alyonka stand up for herself will always be my favorite pastime. But I am concerned about the two of us traveling together, because this will be a lot for Alyonka. And not only physically, but emotionally as well. It would've helped to have Daria along.

"Everything is ready," Timofey says, coming up beside me. Outside of Tatiana and Daria, he's the only other person who knows what we're doing. It seems safest that way, and it's truly the best plan we have to give her this opportunity. Daria packed up a bag for Alyonka before she got sick and Timofey got the carriage ready for us. He'll be driving us to the village.

"Are you sure this is a good idea?" He asks for what seems like the fiftieth time. I understand the concern. If—nyet, when—Tsar finds out about this, I might lose my position, but I can't change my mind now. Not when Alyonka is looking forward to this with pure excitement.

"It's the only idea I have," I reply honestly, and Timofey doesn't seem to need more than that. He clasps me on the shoulder once, just as Alyonka leaves Daria and comes over to me. I reach over and tug her hood over her head, before buttoning the top button of her *shuba*. She's bundled up, but also her face is covered. Not that many people would recognize her, considering she's been away from the castle only a few times. But she is striking as a person, and we need to keep the staring to a minimum.

We take the back hallways and come out at the servants entrance to the stables, that lead out to the check point at the outer wall where staff can enter. We're leaving during breakfast, which means most of the staff has arrived and everyone is otherwise occupied.

Once inside the carriage, Timofey takes the reigns, while I sit beside her at the back. She continues to stare out the window, and I can't help but stare at her. Which is how I notice her wringing her hands together amidst the fur of her coat. I reach over, placing my hand over hers and she jumps, twisting to look at me.

There's so much uncertainty in her gaze it makes my heart hurt.

"Talk to me, Alyonushka," I say, keeping my voice low and her eyes fill up immediately. She drops her head down for a moment and when she looks up at me, the tears are gone. She's always been very good at presenting herself in the proper light, but not for the first time I wish she wouldn't pretend with me. Not when we're alone.

"What if I'm bad at it?" She asks, her voice barely above a whisper. My heart thumps against my chest, filling with so much emotion for her that all I want to do is pull her against me and protect her from the whole world. Instead, I move my fingers against her palm, spreading them out so I can lace my fingers with hers. But I don't speak, letting her organize her thoughts.

"I've only ever been to events with my parents. They tell me what to do and when to speak. I've never made friends outside of Daria. But if I'm being honest, she sort of adopted me before I could even let myself imagine us being friends."

"You made friends with me," I say, making circles with my thumb against her skin. She seems to breathe a little easier, relaxing her shoulders, but holding on tightly to my hand.

"Are you sure? It was so long ago."

"It wasn't that long ago and I'm absolutely sure. You bullied me into being your friend."

That makes her sit up straight, outrage all over her face.

"I did no such thing!"

"Mhhmm, I remember it like it was only yesterday. I was living a peaceful life and then you came barging in—"

"Well, if it was so traumatizing—"

"It really was. I've had to speak with multiple councilors about my troubling childhood."

"Clearly it hasn't helped. You're still a bit baby."

"Ah, so you do remember!" I point a finger at her and she grins.

"You were crying the first time we met," she says, a teasing look in her eyes that makes me think all kinds of inappropriate scenarios that are anything but childish.

"And you punched me in the stomach," I say, which makes her laugh.

It's true. I was crying. Some of the kids at the village were especially mean and I snuck in to see my mama, but she was busy and I didn't feel like getting her into trouble. So I sat under a tree in one of the gardens and cried. Until Alyonka showed up.

She was so clean and proper, I thought she was magic. And when I wouldn't respond to her probing, she went ahead and punched me in the stomach. It didn't hurt, but it shocked me enough that I stopped crying and started telling her how I felt. She listened, like I was talking about the most amazing thing in the world, and when I was done, she reached into her dress's pocket and pulled out a *pirozok*. It was wrapped in a cloth handkerchief and it was one of the ones my mama made.

We stayed together till dinner and when I left to sneak back over to the village, I promised to come back. Which I did.

"I only lightly tapped you on the stomach. You were standing up so straight, I had to make sure you were real."

She squeezes my hand then and does something that nearly sends me into cardiac shock. She leans over and places her head against my shoulder for a moment.

"*Spasibo*, Nikolai," she whispers, before sitting back up and turning to look out the window. I truly fear no matter what happens in the future, I might not survive it at all. She'll marry someone else, become the amazing queen she is destined to be. While I'm not exactly sure how to live without my heart, since she's holding it hostage.

twenty-six

ALYONKA

Going through the portal is the most underwhelming experience. Nikolai greets the man stationed in front of it, gives him some papers and then we're motioned inside. He doesn't even check the bag Nikolai is carrying, which just shows how much status he holds. The portal is just a gate in the middle of the forest. Like abandoned ruins found in the middle of overgrown areas. But then Nikolai takes my hand and walks confidently below the arch and then we're in a forest no longer covered in snow.

I gasp as I stare at the spring time around us and when I glance at Nikolai he's smiling at me. The *shuba* I'm wearing is too hot immediately and I want to take it off.

"Amazing, isn't?" He asks and all I can do is nod. I

pull the coat off me and he takes it from my hands before I can protest. Capturing my hand in his once more, he leads me away from the gate and into the village.

It takes us no time at all to secure a carriage that'll take us to the castle. Since Tetia Tatiana hid the invitation and we had to wait for the weather to clear up, we're arriving right before the coronation. It's not ideal, but it's the best we could do.

"Do you want to change before we head over?" Nikolai asks and I nod. He leads us to another building and I notice a bed and breakfast sign over the door.

"Nikolai?" I tug on his hand and he throws a quick smile my way.

"I'll ask nicely," he says and I'm not sure how he's going to get us a room without renting one, but he does. The man behind the counter lets us in and I immediately reach for the bag Nikolai has been carrying. Daria packed my favorite pink gown. It's mostly tulle, so easily rolled up to fit in a bag.

I pull it out, spreading it on the bed. Nikolai cough once and I turn to find him near the door.

"I'll wait outside," he says, before he steps out. My cheeks are bright red as I turn back to the dress. Pulling the *sarafan* over my head takes some effort but I manage. The under dress is easier. But that's when I realize the real problem. The gown is laced up at the back and there is no way I can do it myself.

I rearrange it on the floor, stepping inside the circle

and pulling the skirt up over my hips, before I tug the sleeves over my arms. The sleeves are tulle and fluffy, leaving my shoulders bare. I keep a hand pressed against my chest, spinning to glance at the mirror on the vanity table. No matter how much I twist and turn, I can't get the dress laced up.

Instead of just my cheeks, my whole body feels like it's burning as I tiptoe over to the door and pull it open just a smidge.

"Nikolai," I say and he turns to glance at me, his eyes raking over my messy hair and the hand over my chest.

"What is it?" He steps closer, concerned.

"I need help," I manage to push past my lips, before I step behind the door and pull the door open wider. He steps back inside and I shut the door, too embarrassed to meet his eyes.

"It's a lace up back," I tell the floor, my back to the door. I pull my braid over my shoulder, keeping it in place with the front of my dress. "I can't do it by myself."

He doesn't speak and doesn't move, so I finally look up to meet his heated gaze. He's as still as a statue, but my movement must spring him into action, because he gives me one tense nod and steps toward me. I push away from the door and move to the center of the room, so I can see him in the mirror.

There's a moment of stillness between us and then his fingers brush against my bare back. An army of goosebumps erupt over my whole body and I suck in a breath, keeping myself as still as possible. He ducks his head, his face full of concentration as he begins to lace up the dress, starting at my lower back and moving up.

Each movement is so gentle it makes me feel dizzy. I watch him in the mirror, the way his eyes track each weaving in and out of the lacing. He seems to be holding his breath, as his fingers move, brushing my skin every so often.

The whole room feels like it is a thousand degrees and I swear he can hear how loudly my heart is beating. Or maybe it's his own. I can't really tell. All coherent thought has left me and it's only the feel of his fingers on my back that's keeping me grounded.

When he reaches the top of the dress, he ties it and then stands there, right behind me, as if he too is unable to move. I watch him start at the one spot on my back and decide to be the one that breaks the tension.

"*Spasibo*," I say, making him jump a little. He clears his throat and bows a little, taking a step back. Quickly, I walk over to my discarded dress and fold it up. Nikolai steps up and helps me put it in the bag, before he swings it over his shoulder. I pick up my shuba, and then turn to study Nikolai's outfit.

"You won't be too hot in the uniform?" I ask and he looks down at his standard blue military garb.

"Oh, I brought a change of clothing," he says and then raises his head. We stare at each other for a moment, before he places the bag on the bed.

"I will wait—" I begin, reaching for the door, but he catches me by the wrist. His touch is so gentle, yet sure, sending a bunch of tingling sensations up my arm.

"I can't let you go out there alone. Can you..." he looks around the room, thinking. The bathroom in this place is a share room down the hall, so I actually have no where to go. "Can you just turn around?"

I nod and turn immediately, facing the door. The room is incredibly quiet, it almost feels like my breathing is being broadcast like an announcement. It's hard not to think about the fact that Nikolai is undressing right behind me. But I'm glad he is—I mean, his uniform is made from heavy material. He would be so uncomfortable in this weather. So really, it's a good thing he's prepared and—

Somehow my senses have become magically enhanced because I swear I can hear the sound of material being pulled over skin. What is this thing happening in my brain? I have the urge to fan myself, but instead, I fold my hands in front of me, underneath the *shuba* that I'm still cradling, trying to mimic the way Nikolai becomes a statue anytime he's watching over me.

Well, it's easy for him. He's built like one of those gorgeous statues I've seen in books. Smooth marble, strong features—I might be having a medical emergency. Again. Should I ask to see a doctor?

"Alyonushka."

Nikolai's voice breaks through my thoughts and I turn

before I can think about it. But he's fully dressed, in a black button up shirt and black slacks. He finishes rolling up his sleeves to his elbows, exposing his forearms and I'm staring all over again. Somehow, he looks even more handsome like this—a tad bit relaxed, yet dangerous. I can't stop staring.

"Are you ready to go?" He asks, clearing his throat for what seems like the tenth time since coming in here.

"Oh, *da*. We should go." I say, and then I step back so he can lead me out of the room. Fresh air is definitely going to do me some good.

NIKOLAI

I<small>F ANYONE</small> ever wanted to torture me, I don't think nothing will come close to being in the room with Alyonka while I changed clothes. I couldn't stop staring at her back—the back I touched—as I buttoned up my own shirt. It's truly madness.

Now, she sits beside me in the carriage we rented, as we're heading for the castle. Thankfully, we can stow our items in the carriage during the coronation and the ball afterward. But right now, she's clutching her *shuba* to her like a blanket of comfort. I want to reach for her again, but then we have arrived and it's time I put the required distance between us.

I step out of the carriage first and offer Alyonka a hand. She follows slowly, her gaze focus on all the people around us and then the castle.

"Are you alright?" I ask and she nods, her whole attention on the castle looming over us. I watch her face, the small wonder that's plainly written all over her face and glance up to see what she sees.

The castle is slightly smaller than that of *Holodnova Tsarstva*, but only that it's not as wide. It's taller. There are multiple towers of different heights, and a lot of windows, especially on the upper floors. While Alyonka's castle keeps growing outward, this one seems to have been growing upward.

"I'm alright," Alyonka says glancing at me. "I guess I just never realized just how close we are. With the portals—the Skazka forest always seems so vast and unexplored, and yet, we're here in the matter of hours."

"The power of magic, right?" I say and something flashes in her gaze, some of the wonder of it all, gone.

"Let's see what the inside looks like," she says and steps forward. I realize then that she's been holding my hand after stepping out of the carriage. It's become so natural for us, this closeness, but as she walks in front of me, I know it's only an illusion. She's the Tsarevna, she walks first and I stay behind her.

Without another word, we head inside.

We follow the other people walking into the large doors at the front, some casting curious looks our way. *Tsarevna* Alyona has only been seen a few times and I'm not sure anyone here would actually recognize her. She's not wearing her royal robes and I'm not dressed in my uniform for this exact reason. We're trying to stay inconspicuous. At least until she starts dancing with the eligible gentlemen at the ball afterwards.

Just the thought of it leaves a bitter taste in my mouth.

I focus on our surroundings, making sure I'm on the lookout for any kind of danger. But honestly, I'm not expecting anything to happen. The stories of soon-to-be Ivanna Sergeevna and her seven warriors has become known across the land the moment she defeated her evil stepmother. If there's one thing Skazka does well it's gossip.

We step inside and Alyona is back to gawking at everything like she's never been inside of a castle before. The walls here are bright with color, blues and greens and reds. Most of the space is adored with paintings of all shapes and sizes, in golden frames. Much like our own castle. It's very tradition in its decor, which isn't all that surprising.

Alyonka and I head inside the open hall, finding a spot near the other royals closer to the front. There's a buzz of conversation around us, but no one is paying any attention as we move forward. Suddenly, Alyonka grabs my arm, her fingers digging into my shirt.

"It's her," she breathes out, her gaze fixed on someone

up front. I step closer to Alyonka so I can see what she sees and that's when I see her. The High Queen of Skazka, Calista herself. Her and her husband are at the front and it looks like she will be performing the coronation. The woman radiates so much power, and not only the magical kind. She holds herself with incredible pose, her husband grinning at her from beside her.

Of course, like everyone else across Skazka, we have hear of Queen Calista's triumph over the Shadowlands and Baba Yaga herself. Her adventures are chronicled in the history books. But I've never been close enough to see her with my own two eyes.

"She's magnificent," Alyonka breathes out and I have to agree. "And that must be the warriors," she continues and nods in the direction of the men coming up to line up on the sides of the throne. The murmur of conversation dies down and then balalaika music fills the space around us. The doors open and the future queen comes in. Alyonka's hand slides down the side of my arm and clasps my fingers tightly. I can't even tell if she knows what she's doing, her attention is on the woman in the yellow gown walking down the aisle toward the throne.

I know words are said and vows are spoken. I know there are tears and laughter and a beautiful speech by the now crowned Queen Ivanna. But I can't concentrate on any of that. My whole attention is on Alyonka's hand gripping my own.

I hear the words friend and love and then Alyonka is

looking up at me, unshed tears collecting on her eyelashes. There's so much emotion in that gaze that it nearly takes me to my knees. The hall erupts in cheers and clapping but Alyonka and I are unmovable. We stay just like that, hands clasped, staring at each other as if this is our last moment on earth.

twenty-seven

ALYONKA

There is so much activity around me I feel intoxicated.

We're in the ballroom now and people are definitely still celebrating even though it's been hours. I met Queen Ivanna right after the coronation, before she was whisked away for some legalities, but I like her already. Nikolai and I were able to eat lunch and walk the grounds before the festivities began. Even though I'm still nervous and very tired, I also feel the most relaxed. It almost feels like I can pretend that I'm someone else for the day, not a girl with a curse hanging over her head.

"Nikolai," I say without turning around, knowing that he's right at my back, "Is that bunny?"

My attention is on the throne placed in front of the

room and the small white fluff ball that's watching everything going on around it.

"I believe that's the magical creature Queen Ivanna found in the forest," Nikolai says, keeping his voice low. He's so close, I can feel his breath teasing my ear and all I want to do is just lean back into him. "I think Skazka is looking out for her queens."

I smile at that, understanding his meaning. Queen Ivanna was sent a magical bunny and I was sent a magical dragon. Chudo probably would've loved coming here and maybe one day I can let him do just that.

"Hello, Your Highness," a man comes up to me, a smile on his face. He's tall, blond, wearing a dark suit and holding out his hand. "I am Leonid from *Vodnova Tsarstva*. Would you care for a dance?"

I can't say no. When it was time to come into the ballroom, I was announced, much to Nikolai's discomfort. But we had to play our part and if we're going to stand in front of my parents and explain ourselves, I had to dance with the eligible suitors.

I take the man's hand, sending one look over my shoulder at Nikolai. He's back to his stoic bodyguard stance, but he does move through the crowd as I move around the dance floor. I can always feel his eyes on me.

So far, I have danced with a handful of men, none of whom sparked any kind of interest in me. When the dance is finished, the man bows, asking if he may have another dance later and I only smile and move back to my bodyguard.

"Not a winner," he says, his voice low at my back.

"Not even close," I reply, my eyes trained back on the room.

"Does your bodyguard keep a running list?" A voice asks from beside me and I didn't even see her approach. I jump a little, placing a hand over my heart. She's dressed in a dark red pantsuit, her hair long and slicked back in a high ponytail. She's tall, even if she wasn't wearing heels and she carries a lot of power around her.

"Sorry, hazard of the job. I have a tendency to just sneak up on people," she flashes me a smile that I can't ignore even if I tried. "I'm Ekaterina. The ambassador's daughter."

"Oh, it is nice to meet you, Ekaterina," I reply, pushing Nikolai back a little behind me. "I'm Alyonka."

He makes a noise of protest and I push even harder on his stomach, to keep him quiet. None of this escapes Ekaterina, of course.

"Everyone knows who you are, Tsarevna," she says, throwing a wink at Nikolai, "even if they didn't announce your presence with an official introduction. You're too beautiful to be just another guest."

I blush because I can't help myself and Ekaterina grins again. I'm not used to being spoken to with such familiarity, but I don't mind one bit. It makes me feel like we can actually be friends.

"Let's go mingle with the rest of these people. Or I see at least three men waiting to dance with you?"

I jump at the chance not to do that.

"Please lead the way."

She does, walking up to Queen Ivanna and Princessa Miraslava of *Zelonovo Korolevstva*, catching the end of their conversation. She jumps right in, as if she's completely at ease with them and I watch, fascinated. Maybe it's her profession, being an ambassador's daughter, she has to be good at people. Queen Nikita of the *Volkovskova Korolevstvo* is right behind us, looking for her four-year-old daughter.

I feel like a bystander, as I watch King Gavriil chase his daughter across the room, only stopping long enough to drop a kiss on Queen Nikita's cheek. The women around me laugh, sharing a comradeship that I can't even imagine being part of, when Queen Ivanna turns to me.

"Princessa Alyona, are you enjoying yourself?" She asks and I smile at her use of the title. My kingdom truly is the only one using the terms of royalty no one else does. The rest of the women look at me and I decide to be honest.

"Would it be too much trouble for you to pretend to require my presence by your side for the next ten dances or so?" I can't deal with these suitors anymore."

Everyone knows my story and I'm used to the combination of curiosity and almost fear I typically receive from others. But these women show me something I'm not used to, they show me sympathy.

"Your parents are very determined to find you a match before your nineteenth birthday, aren't they?" Princessa Miraslava asks and I nod. The fact that we're discussing all of this so naturally should be making me feel something, but all if feel is tired.

"Note for the future: christenings, don't have them. Keep your children away from any witches that might curse them out of spite."

Queen Ivanna is the closest to me, with Ekaterina on the other side and both of them reach for me at the same time. One squeezes my hand while the other pats my upper arm and suddenly, I want to cry. I was so scared of coming here, thinking I wouldn't be able to handle all this. But here I am, starting friendships with women who have overcome their own magical battles and are now standing strong in front of me.

"Noted." Queen Nikita says, her face full of compassion. "When the curse is lifted—" she gives me a look full of confidence, "we'll have a different kind of a party."

"I'll host. If you'll brave the cold," I say and the women agree immediately.

"We can have a slumber party!" Ekaterina announces and I look at her in confusion. "Sorry, I've been spending a lot of time in the human realm and their girl slumber parties are the best parties."

Everyone laughs and agrees and I feel elated somehow.

I can't help but glance over at Nikolai who's wearing his typical bodyguard expression, but with something else attached to it. When he meets my eyes I swear I can see pride in them. And it's directed at me.

When the time comes to leave, each of the women hug me tightly before promising to see me again.

"You sure you won't stay the night?" Queen Ivanna asks and I shake my head.

"We need to get back."

"Then I will see you again."

Just like that, we have formed a friendship. One I hope I can nourish in years to come.

When I climb into the carriage, my body feels like it's completely drained of energy.

"I can't believe I did that!" I say, as Nikolai climbs in beside me. "I mingled! With others my age. With women my age!" I look over at him and he's wearing that expression that would've made me pass out if I wasn't sitting down already. It's like I've suddenly hung the stars in the sky. My heart squeezes and it takes all of my self control not to go to him.

"You didn't think you would?" He asks.

"I didn't think I could," I reply honestly. "I've only done any kind of mingling within the walls of my own castle. It gives me an advantage. And the few times I've traveled with my father, he dis all the talking. I honestly didn't know I could do this."

I was afraid I would make a complete fool of myself,

but it ended up being the opposite. It feels incredible. I'm so hyped up, it feels like my heart is going to jump out of my chest.

"Oh, oh my. Is my heart supposed to be beating so hard?" I ask, placing a hand against it. Nikolai reaches for my hand, taking it in both of his.

"*Da*, it means it's doing its job."

I stare at him like he's lost his mind and then I chuckle.

"Ah, that's better. There she is."

We stay like that for a long tense moment and I feel like we're back at the coronation, with the applause exploding around us, but we're so focused on each other we can't seem to move. My heart finally calms, but only a little, because Nikolai's proximity always makes it act a little crazy.

"Why aren't we moving?" I ask, glancing out the window and realize we haven't. Nikolai frowns and then motions for me to stay, while he goes to check. He's gone but a few minutes, before he returns.

"Our carriage driver has apparently partied too hard and passed out in the stables. I watched the stable hand hitch up the horses, thinking he'll be here next, but *nyet*. He's definitely sleeping in the hay."

"Oh, so what do we do?" I ask. If we don't return when scheduled, I might never be allowed to leave the castle again.

Nikolai thinks it over, before he nods, as if agreeing with something I didn't hear.

"I'll take us. It's only about an hour by carriage. We can—"

"Can we walk?" I interrupt him before I even decide to do so. He looks completely surprised, and I'm surprised by my request as well. But the moment I said it, I really want to do it.

"If we walk, it'll take us a few hours. Also, I'm not sure it's a good idea, it could be dangerous."

"But you'll protect me."

Maybe it's exhaustion mixed with excitement. Maybe I'm just losing my mind, but I suddenly have this idea in my head and I know there will never be another chance for it.

"Nikolai," I say, leaning forward and covering some of that distance between us. "Can we walk and then camp in the woods? Just one night, maybe a few hours, I—I've always wanted to try it."

I'm almost positive he's going to say no. I understand how wild it sounds. But I've read about all these Skazka adventures and I've never even come close to one. Instead of an adventure, I will take an experience. I try to see if I can come up with a more plausible argument, but then I don't need to.

"We can camp in the woods," Nikolai says.

NIKOLAI

I REALLY TRULY AND completely cannot say no to this woman.

"Stay here." I tell her, as I leave the carriage behind and head back inside the castle. It takes me no time at all to sweet-talk one of the ladies in the kitchen to pack us a little package with some pastries, sausages, bread, and tea. With a wink, she also hands me blanket and I thank her, before I head back over to Alyonka. I'm not sure what the woman was picturing is going to happen, but I'm thankful she was so gracious with the supplies.

When we leave the carriage behind, I'm grateful Alyonka is wearing her lace up boots, so there's no issues with her heels getting stuck anywhere. I keep us on the road, with the forest to the right. The moon is out and full, eliminating our way in such a way that makes it seem like it's not even night.

There isn't much when it comes to navigating. The village is a straight path from the castle. Which is probably why I said yes to this middle of the night camping adventure. This isn't exactly in my plan for the trip. Timofey will wonder where we are, but there isn't a way for me to let him know. We always give each other a full day before we get concerned. So if we're not back by tomorrow, he'll send out a search party.

But even so, none of these concerns seem to matter, however, because Alyonka is having the time of her life. She walks a few paces in front of me, clutching her coat, and doing a little dance every now and then. I can't even tell if she knows she's doing it or if it's simply her happiness.

"Alyonka, let's stop here," I finally call out, when I think we're close enough to the village that it won't take much more walking. She comes over to me, looking up expectedly. I shake my head a little and then I step off the main road and lead us to the forest on the right.

The farther we go, the more dense the forest becomes, but Alyonka doesn't complain. She keeps pace with me until we come to a small clearing. It's barely even a clearing, just a small circular space between the trees. Maybe only about two three lengths of me all the way across in a diameter.

"Here?" Alyonka asks and I nod. I place the bag on the ground and she leaves her coat beside it, before looking at me again.

"What?"

"Should we collect some wood for the fire?" She asks and the excitement on her face is blinding. I want her to be this happy all the time.

"*Da*, let's collect some wood. Look for dry sticks and leaves." I advise and the immediately starts looking. I follow her as she heads farther into the woods, keeping an eye on her as I also look. When we both found enough, we walk back to the clearing.

It takes me no time at all to start a fire, after years of military training and living in the coldest kingdom. This weather is definitely such a contrast. I spread out the blanket and Alyonka settles in comfortably.

"Are you sure you don't want to stay at the nearby village?" I ask. Night has fallen fully now, and the forest around us is full of noises.

"I've never been in the forest like this before." Alyonks is shaking her head. "In my kingdom, even if I wanted to camp in the gardens on castle grounds, I'd probably freeze. But here—" she looks around, staring at the trees as if she's seeing them for the first time. "Everything is so different. I'm not...I'm not ready for things to go back to the normal."

I can't fault her in that. She's been so protected, so locked behind those doors, that this must feel like the grandest adventure. And all we're doing is sitting in front of a fire in a dark forest. I thought I'd be more anxious about being out here, but for some reason, I'm not. Almost like Skazka herself I telling me it will be okay.

I shake my head at the absurd thoughts and turn back to Alyonka.

"What are you thinking about?" She asks. She pulls her knees up to her chest, resting her head there as she looks at me. We're close enough that it would take no effort for me to reach out and touch her, and it feels too close and too far at the same time.

"Oh you know, nothing in particular. Just how to keep you safe." I pour Alyonka some tea and she takes the tiny cup gratefully.

"Ah, of course, the bodyguard duty," she says, smiling and take a sip of her tea. "You're very good at that."

"Am I?" I can't help but ask.

"Of course! You're all about my safety. You prevent me from doing all kinds of things!"

"Maybe I should be even better at that," I say, suddenly overcome with sadness. She continues to watch me and I know the question is on the tip of her tongue. But she doesn't ask it. Maybe she reads something in my face, I can't seem to keep my mask in place when I'm around her.

She stretches out her legs, placing the cup beside her and then suddenly stands.

"You know what always makes me feel better?" She asks, looking down at me.

"If you say dancing—" and she interrupts me with one of her free spirited laughs.

"Of course I'm going to say dancing," she replies, doing a little shimmy in place. When I don't move, she reaches down, grabbing my arm and yanking on it hard. I have no choice but to stand up.

"Haven't you danced all night?" I ask and she immediately pouts.

"It doesn't count."

"What do you mean?"

But she doesn't answer. Instead, she does another little dance, and then stops, narrowing her eyes.

"I see." Her face is all seriousness now. "This is how you dance."

She goes into a stance, keeping her back straight and her arms in a locked position. She moves up, to the side, back, side, and up again. When I don't move, she puts her hands on her hips.

"Come on, I'm trying to teach you how to dance," she whines a little and I suppress a smile. "Follow my lead."

She shows me the steps again but I still don't move.

"Nikolai."

"Grand Duchess."

"Don't call me that," she replies immediately. "I like— I like the other nickname better."

She doesn't look me in the eye as she says it and then she's spinning again, dancing to that music she always carries within her soul. But then, a bird begins to sing in the distance and I have no idea what kind of a creature sings in the middle of the night, but it's beautiful and haunting. Alyonka gasps, pointing in the direction of the song, before she claps her hands together and continues to spin. I watch her for a moment, before I step right into her way, catching her mid spin.

"I know how to dance."

She stares at me in shock, as I move one hand behind

her back, while I take the other and lock it at shoulder level. Then, I begin to lead. I move to the melody the bird is singing, doing the steps Alyonka just showed me, except with her in my arms.

"I—how—you know how to dance?"

"*Da.*"

Is all I say, keeping the other part of it to myself—that I learned for her. I continue spinning us more and more, until she begins to laugh, throwing her head back. I can feel all tension leaving her body as I hold her close and my own heart sores.

But only for a moment.

Because tomorrow we'll be back at the castle and she will be back to dating the suitors and I will be her bodyguard. And only her bodyguard.

Yet, for right now, I can't seem to remember any of that as I dance with her in the middle of a magical forest, while a bird sings a song in the moonlight.

twenty-eight

ALYONKA

I wake up with a heavy arm over my waist and a sound of birds chirping. For a moment, I try to reorient myself. I'm in the forest in *Korolevstvo Tsvetov,* sleeping on my *shuba* with Nikolai beside me. It's his arm that's pinning me in place and I can't help myself but run a finger over his skin. He jerks back and then sits up.

"I'm sorry, I must've moved in my sleep." He says, getting off the ground and stretching.

"You actually slept?" I ask and he turns to me with horror on his face. His eyes scan our surroundings, like someone is about to jump out and assassinate me.

"I'm sorry. I—"

"*Nyet,*" I stand in front of him, placing a hand in

front of his face to shock him into silence. "I don't want apologies. I'm glad you slept."

"I shouldn't have."

"You should've."

I think we'll keep arguing about this all day. But the sun isn't even up yet, so it means we barely even slept.

"Let's go, before Tetia Tatiana sends out a search party."

He doesn't argue. We check the fire, grab out stuff, and we're off.

I really want to thank him for indulging me in my little adventure, but I'm still trying to process the fact that he can dance. Not just like a random movement. But someone who was taught. I want to ask him about it, but I'm suddenly a big coward.

We make it back to the castle with no issues. They let us through the gate and Timofey meets us on the other side with the carriage. Him and Nikolai exchange a few hushed words and then we're off. I sit beside Nikolai trying to figure out how I'm supposed to go back to sitting across from the suitors, when nothing about them makes me as excited as doing a little waltz in the middle of the forest with him.

The castle seems to be full of activity when we arrive, so it takes a little sneaking around to get me back to my rooms. We take the back corridor and the secret turret steps up to the roof landing, before going down to my rooms.

I'm a little cold, since I only have my light dress under my *shuba*, so Nikolai walks over to light the fireplace immediately.

"I'll send for Daria," he says.

"If she's feeling better," I reply, and he nods.

"*Da*, I will also—" before he can finish there's a knock on the door and it opens before I can reply. Tetia Tatiana walks in, giving both Nikolai and I once-over with her eyes. She doesn't look like I expect her to look. There's something about her that seems almost smug.

"*Tsarevna* Alyona," she begins, but is interrupted when the door opens behind her and my father walks in. My whole body goes cold, as if a bucket of cold water was dumped on it. "Tsar and Tsarina have returned." Tetia Tatiana finished her announcement and no wonder she looks smug.

"Father, Mother," I greet them, as my mother steps into the room from behind her. Even though the space is large, it feels like it's being overtaken by my father's presence.

He's always been large, about half a head taller than Nikolai, and very broad. He's just big, it's the one thing I can always associate with him. My mother is about my size, but with brown hair and brown eyes. They both look between Nikolai and me, disapproval plainly written on their expressions.

"You have broken rules, Alyona," my father booms, his voice just as large as his size. "It is unacceptable."

I glance over at Tetia Tatiana, not missing her raising her eyebrows at me. This is clearly her doing. She probably sent for them the moment I announced I wanted to go.

"*Da*, father. But it was necessary—"

"What's necessary is your upcoming nuptials. There is really no time to waste."

"I don't understand, my birthday isn't for half a year yet."

"However, the kingdom does not have that kind of time." He keeps talking over me, his hard gaze never leaving my face. "Parts of the kingdom have already begun experiencing the curse. The sooner you marry, the better it will be for the kingdom."

Dread fills me at the words, because I think I know where this is going.

"Father—"

"We have spoken to Tatiana and have decided on a match for you. The wedding is in three days. I suggest you get some rest. Nikolai, a word."

He doesn't wait for a response, simply turns on his heels and walks out of the room. Mother walks over to me, places a hand against my cheeks and shakes her head, as if she's disappointed in me before she's gone as well.

Tetia Tatiana follows, that smug look never leaving her face. After a long tense moment where I forget how to breath, Nikolai moves. I grab his sleeve, holding him in place, desperation coursing through me.

"I can't—" I say, gasping to try and push some air into my lungs.

"You will," he says, and then he gently pries my fingers off his sleeve and walks toward the door. I watch him, sure he'll stop and say something. Maybe come back and hold me for a moment. But he does none of that. He doesn't even turn to look at me. He simply walks out of the room, shutting the door behind him, as I sink onto the floor in front of the fireplace.

Just like that, everything is crashing down around me.

NIKOLAI

No wonder the castle is full of activity. They're preparing for a wedding. There are more people in the halls, everything is being dusted, all the frames and furniture shifted around. I let my eyes roam over the people as they stop what they're doing and bow to the Tsar. Tsarina has walked off in the opposite direction, so it's only Tatiana and I following him to his study.

I feel numb. That's the only way I can describe it.

Maybe later, in the confines of my own room and the shred of darkness I will let myself feel something else. But right now, nothing is allowed in.

I knew this day was coming. I knew Alyonka could never be mine.

But my heart refused to listen to reason regardless. Hope is a terrifying feeling and here it is, blowing up in my face.

"I was told traveling to *Korolevstvo Tsvetov* was your idea," Tsar says, once we're inside his study. This one is about five times bigger than Alyonka's. The walls are lined with books on three different levels. But they look like they've never been touched before. Tatiana is to my left as the Tsar walks over to stand in front of the desk.

"*Da*, Your Imperial Majesty," I reply, bowing a little, before straightening again. He makes a gruff noise, clearly unhappy with this.

"And who gave you the permission to make such a decision?"

Clearly, he knows all of this already. I don't understand the reasoning behind this interrogation, but I decided even before we went that I would take all the blame if necessary.

"As the commander, I made the decision myself," I say and Tatiana huffs loudly. I glance at her sharply and she's not looking at me.

"He's protecting Alyona and her blatant disregard of your order," she says, her full attention on the Tsar. "She was the one who pushed the issue and stated that it is her standing as a future Tsarina that she could do what she deemed correct."

Not how it went down, but now I understand what she's doing. She's painting Alyonka to be the bad guy. But why? To make sure this wedding happens?

"It was my idea," I say, before the Tsar can make a comment. Both of them look at me sharply. "I will accept the consequences for my actions."

Tatiana opens her mouth again, but the Tsar silences her with a wave of a hand. He's looking at me, as if trying to see inside of me and it's only my training that keeps me from fidgeting or turning away.

"You think you are being a hero," the Tsar finally says, turning to the side to look at something on his desk. "Ivan thought he was a hero too."

The Tsar picks up a stack of paper, waving it a little, before dropping it back on his desk.

"He thought he could keep Alyona from marriage if he could solve the curse problem another way. But there is no use for this, she is marrying *Knyaz* Boris Stepnaich in three days time, the curse will be lifted, and you will be sent somewhere...else."

"I'm being reassigned?" Somehow I'm not surprised it's Boris that they choose for her, but I can't even focus on that because I'm being *set away*. "Tsarevna needs protection."

"When the curse is lifted, your services will no longer be required," the Tsar says, walking around his desk so he can sit. The way he says that, the way he's acting, he truly believes that this marriage will be what lifts the curse. I never understood the reasoning behind any of it, but now I understand even less.

He hasn't seen his daughter in half a year, but there's not emotion behind seeing her now. He delivered the news, breaking her heart and then walked away. It's almost like he's simply marrying her off—maybe for some other reason beside the curse? A deal with the other kingdom? Riches? From everything I've heard about the Tsar, he has always been on the lookout for opportunities. Maybe even if the curse isn't broken, he still gets something out of it.

"What if the curse isn't broken?" I ask, because no matter what happens to me I can't just stand by and do nothing. Both the Tsar and Tatiana look at me as if I've lost my mind.

"It is not your concern," the Tsar replies, his eyes hard. He says it like he doesn't even care, but I don't understand how can that be.

"I am her bodyguard. I've been tasked with protecting her and protecting the kingdom. What happens to her once she is married?"

"You have no right to ask these questions," Tatiana snaps and the tsar raises his hand to calm her.

"You are walking on thin ice, Nikolai. I suggest you do your job and keep your mouth shut. Or your reassignment will be just the beginning."

I hold his gaze, wondering what has happened to the man who was so excited to have a daughter. Just like everyone in the kingdom, I have read the account of what happened at the party. People talked about how excited the Tsar was to finally hold his 'precious little girl' in his arms. Now, he's just a man made out of ice—I see no kindness in him.

He waves his hand, breaking the eye contact and I've been dismissed. Tatiana makes sure to send me another smug look, as I bow and walk away. I want to go to her, desperately. But will that help anyone at this point? I'm afraid I'll be reassigned before the wedding, before I can figure how to help her.

Right now, I simply feel tired and helpless and no matter how much I want to march up to her rooms and whisk her away from all of this, I know I can't.

twenty-nine

ALYONKA

I can't even cry. My whole body has shut down, simply going through the motions. Daria arrives to find me still sitting on the floor, trying to remind myself how to breathe. In broken sentences, I tell her what happened and she wraps her arms around me and simply sits with me.

It's what I wanted from Nikolai. But how can I ask that of him? He is not mine to keep.

Tetia Tatiana came by to tell me who I'm marrying and she looked mighty smug saying Boris Stepanich's name. We never did find out what her relationship with him is, but it doesn't seem to matter anyway. It's very hard not to burst into hysterical laughter as she leaves and Daria begins to brush out my hair.

"What was the point of it all?" I ask out loud. Daria meets my eyes in the mirror, poor thing still looking exhausted.

"It doesn't make sense," she says and the fact that she agrees makes me feel slightly less crazy.

When she leaves me for the night, I'm still thinking those words. The storm arrived sometime after I did and the winds are rattling the windows again. But all I can do is lay there, staring at the flames dancing in the fireplace.

I don't sleep at all. The next morning, when Daria arrives to get me dressed for the day, I go through the motions because I know I have to.

Tetia Tatiana arrives to oversee my getting dressed and I wish she was gone. Seeing her reminds me of what will happen in only two days and I don't want the reminder.

When there's a knock on the door I try to ignore the way my stupid heart speeds ups at the sound. Daria finishes rearranging my hair over my dress and I turn toward the entryway just as Timofey steps inside. He bows deeply, before straightening and I glance over his shoulder.

"Where is Nikolai?" I ask and Timofey glances quickly at Tetia Tatiana before he meets my eye. He looks apologetic.

"I'm sorry, *Tsarevna* Alyona, but Nikolai is otherwise occupied today. I will be serving as your bodyguard."

The way he says the words is clearly rehearsed and I

narrow my gaze at Tetia Tatiana as she pivots on her heels and heads for the door.

"We have no time to waste," she says over her shoulder, motioning me to follow. I look over at Daria but she just gives me a quick encouraging smile. I step up to Timofey and head for the door as well, but the moment Tetia Tatiana is on the other side of the doors, I lower my voice and turn toward Timofey.

"Where is he?" I raise an eyebrow at him, almost daring him to give me another excuse Tetia Tatiana came up with, but he gets the hint immediately. His lips twitch for a moment as if he's trying not to smile, before he sobers up.

"He's sick, *Tsarevna*. Came down with fever in the middle of the night."

My vision tunnels for a moment at his words, before I push past the immediate worry and head into action. I nod my head, motioning for the door and we start walking, lest Tetia Tatiana comes back.

When we step out of the room, she's down the hall near the stairs and she glances back at me to make sure I'm following before heading down.

"Has he eaten? Was his mother called?" I ask, keeping my voice low and my face forward. Timofey is right behind my right shoulder and I don't have to see his face to hear the worry in his voice.

"*Nyet* to both. I didn't have a chance before I was summoned."

My mind is working in overdrive. There has to be a way for me to sneak over to see him. But when? After breakfast is the wedding dress fitting and then writing of the vowels. I'm actively refusing to acknowledge the fact that Boris Stepanich is the one my parents choose for me based on all the information Tetia Tatiana has presented them with. Should I really be surprised that it was never my choice to begin?

But what is my choice is seeing Nikolai. So I will make it happen.

I thought I would breakfast alone, with only Timofey watching over me, but Tetia Tatiana seems to have attached herself to me for the day. I can't even discuss my sneaking away with Timofey because she is always watching. Maybe she's waiting for me to loose my cool and speak up against all of this. But no matter how much I want to, it's not something I can do. Years ago, I promised my parents that I would follow their lead when it came to breaking the curse. I thought it would earn me a little of their kindness, if nothing else. It's why I agreed on the competition, why I've endured this loneliness my whole life. They said they wanted to protect me, they said they knew better, so here we are.

No matter how wrong it might feel to me.

"Stand up straight," Tetia Tatiana's voice breaks through my thoughts an hour later, as I'm posted on a stand in the middle of the dressing room. This room is on the first floor, near the kitchens, and it is used specifically for measuring and creating the royal wardrobe. The walls are lined with material and there's an area with large mirrors and a platform to stand on. The seamstress—a woman I have never seen before—is walking around me with a tape measurer, an indifferent look on her face. She's at least in her forties, dark hair and bright eyes, and she looks like it's a chore for her to be here.

Daria stands in the corner of the room, with Timofey next to her, and I can't help but think how much Daria wanted to be the one to help me with my dress. We've discussed it so many times and I loved the vision she created. Now, she gets to watch this woman dress me. It makes me want walk over and hug my friend.

"A very traditional square neckline, open shoulders, long wide skirt," Tetia Tatiana is telling the seamstress. "You have already prepared the gold embroidery for the sleeves, train, and the bodice. We can choose the panels tomorrow morning, after the under the dress portion is complete."

The panels are already prepared? I glance at Tetia Tatiana sharply, but she's not looking at me. I don't understand how my dress could already be in the works when there was no decision until yesterday. I watch as Tetia Tatiana moves off with the seamstress, discussing the hair dressing and veil.

Timofey steps up to me, offering me his arm so I can step down from the platform. I glance back at Tetia Tatiana and then at Timofey.

"We're heading to my rooms," I announce, and ~~Tetia~~ Tatiana turns to face me, ready to argue. I put up my hand, raising my eyebrows at her. "I need to change out of this dress before heading to the chapel. Please finish going over the details of my dress. I will meet you there."

I don't wait for her argue, but motion for Daria to follow as Timofey and I leave. The moment we're away from the dressing room I pivot in the opposite direction of my room.

"Timofey, take me to Nikolai immediately. Daria, I need you to bring my dark maroon dress to Nikolai's room. I'll have to change there."

Neither one of them says anything, but Daria takes off toward my rooms, while Timofey leads me down the hallway. We don't pause as people move out of the way, weaving in and out of the staff corridors until we reach the training courtyard.

The men are immediately at attention, but I don't have time to greet them. I race for Nikolai's room, hoping that the gossip will keep at bay long enough for me to at least see him.

"I'll talk to the guys," Timofey says, opening the door for me, so I can enter ahead of him. I give him a grateful smile and step inside the room.

Nikolai is on the bed, the covers a knotted mess around him, his skin clammy with sweat. I fix the covers first, spreading them out over him before I lean over, placing my the back of my hand on his forehead. He turns into the contact immediately, sighing a little. He's burning up.

I stand up straight, glancing around, looking for something to sooth him with. I need to get water and a towel, at least for some relief. But when I turn to go, his hand catches my wrist, pulling me with surprising force down on the bed beside him.

"Alynoushka—" his voice is barely above a whisper and he doesn't open his eyes. But his hand is wrapped around my wrist, holding me in place.

Just then the door behind me opens and I turn, thinking I've been caught, when Nikolai's mother walks in.

"Oh, *Tsarevna* Alyona!" She bows immediately and that's when I notice a bowl of water in her hands.

"Please, see to your son. I didn't meant to get in the way," I say, motioning her foreward. I try to extract my arm, but Nikolai's hand only tightens. His mother doesn't miss a thing.

"He's called out your name a few times, Your Royal Highness," she says, placing the bowl of water beside the bed on the table.

"He's very good at his job," I reply, glancing over at him. "Knowing how concerned he is for me, he's probably dreaming of some scenario where his services are required."

His mother chuckles and I glance at her in confusion.

But she doesn't offer an explanation, only hands me a wet towel.

"I'm sure you'll both feel better if you do this," she says and I take the towel automatically. Turning back toward Nikolay, I lean over, patting his skin gently and he sighs again, flexing his fingers over my wrist. Surprisingly, I do feel better.

"Am I truly so transparent?" I ask, not looking at his mother, but at him. I'm not sure if I'm actually asking the question to get an answer from her or from myself.

Has he always been this important to me? Did I spend my years missing him in my presence? I honestly can't remember what my life looked like before him? It's almost like he's always been here.

"You are very alike in that sense," his mother says and I glance at her then. She's watching her son with such fondness in her eyes, I wonder just how difficult it was for them to be apart.

"What do you mean?"

She looks over at me, that same fondness never leaving her expression and it makes me want to cry all of a sudden.

"You are both so stubborn, so against being honest with yourself on where you stand. Both so bound by duty, that you would sacrifice yourself without a second thought." She watches me, a sadness entering her eyes that make my own fill with tears. "You care about him, don't you?"

I glance back at the man in front of me, his brow furrowed a little, as if he's fighting some demon in his sleep. I think back to all the time we've spend together, as kids and as adults, of all the ways he's always encouraged me to be myself and seemed to appreciate those parts of me the most.

A tear slips down my cheek, my heart heavy with the words I can't say out loud. So I settle for the next best thing.

"I don't know how not to care," I reply, another tear escaping down my cheek. I turn back to his mother and watch as she stands, leaning over to wipe the tears off my cheek with a handkerchief. She's so gentle, it makes me want to cry harder. She pushes a wisp of hair off my cheek and pats my skin dry in a way I would imagine a mother to do.

"You are going to be a wonderful ruler," she says, her own eyes filling up, "And I am proud that you will be our queen."

She doesn't say the words, but I hear them anyway—thank you for your sacrifice.

NIKOLAI

I'M in and out of delirium for hours. Dreams continue to assault me and in the center of it all is Alyonka. The sight of her in a wedding dress, tears streaming down her face, surrounded by sleeping bodies everywhere. Me, trying to get to her, but no matter how hard I fight, I can't get near her.

But then in the midst of it all, I hear hear voice and I feel her touch and I finally—finally rest.

When I do open my eyes, it's dark outside. I have no idea how long I've been out. Timofey is in the bed, fully asleep. There's a glass of water on the table near me, so I reach for it and drain it. I feel completely back to normal.

Keeping as quiet as possible, I get out of bed, grab a fresh set of clothes and head for the showers. After I wash off the fever sweat, I dress in slacks and a pullover sweater, donning on my boots. My mind is filled entirely with Alyonka and I know I have to see her.

When I glance at the clock in the room, I see that it's past one in the morning, but even so, I don't think she's sleeping. I can't tell if it's wishful thinking or some of that otherworldly pull that I always feel toward her. Either way, I leave my room behind and head for the moonlight ballroom.

If there is one thing that always helps her clear her mind, it's dance.

Once I reach the ballroom, I pull the door open carefully, slipping inside. The moon is full and bright tonight, because the whole room is illuminated. For once, there are no clouds in the sky, no storm keeping us locked inside this castle. So I see her clearly.

She's in the middle of the ballroom, swaying gently to the music she always carries within herself.

I don't think I make a noise, but she turns my way anyway, a little gasp on her lips. There's a moment when she jerks towards me, as if she's going to run, but then stops, as if frozen by my presence and it's I who walks in her direction.

"You're better," she says, when I'm about two and a half meters away. Her eyes roam over me, and I think I see her tiny relieved exhale.

"I'm sorry for the inconvenience," I say, and she raises her eyebrows in surprise.

"What a strange thing to say," she replies, shaking her head. But I don't know what to say to her, except all the things I'm supposed to as her bodyguard in this situation. Because if I speak on anything else, I'm not sure either of us will come out unscathed.

"I'm—"

"You were asleep for two days. It truly was inconvenient. Don't do that again," she interrupts me and now I have nothing to say, because two days? That means—

"Tomorrow?"

She's not looking at me again. "*Da*, tomorrow."

It's like a crushing weight inside of my chest. Will I have to live with it for the rest of my life? When the tsar has his way, I'll be stationed in the middle of some part of the Skazka forest, but still dreaming of her every night, just like I did for the last two days. I can see my future clearly now and it's so empty without her in it.

"Do you think—" she begins and then pauses before taking a deep breath and trying again, "Do you think the curse will break the way my parents believe it will?"

It's such a loaded question and one I've been asking myself for months since my return. Maybe even before then. I don't know the logistics of the curse, no one really does beside the Tsar and Tsarina. But they literally abandoned their daughter to lock her away from the world for the last eighteen and a half years of her life, so wouldn't it stand to think that they believe it will?

"You have your doubts," I say, because of course I have my own as well.

"I never understood the way it worked or the reasons behind why I would need to marry," she replies honestly, turning to face the large windows so she can look up at the sky. "It's never how I pictured it."

"How did you picture it?"

She chuckles a little and at first I don't think she'll tell me, but then she does.

"You've read about High Queen Calista's fierce defeat of Baba Yaga, right?"

"Of course."

"But do you know what part of that history I love the most?" She sighs, her eyes still on the moon lit sky. "The part where King Brendan was by her side through it all.

They have such an epic love story. A forbidden romance, a friendship that changed them both—a bond that saved our land from destruction. Isn't that what every person wants the other to be to them on their wedding day?"

When she finally looks at me, her eyes are glittering. I curl my fingers against my slacks to keep myself from reaching for her. I have no right to comfort her. Not when I can't give her the promises we both want.

"I guess it was foolish of me to ever hope for some epic love story," she whispers, her smile sad. "I've always wanted to be strong and brave like Queen Calista, but I guess I'm not—"

"You are," I can't help but move toward her just a fraction. "You're the bravest and strongest person I know. Wanting to be loved does not make you weak. It's the exact opposite."

My voice sounds rough even to my own ears and I nearly choke on all the words I want to say to her. But will that help anyone? Or will it simply break us both.

We stand with our eyes locked, as if time has frozen us in this moment. A gift to remember and to try to forget. But then I break the stillness with words that surprise even me.

"Dance for me, Alyonushka."

thirty

ALYONKA

It's taking every ounce of my self control for me not to reach for him. When he walked through those doors, I felt the most at peace I've had in days. But now, only a storm of emotions rages inside of me and he adds fuel to the fire with his words.

"Are you sure you aren't tired of watching me do this almost every night?" I push the hair out of my face, hoping to find some of the lightness in this situation, before it drags us both down. I feel, rather than see him move toward me. When I glance up, he's barely an arm length away, his eyes shining in the moonlight.

"I can watch you dance for a thousand lifetimes and never get tired."

That pain in my heart intensifies and I place a hand

over it, if only to keep it from spilling out around us. The air is so heavy with all the words we can't say to each other, but he's walking that line dangerously close.

"I—"

"Please," his voice is barely above a whisper, shaky with that one word. "Dance for me."

Just like that, I have no power over my own body, as it answers his request almost on its own.

I step back, putting my weight on my left leg, as I point my right and then I step forward, arms raised. My feet move to the rhythm of my heart as I keep my eyes on Nikolai.

He watches me, completely stripped off any defenses that he's so good at keeping between us. His eyes track my every movement and I feel them like the caress of a dance partner.

When I spin around him, he turns to follow the motion. I'm closer than I should be, the skirt of my dress & the ends of my hair brushing against him as I move.

If I let myself, I can almost believe that we're dancing together. The only dance partner I've ever wanted.

I spin again, faster this time, circling him as I go and I'm out of breath, the shadows blurring together, but I don't stop.

Faster and faster, with the moonlight pouring over me and the sound of our hearts beating filling my ears, I pour my whole heart into this one dance.

My last spin brings me back in front of him and I

reach out with my right hand to the right, before I do the same to the left, swaying my body with the movement.

Nikolai's hand reaches out toward me, hovering just above my hip near my waist, where a dance partner would normally support this move. His fingers are more than a dozen centimeters away, but I can feel the ghost of the touch as if it reaches out to me.

My eyes lock on his once more and then, as if we've always done this, he moves with me. His hand, still hovering near my waist, as he steps forward and then back, taking me with him.

It's only about ten steps before we stop, staring at each other, both out of breath. This moment feels like it carries the weight of a thousand moments and it would take no movement at all to close what little distance there is between us.

A dream that can only ever be a dream.

He drops his hand to his side, and I watch as he flexes it briefly before he locks his hands behind his back, straightening his shoulders.

I want to say something, anything, but I know my place. And it can never be next to him.

He called me brave, he called me strong, but all I feel is hopeless. Yet, even after all that, how I feel doesn't matter.

Tomorrow, I will walk down the isle toward a man I do not love to marry him in front of my parents and the courts. To protect this kingdom, to save Nikolai from this curse, I will do what is required of me.

Even when it breaks both of our hearts.

NIKOLAI

I DRESS for the day without much thought. Food is consumed, the soldiers are checked and assigned their duties, but I'm mostly going through the motions. So much is riding on today—the fate of the whole kingdom. And all I want to do is take Alyonka and run.

There are more people inside these walls than the castle has seen in years. The front doors are opened for the first time since the baby presentation ceremony, with so many people pouring it, even I'm feeling slightly overwhelmed. The throne room on the first floor has been specifically designed for these type of events. There's a balcony that hangs over the back entrance, a large walkway in the middle of the room that splits it in two and a set of stairs and a platform where the thrones sit. The guests are ushered through the side entrance, leaving the back open for Alyonka to walk in. The opposite side of the room has giant glass doors that lead out to the courtyard and since the weather is perfect today, they're open to allow more people into the room.

I'm honestly surprised by how many people are here,

Tatiana must've worked overtime to send out invitations. Although, I suppose one word of it and people would come flocking in since everyone wants to know how this turns out.

At first, after the curse was spoken, people left the kingdom in fear of being stuck here. But no one knew if the curse would follow if the person was originally from *Holodnova Tsarstva*, so they weren't exactly accepted. As the time past, and people forgot to actively think about the curse, they've come back.

After I've checked over the downstairs area, I head for Alyona's rooms. I wasn't with her at her fitting, so this is my first time seeing her in the wedding dress. I'm not prepared for it.

She turns when I step inside the room, the material spilling out around her. It's white, with gold embroidery stitched into the bodice, sleeves and skirt. It looks like the dresses I've seen in history books, not an ounce of her personality stitched into it. Her hair is braided, a diamond filled tiara sits on top, with a very long veil spilling from it.

Even though she looks like she's wearing clothes meant for someone else, she is still the most beautiful woman I have ever seen. And it's killing me. This feeling inside of me, it's as if it's eating me up, ready to swallow me whole. I feel nothing and everything at the same time. I would give up everything—my position, my future—if only I could be the one to meet her at the end of that aisle.

I think we're both holding our breaths as we stare at

each other and I have no idea how long we would've stood like that if Tatiana didn't clap her hands.

"Shall we?" She asks, her hard gaze on me and I nod, before stepping back out into the hallway. Tatiana steps out next, and then Alyona. Daria and three other girls are right behind Alyona, carrying her train and veil so it doesn't drag on the floor. Tatiana leads the way and I stay behind them, as we reach the entrance to the great throne room.

I step to the side as the girls rearrange the veil and the train and Tatiana utters some last minute instructions, before they all leave, leaving Alyonka and me by ourselves.

Her hands are folded in front of her, as she stares at the double doors like she's about to walk in front of the firing squad. What I wouldn't give to be able to take her hand and whisk her away from here. But she would never walk away from her responsibility and neither can I.

When I notice her hands trembling, I can't take it. I step right in front of her and she gasps, glancing up at me. It's just the two of us right here, but even if it wasn't, I still would take her hands in mine. Bringing them up to my lips, I leave a tiny kiss on her knuckles, before I look into her eyes. She's staring at me as if I've lost my mind, but I see the glimmer of emotion I won't name behind them.

"Don't ever forget who you are," I whisper, holding our hands between us. "The same fearless girl who would climb trees too tall for her to handle, who would force her friendship on a sad boy who was too scared to make friends, who could handle a room of men and Tatiana, who has a magical dragon gifted to her from Skazka herself because Skazka believes in you as a person and a ruler."

A lone tear escapes down her cheek and I reach over to flick it away. But she catches my hand, placing it against her cheek for just a moment. We stand like that, while I try to remember how to breathe.

This is a goodbye for us. We both know it.

She will no longer need my presence when the curse is broken and even though I haven't told her what her father said, I think she knows it anyway. My assignment comes to an end the moment the curse is gone. Neither one of us wants to admit it out loud, but we hold still as long as we can. It's only when the music begins to play behind the doors that we finally break apart.

I take a step back, blending into the shadows to her left as the double doors open wide. She holds my gaze and then raises her chin and walks forward. A hush falls over the throne room as she makes her way forward down the long walkway. I watch, until the doors close, putting a final chapter on the two of us.

thirty-one

ALYONKA

There are so many faces in the room, I'm finding it difficult to breathe. I walk forward on sheer willpower, wondering how someone could survive when her heart is no longer her own.

My parents are seated on the thrones in front of the room, with Boris Stepanich standing to the left, and a priest standing to the right. The two of them come forward when I reach the steps, with Boris Stepanich coming to stand beside me on the right, while the priest stays a step above us.

A movement catches my attention of Boris's shoulder and I watch as Nikolai comes to stand near the front, near Timofey. Since the doors to the courtyard are open, he's mostly outside and he doesn't have his coat on. If he meet-

sHe's not looking at me and maybe that's for the best. I tear my gaze away and look up at Boris Stepanich.

It's the first time I've seen him in over a week and he looks more tired than anything else. We weren't allowed to meet after my father made the announcement, but I kind of wish we did. There are so many things I wanted to discuss with him. The priest says a few words of greeting and then stops abruptly.

I turn toward the isle I just walked down to see Tetia Tatiana coming up the middle. We didn't go over this part. I glance at my parents who are also looking confused.

"I'm sorry to interrupt," Tetia Tatiana says, bowing deeply to my parents. "But it is tradition, on the wedding day, to receive a gift of abundance, given to the bride before she takes her vows."

Tradition? Maybe from her kingdom. I glance at Boris Stepanich, but he looks indifferent to the whole thing.

"Go ahead," my father booms and Tetia Tatiana moves forward immediately. She produces a velvet box, opening it so I can see. Inside is a golden brooch, with diamonds. A half crescent moon, with six stars and what looks like vines growing through and around it. She steps up on the stairs near the priest, and I turn toward her as she takes out the brooch and leans toward me. Seeing no other option, I stay still as she pins the brooch near the neckline of my dress, right over my heart.

"It's beautiful, don't you think?" She asks. There's something about the way she's looking at me, but I can't really concentrate on it, because the brooch on my chest twinkles in the light, pulling my attention to it.

It really is beautiful—almost magical in its beauty. I smile, staring at it, as it continues to sparkle in the light. Reaching for it, I can't help but fun my finger, following the vines when I feel it. A tiny prickle and I pull away to find a bead of blood at the edge of my finger. Confused, I look at the brooch and realize the vines aren't covered in leaves, they're covered in thorns.

"There it is," Tetia Tatiana says, before she falls. Except she doesn't.

I blink at the sight of Tetia Tatiana's body hitting the stairs and rolling down, while a woman I've never seen before stands in her place.

Strikingly beautiful, her hair is bright white and falling down her back in loose curls. Her dress is gold, which matches the color of her eyes. Her lips are full and red, pulled at the corners in an awfully smug smile.

"You!" This comes from my father who has risen from the throne, staring at the woman in front of me.

"Me!" She spreads her arms wide and grins at the crowd. "Welcome to your curse!"

There's a commotion, as people start screaming and the soldiers move forward. My eyes find Nikolai's as he pushes to get to me and then everything goes dark.

NIKOLAI

I WATCH Alyonka drop to the floor just as a gust of wind rushes through the room, so powerful that it knocks everyone off their feet. I slam hard against the stone ground of the courtyard, pushing to my knees to see the front of the room.

"It's not time yet. You said—"

"That in her ninetieth year of life, a curse will come upon her," the woman who is definitely not Tatiana speaks, glancing down to where Alyonka has fallen. "To tell you the truth, I was generous. Time moves so differently across realms, I could've come for her months ago, but this was just so much more fun."

She walks up the few stairs, glancing around the throne room. No one can move, no matter how hard I fight against it, I'm frozen on all fours, just watching it all unfold.

"Before you sleep, is there anything you'd like to say to me?" The woman asks, addressing the tsar. He stares up at her from his position on the floor, such a big man and so helpless. "*Nyet*? What about you?" The woman turns to the *tsarina*.

"Why?" *Tsarina* manages and the woman laughs.

"Because you deserve it, of course. You humiliated me in front of all of Skakza and you thought I wouldn't take my revenge. It's annoying that I can't simply kill you, but those melding fairies are always messing up my best plans. But to tell you the truth, this actually works in my favor. I can spend the next thousand years feasting off your energy."

She laughs then, but a memory of something I read in the books Ivan Popyalof asked me to look over flashes in my mind. A creature who comes in the night and siphons energy off sleeping people. There was one who was thought to be the sister of Baba Yaga, a creature as vile as the other, but instead of feasting on children, she feasted on the dreams of those she visited. No one has ever seen her, only rumors were written in the accounts, but there was a name. I know there was a name.

I fight against whatever magic is keeping me in place, desperate to get to Alyonka. I can no longer see her from where she'd fallen. The woman continues her speech, kicking the tsar out of the way, so she can sit on the throne.

"You will never get away with this," the tsar says and the woman laughs.

"What a cliche thing to say. I already have. The moment she pricked her little finger, the kingdom had succumbed to the spell. Soon, it will overtake you. Can't you feel it?" She leans down to smile at the tsar. "Your limbs are getting heavier by the moment, you won't be able to fight the pull of it for much longer."

I could feel it too, exactly as she describes, but I'm not giving up. I can't give up. My whole attention is on getting to Alyonka, but I'm momentarily distracted by the tsar's next question.

"Did you stop the marriage because it would save us?" He asks and the woman laughs so loudly the sound rings in my ears.

"*Nyet*, you were never going to break the curse with your stupid little games. It was entertaining to watch. Don't worry, I didn't posses her for long. I just used her as my eyes and ears. But I liked watching you try. I especially liked watching you be so afraid of your own daughter that you shut her away behind these walls. Your precious baby girl, and you couldn't even watch her grown up. You really are such a weak man, aren't you?"

The woman cocks her head to the side, looking down at the tsar, before she finally stands.

"But I felt a shift here," she says, looking around the room, as if she's looking for something. "I didn't know what it was, but I wasn't about to let it ruin my plans. So I simply accelerated the timeline a little. Plus, I'm hungry."

She starts laughing again, as she steps over the tsar and heads for the stairs. She waves her hand and Alyonka's body rises from the floor, floating in mid air. The woman walks out of the room, with Alyonka's unconscious form trailing behind her, just as I manage to straighten from all fours.

"Sweet dreams," the woman calls behind her and I watch as people start to drop, one by one. Suddenly, something grabs me from behind and I'm ripped away and up into the sky. I glance up and find Chudo above me, looking larger than the last time I saw him. He carries me straight out of the courtyard and up above the castle, his large talons wrapped around my upper body. He doesn't stop flying until he crosses the Rusalka River, leaving the kingdom behind.

thirty-two

NIKOLAI

I have no idea where he's taking me, I just know we're not in *Holodnoye Tsarstvo* anymore. The weather changes drastically, winter turning into a much warmer climate. It feels like we're airborne for hours, but I can't really focus on anything except seeing Alyonka's body hitting the floor. It's like it's on a loop in my mind.

Suddenly, the forest below us opens up and I see our destination. We were just here.

"Woah!" Two men shout, jumping back and reaching for their swords as Chudo descends into a courtyard unannounced. He lets me go as soon as my feet graze the ground and I roll, before coming up in a crouch. The two men rush over, pointing their swords at me and Chudo, who lands behind me and folds his wings against him, looking very smug.

"Are you proud of yourself?" I ask the dragon and he huffs hot air at me, before he raises his chin and puffs out his chest.

"He is very proud of himself because he saved you."

The voice comes from behind me and I turn to watch Queen Ivanna step out from behind the trees. Dimitri is beside her, with his sword drawn, but she nudges his hand down with her own.

"You can talk to him too?" I ask, standing up slowly as not to spook the two men who still have their swords drawn on me.

"I can't, but Kroshka can." She glanced down and I follow her gaze to the small creature she has cradled against her with one arm. The bunny we saw at the coronation party.

"Do all the queens of Skazka have their own magical familiars?" The blond guys to my left asks, shaking his head. "That's so unfair."

"Coming from the one who spends the most time with Kroshka. Do you really need your own, Maxim?" Queen Ivanna asks and the man—Maxim—shakes his head. "Now, put away your swords and let's sit down. You look like you might fall over."

She addresses the last part to me and I take a seat on the bench she indicates gratefully. I think I should be more emotional about this, but I might be in shock. The curse—Alyonka—I don't know how to process any of it.

A glass of water appears in front of me and I glance up to find another man, this one almost blond compared to the others, who looks familiar holding it out to me. That's when I realize these were the men in front of the coronation hall, near Queen Ivanna. The warriors she thanked publicly.

"*Spasibo*," I say, taking the water and draining it in one go.

Queen Ivanna hands her bunny over to Maxim and then takes a seat beside me. Chudo stays right where he is, watching the rest of us. Dimitri and his three man stay standing near Queen Ivanna, eyes watchful.

"Tell us what happened," she says, offering me a kind smile and I do. The whole day spills out of me in one breath, almost like I'm afraid that something will prevent me from speaking all of it. Clearly, leaving the kingdom could've been a way to avoid the curse. Or maybe it was Chudo's magic that kept me from succumbing to it. I don't actually understand any of this or how it works.

"So the marriage wasn't the answer," Queen Ivanna says when I finish and I shake my head.

"I've been reading over all the books Ivan Popyalof, her previous bodyguard, has been able to find, but I've never found anything that could speak on breaking the curse."

"The magic of Skazka isn't about rules," the man who brought me water speaks up.

"What do you mean, Kostya?" Queen Ivanna asks.

"I mean, think of your own history. It's never about making sense or putting people rules on the situation."

"People rules?" Maxim chuckles and Kostya sends him a glare.

"I mean, we tend to put our own ideas on things that we do not understand. The magic that exists in Skazka, regardless of who wields it isn't about rules. It's always about what drives those rules."

"You mean emotion," Dimitri says and Kostya nods.

"Think back to finding Ivanna in the cave, did you follow rules?"

"*Nyet*," Dimitri answers, looking over at Queen Ivanna and giving her a smile that makes me feel like I'm intruding on something private. "I followed my heart."

"Your heart?"

"If the curse spoke of being bound, maybe it wasn't about being bound in marriage. But being bound in the heart."

"That doesn't make sense," the man who hasn't spoken says, but I'm shaking my head.

"I think it does. I can't explain it, but the woman, she spoke of something changing. Like there was a force that shifted and she didn't want to risk it."

"So how does that help?"

"Shh, Arseniy," Queen Ivanna says, "Let him figure it out."

I think back to the last few weeks, of how things between Alyonka and I began to grow out of control of either of us. Neither of us could understand, but we felt it.

"We changed," I say, glancing up at the faces watching me. "Alyonka and I. We changed."

Chudo makes a noise and flaps his wings one, startling all of us. Then he glares at me.

"I don't speak dragon," Maxim says, "But I think that was his way of saying "took you long enough"".

I agree. How could I not see it? Alyonka and I, we were bound by heart. Our souls have become one before we knew what was happening.

"I need to go back."

"We can ride with you," Dimitri says and motions to the other men beside him. I know they can, but this feels like something I need to do alone.

"I'm not sure Chudo can take us all. And I need to get back to her now." I reply. The urgency of it feels overwhelming. If that women is sucking the energy off of the people while they sleep, what happens to them when they have no energy left? I don't want to think about it.

"What if you need back up?" Arseniy asks and I can

see why Queen Ivanna honored them in front of her kingdom. They seem like very good men and someone I would love to go into battle with, but I can't risk it.

"We don't know what happens if you enter the kingdom while it's under the curse. Or if you even can. With Chudo," I look at the dragon who currently has his head to the ground so he can be eye to eye with Queen Ivanna's bunny. I shake my head. "He might be able to get me back in, since he's magic."

"She might be somewhere in the castle, protected." Kostya offers and I look at him in question. "If the curse is attached to her, then she would be preserved. To keep it going."

I don't like the sound of that, but it makes sense. It's better than me thinking the woman is going to drain Alyonka of energy immediately.

"It'll be dark soon," Dimitri says, "If you can't enter the kingdom, come back. We'll figure out another way." He hands me a sheath and a sword, since I wasn't carrying one at the wedding. I take it gratefully, strapping it around my waist.

"I am thankful for your kindness," I bow to the queen and she steps up to offer me her hand. I take it and she clasps it with both of hers.

"Don't hesitate, if you need anything."

I nod once and turn to the dragon. The bunny eyes me and I honestly can't tell if it's good or bad, but I don't ask. Chudo stands up straighter and I freeze in my tracks.

"Did the dragon get bigger?" Kostya asks from behind me and all I can do is nod. He started out as big as a bear, but now I'd say he's grown about half of that size bigger. Chudo looks at me and I look at him and I can't communicate, but I think he's impatient to get back as well. I walk up to him, expecting him to take off and grab me around my torso again, but instead, he almost squats, offering up his back.

"You want me to ride on your back?" I ask and he huffs ones. Glancing back at the queen and her men I find that they all took a step back and watching expectedly. "Here goes nothing."

I walk up and swing my leg over, much like I would over a horse. Surprisingly, it's not uncomfortable, but Chudo doesn't even wait for me to settle, before he jumps straight into the air. I grab onto the fur around his neck and hold on. He seems to fly even faster than last time, or maybe it's because I'm actually aware of it now.

The shock has settled into a firm determination. I'm not leaving Alyonka to that curse for more than a few hours. I don't know what awaits us, but I know that I will do whatever it takes.

When we cross the river, I can tell immediately that we're back. Even the air around us seems to be at a standstill. We pass over a village and we're low enough that I can see people lying where they fell. Chudo descends closer to the tops of the trees and there's no sound. No birds, no animals, nothing.

We reach the castle, and there are more people on the lawn in front. We circle the building, looking for any signs of movement. Not that I expect any of the people to be awake. Mostly I want to see where that woman went. Hopefully, we're far enough above it all for her not to be looking up here.

"Land where you normally do," I say, leaning forward a little to make sure he hears me. He turns, flying around the front of the castle and to the back. The landing comes into view and I don't see any signs of danger. The snow that covers the space is undisturbed, until Chudo descends.

"I'll get her," I tell him, as I slide off his back. He nods at me and I nod in return, turning toward the steps near the vines. I have no idea where the woman took Alyona, but it feels right somehow that I start in her rooms. Or maybe I can feel her, like I always seem to feel her presence.

Pulling the vines to the side, I descend the stairs carefully. I'm not sure what I'm expecting but it's not thorns growing over her windows. Clearly, I'm in the right place. I have no idea ho much time I'll have once I start chopping at the thorns, but I'm hoping the woman is somewhere else and won't hear it or feel any disturbance in her magic. At this point, the craziest thoughts are probably the most plausible ones.

I begin to hack at the thorns, trying to make a hole large enough that I can get through it. But no matter how many thorns I cut, they don't seem to make any kind of an opening. Still, I don't stop. I hack at them until sweat is pouring down my back, refusing to pause for even a moment in case it undoes my progress somehow. When it feels like I'll be doing this for the rest of my life, suddenly, there's small clink of my sword against the glass.

I stop then, to see that yes, I've actually reached the window. Unbuttoning my outer jacket, I roll up the sleeves of my dress shirt and with renewed determination, I keep going. The sun has gone down, the night turning chilly, but I keep going. When I finally see more of the glass, I drop my sword and grab between the thorns, pulling and tugging on them. Some cut my upper arms, where I rolled up my sleeves, but it doesn't matter, because after a few more tugs, the opening is big enough that I can slip through. I push the window, thankful it opens inward, grab my sword and toss it inside, before I follow in.

thirty-three

ALYONKA

I find myself in the middle of a meadow in the middle of the forest, surrounded by a million tiny sparkles. Mesmerized, I watch them dance around me in unmapped patterns. The space around me feels peaceful and I smile to myself, as I reach a hand out to try and touch the magic.

A voice calls my name from somewhere far away and I turn, trying to find where it's coming from. It seems to echo all around me, disturbing the blissful state of my being. Maybe I can simply lay down and stay here forever.

But *nyet*, that doesn't seem right. This is not where I'm supposed to be.

For some reason, however, I can't remember where

I'm supposed to be. It's like my mind is dimming with each passing moment. I try to shake it off, but I can't seem to.

Maybe if I simply lay down for a little bit, the grass seems very inviting. Unlike in my own kingdom, there is no snow here, only green grass and green trees.

Wait, I have a kingdom. Responsibilities. I can't lay down in some unknown place.

But, oh, the pull is difficult to ignore.

The sound of my name reaches me again, and I do a quick scan of my surroundings. Just when I think nothing is there, the sparkles that are dancing around me change colors.

Green, blue, yellow, red, pink, and lavender.

These lights shine brighter and bigger than the rest, spinning around me in a circle. There's a buzz that feels the air, almost like a song that's sung behind closed doors. I want to reach out and touch them and then I hear my name for the third time and I know that voice.

Nikolai.

Pain suddenly fills my chest, as if I've been pierced through the heart and I bend over, holding my hand over the spot. Memories of the wedding ceremony, Tetia Tatiana who isn't Tetia Tatiana, the curse, and Nikolai— across the room, his eyes on me, desperately trying to get to me. I hear his voice speaking words I've longed to hear, words I want to be able to say in return.

"I remember," I say out loud, standing up straight again. This is my curse, the slumber promised by the curse. I always imagined it would be a nightmare land, but this feels peaceful, as if I could stay here forever.

The colorful bits of light congregate in front of my face, creating different patterns and I watch confused. I have no idea what they're trying to tell me or how I'm supposed to get out of here.

"Is this the final gift?" I ask the lights, because it's the only thing I can think of. "In the stories, the sleep like death was turned into an actual sleep. Is this my place of slumber?"

One of the lights grows brighter, the lavender one, coming away from the group and toward me. It's so bright I can't look at it directly, but I also can't turn my gaze away, so I shut my eyes. I feel a breeze caress my cheek and I think it's the light. It's trying to tell me something, of that I am sure. So I keep my eyes closed and I concentrate on the buzz around me.

But it's not a buzz at all, it *is* a song and it seems to be sung by the air around me.

> "A name calls through darkness,
> A power lies within,
> Utter the words,
> Destroy the evil,
> Let new life begin."

"A name?" I whisper, "A name has power."

It's not a question because I remember reading such a statement in the books in my study. My bodyguard—a man who raised me—was looking for a name that would change everything.

"What is it?" I ask the air around me, "*Pozhalusta*, tell me."

For a moment, I hear nothing but the song, the words repeated over and over. And then, a light touch on my forehead sends sparks through my body and I hear one word,

"Carabosse."

NIKOLAI

THE ROOM INSIDE IS DARK, and it's only because I've spent so much time here that I know my way around. Moving toward the door to the bedroom, I try to keep an ear out for any movement, anywhere, but the whole castle is completely silent. I think if the woman was anywhere near here, she would've heard me by now. I have no idea where she is or why she wouldn't be here, but right now, I don't care. All I care about is getting to Alyonka.

When I pull the door to the bedroom open, I'm not sure what to expect. It certainly isn't Alyonka, placed directly in the center of her bed, still in her wedding dress, her arms crossed over her stomach. The fireplace is lit, casting shadows across the room. The thorns that are outside the room are also in here. They cover the walls all around the room, including the door. It's so much warmer in here and I wonder if the thorns purpose isn't only to keep out anyone who might want to get in, but also to preserve her. Kostya must be right about the way the curse is attached to her.

I walk forward slowly, but even though I'm trying to be careful, some of the thorns still manage to get me. I grit my teeth against the pain and when I reach the bed, all of that fades to the background.

Even asleep, she's beautiful. But then, I've always thought so. Even when she was no more than a memory to me, I always found her to be the most beautiful person alive. Her chest rises and falls, as if she's in peaceful slumber and maybe I should be at least thankful it's not some nightmare world that she's stuck in.

Sitting down on the bed beside her, I reach for her hand. Even though it's warm in the room, her fingers are surprisingly cold.

I curl my own fingers over her hand, desperate to get some warmth back into her.

"I'm sorry," I say, before any other words can pass my lips. I don't realize I'm crying until a tear falls onto the bed. "I've turned out to be a pretty lousy bodyguard."

The feeling of failure is nearly overwhelming. The despair of it following close behind and somewhere at the back of my mind, I know this is not my emotions. Maybe it's hers, or maybe it's protective mechanism so I'm too caught up to do anything, but I fight agains it.

"Alyonushka, I'm going to say something that I was never brave enough to say before. I don't want to simply be the friend you had when you were little. I don't want to only be your bodyguard, although I intend to be there to protect you always. I want to be yours.

I want to share every high and every low with you. I want to cheer you on when you take on a challenge and celebrate when you achieve it. I want to comfort you when the world feels like too much. I want to braid your hair when you're too tired to do it yourself and watch you watch the sky as if you've never seen it before.

So please wake up, so we can go dance under the moonlight until we're a hundred years old. Let me be your forever dance partner."

I move some of the wisps of hair off her skin and lean forward, placing a gentle kiss to her forehead. She doesn't stir and the tears are there again, as I lean my own forehead against hers, cradling her cheek. My whole heart burns for her and only her. No one has ever or will ever come close.

"You call that a kiss?"

I jerk upright, my eyes flying up to meet her beautiful green ones. There's a gentle smile on her face, her gaze heavy from sleep.

"If you're going to save the girl, you should kiss her proper," she says, before she reaches up and pulls me by my shirt. Her lips meet mine and whatever shock I just felt intensifies and then melts into complete wonder. My arms wrap around her lifting her off the bed and against me as my mouth explores hers.

She's just as hungry for me as I am for her. She angles her head, her grip on my shirt tightening, as if she wants to bring me even closer. I match her beat for beat, my head spinning with the taste of her. Alyonka's hand leaves my shirt, ending up in my hair, as she tugs me even closer. I groan as she opens her mouth just a little, diving fully in. She's just as wild for me as I am for her and I could stay like this, with her in my arms, forever.

A loud bang jerks us apart and we turn as the doors to her room burst open, sending the thorns flying everywhere. I dive on top of Alyonka, shielding her with my body as a pain slams into my side. Alyonka pushes against me as I grunt.

"Where are you hurt?" She grabs my face in her hands and I glance down at my hand, sticking with blood.

"I should have known! Those stupid fairies could not leave my curse alone! I should have destroyed the whole kingdom!"

The screech comes from behind me and I turn just as the dark fairy steps into the room. Her eyes are full of rage, trained completely on me. Alyonka pushes away from me, placing her body in front of mine.

"Oh, how cute. Now the little princess is going to protect her bodyguard. Isn't that his job?" The dark fairy asks and Alyonka stands up, her own eyes flashing.

"We protect each other," Alyonka says and I reach for her, but she won't back down. I feel the thorn that impeded itself in my side and I do my best to ignore the pain as I try to get to my feet. Except Alyonka is standing in the way.

"Very cute," the dark fairy spits out, raising her hands.

"Isn't it though...Carabosse," Alyonka says.

The unfamiliar name stops the dark fairy in her tracks. She tries to raise her hands in the air, but she seems to be frozen in one spot.

"How?" The dark fairy manages and I can't see Alyonka's face, but I can hear the smile in her voice.

"Does it matter? I know who you are, Carabosse. The dark fairy, the one who cursed me." I reach for Alyonka, but she moves toward the woman, her shoulders back, her head raised high.

"You cannot hide any longer, Carabosse, because now, the curse is broken and I can find you. No matter where you go—"

Suddenly, a gust of wind rushes through the room, nearly knocking Alyonka off her feet. She steps back, reaching for my hand and I pull her down on the bed beside me as a storm begins in the middle of her bedroom.

"You will not disrespect me again!" Carabosse screams, the wind spinning around her, as dark smoke begins to rise from her. The contrast of her white hair and dress outlined in the black smoke is terrifying. I try to push Alyonka behind me, but she won't budge, determined to be the one to protect me.

"This is not over! I will not rest until you are destroyed!"

"You have no power here," Alyonka says, her voice firm despite the storm happening right in front of her eyes. "You are just a sad woman whose feelings got her. You really need to get over that."

Carabosse's eyes flash in anger, dark as the night, and if I don't get Alyonka out of here now, we'll be pulled into the whirlwind Carabosse is creating in the middle of the room. But then, her attention is pulled to the open window, just as Chudo appears.

Carabosse grins as if greeting an old friend, just as the dragon lands in the middle of Alyonka's room. But as the dark fairy stares at the dragon, her expression changed from glee to actual fear.

"Nyet! You cannot choose her!" Carabosse screams, as the dragon opens his mouth and let's out the scariest growl I have ever heard in my life. The bed we're sitting on shakes under the noise.

Carabosse screams and then, out of thin air, a mortar and pestle appear, large enough to fit a person inside. She reaches for the pestle and then steps inside the mortar and with one spin, she disappears into thin air.

The storm disappears with her and I stare at Chudo, who is now sitting in front of the bed, looking very smug.

"Where did she go?" I ask, turning my attention to Alyonka. "I need to go after her."

"You need a doctor," Alyonka replies, reaching over and dropping a kiss to my lips.

thirty-four

ALYONKA

My mind and heart are so overwhelmed, I'm finding it hard to breathe. Chudo is very pleased with himself and after I make sure Nikolai is taken care of, my dragon is getting all the treats he wants.

"*I good. Did good. Save favorite you.*" Chudo says and I give him a quick smile.

"You did very good, Chudo. You saved us." He thumps his tail on the floor a few times, very pleased, before he looks at Nikolai.

"*Smells funny. Don't like.*" And with that, the dragon jumps back out of the window.

"Are you okay?" I focus on Nikolai, looking him over. The thorn is sticking out from his lower back, bleeding through his shirt. I need to get him to a doctor. I can't fix this, all I know is not to pull it out, lest he bleed out.

"Did your dragon gloat a little?" Nikolai asks and I roll my eyes.

"Don't try to be a tough guy." I push him down when he tries to get up again.

"But I am a tough guy," he says.

"Nikolai, I need to go find help. If the curse is broken, others will be awake. Just stay here." I push away from him, but I don't go far before he grabs me by the wrist and pulls me down halfway on top of him.

"You can't go. What if it's dangerous? What is she's still out there? I need to go check—"

"You need to lay down and let me do my part. She won't be back. Not right now. But it doesn't matter, because we can find her now."

"How...how did you know her name?" He asks. Even though Ivan Popyalof never told me, I know he's been looking for her name. Ever since I could, I've been looking for. It's the one thing that has power over her. But could never find it.

"It came to me in a dream," I say, before I lean over and place a quick kiss to his lips. "Now, let me go get help."

I try to get up again, but he still won't let me go, tugging me against him.

"Nikolai!"

"First, I have to tell you something." I push the hair

plastered to his forehead and leave my hand against his cheek, so I can look him directly in the eye.

"I already know. You love me, obviously. I love you too, obviously. Now let me go so I can save your life!"

With otherworldly strength he sits up suddenly, his arms still wrapped around my waist.

"Say it again."

The desperation in his voice will be my undoing. I place my hands on both of his cheeks, staring deeply into his eyes.

"I love you."

He exhales, like he's been holding his breath this whole time and leans his forehead against mine. We stay like that for a moment, breathing each other in, before he raises his head and looks me in the eye.

"I love you."

I grin, pulling his mouth to mine and kiss him long and hard. Then, I wiggle out of his hold, and jump back.

"Now, I need to find you—"

"Alyonka!"

I twist around to find Daria and Timofey at my door. They both rush inside and Daria grabs me in a hug, holding me tightly.

"Timofey, help Nikolai," I say, my voice muffled against Daria's hair.

"I'm on it," I hear his response and then suddenly there are more people pouring. Oleg and Daniil rush in, and one of them runs out to grab a doctor. Before I know what else to do, my parents are suddenly there.

They step inside the room, a look on their faces I've never seen before. They look ashamed.

I don't know what happened after I feel asleep, but no matter how lonely I've been my whole life, or how much my parents kept a distance between us, I've never blamed them. When I was little, I wanted to. Because how could they think that abandoning me was the right answer?

But I see now, that they have always thought they were doing what they needed to do to keep me and the rest of the kingdom safe. And I can blame them even less now knowing that at least part of that time, Tetia Tatiana was used as a puppet to control them. My parents never had a chance to learn how to be parents, but maybe I can bridge some of that distance between us now.

So I let go of Daria and walk toward them, throwing my arms around both of them at the same time. My mother is already crying, her body shaking as I hold them. My father doesn't really know where to put his hands and I don't know if we can ever have a good relationship, but I will try. It will need a lot of healing, but now that the worst is over, I believe we can get there.

Oleg comes back with the doctor hot on his heels and I let go of my parents, moving back toward the bed. They don't stop me and I'm thankful for that. Because no one can ever keep me away from Nikolai ever again.

I can still hear his words echoing in side my head.

They were faint when I was in that dream, but somehow, I hear them clearly now. Maybe it's another gift the fairies have given me, just like the dark fairy's name. For some reason, I have no doubt that is who the lights were. The last gift I was given by the fairies might've been infused with the gift of understanding.

Because we were all wrong. We were never going to find answers in any of the books. The answer was always inside of our hearts. Mine and Nikolai's. Because for as long as I've known him, we have always belonged to each other.

ALYONKA

"Are you sure he's allowed to eat that many?" Timofey asks me three days later, as he stares at Chudo sitting in the middle of the courtyard. We're in the first floor gardens, with Nikolai sitting on the bench by my side, and Chudo reaching over to sneak *pirozki* from my hands every now and then.

"Hmm, are you going to tell him how many he should have?" I ask and Chudo immediately turns his head toward Timofey, throwing him a glare as he bares his teeth a little. Timofey immediately takes a step back, raising his hands.

"I would never."

"*Human. Puny. My. Treat.*"

"*Da*, your treat," I reach over to scratch him between the eyes, as he begins to purr. He saved Nikolai for me. There was a point, right before I fell, where I screamed for him to get Nikolai out. I had no idea if it would work, only that if this kingdom was going to sleep for a thousand years, I didn't want that fate to befall on the man I loved. But Chudo came through. My little—giant and still growing—dragon hero.

And then, he saved us both when he burst into my room. I never would've imagined that Chudo knew the dark fairy, but there's history there that he won't share and I won't pry about. For now. Maybe one day.

The moment Chudo leans back to eat his *pirozok*, he throws another glare at Timofey. The soldier takes another step back, while Daria giggles. She's sitting beside me, working on a new scarf for Chudo as a gift. He wants a green one and he needs a new scarf, since he's grown so much the other doesn't fit anymore. Which he made sure Nikolai knew when he dumped it on his lap this morning.

The four of us, well, five including Chudo, have congregated in the garden for some quality time. The last three days have been full of official activities—anything from speeches to visiting the noble's families to going to the nearby villages to meet with the people. The kingdom and its people experienced a shock and even though the curse lasted a day instead of a thousand years, there's still a lot to take in. Some people didn't even believe magic was real, let alone that they are part of a curse.

"Well, at least he's not glaring at me anymore," Nikolai leans over to whisper in my ear, sending pleasant goosebumps up my arm. Chudo turns his head toward him immediately, but it's more playful than menacing this time. Apparently, Nikolai was a very proper passenger and didn't pull on Chudo's hair or hurt him in any way. Therefore, they're something close to…comrades.

"Good. Squirrel."

It's what he calls Nikolai. That's the highest complement Chudo can give because squirrels are his friends. Apparently, they bring him nuts and mushrooms they find and they have feasts together when Chudo is exploring the forest. It's something I very much would like to witness for myself.

"What is it?" Nikolai asks and I realize Daniil has come into the courtyard. He bows to me before speaking.

"Baron Denis is leaving and he would like to see the Grand Duchess."

"Oh! Right, of course," I motion for Daniil to bring him in, as I stand.

"Should you be this excited to see another man?" Nikolai stand up beside me and I wave him away.

"Hush you, and sit."

"Not a chance."

Denis Alexandrovich is led in by Daniil and he stops in his tracks at the sight of Chudo munching on bread.

"Please don't worry about him," I say, stepping forward and drawing the attention away. "You have everything you need?"

Denis Alexandrovich pulls his gaze away from the dragon, before he bows to me.

"I appreciate your kindness, *Tsarevna* Alyona. I wish you...both well." He glances at Nikolai and then bows again and leaves. He's the last of the suitors to go and I fell somehow disconnected from the competition already. It's like it didn't even happen to me.

"He was my favorite of the bunch," Daria calls out and Nikolai growls a little as I laugh.

"Mine too," I reply, placing a hand on Nikolai's stomach and leading him back to the bench. "Turns out, that just means I'm a good judge of character."

In the end, we found out that Lev Ignatovich already had a woman he wanted to marry. Which made sense why the poem he wrote was so full of emotion. Georgiy Leonidovich made a bit scene about wasting his time, before he left. But thankfully, Sergey Vladimirovich was only quietly disappointed. He seemed to genuinely be interested in me.

Nikolai finally heard from his contacts and it turns out that Boris Stepanich was Tetia Tatiana's step nephew, however that's supposed to work. Even when she wasn't mind controlled by Carabosse, she was still scheming to get him into the final. He only wanted to rule, since he's about seventeenth in line for the throne and didn't care how to get there. She wanted him in the running from the beginning, but after the first batch of suitors realized that the later ones would work more in their favor. Needless to say, she left with the *knyaz*. I don't need a matchmaker anymore.

I still don't quite understand how Carabosse was able to use Tetia Tatiana's body on the day of coronation or how long she's been whispering to her in her dreams. But Tetia Tatiana apologized for the part she played and the way her ambition opened the door for her to be used.

"How long will your parents be gone?" Nikolai asks as I snuggle carefully into his side. He's still healing from the thorn, but thankfully it wasn't as deep of an impale as we first thought. The doctor was able to close up the wound pretty quickly. It's the resting part of the healing process that seems to be so difficult for him. He wraps his arm around my waist, pulling me close.

"I'm not sure. They wanted to visit the whole kingdom and spend time in the villages."

After the initial council meetings, my father decided that it would be best for me to stay here and do things I wanted to do, while he and mother took care of the officials side of things. I suppose it's their way of trying to be parents, even if it feels like the opposite. I'm not complaining. I much rather be here than meeting with officials. That day will come, I'm sure.

For now, I want to make my own plans and spend time with the people I care about. I watch as Timofey offers Chudo another treat and the dragon does a little leap in the air in happiness. The sound of his little squeal, coupled with Daria and Timofey's laughter brings me immense amount of comfort.

So do Nikolai's arms wrapped tightly around me. Whatever happens next, I know that as long as we're together, there isn't anything we can't handle.

thirty-five

NIKOLAI

It still feels absolutely wild to me that she loves me. Every time I look at Alyonka, I'm amazed all over again. Especially right now, as she spreads out blanket after blanket in front of the fire. The room has been through a lot, but thankfully, all the repairs took less time than I thought. The fireplace didn't sustain much damage at all.

"Is this really a good idea?" I ask, standing in the middle of her bedroom as she chucks a bunch of pillow on the floor.

"Of course! I bet you've never had a blanket picnic time, have you?" She places her hands on her hips, cocking her head to one side and then the other. I shake my head and she claps her hands a few times.

"Then you must experience it! We have food," she points to a basket my mother prepared for her, "We have games," she say and we both look at a stack of cards near the basket. "And most importantly, we have paint!"

I take a step back immediately as she steps toward me.

"Will you let me paint your face?" She asks, smiling sweetly. Even though my whole body says it's the last thing I want, my mouth forms a single,

"*Da*."

I am incapable of saying no to her. She laughs and then walks over to wrap her arms round my middle and look up at me.

"You should see your face. You look like you're about to step in front of a firing squad."

"I do not."

"You do. And you're very sweet for agreeing, but actually, the most important part of the blanket picnic are comfy clothes." She steps back and walks over to the bench at the end of her bed. "Here, change into these."

She hands me the clothes and I unfold it to find a pair of pants and a button up shirt, both made from the softest material and at least a size too big.

"Did you just have this lying around?" I ask, looking up at her.

"Of course, don't most people have an extra man's pajamas in their wardrobe?"

I glance up at her and find her smiling.

"I asked Daria to make some a month ago. It was going to be a birthday gift."

"Oh but my birthday isn't—"I stop, thinking of what time of the year it is. "It's next week."

"That it is. Now go change."

She turns me around, pushing me toward the bathroom and I have no choice but to do as she says. Once inside, I strip off my uniform and pull on the pajamas. The material feels amazing against my skin and I feel comforted somehow.

When I step back out into the room, I find Alyonka has also changed and is now wearing a matching outfit. While mine is dark blue, hers is her signature pink. She's also wearing very fuzzy socks and she looks so adorable my vision swims for a moment.

"Is this part of my gift as well?" I ask, my throat suddenly thick.

"Absolutely," she replies.

I can't stand it anymore. I close the distance between us in a few strides and then I sweep her right into my arms. She squeals, wrapping her legs around my middle and locking them behind my back, as I hold her in place.

"Hi," I say, as her hair spills forward over both of our shoulders.

"Hi," she replies, a soft smile on her face. She runs her fingers over my forehead, pushing at the hair there, before she lets her fingers travel down over my temples and then my cheek. The whole time, my eyes stay on her as she continues to explore. Her fingers trace my eyebrows and then my nose, as if she's memorizing me with her touch.

"I always wondered what you looked like after you grew up," she say, as her touch continues to dance over my skin. "I wondered where you were, if you were eating well, if you had enough blankets to keep your warm at night."

She meets my eyes then, her honesty disarming me like it normally does. I've never been this comfortable with sharing my feelings, but it seems like with her, I want to.

"I wondered about you too. No one has seen the cursed princess in so long, I couldn't even ask anyone about it. I never thought I'd see you again."

"Why did you learn to braid then?" She asks and I chuckle. I really should always remember how smart she is.

"Because if on the off chance that I did, I would have all the skills required of me."

"Like braiding hair and dancing the waltz?" Drops a quick to the tip of my nose, making my head spin all over again.

"The foundation to any good relationship. I figured you'd teach me anything else I might need to know."

"Oh I will," she says and I can't stand it anymore, I kiss her. She smiles again my lips, just as ready for me as I am for her. I kiss her with the utmost gentleness, worshiping her with my mouth with each stroke of the lips. When I come up for air, we're both gasping.

"I love you," I say and she smile, before dropping another quick kiss to my lips.

"I love you," Alyonka replies. "But I'm still going to crush you in this game."

ALYONKA

W E'VE EATEN ALL our snacks and we tied in points for the game. I spent over an hour asking Nikolai about the flowers he's collected, as we leafed through his book with them pressed inside. I really want him to have the space to continue his hobby and I think it will be fun for him when we start traveling together.

By the time both of us are too exhausted to keep our eyes open. The fire is the only light in the room, as I lay snuggled into Nikolai's side. He's still healing, so I want to be considerate, but he won't hear of it as he tucks me snuggly against him.

"For survival," he says, placing a kiss to the top of my head and I feel myself relax even more. I never imagined this for myself. The way my heart feels at peace when I'm near him, the comfort I find in his arms.

All my life I expected a marriage of convenience, something that was approved by my parents, saved the kingdom, and left me with someone to sit beside me at public events. I should I would have a work colleague, not a real love story.

It's that thought that finally lulls me to sleep.

But I don't sleep long.

"Nikolai, wake up," I say, trying to pull myself into a sitting position. He's awake immediately, sitting up and giving me a once over.

"Is everything okay?"

"*Da*," I nod, "But we have to go somewhere. Now."

"Go? Where are we going?" Even as he asks, he's already pulling me up to stand beside him.

"We have to go meet the fairies."

He doesn't question me, as we get ready. It's barely starting to get light out, but I don't want to miss anything if we wait any longer. I step out of my bathroom with a winter *sarafan* and my boots laced up. Nikolai holds out my *shuba* and I step into it gratefully. He's wearing his dark blue uniform again, with a long heavy coat over it.

"Should I get the horses ready?" He asks, dropping a kiss to my cheek after giving my clothes a once over.

"*Nyet*," I reply, taking his hand and pulling him toward the bathroom. "We're taking Chudo."

We head for the landing and when we reach it, Chudo is already landing.

"Hello my handsome boy, did you sleep well?"

"*Treat! Pets!*"

"Of course," I say, pulling out one of the *pirozkov* I

saved from the picnic basket. I have to have one on standby at all times now, but it's a good problem to have. He takes the bread and proceeds to chew, as he leans over so I can scratch him between his eyes.

"Alyonka, does he seem bigger to you?" Nikolai asks and I actually take a moment to study my dragon. I see what Nikolai means. He has grown. Even his fir is bushier around his legs and neck.

"*Good Chudo. Big!*"

"The best," I say, giving him another scratch. "Will you take us to see the fairies?" I asks and he nods eagerly.

"*Miss colors. Pretty. Must go!*"

"Colors?"

But he only puffs hot air our way and crouches down so we can get on. Nikolai goes first, and then he lifts me to sit in front of him.

"Hold onto his fur or to me," Nikolai whispers in my ear and then Chudo flies straight into the sky. There's no in between, one moment we're on the roof, the next, we're airborne. I gasp, the air rushing into my face.

Seeing my kingdom from up above, I marvel once again at how beautiful it is. I've always thought so. Some may think that a kingdom that's snowy and cold eighty percent of the time is boring, but I find it breathtaking.

Nikolai tugs me closer to him and I give myself the moment to enjoy it all. I have no idea what awaits us with the fairies, but I know I can't ignore their request. After all, this is the second time they showed up in my dreams.

The first time was when they gave me Carabosse name.

I haven't told anyone about that, not even Nikolai. Everything happened so fast, I didn't have a chance. But now he'll know it all.

In another ten minutes or so, a clearing opens up ahead and Chudo descends immediately. We land softly, our feet the first to disturb the freshly fallen snow. The sun is up now, and it brings an extra shine to our surroundings. It looks like the snow is full of jewels, twinkling up at us.

"Friends!" Chudo suddenly shouts and races off toward something I can't see.

"Where is he going?" Nikolai asks, while he continues to scan our surroundings. I really don't make this whole protecting me easy. I step close to him, lacing out hands together and that's when he finally looks at me, his expression softening.

"I'm the worst bodyguard-ee you've ever had, aren't I?" I ask and he smiles, before he goes back to guarding his expression.

"I'm pretty sure that's not a word," he says but I'm already shaking my head.

"I kind of like it. Do you think I can write it in the officially dictionary? Is that a queen's duty?"

"Maybe we should get you a tutor. Just to be on the safe side, before you start writing any new words into dictionaries...for all too see." I stick out my tongue at him in a very un-princess like manner and he reaches for me as I dart away.

"Adorable."

Nikolai and I jerk in the direction of the voice, but we don't see anything. Then, the space ripples, as if someone thrown a pebble into the water, and a gorgeous woman dressed in lavender steps out. Her hair is light purple, and she's wearing only golden jewelry: rings, necklaces, bracelets, and a headdress. Her gown seems to shimmer as she moves toward us.

Nikolai is immediately in front of me, tucking me behind him, but I push his arm down, my eyes on the woman.

"*Zdrastvui*, Alyona," the woman says and I smile in return. Nikolai glances between myself and the woman, looking to me to make the decision on what to do. I reach for his hand, entwining our fingers together and tug him toward the woman.

"You are her, aren't you?" I can't stop staring at her. She's so strikingly beautiful.

"I am the Lilac Fairy," she replies, "It is a pleasure to finally meet you."

The space behind her ripples again and one by one more women step out. One in all green, one in all blue, one in all yellow, and one in all red. Then, finally, on in all pink. They all wear golden jewelry, their hair matching their gowns.

"The fairies," Nikolai whispers, his voice full of awe.

The fairy of tenderness, the fairy of playfulness, the fairy of generosity, the fairy of serenity, and the fairy of courage. With the Lilac Fairy, they are the ones who gifted me with a blessing on my dedication day.

"I'm sorry we could not come sooner," The Lilac Fairy speaks up. "The curse prevented us from reaching you with our magic, in helping in any way."

"But you did," I say, "You came to me in a dream and you told me her name, Carabosse. Who is she?"

"The one who carries darkness," the fairy of courage says. "She is Baba Yaga's younger sister. Instead of feeding on children, she feeds on dreams."

"Baba Yaga?" Of course I know of the dark enchantress that has plagued Skazka for as long as Skazka has been around. But she was defeated by High Queen Calista, eventually stripped of her powers. "I didn't know she had a sister."

"She has many secrets, some we're only discovering now. Her powers grow and that is why she was able to whisk Carabosse away."

"I thought Baba Yaga's magic was bound?"

"Magic is a living and breathing thing, Alyona," the fairy of playfulness says, "Even when it is bound, it one day adapts and breaks through those bounds to become something else. Something more. It's why Skazka needs good people like yourself to stand at the front, leading the people toward good."

"I couldn't stop her all those years ago," The Lilac

Fairy says, coming to stand in front of me and reaching for my hands. Nikolai takes a step back, but staying right over my right shoulder, like he usually does. "She is full of bitterness and hatred and we were not prepared for her. The rest of my sisters have given their gift, and I was the only one left. So I made a magical failsafe. That when you slept, I could reach you and give you the ultimate power—her name."

"But how did you know I'd wake up? My parents got the curse all wrong."

"I knew you would because love has always been the most powerful magic in the world. No matter what we may try to say and do, at the end of it all is a love that overcomes all curses."

She glances at Nikolai and then holds out her hand. He takes a step forward, reaching for it and she holds in place, a smile on her face.

"You have nothing to worry about when it comes to Carabosse anymore," The Lilac Fairy says. "She is powerless in this kingdom and she is powerless against you. We have dampened her powers and it will take her a long time to recover."

"Wait, you found her?"

"We did. Once the curse was lifted and her true name was spoken in Skazka, she could no longer hide from us."

My knees feel weak from the information, but I don't sway. I knew at the back of my mind that danger wasn't over. I was preparing to do whatever it took to keep my people safe if she returned again. But now, I don't have to worry about that.

"We couldn't help you before, but we can help you now. You will be a wonderful queen one day and the kingdom will flourish under your rule. Don't ever doubt yourself. And don't even doubt the love you have for each other. It will take you far."

Tears come to my eyes at her words, and Nikolai is there to wipe them away. Suddenly, a gust of wind sends the fallen snow into the sky and then Chudo is there. He's flapping his wings, his face full of glee. He jumps up and down like a puppy, but he's not circling us. He's circling the fairies.

I feel incredible happiness radiating off him as the fairy laugh and pet him and I realize something else.

"You sent him to me," I say and the Lilac Fairy smiles.

"He chose to go," she replies. "Did you know that his lineage is in your story books? Chudo-Yudo is believed to be a descendant from Baba Yaga herself. A dragon who grows into a monster with many heads and controls the weather to keep the rain away."

I gasp, because I can't help it. Watching this gorgeous purple and blue bundle of happiness jump around the fairies like a big puppy does not agree with anything the Lilac Fairy says.

"But he's not evil?"

"Of course not. Magic is not evil and it is not good. It is what we make it to be. His power comes from his bond to you. The closer you grow, the more you share, the bigger he grows. In size and in goodness."

I watch him roll around in the snow as the fairies descend on him and I can't help but smile. My life is nothing as I thought it would be and I couldn't be happier.

"*Spasibo*," I say, gratefulness pouring out of me as I look at the Lilac Fairy. "Thank you, for giving me a chance, for giving me an opportunity. I won't fail."

"I believe you."

thirty-six

FOUR MONTHS LATER

NIKOLAI

The picnics in front of the fire have become a tradition. Even when our days are busy, we try to have a standing picnic date once a week. However, today, I want to do something a little different.

The past three months have been full of activities. Alyonka decided that one of the things she wanted to do most is visit all the places she's only read about. We went back to *Korolevstvo Tsvetov* and visited with Queen Ivanna and Dimitri for a whole week. They have become close friends, which I love to see for Alyonka. Outside of Daria, she's never had girl friendships before, but now she has many.

We went south after that to visit King Gavriil and Queen Nikita. That was an interesting experiences, because they were hosting the princess from *Vonoye Tsarstvo*. I've never met anyone from the water kingdom, as they do tend to keep to themselves. There are many predisposed notions about them, such as the lore that the people there lure others to their death through song. But Alyonka took to the princess immediately. They seem to share an adventure spirit and she will be visiting our kingdom eventually.

After all that, we visited Ivan Popyalof who is settling very nicely at being the biggest pushover when it comes to his baby nephew. He even started to see a woman in the village and now that Alyona is safe, he can actually live a peaceful life. I'm sure we'll be visiting him often.

We'll be heading to visit High Queen Calista and her family next, but since we're back home for a moment, I think it's time to put my little plan to the test.

"Did you take another shower? You look a little drenched," Timofey comments, a big grin on his face. We're standing side by side near the training field to oversea today's sparing matches. Alyonka is in a meeting with her father, so I'm waiting until she finishes. But the waiting is apparently making me a mess.

"Shut up, before I throw you to the wolves," I say, not taking my eyes off the two soldiers in front of me.

"You wouldn't. You're a big softy now."

"Where did you get that idea?"

"Please, if Daniil ran up to you right now asking for a hug, you'd hug him immediately."

Which is true. I've learned a lot in the last few months and one of those things is that different people need different things. Some of the soldiers appreciate words of encouragement, but others just need a big brother moment and they're good to go.

"I hugged him one time. He was crying, I wasn't going to punch him."

"Well, maybe nothing that drastic," I glance at Timofey our of the corner of my eye as he rolls his own. "But you would've just sent him to his room and brought him a pastry. Now you're all kinds of fatherly. A big, big softy."

This time, I do push Timofey away from ne and he stumbles, laughing. He's not wrong, of course. But that doesn't mean I'll let him just be.

"Relax, dude. You've prepared, it'll be okay."

I nod, but don't say anything else. Just then, Daria comes into the yard and waves me over.

"Make sure the rest of them finish," I say to Timofey as he claps me on the back.

"Go see your girl," he replies and this time I do grin.

Daria hands me a bag as we walk back into the castle.

"She'll be up on the balcony landing in about fifteen minutes. Your mom said you owe her a family dinner," Daria smile and I return it. The family dinner means not only me, but Alyona, Timofey, and Daria as well. The four of us come as a package now, although I have no idea if anything is going on between Timofey and Daria. They've been slightly hostile toward each other the past few weeks.

"I'll see you in a few." I say and then we separate. I reach the landing first and call out to Chudo. He's been circling for exercise, so he's close by. When he lands, he reaches for the bag immediately. Probably because he can sniff out his favorite *pirozki* from half a kingdom away.

"Hey, not yet!" I say, grabbing the bag away. He turns on me immediately, his eyes narrowed, but I don't back down. "Don't look at me like that."

Since intimidation doesn't work, he goes for the next best thing. He pouts.

How a giant terrifying dragon can look like such a baby with that pout I will never understand. He leans closer to me, until our foreheads are lined up, his pleading face fully on display. I lean closer as well, before poking him gently on the snout.

"Stop being a big baby," I say and he huffs, right before he drops to his back, legs up in the air and wiggles, shaking the whole landing in the process. I jump out of the way, trying to keep my own stern look on my face because he looks ridiculously cute.

"Not going to work," I call out. "I can do that too." And then I proceed to make a cute pouty face at him. He's looking at me upside down, but I know I got him. Alyonka says this is my best pouty face.

"Are you two fighting by trying to out-cute each other?"

Chudo and I turn as one toward Alyonka, as she looks between the two of us. Chudo twists around, sitting up very proper and I roll my eyes.

"Obviously, nyet," I say, running a hand over my hair. "But obviously, I would win."

Chudo leans over and puffs a gust of hot wind at me, sending my hair into disarray. Alyonka laughs and I can't concentrate on the dragon anymore, because that's my favorite sound.

Well, that and when she talks, or when she hums while dancing, or while eating. Sometimes she yells really loud in frustration at herself and that's cute too.

I think Timofey might be correct, I am a big softie now.

"So what is all this secret sneaking around?" Alyonka asks, coming up to drop a kiss to my lips before she pets Chudo.

"Secret? What? Sneaking around? What?"

She raises her eyebrow at me and shakes her head.

"You are terrible at this," she says and Chudo laughs. I glare at the dragon, before I motion for him to get down.

"I'm taking you to a very special place," I say, reaching for Alyonka's hand. "Trust me?"

"Always."

ALYONKA

Riding around on Chudo with Nikolai's arms wrapped tightly around me might be my favorite thing in the world. Well, I have a lot of them actually and they all involved Nikolai.

"*Funny human. Sweaty.*" Chudo says and I try not to laugh out loud. Nikolai has been a bit nervous the last few days and Daria and Timofey have been tough nuts to crack. Although Daniil and Oleg did mention a few times that Nikolai was working on something behind scenes. And then they would proceed to smile about it.

It doesn't matter what he's planing, because I can just stay snuggled into his arms for the rest of my life.

"Are we leaving *Holodnoye Tsarstvo*?" I ask, when we've been flying for a little bit.

"*Nyet*, just heading toward the north border."

I haven't been that far yet. There's so much of my own kingdom that's unexplored. It makes me so excited to see more of it.

We descend into a small clearing in the forest. Once we're off Chudo, the dragon doesn't leave, but instead walks over to the edge of the trees and curls up.

"*Take nap. Right here.*" He says and then closes his eyes.

I glance over at Nikolai but he simply shrugs, before taking my hand and pulling me into the forest. We walk a few paces when we come up to a cave opening. It's so overgrown with trees, I never would've found it.

"What is this?"

Nikolai doesn't respond, but simply leads me farther in. It's dark for a few meters, but then suddenly, there's a light coming from somewhere in front of us. We turn to the left, walk through another small opening and suddenly, I feel like I'm in a completely different world.

"Oh—" Is all I can manage.

The space around me looks like a large dome. There's a large willow tree to the right and a pond of the clearest blue water I've ever seen right in front of it. What I notice immediately, is how warm it is inside.

"Here," Nikolai is behind me, reaching for my *shuba* and I let him take it off my shoulders.

"Is this why Daria dressed me in this?" I point to my pink gown. It's mostly tulle, with open neckline and long sleeves, but everything very light. It's definitely more of a summer time dress for me.

"*Da.*"

Nikolai doesn't move as he watches me explore.

The ceiling of the dome is filled with something sparkly, it also reflects in the pool. There are patches of green and white and when I look closer I see that they're snowdrops. The space is littered with them.

A tiny white butterfly flutters in front of me, pausing as if looking me over, before it continues on. The closer I walk to the pond, the more butterflies I see. They're flying everywhere. There are also tiny sparkly bugs, chasing each other around.

When I stop near the pond I realize the heat is radiating off of the water.

"What is this place?" I ask, turning to look at Nikolai.

"One of Skazka's many secrets," he replies. "There's a year around hot spring here, so it almost like a little world on its own. I thought that maybe, you'd like to have a sleepover here for a change. I brought food and games, as is always requested." He motions to the bag at his feet and my heart is so overwhelmed with my love for him, I think I'm going to burst. Instead, I run at him and he meets me halfway, catching me in his arms.

"You are amazing," I say, holding his face in both of my hands. "But you're amazing even when you're not doing these ridiculously romantic things for me. You're amazing because you're you."

"But I want to do these ridiculously romantic things for you."

I kiss him, because I can't help myself and he answers in kind. He is always meeting right where I am, almost like we're two pieces of each other—a perfect fit. I pour my whole heart into the kiss, holding him as close as possible, while I feel like everything around us is spinning.

"Alyonushka, will you dance with me?" He whispers into my ear, sending goosebumps over my body. I nod, and he gently lowers me to the ground, his arms staying wrapped around my back. I reach up and push some of the hair out of his eyes, before I trail that hand to one of his, pulling him into a proper hold.

We start to move together, our steps in perfect sync. Whatever comes our way, when we're together, I feel as if we're unstoppable.

"Nikolai."

"Mhhm."

"Do you remember that awful poem competition?"

He groans, throwing his head back for a moment. "Why must you remind me of the most terrible time in my life?"

"Worse than your military training?"

"Absolute. At least there I could punch people back. Here I just kept getting slapped and slapped—"

"No one touched you."

"In the heart," he rolls his eyes dramatically. "Obviously."

I chuckle, because this side of him is just as adorable as all the others.

"Well, while you were getting slapped in the heart, I wrote you a poem."

He stops in his tracks, gapping down at me.

"What? Even back then?" His gaze if full of shock and a bit of something else I can't quite identify.

"*Da*, even back then," I say, because I don't think he realizes just how long he has been plaguing me.

"Let me hear it."

"It's probably terrible."

"I don't care."

Suddenly shy, I almost back out. But he's looking at me with such earnest expression that I can't help myself. So I begin to speak.

> "A world of magic,
> But full of darkness,
> When you're not here,
> The sun won't shine.
> I fear tomorrow,
> I fear the thunder,
> But when you come,
> I feel at home.
> My peace, my wonder,
> My one true hope,
> Come stay beside me
> Come hold me close."

When I finish, there are tears in his eyes. I reach over, running my thumb over his cheeks, as my own tears threaten to fall.

"Wow." He says, a small smile on his lips. "That *is* terrible."

I gasp, pushing at him, but he catches me around the waist pulling me against him as he drops a quick kiss to my cheek. I know he's kidding, but we both can play this game.

"Let me go. We're done. I'm taking Chudo and leaving you to live in this warm oasis."

"You can't do that."

"Sure, I can. I am the future queen."

"But don't you want to hear my poem for you?"

I stop wiggling immediately, glancing up at him in shock that I'm sure matches his own from earlier.

"You wrote me one too?" He nods. "Back then?" He nods again and I start crying immediately.

"Alyonushka, you haven't even heard it yet." He chuckles, lifting my head to cradle it between his hands.

"I want to hear it," I say, my voice coming out muffled because he squishes my cheeks together. He holds me like that for a moment, grinning down at me. "Nikolai."

"I'm sorry, I got distracted by your cuteness."

I swat at his arms, but I don't move away. I just look at him expectedly. He sighs dramatically and then begins to recite.

"Do you know what love is?
A feeling unlike any other.
But it's more than that,

It's a promise we make to each other.
I look at you and I see the years beyond,
The calm mornings together
The laughter, the tears, the fights.
In all of those moments,
In good times and bad,
We'll walk hand in hand, we'll stay to the end.
My heart has been yours before I knew it was gone,
I want a forever, I want you for always,
I want us to dance to the song in our hearts."

I'm crying openly now, making a completely mess of myself, but I can't hold back. Not when every single word Nikolai speaks is full of emotion. My body feels like it's no longer my own. I can see it too, the years to come and no matter what I'm doing—ruling the kingdom or sneaking over to the ballroom to dance—Nikolai is always there.

"You are the best bodyguard in the history of bodyguard," I say, hiccuping over my words. He grins, leaning down to kiss me gently on the lips, before he moves to kiss me on the forehead.

"Then I guess that means I have the job for the rest of my life?"

"*Da*," I reply, wrapping my arms around his middle, and tugging him closer. "You're stuck with me for life."

epilogue

FIVE MONTHS LATER

ALYONKA

Being the next Tsarina of *Holodnova Tsarstva* has kept me incredibly busy. But no matter how busy I am, there is no way I'm missing today. I've been planning this for a while now and I think it's time. Everything has lined up accordingly.

"You can definitely make the snow fall when I signal you, right?" I ask Chudo as he lands in front of me in the snow. We're at the pond and I managed to get here with few minutes to spare before Nikolai shows up.

"*Chudo good. Chudo make snow. Pretty, pretty.*"

The dragon has stopped growing as rapidly as he was,

but he's doubled in size since I first met him. Still, he's the most cuddly dragon in the history of dragons and I love the time I can spend with him purring beside like a cat.

I glance behind me as I hear someone approach and then Nikolai is there. Just as always the sight of him makes my chest tight for a moment, as if I can't believe he's real. His eyes meet mine and the serious furrow of his brow transforms immediately as he smiles. He moves toward me, dropping the bag he's carrying in the snow, at the same time I move toward him. He catches me in his arms, picking me straight off the ground, his arms locked against my thighs as I cradle his face in my hands.

"What took you so long? It's been ages since I've seen you!" I exclaim and drop a kiss to his lips.

"Ages and ages," he murmurs against my lips as he sets me back on the ground.

"*Saw squirrel. Now. At castle too.*" Chudo makes a noise and Nikolai smiles.

"Is your dragon laughing at us?" He asks.

"I think so. Apparently, an hour does not qualify as 'ages and ages' in his eyes," I say and turn to glance at Chudo, who gives me one look and then proceeds to fall onto his back and rub his back in the snow, kicking his legs in the air.

"He's so big, but he's such a baby," Nikolai says as I turn to face him again and I nod.

"Let him play in the snow while we skate!" I say,

taking Nikolai's hand in mine and pulling him toward the bench.

"So that's what we're doing," my bodyguard grins, settling down beside me. I pull my fur lined boots off my feet and stick them into the skates as fast as I can. The weather has been getting colder by the day, even though spring is right around the corner. The cold kingdom always plays by its own rules. The sun will set soon, so we need to get moving.

I love the feeling I get when I'm skating and I love even more when Nikolai is beside me, holding my hand. He catches up to me with no problem, but I dodge him for a moment, and he laugh as he chases after me. I weave around him, my dress and cloak fluttering around me as I spin in a fill circle. Even on skates, all I want to do is dance.

Nikolai reaches for me and this time I let him catch me. We spin together, face to face, as we hold our gaze. When we finally stop, we're in the middle of the pond, and the snow begins to fall. The space around us seems to dim, just enough that the snowflakes sparkle with something extra.

"Why is it only snowing over the pond?" Nikolai asks, his eyes not leaving my face.

"Why is it you're so observant?" I reply.

"Hazard of the job." He smiles and then finally looks up at the sparkling snow. I follow the direction of his gaze, taking in the beauty around me. He glances down again at me and grow bolder.

"Do you remember when you asked if if you had your bodyguard job for the rest of your life?" I ask and he nods slowly. "Well, I think it's time I fired you."

"What?" He narrows his eyes in confusion as I duck my face into his chest.

"Well, maybe not fire. Possibly a promotion? Da, that's a good word for it. A promotion. Like a better position than you previous one. But you can still have the responsibilities of the previous one, but also it's different. You're my best friend, and you are everything to me, and I can't imagine, wait, I mean—"

"Alyonushka, are you proposing right now?"

I jerk my head up, my mouth agape. Nikolai's lips are curled at the corners and he looks like he's trying not to laugh.

"What? Nyet! I would—don't laugh at me!" I slap his shoulder when his laugh rings out around me.

"You precious gorgeous creature, I'm not laughing at you. I'm laughing because I'm happy and slightly frustrated."

"What do you mean?" I pull back immediately so I can see his face fully. He takes my hand and skates us back to the edge of the pond, leading me out into the snow and toward the bench. When I meet his gaze, he's smiling down at me with so much love shining in his eyes, I think I'm going to cry. "I don't understand."

Nikolai reaches inside his coat pocket and pulls something out. I look at the snowdrop between his fingers and then at him.

"I picked this for you on the way here," he says and I take the offering, he lowers himself beside me on the bench, as I hold the flower with both hands. "Do you know the symbolizm behind snowdrops?'

I shake my head, swirling the flower between my fingers.

"It's a flower associated with new beginnings, of overcoming challenges and of hope. It's a flower that makes me think of you."

I glance up at him then, as he reaches up and tucks a stray hair under my fur headband.

"But this time, I don't want it to simply be a representation of how strong and resilient you are. I picked it because I want it to symbolize our new beginning."

"Nikolai?"

He reaches for my hands and places a soft kiss to my mitten covered knuckles, before he slowly lowers himself to one knee in front of the bench.

"You are my new beginning, my best friend, my favorite flower, and the queen of my heart. Will you marry me?"

There's a moment of stillness all around us and then I launch myself into his arms, falling into the snow. I place kisses all of his face, as I try to hold the tears of happiness at bay.

"Is that a yes?" He says, laughing.

"It's a yes and a hundred times yes," I reply and he captures my lips in a soul sealing kiss. My arms sneak inside of his coat, pulling him closer to me and keeps me right against him, as he kisses me back with so much love I think I'm going to burst.

A gust of hot air slaps us in the face and we turn to the right to see Chudo looming over us.

"*Cold. Snow. No sick!*" He says and I realize he's concerned about us tumbling in the snow. I lean back, pulling Nikolai with me to a sitting position. He does one better, and stands, picking me up with him.

"I assume he wasn't happy with us laying in the snow," Nikolai says and I nod. We watch as Chudo curls himself around the bench and I take that as an invitation to sit down and change my shoes. Nikolai beats me to it, as he reaches to unlace my skates and pulls my boots back on my feet.

Then he stands, reaches into his bag and produces a quilt Daria made me recently, placing it over my knees. Before I can ask any more questions, he also hands me a cup and pours hot chocolate into it.

"Oh!" I sit up straighter immediately, grinning as I breath in the sweet aroma. Nikolai changes into his own boots as I take a sip of the rich goodness. Then, I tug the blanket over Nikolai's knees as well, as he settles beside me. With Chudo's warmth at my back and Nikolai beside me, I'm surrounded in the most perfect way.

"You really planned this out," I comment as he takes a sip of his drink as well.

"I did. What was your plan? Make Chudo sprinkle us with snow as you offered me a promotion? Then what? Did you even have a ring for me?"

I bump him with my shoulder as I bring the cup back to my face.

"Are you going to tease me about this forever?" I ask and Nikolai laughs.

"Only for the next fifty years or so."

"Okay, so I thought it would be romantic with the snow and the skating. I've never proposed to anyone before."

"Neither have I," Nikolai says, "But I at least brought a ring."

And then he holds it up right in front of my eyes. I gasp and he quickly takes my cup as I reach for the ring. It's a snowflake, with a diamond inside and tiny diamonds decorating the little branches that grow out of the middle. It's gorgeous.

I hold out my hand and the ring and Nikolai chuckles as he removes my mitten and places the ring on my finger.

A perfect fit.

I lean forward, taking his face into my hands and pulling him down toward me. I kiss him with all the love in my heart and he meets my intensity, just like he always does.

"Does this mean I got the promotion?" He asks and I chuckles.

"Da, you've got the promotion. Your new title is 'my husband'."

"That is the best title I have ever received," Nikolai says, kissing me lightly on the nose. "I can't wait to be your husband, my wife."

I grin and kiss him again, and when we finally come up for air, he opens up his coat and I snuggle inside, wrapping my arms around his middle. Chudo purrs against our backs, as the sun begins to set and I think I am the luckiest person in Skazka.

"Nikolai," I say, looking up at him from my position against his chest.

"Hmm."

"I love you, forever and ever."

He grins, dropping a kiss to my forehead.

"And I love you, forever and ever."

Then, we seal that promise with a kiss.

THANK you so much for reading! If you're not ready to say goodbye to the world of Skazka yet, you can read ***The Princess Test: A Princess and the Pea Retelling*** for FREE when you subscribe to my newsletter. Click HERE.

The next book in the Skazka Fairy Tales series is a Little Mermaid retelling that follows a grumpy water princess, sunshine prince, fake dating, and all the cozy feels! Click HERE.

glossary of russian words and phrases:

Dobrii den - good afternoon

sistrichka - sweet term for a sister

krasavitz - handsome

Prosti nas pozhalusta - Please forgive us

Zdrastvuite/Zdrastvui - hello

pirozok/pirozki - pie (typically baked in individual portions, like buns with stuffing)

Dobroye utro - good morning

Tsarevna - daughter of a tsar

Knyaz - prince, typically a titled nobility

Podpolkovnik - lieutenant colonel

Pozdravlyayu tebya - Congratulations to you

Spasibo - thank you

Marshal - the highest ranking officer in the army

kislaya kapusta - sour cabbage, sauerkraut, a very popular dish in Russia

shuba - long fur coat

Priyatno poznakomitsiya - Nice to meet you

Dobrii den - good afternoon

pozhalusta - please

oladi- Russian buttermilk pancake

vatrushki - pastry, a sweet yeast bread baked in a ring with a white cheese filling.

ploskiy blin - flat pancake

pelmeni - meat dumplings

brusnika - lingonberry/cranberry

Moya - mine

Sinok - son, said in a sweet way

kingdoms of skazka

Holodnoye Tsarstvo - Cold Kingdom - Alyonka and Nikolai's kingdom

Korolevstvo Tsvetov - Kingdom of Flowers

Tsarstvo Vesniy - Autumn Kingdom (Second)

Zelonoye Korolevstvo - Green Kingdom

Volkovskoye Korolevstvo - Kingdom of the Wolf

Oceniye Tsarstvo - Autumn Kingdom (First)

Vodnoye Tsarstvo - Kingdom of Water

don't miss the snow white retelling!

The Poisoned Princess is the retelling of the traditional Russian Snow White fairytale, where you meet Queen Ivanna and her seven warriors!

Read their story now!

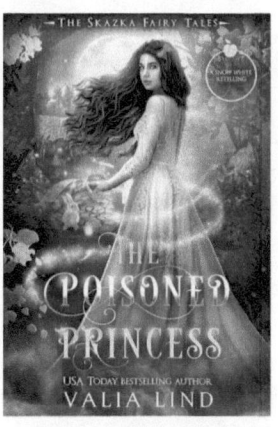

what more from the land of skazka?

Discover how Calista became the Queen of *Zelenovo Korolevstva* and learn more about the land of Russian fairytales in The Skazka Chronicles trilogy.

also by valia lind

The Skazka Fairy Tales

The Scarlet Rose (A Beauty and the Beast Retelling)

The Golden Slipper (A Cinderella Retelling)

The Poisoned Princess (A Snow White Retelling)

The Cursed Beauty (A Sleeping Beauty Retelling)

The Storm Dancer (A Little Mermaid Retelling) - coming 2025!

Witches of Edinburgh

How Not to Hex a Gentleman

The Skazka Chronicles

The Complete trilogy Boxset

Remembering Majyk (The Skazka Chronicles, #1)

Majyk Reborn (The Skazka Chronicles, #2)

The Faithful Soldier (The Skazka Chronicles, #2.5)

Majyk Reclaimed (The Skazka Chronicles, #3)

Thunderbird Academy

The Complete trilogy Boxset

Of Water and Moonlight (Thunderbird Academy, #1)

Of Destiny and Illusions (Thunderbird Academy, #2)

Of Storms and Triumphs (Thunderbird Academy, #3)

Of Holidays and Soulmates: A Christmas Novella

Fae Chronicles

The Complete trilogy Boxset

Shadow of the Fae (#1)

Blood of the Fae (#2)

Revenge of the Fae (#3)

Hawthorne Chronicles

The Complete Season One Box Set

Guardian Witch (Hawthorne Chronicles, #1)

Witch's Fire (Hawthorne Chronicles, #2)

Witch's Heart (Hawthorne Chronicles, #3)

Tempest Witch (Hawthorne Chronicles, #4)

Crooked Windows Inn Cozy Mysteries

Books 1-3 Boxset

Once Upon a Witch #1

Two Can Witch the Game #2

Witch's First Zombie - FREE short story

Third Witch's the Charm #3

Witches Four the Win #4

The White Wolf Saga

The complete series boxset

Moonlight Mate (#1)

Wolf Untamed (#2)

Shifted Hunted (#3)

Blackwood Supernatural Prison Series

The Complete series Boxset

Witch Condemned (#1)

Witch Unchained (#2)

Witch Awakened (#3)

Witch Ascendant (#4)

about the author

USA Today bestselling author. Photographer. Artist. Born and raised in St. Petersburg, Russia, Valia Lind has always had a love for the written word. She wrote her first published book on the bathroom floor of her dormitory, while procrastinating to study for her college classes. Upon graduation, she has moved her writing to more respectable places, and has found her voice in Young Adult and cozy mysteries.

Sign up to receive updates, behind the scenes, & more!
CLICK HERE

www.ingramcontent.com/pod-product-compliance
Lightning Source LLC
LaVergne TN
LVHW041738060526
838201LV00046B/846